PRAISE FOR

SEAL's Honor

"Megan Crane's mix of tortured ex–special ops heroes, their dangerous missions, and the rugged Alaskan wilderness is a sexy, breathtaking ride!"

—*New York Times* bestselling author Karen Rose

Also by Megan Crane

SEAL'S HONOR
SNIPER'S PRIDE

SERGEANT's *Christmas* SIEGE

AN ALASKA FORCE NOVEL

MEGAN CRANE

JOVE
New York

A JOVE BOOK
Published by Berkley
An imprint of Penguin Random House LLC
penguinrandomhouse.com

ISBN: 9781984805508

First Edition: October 2019

Printed in the United States of America
1 3 5 7 9 10 8 6 4 2

Cover images: Couple © Claudio Marinesco; Chalet and trees © Sandra Cunningham / Trevillion Images
Cover design by Sarah Oberrender
Book design by Tiffany Estreicher

This book is dedicated to the incomparable Karen Rose, who dared me to write a local cop heroine paired with one of my over-the-top Alaska Force heroes. Challenge accepted.

One

The man she was supposed to meet was late.

Deliberately, she assumed.

Investigator Kate Holiday of the Alaska State Troopers noted the time, then sat straighter in the chair she'd chosen specifically because it faced the door of the only café she'd found open in tiny Grizzly Harbor, one of Southeast Alaska's rugged fishing villages that was accessible only by personal boat, ferry—which at this time of year ran seldomly—or air.

Another minute passed. Five minutes. Ten.

This was not a particularly auspicious beginning to her investigation into the strange goings-on in and around this remote town, tucked away on one of the thousand or so islands along the state's southeastern coast. Kate took a dim view of strange goings-on in general, but particularly when they consistently involved a band of ex-military operatives running around and calling themselves "Alaska Force."

Of all things.

Kate was not impressed with groups of armed, dangerous, unsupervised men in general. Much less with those who gave themselves cute names, seemed to expend entirely too much energy attempting to keep the bulk of their activities off the official radar, and yet kept turning up in the middle of all kinds of trouble. Which they then lied about.

She had been unimpressed the moment she'd read the file that carefully detailed the list of potential transgressions her department at the Alaska Bureau of Investigation believed the members of Alaska Force had committed. But then, Kate had a thing about the men up here, on this island and all over the state, who seemed to think that the law did not apply to them. It was a time-honored part of the Alaskan frontier spirit, and Kate had hated it pretty much all her life.

But this was not the time to think about her unpleasant childhood. What mattered was that Kate had grown up. She had escaped from the armed, dangerous, and unsupervised men who had run roughshod over her early years, helped put them away, and had thereafter dedicated herself to upholding the rule of law in the most defiantly, gleefully lawless place in the United States.

This introductory interview with the supposed public relations point person of Alaska Force was only the opening shot. Kate was unamused that the group—who secreted themselves away on the near-inaccessible back side of the island, and when had anything good come from groups of dangerous men with hideouts?—considered it necessary to have a public relations point person in the first place.

She had every intention of taking them down if they were responsible for the escalating series of disturbances that had culminated in an act of arson two days ago, which had amped up her department's interest in what was happening out here in Grizzly Harbor. Because she had no tolerance whatsoever for people who imagined themselves above the law.

Much less people who thought it was entertaining to

blow up fishing boats in the sounds and inlets that made up so much of Southeast Alaska, where summer brought cruise ships filled with tourists. This time there had been no one aboard, likely because it was the first week of a dark December.

But it wouldn't always be December.

The door to the café opened then, letting in a blast of frigid air from outside, where the temperature hovered at a relatively balmy thirty-three degrees. Or likely less than that now that the gray, moody daylight was eking away into the winter dark and the coming sunset at three fifteen.

Kate glanced up, expecting the usual local in typical winter clothes.

But the man who sauntered in from the cold was more like a mountain.

She sat at attention, unable to help herself, her body responding unconsciously to the authority the man exuded the way other men—and the many deadly wild animals who roamed these islands—threw off scent. And she deeply loathed herself for the silly, embarrassingly feminine part of her that wanted to flutter about, straightening her blue uniform. She refrained.

The man before her was dressed for the cold and the coming dark, which should have made him look bulky and misshapen. But it didn't, because all his gear was very clearly tactical. He was big. Very big. She put him at about six four, and that wasn't taking into account the width of his shoulders or the way he held himself, as if he fully expected anyone looking at him to either cower in fear or applaud. Possibly both.

Kate did neither.

It was December on a steep, rugged island made from the top of a submerged mountain and covered in dense evergreen trees, perched there in the treacherous northern Pacific with glaciers all around. One of the most beautiful, if inhospitable, parts of the world. There were only about 150 or so year-round residents of this particular village, and Kate was the only person in the café besides the distinctly unfriendly owner, who had provided her a cup of coffee without comment, then disappeared into the kitchen.

Meaning she was, for all intents and purposes, alone with a man who made her feel as instantly on edge as she would if she'd come face-to-face with a grizzly.

Kate didn't speak as she eyed the new arrival. She'd joined the Troopers after college and had been on the job ever since, helping her fellow Alaskans in all parts of this great state. And sometimes providing that help had involved finding herself in all kinds of questionable situations. The man standing before her radiated power, but Kate knew a thing or two about it herself.

She watched, expressionless, as he stuffed his hat and gloves in the arm of his jacket, like a normal person when he wasn't, then hung it up on one of the hooks near the door. All with what seemed to Kate entirely too much languid indifference for a man who was clearly well aware he was nothing less than a loaded weapon.

He looked around the café, as if he expected to see a crowd on this dreary, cold Friday afternoon in the darkest stretch of the year. Then he finally looked straight at Kate.

For a moment, she felt wildly, bizarrely dizzy. As if the chair she was in had started to spin. She went to sit down, then realized three things, one on top of the next. One, she was already sitting down. Two, the man might have made a big show of looking around, but he'd taken in every single detail about her before he'd fully crossed the threshold. She knew it. She could tell.

And three, the man in front of her wasn't only big and powerful, and incredibly dangerous if the file on him was even partially correct; he was also beautiful.

Shockingly, astonishingly, absurdly beautiful, in a

way that struck her as too masculine, too physical, and too carnal all at once.

He had thick black hair that didn't look the least bit military and that he made no attempt to smooth now that he'd pulled his hat off. His eyebrows were arched and distinctly wicked. His eyes were as dark as strong coffee, his mouth was implausibly distracting, and his cheekbones were like weapons. He looked the way Kate imagined a Hawaiian god might.

Which was a fanciful notion that she couldn't believe she'd just entertained about a person of interest in a recurring series of questionable events.

His gaze was locked to hers, and she wondered if people mistook all that inarguable male beauty for softness, when she could see the gravity in those dark eyes. And a certain sternness in his expression.

But in the next second he smiled, big and wide, and Kate was almost . . . dazzled.

"You must be Alaska State Trooper Kate Holiday," he said in a booming voice. "Come all the way out to Grizzly Harbor to sniff around Alaska Force. I'm Templeton Cross, at your service."

And when he moved, his strides were liquid and easy, two steps to cover the distance and extend his hand to Kate as if he were welcoming her to his home like some cheerful, oversized patriarch. As if he weren't on the wrong side of an interview with law enforcement.

As if he weren't very likely responsible for—or complicit in—a string of hospitalizations, explosions, and other dubious events as far away as Juneau, but mostly concentrated in Grizzly Harbor, going back years. With a noted and concerning uptick over the past year.

But being a trooper wasn't like other kinds of policing, or so Kate gathered from watching police shows based in the Lower 48. Alaska State Troopers had to get used to roles that defied proper job descriptions, because anything could and would happen in the course of a shift when that shift took place somewhere out in the Last Frontier. Kate knew how to play her part. She stood, smiled nonthreateningly, and took his hand.

And told herself that she was cataloging how hard and big it was, that was all. How it wrapped around hers. How Templeton Cross, whose military record stated he had been an Army Ranger until he'd moved off into something too classified to name, made no attempt to overpower her. He didn't shake too hard. He didn't try to crush the bones in her hand, to let her know who was boss. There was no he-man, Neanderthal moment, the way there too often was in situations like these.

He shook her hand like a good man might, and she filed that away because she suspected he wasn't a good man at all. And a man who could fake it was exponentially more dangerous than one who oozed his evil everywhere, like a fuel leak.

She angled her head toward the table she'd claimed, removing her hand from his and waving it in invitation. Because she could act like this was her home, too. No matter that the hand he'd shaken . . . tingled. "Please. Sit down."

"Right to business," Templeton said, with a big laugh that jolted through Kate. She told herself it was an unpleasant sensation, especially the way it wound around and around inside her and heated her up from within. "Caradine!"

The unfriendly owner of the café was a woman with a dark ponytail and a scowl, who appeared in the doorway to the kitchen and glared. "I can't think of a single reason you should yell my name. Not like that. Or at all."

"Deep down," Templeton said to Kate, with a conspiratorial grin, "I'm convinced that Caradine is a marshmallow. Just wrapped up in all that barbed wire."

"No marshmallow. No barbed wire. And no interest whatsoever in being psychologically profiled."

Caradine came over to the table as she spoke, then

plunked down what looked like straight black coffee at the place across from Kate.

"Thank you for opening today," Templeton drawled, grinning wide, as if this was all a complicated friendship ritual. Which maybe it was, if Caradine had opened the café for this meeting on a day that she likely wouldn't see much other business, if any. "And you know you love my psychological profiles."

Caradine did not grin back. "I love nothing, Templeton, except your money."

Kate couldn't decide which one of them was putting on a show. Or was this a coordinated performance for her benefit? Yet somehow, as Caradine stomped back toward her kitchen, she didn't think so. Caradine struck her as a typical sort of resident found all over the wildest, largest state in the union: happy to mind her own business and downright ornery when someone else attempted to mind it for her.

Templeton struck her as a problem.

She smiled at him anyway as he threw himself down into the seat across from her, taking up more than his fair share of space. And his big arms, clad in a tight henley, showed her exactly how seriously he took his physique.

"Do you think this will make you seem more approachable?" she asked.

He belted out another laugh. "Do I seem approachable? I must be slipping."

And for a moment they both smiled at each other, competing to see who could be more pleasant.

"You must know that I'm here after the rash of incidents that seemed to stem entirely from your little group," Kate said, folding her hands on the table and watching his face. His expression didn't change at all. "You've chosen to show up for this conversation late, then engage in what I imagine you think is charming small talk. Your military record goes to great lengths not to say what sort of classified things you engaged in after you were a Ranger, but I'm going to guess it was Delta Force."

"I don't like that name," Templeton said, almost helpfully. "It's so dramatic, don't you think?"

"Now you're being funny," Kate observed. "Which suggests you find yourself entertaining. What interests me, Mr. Cross, is that you think comedy is the appropriate way to handle the situation you find yourself in."

She knew a lot of things about Templeton Cross. Among them, that he'd achieved the rank of master sergeant—but unlike many people with military backgrounds she'd encountered, he didn't correct her when she failed to address him by his rank.

"And what situation is that?" he asked instead. "I'm having a cup of coffee with a law enforcement officer. As a former soldier myself, I have nothing but respect for a badge. I didn't realize there was an expectation that this conversation stay grumpy. But we can do that, too."

"Fascinating," Kate murmured, though he was being evasive, and she was certain that was intentional. "Why don't we start with you explaining Alaska Force to me."

"Alaska Force isn't anything but a group of combat vets who run a little business together," Templeton said genially. "It's all apple pie and Uncle Sam around here, I promise."

"Mercenaries, in other words."

"Not quite mercenaries," Templeton said, and she thought she saw something in his gaze then, some flash of heat, but it was gone almost as soon as she identified it. "I can't say I like that word."

"Is there a better word to describe what you do?"

"We like to consider ourselves problem solvers," Templeton said, sounding friendly and at his ease. He looked it, too. Yet Kate didn't believe he was either of those things. "You start throwing around words like *mercenary*, and people think we're straight-up soldiers of fortune. Soulless men who whore themselves out to the highest bidder. That's not us."

"And yet Alaska Force has, to my count, been involved in no less than six disturbing incidents in the past six months." Kate replied in the same friendly tone he'd used. She even sat back a little, mirroring his ease and supposed laziness right back at him. "There was a member of your own team, if I'm not mistaken, who presented at the hospital in Juneau with injuries consistent with being beaten over the head and forcibly restrained. He claimed he tripped and fell."

"Green Berets are notoriously clumsy," Templeton replied blandly.

"Right around that time, an individual known to be a self-styled doomsday preacher, who Alaska Force interfered with years back—"

"If you mean we made sure he couldn't hurt the women and children he was terrorizing."

"—stole a boat and then rendezvoused with your team this past spring. And with you, if I'm not mistaken." Kate knew she was not mistaken about anything involving this case. She didn't even have to glance at the notepad in front of her to refresh her memory, though she pretended she did. "This interaction involved a high-speed chase in the middle of the night, followed by an explosion." Kate nodded toward the front windows but didn't take her eyes off Templeton. "You claimed he blew up his own boat a few yards outside this harbor and then jumped in the water. Where you saved him out of the goodness of your heart. His story has always been more complicated."

"His story changes every hour on the hour." Templeton's smile struck her as more edgy than before, his eyes more narrow. "We happened to be in place to contain a potentially far more threatening incident. You're welcome."

"Since then, there have been four more incidents involving property damage in and around this island and the surrounding area. Culminating in what happened two nights ago, when a boat that shouldn't have been in the harbor in the first place blew up within sight of the ferry terminal. The anonymous tip that we received suggested Alaska Force was responsible."

Templeton looked unconcerned. "We're not."

"That's it? That's the whole defense you intend to mount?"

"I'm not going to waste my time defending something we didn't do," Templeton said in that amiable, friendly, excessively mild way that was beginning to grate on Kate's nerves. "A reasonable person might ask herself why Alaska Force would blow things up right here in our own backyard. If we were the kind of mercenaries you seem to think we are, that would only draw unwanted attention. Like this meeting."

It was the first hint of anything other than excessive friendliness in his voice. Kate was delighted she was finally getting somewhere.

"You claim you're not that kind of mercenary," she said. "So what kind of mercenary are you? The kind who thinks it's fun to blow things up, maybe? Just because you can?"

"Are you accusing me of something?" Templeton looked and sounded as if he were asking for a menu. Not as if he was facing down an officer of the law and defending himself, whether he wanted to admit that was what he was doing or not.

"Who are the other members of Alaska Force?" Kate asked, instead of answering his question.

Templeton studied her for a moment.

"We tend to be a reclusive bunch," he said after a moment. "I wouldn't want to give you any false impressions. What if I told you what a man calls himself only to be accused of making up a name for villainous purposes? That strikes me as a quagmire I'd be better off avoiding."

Kate smiled. "Isaac Gentry, your leader. Benjamin

Hendricks, otherwise known as Blue. Jonas Crow. Rory Lockwood, the former Green Beret who lied about how he got his injuries last spring. Alexander Oswald."

Templeton laughed. "Who?"

"Otherwise known as Oz." Templeton blinked, and Kate made a show of looking at her notes as she rattled off the rest of the list of names she'd memorized. Then she lifted her gaze to his again. "Up to and including Alaska Force's latest and first female hire, Bethan Wilcox, who joined your team in late August. Did I miss anyone?"

"I don't know why you asked me for a roster when you already have one memorized."

She couldn't tell if that was a figure of speech or if he knew she wasn't really checking her notes. "Are you a doomsday cult of your own? Is Alaska Force involved in some kind of territorial squabble with other less-than-savory groups?"

"A doomsday cult," Templeton repeated, and then let out that laugh again. It was big and bright, and most irritatingly, it seemed to lodge itself inside Kate's chest. She told herself that was the strong coffee the surly Caradine had brought her, warming her from the inside out. "I can't wait to tell everyone you said that."

Then he angled himself forward a little, which seemed to make him that much bigger. That much *more*.

Kate did not allow herself to betray so much as a flicker of reaction. Or to shift herself back at all.

"I've always wanted to be in a cult," Templeton told her, as if they were sharing their hopes and dreams. "Seems like it would be one of those can't-miss life experiences."

"It's not a life experience any reasonable person would want."

For the first time since he'd sat down opposite her, Templeton Cross looked intrigued. "You were in a cult? And they let you be a trooper?"

"I have experience with fringe survivalist groups, yes.

Some might call them cults. I personally view them as criminals, the same as any others."

It had been so long now that Kate knew her voice stayed cool. Even. She could easily have been talking about any old experience she might have had on the job, and she didn't know why she had the distinct impression that this man could see right through her. That he could tell, when so many others hadn't had a clue, that she was talking about herself. Her own experiences. Her personal life that she talked about with no one of her own volition.

That notion chilled her straight through.

"Are you asking if Isaac Gentry has cobbled together a group of fringe survivalists?" Templeton asked. "I'm not sure I know what that even means. This is Alaska. Isn't everyone here a survivalist by default the minute they make it through their first winter? What makes them 'fringe'?"

"There's a difference between what I would call a dangerous survivalist mentality and regular folks who like to keep to themselves, stay off the grid, and conduct their own lives as they see fit."

"If you say so."

Kate leaned forward. "Grizzly Harbor has become the epicenter of an ongoing series of violent incidents. And involved in each and every one of these incidents is this group of yours. A band of men with military skills, who like to get themselves in trouble and then tell lies to the authorities about what happened. This is an unacceptable situation."

"Lies?" Templeton looked innocent—or tried to, anyway, though his face looked purely wicked. "That seems like a harsh word."

"Everybody lies," Kate assured him. "Especially to the police."

"*Everybody* does? Have you interviewed *everybody*?"

"It's the quality, quantity, and kind of lies that you and your friends keep telling that concern me. I have to ask myself what exactly you're hiding out there in Fool's Cove. It's supposed to be nothing more than an old family fishing lodge and a few cabins."

"Fishing is very relaxing. You should try it sometime."

"The thing about a basically inaccessible Alaskan cove that no one can sneak up on is that from where I'm sitting, it looks a lot like a fortress." Kate smiled again. This time, Templeton didn't return it. "And I have yet to discover something that looks that much like a fortress that isn't filled with men who are prepared to defend it like one, too. No matter who comes calling."

"If you're so interested in whether or not Fool's Cove is an armed fortress," Templeton said with a drawl, "why didn't you just show up there and see for yourself? Isn't that what police officers do?"

"This conversation is step one," Kate said. "The friendly approach. I invite you to consider it a warning."

"I'd better behave, then," Templeton murmured, and there was a heat in his voice that made her wonder if he even knew what the word *behave* meant. "You sound like my mama used to. It was best that she never did count all the way to three, if you know what I mean."

"When we asked for this meeting, we expected to meet with Isaac Gentry," Kate said, because she found it oddly disconcerting to imagine the woman a man like this would call *Mama*. "Why isn't he here? Is he too intimidated to have this conversation himself?"

There was what sounded like a snort from the kitchen. Kate didn't turn around, but Templeton's mouth curved the slightest bit in one corner.

"There must be some misunderstanding," he said after a moment, and a deepening of that small curve. "I'm here as a representative of Alaska Force, and also as its first, best member. Isaac and I go way back."

"You and Isaac served together, didn't you?"

"I consider him a brother," Templeton said. Which was a touching way to not answer the question, much less talk about what he and Isaac had done while active-duty members of the military. Kate suspected it was part of that highly classified section of his record. "But if you feel more comfortable talking to him directly, I'm sure we can arrange that." He glanced at his wrist, where he wore a technical watch that looked as if it controlled a fleet of space shuttles. "Thing is, it's getting dark. It's a miserable boat ride this time of year, and it's next-level suffering at night. But I'm game if you are."

And Kate knew she didn't mistake the challenge in the way he looked at her, in his glinting gaze that made her body temperature click up a few degrees, though she refused to acknowledge it.

"No, thank you," she said. "I think I'll pass on the offer to travel in the dark, over rough December seas, on a boat of unknown provenance, with a man I suspect to be involved in criminal activity. Much less to a heavily armed fortress in the middle of nowhere."

"Technically, you just described almost every house in rural Alaska."

"Do you know what sort of people don't turn up to meetings like this? Ones who have something to hide. Or, say, your run-of-the-mill cult leader who feels he's far above such mundane concerns. Which is Isaac?"

Templeton tipped his head back and laughed uproariously at that.

He took his time looking at her again, and when he did, he shook his head a little, as if the hilarity had all but overcome him. Somehow, Kate doubted it.

"He's working, Ms. Holiday. He's a busy man."

"You can call me Trooper Holiday, thank you," Kate corrected him. "But I suspect you know that. Or did they not teach you proper forms of address when you were in the army?" She tilted her head slightly. "Sergeant?"

"I apologize." Though he looked, if anything, amused that she'd used his title in return. Entertained, even. He did not look apologetic. "We keep it pretty informal around here. It helps remind us we're not active duty anymore. Trooper Holiday."

And there was . . . something else in the way he said that. It shivered all the way down the length of her back. Kate sat taller, but the glint in his dark eyes told her he knew why.

When he couldn't. Of course he couldn't.

"Let's get back to this latest incident two nights ago. I'm assuming you know the details."

"I know the details because I know a thing or two about explosives," Templeton said, which was agreeing without incriminating himself, as Kate was certain he knew. "And I tend to take a dim view of them being used in the place where I live. Call it a weird preference of mine if you want. So, yeah, I'm aware that some joker blew up a boat. Until your office called us, we figured it was the usual drunk nonsense. Because, let's face it, out here it usually is."

"Was it drunk nonsense that knocked your friend Rory on the head and left him tied up for a few hours last spring?"

"My recollection is that he fell."

"That's not even a good lie. A man like you can do better. I'm sure of it."

"First, how can a recollection be a lie? You know what memories are like. So unreliable. And second, what do you mean by 'a man like me'?"

Kate smiled. "This whole performance. Swaggering in late. Lounging around like you don't have a care in the world. I understand why they picked you to be their ambassador. You seem so friendly. So approachable, until a person realizes that it's all a show. And I saw your face when you walked in the door. Before you started smiling so much. I think that's probably a whole lot closer to the real Templeton Cross."

She didn't know when the tension between them had gotten so thick, but she didn't do anything to break it. She waited, her gaze steady on his, to see what he would do.

To see who he was.

"I'm pretty sure there's only one Templeton Cross," he said after a beat, his voice a deep, amused rumble. "I don't keep extra ones in a jar by the door." He tapped a lazy finger on the table between them. Kate figured he was reminding her of his intense physicality, the way men often did. Though she didn't usually feel it inside her, as if he'd stroked her with that finger. "Life isn't a Beatles song, you know."

"I read your military file, and what wasn't classified made it pretty clear that you're one of the most dangerous men alive today. And what I have to ask myself is why a man with your background would spend so much time trying to convince me that he's a tabby cat."

"A tabby cat?" Kate thought she heard another snort from the kitchen. "I can tell you with one hundred percent honesty that I have never attempted to act like a tabby cat in my entire life."

"You're only making this worse for yourself," Kate said softly. "You're making me wonder what you're trying to hide. And here's the thing about me that you should know because, of course, you don't have access to *my* file."

But when she said that, something in his face changed. And she wondered if that little flicker she saw in his dark eyes meant that he did indeed have a file on her. The way ex-military types probably would. She would have to assume he did.

Kate kept going. "When I start wondering about things, it tends to lead to investigations. And those investigations tend to lead to convictions. Incarcerations. You get where I'm going with this."

"I can't say I'm a big fan of cages. Or courtrooms."

"Then I suggest you help me."

"I'm nothing if not helpful." His gaze got significantly more intense when he stopped smiling. "How about this? Alaska Force is being framed."

Templeton Cross was not a man who indulged his temper.

If he had been, he wouldn't have been here now. He would have been off venting his spleen in the manner he knew best—which usually involved kicking butt, taking names, and making sure he utilized each and every lethal skill he'd been taught so well in the United States Army.

But it didn't matter that someone had dared to come for his brothers-in-arms. It didn't matter that whoever it was had been circling around Alaska Force and Grizzly Harbor since sometime in the summer, the best they could figure.

It didn't matter that Templeton was a man of action who far too often these days found himself shoehorned into his alternate persona. The one where he was so freaking charming he sometimes thought he might choke on his own smile.

None of that mattered, because the Alaska State Troopers had come calling, and it was Templeton's job to handle it. He'd learned a long time ago that the only thing that mattered was his mission. Usually he believed that totally.

Today shouldn't have been any different.

"You think you're being framed," said the woman across from him at an exposed table in the Water's Edge Café instead of the more private table Templeton preferred. As if she was humoring him.

Trooper Holiday kept a pleasant expression on her face, but her cool brown eyes were cop straight through. And it had been a long, long while since Templeton had seen that particular look directed his way. It amazed him that he could still feel the same kick he had when he'd been an angry, grieving teenager on a self-destructive rampage. Back then he'd seen that look all the time from every police officer in the greater Vidalia, Louisiana, area.

He couldn't say he cared for the sensation. Nostalgia wasn't his thing. So he smiled instead.

Her intense expression only cooled further. "And who do you think would go to the trouble of framing a bunch of men with violent, antisocial predilections when it seems clear to me you and your friends are good at doing it on your own?"

Templeton was good at charming people. It was one of the reasons he'd succeeded in his chosen profession. Well. He hadn't so much *chosen* the army as he'd been advised by a judge that he'd better get right with the Lord, Uncle Sam, or any combination thereof, because if he showed his face in the courtroom again he'd end up doing hard time.

He might have been basically feral at that point of his life, having been shuttled from one foster care placement to another after his mother died—because Templeton had already been gaining on six feet and was called *scary* at twelve years old when really, he was half-crazy with grief—but he'd had no interest in being yet another brown man behind bars. Like his own father. No, thank you. He'd introduced himself to Uncle Sam down at the recruiter's office later that same afternoon and had changed the course of his life forever.

And now here he was. All these years later, telling lies to another cop.

At least this time around, he was better at it.

"If we knew who was framing us," he said, pleasantly enough, "we'd probably go on out and apprehend them."

"And by 'apprehend them,' can I assume you mean something along the lines of what happened that night last spring out in the sound when yet another boat blew up?" Her voice was as cool as her gaze. And it made Templeton remember being smaller, skinnier, angrier. And so much less in control of himself that he'd been a different person entirely. "That being the night you claim you were out fishing in the predawn hours and just happened to catch the very preacher whose compound you'd disrupted heading for Grizzly Harbor. Loaded up with bad intentions."

The boat had been packed with C-4 as well as bad intentions, but Templeton only smiled wider. "Fishing is my life."

Templeton had never fished, unless it was back in the hazy days of his early childhood in Mississippi before his father had started his life sentence, no possibility of parole, thanks to the state's three-strikes law. If so, Templeton had gone ahead and buried it along with any other stray memory of the man who'd disappeared into Mississippi's notorious Parchman prison and had refused to let anyone visit him there. Ever. Because he might as well be dead, he'd said, and they needed to grieve him and move on.

Thinking about his father made Templeton want to hit something. Preferably Isaac Gentry—founder of Alaska Force and also Templeton's best friend and brother-by-battle, a relationship forged in some of the worst fires imaginable. They had both been recruited into what was sometimes called Delta Force. Isaac had come from Marine Force Recon and Templeton from the Army Rangers, and they'd both made it through separate, grueling selection processes to the same qualification course. They'd both managed not to wash out of that six-month adventure into what a man was really made of—otherwise known as hell—and they'd been working together in one form or another ever since.

Templeton would die for Isaac in a heartbeat, but that didn't mean he enjoyed being sent on this errand to play cops and robbers with a trooper while the rest of the team tried to figure out who was trying to come at them. It made him wish he could indulge his temper after all.

Or, worse, the other appetites he kept on lockdown while on a job, because he liked his life free of complications.

The thing was, Templeton couldn't help but notice, *Trooper Holiday* had a seriously complicated mouth.

It was distracting.

Templeton had taken her number before he'd walked in, since she'd chosen to sit at a table where he could study her through the window without being seen. And while he'd messed around with his coat, hanging it up neatly like he was in any way domesticated, he'd been comparing what Oz, Alaska Force's computer whiz, had told them about Investigator Kate Holiday of the Alaska Bureau of Investigation to the actual flesh-and-blood woman waiting for him in Caradine's Water's Edge Café.

Caradine might have been the most relentlessly unfriendly person Templeton had ever met, which was only one of the reasons he liked her, but she could always be depended on to open up the café if needed. Even on slow winter afternoons, because she was always happy to be paid for her trouble. And Templeton preferred the home-court advantage.

Kate Holiday was exactly who he was expecting. Trim build, with lean curves that told him how dedicated she was to keeping fit. It was another way of letting him know that she cared deeply about her competence, and he approved. Templeton knew she'd flown herself here in one of the little jumper seaplanes that everybody and their uncle seemed to have in this part of the world, which told him she was practical and independent. Because the Alaska State Troopers were spread thin as it was, like a bunch of shiny blue marbles flung across a big, wide, endlessly wild and rugged table. Templeton was always hearing stories about the troopers having to take commercial flights or ferries to conduct their investigations. Unless, of course, they had their own transportation at the ready.

In the file Oz had compiled, Templeton had seen a picture of her in the traditional Trooper uniform, her brown hair pulled back severely and that unsmiling, authoritative cop look on her face. It didn't make her any less pretty, but it suggested that her prettiness came with a punch.

In person, she was less severe. She still had her hair scraped back, but there was something about her face in motion that got to him. That generous mouth, maybe, that made him want to keep looking. Made him want to reach out and touch.

He didn't. And not only because it was clear that Trooper Holiday took her boundaries seriously. Very seriously, if the stiff way she was sitting was any indication.

The thing was, Templeton shouldn't have *wanted* to touch her. He had strict rules against getting involved with women he met through work and might have to contend with in his professional sphere.

One disaster in that arena was enough, he'd always thought. He'd had his already.

"You seem to have drifted off there," she commented in that cool voice that reminded him that whatever else she was, she was sharp. And not particularly charmed by him, which, perversely, made him think more highly of her. After all, an act was an act, and Templeton never could bring himself to unreservedly like anyone who bought his. "Dreaming of fishing?"

Templeton smiled. "All the time. Even in the middle of rousing conversations with law enforcement officials, my heart is out there with my bait and tackle. Makes a man feel alive inside."

"I'm thrilled for you." She folded her hands before her on the table, and the smile she aimed back at him was laced with steel. He liked that, too. "So what is it you think someone would gain by framing you?"

"Off the top of my head, I think the first thing they'd gain was the Alaska State Troopers all up in our business." He tipped his head toward her. "And check it out. Here you are."

"I like to flatter myself that our reputation is fierce indeed, but I somehow doubt that we're an endgame."

So did Templeton. Which begged the obvious question. If siccing the Troopers on Alaska Force wasn't the endgame, what was?

"You're skeptical. I get it. But ask yourself this. Who stands to gain from Alaska Force being taken apart?"

She regarded him steadily, in a manner calibrated to induce spontaneous confessions of wrongdoing. "You mean aside from the citizens of the great state of Alaska, who can look forward to healthier and happier lives with a band of petty criminals taken off the streets?"

"For the sake of argument, pretend that Alaska Force isn't your run-of-the-mill survivalist cult," Templeton suggested, and it cost him to keep that smile in his voice and on his face. "Pretend that instead, we are men of honor. Men who served their country well and aren't quite ready to become civilians. Men who instead dedicated their lives to solving problems law enforcement can't."

"That's very stirring. But if law enforcement can't

solve the problem, that suggests that any civilian-led solutions are illegal."

"Not illegal." Templeton considered. "Really, we operate in more of a gray area."

"I don't believe in gray areas."

Templeton didn't have to pretend to be amused then. He laughed. "You don't have to believe in gray areas. They're still there."

"There's wrong and there's right," Kate replied. "It's actually simple."

"Unfortunately, life is very rarely simple."

"On the contrary. We all want to make life complicated, and we often go to great lengths to do it. But the right choice is always obvious." Her brown eyes glittered. "People don't want to take it."

"That's easy to say."

"I'm sure that you tell yourself all kinds of lies to make it okay that you bend the rules, Mr. Cross."

Once again, her gaze was steady on his. *Sure*. Most people were intimidated by him. Cowed, whether they wanted to show it or not. But not this woman. She stared right back at him as if they were the same size. As if, should she feel like it, she could surge to her feet and engage him in hand-to-hand combat and who knows? Maybe land a few punches.

It was about the hottest thing Templeton had ever seen.

"But rules exist for a reason," she said steadily. With that same look that suggested she was wholly unaware that he outweighed her by at least a hundred pounds of pure muscle. "Everybody thinks it's okay if *they* cheat a little or tell a white lie. But then before you know it, we find ourselves here. Where a group of mercenaries with combat training can call themselves patriots and terrorize whole islands in Southeast Alaska."

Templeton studied her. "Black and white. Right and wrong. No deviation. Got it."

"It's not a character flaw. It's called the law."

"Alaska Force exists because people are always coming to us for help. Not hired muscle or combat-trained terrorists." He shook his head. "It seems to me that if you take us out of the picture, you allow other people far less cute and cuddly than we are to move in and do a whole lot worse."

Again, that smile, as if she were humoring someone remarkably dim-witted. If Templeton had been possessed of the slightest shred of self-doubt where his intellect and abilities were concerned, that smile might have inspired him into unfortunate displays. Luckily, he could sit there and enjoy it as the weapon it was.

"Do you have examples of other bands of desperadoes roaming around the Alexander Archipelago, wreaking havoc?" she asked. "Because so far, the only group by that description I'm aware of is yours."

Templeton reviewed the situation. The first time something had blown up a little too close to Grizzly Harbor, they'd considered it an isolated incident. That preacher had vowed he'd get his revenge, and there he was, trying to get it. They'd intercepted him, taken him out, and presented him to the authorities—practically with a bow on top.

But the next time it had been a storage facility in Sitka, one of the larger cities out here in Alaska's rugged southeast islands, which Isaac and Templeton had set up when they'd first started to put this funny idea of theirs into action. Only three of their team had walked back off the field after that last, terrible op, and that was it. They were all done.

Jonas Crow had disappeared as soon as the briefing was done. Like the ghost he was.

Templeton had gone back to Vidalia, but there was nothing for him there. He barely remembered that feral teenager he'd been. He had aunts and uncles he'd never met scattered all over Mississippi, and a father still doing that life sentence in Parchman, but his mother had walked away from all of them when Templeton was still small, blaming everyone and everything in the state for what had happened to her husband. That meant Templeton had never had any use for them, either, in solidarity.

And the truth was that none of that mattered to him now. Not the way the men he considered his real brothers did.

Templeton had never been one for the cold, but he found himself in Alaska anyway, because he remembered the stories Isaac had told him during all the dark nights—of the soul or otherwise—they'd bare-knuckled it through together. Stories of growing up in a place called Grizzly Harbor, where the men were hardy and the women were far tougher, winter came like it planned to stay forever, and summer felt like a dream even while it was happening.

It seemed like the least likely place to build something. And therefore the best.

After a while, they'd gone out and found Jonas, too.

And what the three of them were particularly good at was anticipating trouble, so it made sense to spread things out. The storage facility in Sitka was only one of the places they used to stash equipment. It had been empty that July night when a fire broke out and burned the building down. The fire had been put out before it could spread, but their unit had been damaged beyond repair.

But fires happened. It wasn't until a second storage unit went up in flames, this one farther afield in Ketchikan, that it occurred to everyone that the first one probably wasn't an accident. And more concerning, that to target storage units at all meant that someone knew more about Alaska Force's operation than they should.

They'd moved swiftly. They'd stopped using commercial storage space for equipment drops years back, and it was high time they stopped using them altogether.

They'd taken the fires as a sign to do just that and closed out their contracts with the remaining few storage facilities within weeks.

It was hard to say if things kept happening, or if they were all so paranoid that they started to worry if everyday, minor inconveniences were actually something more ominous. A fuel gauge that quit working and registered full when it wasn't, leading to a dramatic set down of a seaplane outside Anchorage. An accident or sabotage? No one knew.

Summer had ended and things quieted down, likely because it wasn't exactly easy to creep around a tiny village in the high tourist season of summer, much less when the weather started to turn, all the tourists went home, and the only ones left were the real residents who weathered the winters. And knew one another on sight.

Until the end of October, that was, when hikers on one of the neighboring islands found the charred remains of what had once been an off-the-grid residence. That the house had been torched was obvious even to a casual observer, but no motive had ever been found. Except that, on a clear day, the rickety old cabin had enjoyed a view over the water and straight toward Fool's Cove, the Alaska Force headquarters.

But by that point, they were all convinced that they were running on too much paranoia. Because this was Alaska, where weird things happened all the time. It really could have been a big coincidence.

Burning a boat right here in the harbor felt a whole lot like someone was changing the game. Still, Templeton was here today because Isaac wanted to keep a low profile in the place where he lived as long as he could. And given that the Troopers weren't exactly idiots, Isaac wasn't likely to convince them that he was just a regular guy despite his classified military record. No one ever thought that Templeton was a regular guy, either. But he could often convince them that he was nothing more than big and loud, all laugh and no substance.

Though it had been clear from the moment he'd walked in here that Kate wasn't fooled.

That made her fascinating. And hot, God help him.

And more to the point, dangerous.

"Alaska Force deals with desperate people," he told her now, because the staring contest looked like it could drag on forever. She didn't seem to have any give in her at all. Which Templeton obviously took as a challenge, instantly wondering where and how he could find some—he stopped himself. "Desperation tends to breed enemies."

"Enemies do not breed. They're made by our choices." The way she said that caught at him, but she kept going. "Have you and your friends made the kind of choices that make enemies?"

"You tell me. You're a cop. When you put people in jail, do you explain to them that there's a choice between right and wrong and they should be grateful to you for making sure they didn't go too far down the road of the wrong choice?"

She didn't flinch at that. She didn't even blink. But Templeton thought he got to her all the same. "Not in so many words."

"Do you think those people appreciate you for locking them up? Or do you think, given the opportunity, they might try to get their own back?"

"The more you talk about enemies, the more I think that what I'm hearing is unhinged paranoia," she said. Conversationally. Though her gaze was hard. "And the more I hear unhinged paranoia, the more convinced I become that you and your friends are dangerous. More dangerous, I should say."

"We might be paranoid." Templeton grinned lazily. "But that doesn't mean someone isn't out to get us."

She smiled a steely cop smile and held her hands more tightly on the table between them.

And Templeton did not give in to the urge he had to reach over and cover her hands with his.

He was a man who enjoyed his appetites, heartily. That didn't mean he wandered around, indiscriminately touching people. But something about the starchy way this woman sat across from him, with that sinful mouth of hers and cool challenge in her gaze, made him feel . . . born-again tactile.

Templeton didn't mess around with women he worked with. It was his one cardinal rule. But Kate Holiday made him wonder if he ought to make a special dispensation to the *no women met through work* rule for a woman who wanted him behind bars.

"I'd encourage you to view this as an opportunity," she was saying, clearly unaware of the direction of his thoughts. Or prepared to ignore him. "One that may not be repeated. You have the chance, here and now, to clear this whole thing up. To tell me what's actually going on and work with me to come to some kind of solution."

"I thought that's what I was doing."

"You have a choice." She smiled as if they shared something now. As if they'd built that rapport. "You can help me out and make this all go smoothly. Or you can continue to play these games, and I can promise you that smooth is not how it's going to go."

"I told you the situation." Templeton ordered himself not to think of the things he'd like to share with this trooper. "You're basically accusing the local VFW of being a terrorist cell."

"Is that what you consider yourselves? The local chapter of a VFW?"

"Essentially. Seems to me you should be more concerned with protecting veterans than accusing them."

"You appear to think that your status as a veteran

should accord you special treatment when you break the law. I assure you, it will not."

"Tough room." Templeton wanted to reach out to her, so he sprawled back in his chair instead. He thrust his legs out before him as if he were settling in to watch a game or get his drink on.

"Once again, I would strongly caution you against throwing this opportunity away." She looked like a Kate, no-nonsense and direct, with all that intriguing fire simmering beneath the surface. "The more I uncover about what's going on around here, the less interested I'm going to be in doing anything the easy way. You need to understand that now."

"I was in the Rangers, ma'am," Templeton drawled. "There is no easy way."

Though he found that the longer he looked at her, the more he could think of a few very easy ways to get his point across.

And this time, he was positive she fully grasped the direction of his thoughts. She flushed a fascinating ruddy shade, though she didn't otherwise change her expression. Or even sit back.

Maybe Templeton would have continued to nobly ignore that urge to put his hands on hers, because that was the smart thing to do. Then again, maybe he wouldn't have, because he'd made a career out of thinking outside arbitrary lines—if not usually the ones he drew himself. But it didn't matter either way because Caradine was there at the table, scowling, like the prickly little black cloud she was.

Templeton knew of only one man who wanted to get his hands in all that rain. But then, Isaac had always been a breed apart.

"Fog's coming in fast," Caradine said flatly. "Doesn't look like either one of you is leaving Grizzly Harbor tonight. And don't think I'm cooking dinner for you."

Templeton only shrugged. Caradine stomped off, likely to work on that thunderous scowl, and he watched his new favorite trooper fuss around with her phone.

"If the fog's bad, you shouldn't fly in it." He smiled when she frowned at him. "No worries. We can find you somewhere to stay."

"I can find my own accommodations, thank you."

"I'm sure you can, but Alaska Force keeps a room ready for clients at the Blue Bear Inn. It's empty right now. You're welcome to it tonight."

He told himself there was no reason why his skin felt tight the longer she looked at him.

"Thank you," she said, nothing in her voice betraying the slightest hint of emotion. Or reaction. As if he'd made up that flush of heat on her cheeks when he knew he hadn't. "I may have to take you up on that offer."

"Just promise me you won't try to outfly the fog," he said, as if they were buddies. "That tends to end badly."

"Your concern for my well-being is touching," Kate replied, evenly enough. But he could tell she didn't find it touching at all. "If you'll excuse me."

She stood up, taking her phone with her as she headed toward the back of the café, where there was a bathroom—and privacy.

Templeton stayed where he was, lounging at the table until she disappeared. Then he fished out his own mobile and called in.

"Report," Isaac said when he picked up.

"Nothing to report," Templeton replied. "Looks like I might be fogged in here tonight. Can't say whether that will help or hinder the investigation."

"And Alaska Force is the target of that investigation? Or is this a fishing expedition?"

"You have two choices, Isaac. The right one or the wrong one. It's that simple."

"Great." Isaac sighed. "One of those."

"The trooper has put in a request to visit the heavily

armed fortress that is Fool's Cove," Templeton said. "Assuming we get a break in the fog tomorrow, I'll bring her out."

"Do you have a sense of what she's looking for?"

"Aside from a scapegoat? No."

"Maybe try charming her, Templeton. If you think you can manage it."

Templeton made a genial, anatomically impossible suggestion, which only made his friend laugh.

And he was sliding his phone back into his pocket when his own personal trooper emerged from the back of the café, her uniform looking even more crisp than it had when she'd gone back there. Armor, he thought.

He liked the fact that she thought she needed it around him.

And he ignored the alarm that sounded deep within him. Because enjoying something wasn't the same as breaking his own rules.

"Visibility is deteriorating by the moment," Kate said briskly. "It looks like I'll be utilizing that room after all."

"Fantastic. I'll just—"

"I don't need anything further from you, Mr. Cross," she said in that smooth, certain cop way that he definitely shouldn't find so . . . stirring. "I can handle things from here. What I'd like you to do is use this evening to reflect on the things we talked about and see if you can find your way to a different conclusion."

"I'll be sure to do that," Templeton drawled. "I get real reflective down at the Fairweather. By the third drink, I'm practically a philosopher."

"Wonderful," she replied crisply. "Because what everybody wants from the local neighborhood commando is drunken philosophy."

She turned to Caradine then, who was lounging in the door to the kitchen like she was watching premium cable play out there before her. "I'd like to ask you a few questions, if I could."

Caradine's brows rose. "I don't really do questions."

"Nonetheless," Kate said, in that friendly yet implacable way Templeton figured they had to teach them at the academy over in Sitka, "I'd like to chat with you all the same."

Caradine scowled but nodded. Once, and clearly with reluctance.

Templeton's trooper turned to him and lifted a brow. "Can I anticipate that when I arrive at the Blue Bear Inn, my accommodations will be ready for me? Or are there more hoops to jump through first?"

"I can call Madeleine. She's usually on the front desk when there's someone staying, though it's the off-season."

"You do that. And I'll take your mobile number, so that I can reach you, should I need to."

Templeton obediently rattled off his cell phone number and watched her jot it down in her notebook. Then she tucked it back into her pocket.

"Does this mean we're dating?" he asked.

Because he couldn't seem to help himself.

"It means I'll let you know when I'm ready to see you again, Sergeant," Kate said. And then she nodded toward the door, dismissing him. "But for now? You can leave."

Templeton met Caradine's gaze and assumed he looked as astonished as she did entertained. Because he couldn't recall the last time anyone had ordered him around. Not even Isaac, and that was only because they'd worked together so long that Templeton tended to anticipate his orders.

He didn't argue. He sauntered over to the hook where he'd left his jacket, shrugged it on, and then offered a theatric salute before he let himself out into the dark.

And waited to see what his brand-new favorite Alaska State Trooper was going to do next.

Three

The door slammed behind Templeton, and for a strange, dizzy little moment, it was like all the air, light, and heat went with him.

But that was absurd. And more of that fanciful nonsense from which Kate normally steered clear. She ordered herself to get it together and focused her attention on Caradine, who still stood in the kitchen doorway with reluctance written all over her.

For a moment, Kate only gazed at the other woman, because the scowl on her face was interesting and Kate knew well the power of an awkward silence.

But all Caradine did was continue to scowl, without saying a word. Which was very unusual in the average civilian with no experience being interrogated by law enforcement. Then again, out here in remotest Alaska, people tended toward prickly and uncooperative by nature. It didn't make them criminals.

"What is your relationship to Alaska Force?" Kate asked crisply when it was clear the silence wasn't going to prod the other woman into revealing anything.

If possible, the scowl on Caradine's face deepened. "I would never call anything between me and them a *relationship*."

"Call it whatever you like. What is the nature of it?"

Caradine looked as if she'd swallowed something sour. "I run a café in a very small village. They live in and around the same small village, and they eat at my café. The end."

"Mr. Cross mentioned that you opened today, just for him. Or did I misinterpret something?"

Caradine crossed her arms, and Kate wondered if she knew that the gesture on her looked belligerent more than defensive. She suspected she did know. But Caradine's surliness didn't bother her. Alaskans weren't always fit for human interaction. It was a side effect of living in the midst of so much relentless nature. Besides, while many people came to Alaska for a job or because they loved the idea of all that nature, Alaska was also a place a lot of folks came to disappear.

Kate would stake her reputation on the likelihood that Caradine was one of the latter.

She studied the café owner carefully. Caradine, which Kate very much doubted was the name she'd been born with, was a beautiful woman, though she clearly preferred to downplay that fact. Her dark hair was pulled back in a careless ponytail that looked as if she'd slept in it. There wasn't a trace of makeup on her face, her nail polish was black and chipped, and the jeans she wore were at least a size too big. Her baggy T-shirt used a cartoon fox in place of a curse and the apron she wore wrapped around her waist looked about as battered as her jeans. And of course, there was the deeply prickly body language turning all those things into a deliberate suit of armor.

But it was the wary, combative light in the other woman's eyes that made the back of Kate's neck itch.

"If someone in the village calls and asks me to open,

I usually do," Caradine said flatly. "That's just part and parcel of the service I provide to my friends and neighbors."

"And you consider Alaska Force friends? Neighbors? Both?"

"I try not to consider Alaska Force at all."

Kate smiled. "This is not a productive conversation. The question is, are you being unhelpful out of loyalty to Mr. Cross and his associates? Or are you trying to make it extra clear to me that you don't like the police?"

"I don't like anyone, Trooper," Caradine said. "I wasn't aware that was a crime."

"How long have you lived in Grizzly Harbor?"

"Am I under investigation now? Because let me be the first to tell you, I'm no commando. When danger comes calling, I hide."

Kate studied the woman before her. "Now, why do I find that so hard to believe?"

"I'm a cook," Caradine said, and she even smiled. "I live on an island in Alaska, where nobody is going to irritate me by demanding gluten-free, dairy-free, food-free alternatives, and if they do, I can tell them to leave. I can serve what I want. I can open when I want. I don't have to make small talk, or chitchat with anyone. I can just cook. That's it. That's my whole story."

"Do you live alone?"

"I can barely tolerate my own company, much less anyone else's." Caradine sighed when Kate only gazed at her. "Yes, I live alone. And no, I don't have any kind of relationship with anyone in Alaska Force. Thank the Lord."

But that was a lie. Kate could see it on her face. She didn't go after it, but she did take out her pad and make an ostentatious note in it, just to watch Caradine stiffen in response.

"And where did you live before you came to Alaska?"

"What makes you think I haven't always been right here, marking my territory in the Last Frontier?"

"I'm from here," Kate said. "It's not hard to tell who's from Outside. No matter how long it's been since they came." She smiled. "Besides, I'm assuming you would have had to live somewhere with a lot of gluten- and dairy-free options to find it so annoying."

Caradine's gaze glittered. "And here I thought I blended."

"Okay, let's try this." Kate considered the stubborn, mulish set to Caradine's jaw. "What are your impressions of the members of Alaska Force? Like Templeton Cross, for example. Or what about Isaac Gentry, their leader?"

Something flashed in Caradine's gaze. "I don't have anything nice to say about them. But I don't have anything not nice to say, either. I can't stress to you the extent to which I don't like people and am therefore entirely neutral about them and what they do. But they're not a cult. They're not really commandos. People come to them for help, and they help them."

"Why does it sound like you're telling me these things under duress?"

"Look, I'll deny it if you ever bring it up again, particularly in front of anyone connected to Alaska Force, but the truth is that none of them are bad men." And the look Caradine gave her then was frank. There was a kind of dark knowledge there that made Kate stand a little straighter. "I know about bad men. This is not that."

Kate hoped her own dark knowledge wasn't showing on her face. "There are a lot of ways to be a bad man, don't you think?"

"There are a lot of ways to break a law, sure. But a bad man is a bad man. Inside. Whether he breaks the law or doesn't. Are you going to tell me you don't know the difference?"

Kate wanted to smile her cool, unbothered cop smile. Brush off the question and carry on firing questions at Caradine. But somehow, she couldn't. There was something about the stark honesty of the question. About that too-certain expression on the other woman's face.

It was this time of year, she told herself. This endless dark and the run-up to Christmas and New Year's, which always got to her. Too many anniversaries this time of year. Too many memories she blocked out a lot better the rest of the time. Every year she told herself she wouldn't let the darkness and the holidays get to her. And yet every year they did anyway.

Whatever the reason, she found she couldn't brush Caradine off.

"I know from bad men, if that's what you're asking," Kate heard herself say, as if she weren't here on business. As if she were having a conversation like a regular person.

Caradine's gaze gleamed. "Of course you do. Welcome to being female."

"But I don't make the distinctions you do when it comes to breaking laws. There's right and there's wrong. Or there's chaos."

The corner of Caradine's mouth kicked up into something a little too wry to be a smile. "This is Alaska, Trooper. What other people call chaos, we call a pissant little winter storm."

"But that's why I'm a trooper, Ms. . . . ?"

"Scott," Caradine supplied. Grudgingly. "Caradine Scott."

"That's why I'm a trooper, Ms. Scott," Kate repeated, and something seemed to pass between them then, woman to woman on an already too-dark December afternoon. "I can tell the difference between weather and major crimes."

They went around and around a few more times, but after that moment of telling honesty, Caradine seemed to fall into her scowl with a vengeance and stay there. Kate thanked her for her time, shot off a note to one of her friends in the department to pull up information on one Caradine Scott, currently of Grizzly Harbor though clearly from the Lower 48 originally, and smiled as she let herself out.

Night had come down, hard. It was after four p.m., and it could as easily have been four in the morning. And Kate didn't have to go check her instruments or check the flight databases, because she could see how bad the fog was with her own eyes. It was a heavy curtain in and around everything, making the dark thicker. As if December had teeth and weight.

Kate had always thought so.

And Kate was more than capable of flying by her instruments, but she didn't like to risk it when the weather got questionable. She wasn't much for taking risks, full stop. There were too many stories of small crafts like hers going down in weather like this because the pilot had depended too much on the instruments and run straight into the side of a mountain.

That was the thing with mountains, especially here. They were wily. And not always where they were supposed to be.

It looked like she'd be spending the night in Grizzly Harbor.

She tucked her hands into her jacket, grateful that the village was on the water, making the temperature more reasonable than the winters she remembered off in the interior of the state, out there in the frigid, subzero bush. She'd seen snow on the mountains here as she'd flown in, but there was none on the ground. Then again, it was early yet. She'd expect any serious snow to set in after the New Year.

Even in the foggy afternoon, Grizzly Harbor was pretty. The buildings were clustered together, lit up against the pressing night and the creeping fog. Lights punched out into the dark, some of them brightly colored to announce the coming holiday, others there to make sure the residents could find their way. But either way, it felt festive today. Or at least, that cross section of festive and functional that was an Alaskan winter.

The wooden pathway that took the place of a street was easy enough to navigate from light to light. Kate followed it all the way down to the docks at the bottom of the hill, where she'd left her seaplane. She called in her position and her plans, shared a few of her observations, then retrieved the go bag she kept in her little plane. Because getting stranded out on a job was par for the course, and troopers always came prepared.

Kate slung her bag over her shoulder and settled it against her hip, but when she went to start the steep walk back up the hill toward the inn she'd seen earlier, she paused.

Because Grizzly Harbor clung to the side of the mountain, covered in fog but gleaming like a Christmas card. The weathered houses were clustered together, as if huddling for warmth. In the weak daylight earlier, Kate had noticed how ramshackle they were. How rugged.

But night and fog were kinder, softening all the edges, and Kate's breath left her in a rush.

Once again, she blamed the time of year.

This was always when she was at her weakest. And weakness led to outrageous reactions, like the outsized one she'd had to Templeton Cross. She flushed again, here in the dark, where at least this time no one could see her betray herself so thoroughly. She told herself it was temper, but she could feel that heat all over her body. Even in places she'd decided long ago didn't work for her the way they did for others. She was hot. Everywhere.

It was him. Templeton Cross.

That too big, too loud, too deliberately inappropriate man who was very likely a criminal . . . got to her. He made her body behave like it belonged to someone else. Someone significantly less disciplined than Kate.

Someone who would actually consider a man on the

wrong side of the law, which was so decidedly *not her* that something like a sob welled up deep inside Kate, as though her body was trying to rebel against the things it felt.

"It's just Christmas," Kate muttered out loud to herself. To the fog. To whatever was happening inside her. "All you have to do is get through it."

She forced herself to stop gaping at the pretty village posed there before her like her very own Christmas carol, complete with the musical accompaniment from the rising tide at the water's edge. She started walking up the hill, wishing there were some way she could stop feeling that terrible hollowness that always marked this time of year for her.

She would have been perfectly happy to stay numb. To feel nothing at all, the way she did the rest of the year.

People loved to talk about the power of family. And they never seemed to talk about it more than when Christmas approached, as if the presence of an Advent calendar made them forget what world they lived in. As if hokey songs and a fat man in a red suit erased all the terrible things that went on all around them, all the time.

Kate hadn't grown up with Christmas. Not the way people talked about it, anyway. There had been no tree, decorated or otherwise. Certainly no gifts. Her father—a term Kate only used because it was biologically correct—had never trucked with any notion of holidays. Christmas was a workday like any other out there in the family compound, where their version of off-the-grid subsistence living in the frigid bush came with a whole lot of daily hard labor, regardless of the lack of daylight. And on Christmas, that workload came with an extra helping of unhinged ranting.

What Kate knew about Christmas she'd learned from her father's bitter rants against capitalism, materialism, commercialization, and the sick and bloated masses who were too stupid to see the truth that had led him and his brothers away from all that corruption to make their own world as they liked it.

When she'd finally escaped that tangled mess, it had been under cover of the darkness that characterized this time of year. On a subzero Christmas Day up north. Before that day fifteen years ago, Christmas had always been the horror of what her father would do and how long he would make them all sit there, cold and hungry, while he screamed and yelled and carried on about a world none of the kids growing up in the compound could remember. Then it had been the longest day of her life, when she'd escaped all of that. And then, later, it had been the difference between what Kate knew Christmas was and what everyone out there in the so-called real world claimed it was while manic and overtly cheerful.

It all led to that hollowness inside her, which made her suspect that her childhood had broken something crucial within her. And that she would always be an alien, unable to feel the things normal humans did. Especially where family was concerned.

Her solution had always been to work. Everyone else wanted the holidays off, but not Kate. Never Kate. It was one of the reasons, she was sure, that she'd advanced as quickly as she had through the ranks.

And so she had no idea why, despite all of that, she still found herself susceptible to colored lights strung up on an evergreen tree. Candles and lanterns lighting up windows. And houses lit up against the smothering Alaskan night.

She headed up the hill, making it to the wooden pathway that led toward the inn. She heard the sound of a door slamming in the distance. A dog barking. The hum of generators. The sea in the distance, surging against the rocks.

And the sudden, bright splash of music and laughter when the door to the local bar swung open, spilling noise out into the street.

Kate stopped where she was, several doors down, because she recognized the man who shouldered his way out into the night.

Templeton.

She watched her own breath against the night, escaping in a gust like she'd been socked in the stomach.

He finished zipping up his coat, then jerked his gloves on. He lifted his head and stood there a moment, as if he were listening to all the same sounds of the town she was. He tugged his hat down on his head, turned, and headed off around the back of the bar. Then up the steep little hill that led to the next so-called street.

Kate didn't question her instincts. She followed him.

There wasn't much to the village, but it was dark and the fog was only thickening, providing Kate with all the cover she could possibly need. Templeton moved silently for such a big man, and there was nothing loud or gregarious about him as he slipped through the night. The way he moved reminded her of the look she'd seen on his face when he'd first pushed his way into the café today. That leashed power that made him the man she'd read about in the files, not the performer she'd met at their interview.

The contrast made her shiver.

Kate followed him up the hill, then waited as he made his way to a house set back in the trees, away from the main clump of the village. She stayed where she was, some ways behind him and covered by the shroud of fog. She watched him as he knocked twice on the front door, then let himself in.

One breath. Another. Then a third, and only then did Kate ease herself out from behind the tree she'd been waiting behind. She picked her way toward the house.

She didn't know what she expected to find. Or maybe she did know, she thought, when she peeked through the window and saw what was inside. She'd expected something out of her own childhood. Bare walls and hard floors, because possessions were a distraction, the mission was everything, and the more it hurt, the better.

She blinked at her father's voice wedged deep inside her, then focused on what was actually happening in the house before her.

It looked comfortable. Cozy, even. She was looking into a living room that opened up into a cheerful kitchen behind it. The walls were filled with bookshelves, not machine guns, swastikas, or any of the other weird and creepy things she'd have expected. And in the kitchen, Templeton was kicked back against one of the counters, a bottle of beer in his hands, looking relaxed and at ease.

Not that lazy watchfulness he'd put on for her benefit in the café earlier, but actually relaxed. She was shocked at what a difference it was even though she'd known he was performing.

It looked like the beginnings of the making of dinner. A cozy, domestic scene. Another man was chopping up spices and vegetables and adding them to a pot, the way he held himself and his body language—like the very precise way he wielded his knife—suggesting that he was another elite, special forces kind of guy like Templeton.

The other person in the room was a stunningly gorgeous, elegant blond woman, who wore a black turtleneck sweater that even from this side of the window Kate could tell was made of the finest cashmere. There was a hint of gold at her wrist where the sleeve fell back as she held a glass of wine. Her hair was tossed up into the kind of hairstyle that likely came with a fancy French word to describe it. She looked entirely too elegant for a remote fishing village clinging to the side of an Alaskan mountain.

It took Kate a moment, but she knew who the woman was. Mariah McKenna, a former Alaska Force client turned main prosecution witness in a highly publicized upcoming trial against her rich and powerful former father-in-law. As Kate watched, Mariah leaned in to kiss the man at the stove's jaw with all the possessive certainty of an established lover. And Kate wasn't sure how she'd missed the fact that Mariah had very obviously started shacking up with the man who had to be Griffin Cisneros, former marine sniper, who'd been involved in foiling the kidnap and murder plot against Mariah this past spring.

Just as Kate wasn't sure why the sight of them as a couple made her heart kick at her a little, since Kate would certainly never start dating someone she was investigating. The very idea was absurd.

Or the idea had seemed more absurd before today, anyway.

The thing was, if Kate hadn't known how deadly the two men in the kitchen were, she might have imagined she was looking in at a perfectly normal, unobjectionable evening among normal everyday friends. A glass of wine, a beer. A shared meal.

Like regular people.

Something in her flipped over, and she backed away from the window, feeling flushed again. And disconcerted, somehow. As if something inside her had shifted out of place.

Without Templeton's big, confident form to follow, it took Kate a lot longer to make it back to the main stretch of town. But she did, and then she finally made her way to the Blue Bear Inn, which, except for a light on out front, looked dark and unwelcoming. When she got to the door, she found an envelope pinned to the wood with *TROOPER* scrawled across the front.

Inside the envelope she found a note inviting her to make herself at home in whatever room she liked.

Kate wasn't surprised to find the front door to the inn unlocked, because this was about the worst place in the world she could think to rob. There was nowhere to go. Everybody knew everybody, and at this time of year, there was no getting away with any stolen goods. There was only huddling somewhere and waiting to be discovered.

But that didn't mean she was particularly thrilled to walk into a dark, unfamiliar building. She was relieved to find, when she pushed the door open, that there were a few solitary lights on inside, showing her a small reception area and a quintessentially Alaskan lounge area, complete with a cute little grizzly to one side of the fireplace. Kate took her time finding her way to a room, making sure to check all over the inn first, in case there were any lurking surprises. But everything was as it should have been, which meant that she could breathe easy when she found a room she liked. She took the key out of the lock to shut herself inside and made sure to pull the curtains tight so there was no possibility anyone could watch her the way she'd just watched Templeton and his friends.

Only then did Kate allow herself to relax.

She took off her uniform, carefully hanging it in the closet so it would look as crisp as possible in the morning. Though she might have to use the ancient-looking iron she found there. She pulled her hair out of its tight, serviceable bun and rubbed her fingertips over her scalp, releasing the tension. She always packed a merino wool base layer in her go bag, because she never knew where she might have to spend the night or under what conditions, and she pulled it on now as pajamas. Her room had a hot plate and a couple of packages of Top Ramen, so she made herself a little bowl of noodles instead of eating one of the energy bars she kept stashed in her bag.

She settled in on the four-poster bed, slurping up ramen and writing down her impressions and thoughts on everything she'd discovered today. She charged her phone. She checked her messages and responded to her colleagues and her captain, making sure to note her location and schedule as much as humanly possible. Just to make sure she left a very clear trail while she was off investigating.

When she opened the curtains and looked out the

window later, the fog was so intense she couldn't see more than a few inches, and she blew out a breath, happy she hadn't found it necessary to attempt flight under these conditions. Just because she could fly—and knew many other local pilots who would fly under any circumstances at all, as long as they had the fuel—didn't mean it was a good idea.

Kate hadn't escaped her childhood to go around unnecessarily risking her life now.

The Blue Bear Inn was hushed. The town outside her windows was quiet. The dark and the fog muffled everything, so it almost felt as if Kate were suspended in space or lost in some kind of sensory deprivation tank, and she chose to find that relaxing. Not creepy.

The old television propped up on the dresser in the corner had an ancient VHS player attached to it, so she picked one of the tapes sitting in a tidy stack beside it, stuck it in, and then climbed into her bed to watch a remarkably bad movie starring people she'd never heard of before.

And as she drifted off, she congratulated herself, sleepily, for not thinking about Templeton.

But her subconscious got the last laugh, because she dreamed about him.

And not about the interview or all the things he'd adroitly, deliberately, failed to tell her.

Oh no. Her subconscious treated her to an erotic tour of the man's powerful body that felt so real that she woke up, her heart pounding, sweating all over, and with a slick heat between her legs.

It was so real that she sat up straight, staring around the room in a panic, convinced that she'd somehow slipped, maybe gone off and gotten drunk somewhere and had actually brought suspected domestic terrorist Templeton Cross back to her room to do all the wild, acrobatic, deliriously wicked things she dreamed—

But no.

Thank God, no.

She was still alone. The inn was still as quiet all around her as it had been. Her watch told her it was four thirty, which meant she'd slept through much of the night.

She kicked off her covers and lay there, ordering herself to stop the madness storming through her. To get her pulse under control. To go back to sleep. But the dream was so real she could feel his big, hard hands, streaking down her body to cup her butt, then pull her flush against his—

"Enough," she ordered herself, her voice sounding scratchy there in the darkness of her room.

But she couldn't get back to sleep.

When it finally got to around six—long after Kate had given up and read through her notes again, then found herself scrolling through her phone, idly looking up the names of various members of Alaska Force online, to no avail—she decided she'd had enough.

Feeling jittery and over-caffeinated when all she'd had was some of the weak, watery coffee she'd made there in the room, she pulled on what she needed to face the chilly Alaska morning hours before the sun was due to make an appearance. A few thin, technical layers, complete with a light strapped to her head. She laced herself into her hardy trail shoes and headed outside. If the maps she'd studied online were correct, there was a staircase that led up the hill to a lookout over the town. That seemed like a much safer option in the dark than trying her luck on a trail that could be actively treacherous. If not, she could always run up and down the main street until she worked off some of her excess energy.

Because that dream still clung to her.

She found the stairs and set off at a brisk jog, enjoying the slap of the cold morning against her face. The sound of her breath against the dark. The fog had thinned in some places, though the higher she climbed, thicker patches came in like clouds.

The altitude and the incline made a nice challenge,

and Kate picked up her speed, enjoying the physical exertion.

And for a moment, in motion, in tune with her breath and the sound of her feet against the cold earth, Kate didn't feel hollow at all. She didn't feel alien.

She felt very nearly whole.

Kate was grinning with the sharp, sweet joy of that when she sensed someone coming toward her, hurtling down from the top in a liquid streak—

But he stopped. So precisely it was clear he hadn't been *hurtling* at all but had been completely under control. And though she could see his breath dance against the light from her headlamp and his, he didn't look winded.

On the contrary, he looked beautiful. As if she'd conjured him up, straight out of those tangled, dirty dreams she'd had.

For the first time in a very long while, Kate found herself incapable of speech.

But Templeton had no such problem. His mouth moved into that endlessly wicked curve that she'd dreamed she'd tasted. That she'd dreamed had moved all over her body with lazy certainty and no apparent goal.

"Good morning, Officer," he drawled, lazy and lethal and much too smug, as if he knew.

When he couldn't possibly know. He couldn't possibly see what her dream had done to both of them. He couldn't possibly know how she *felt.* Or how completely her body was betraying her, even now. She hoped he chalked up all the heat she was putting out as the exertion, nothing more.

But the way Templeton smiled, she doubted it.

"Nice morning for a run," he said.

That was all he said.

It was her problem that all she heard was a sinful invitation.

Four

"Are you following me, Mr. Cross?"

His trooper asked the question in her usual matter-of-fact, direct way, but Templeton could have sworn that there'd been something intriguingly molten and hot in her gaze just a moment before.

Then again, it was possible he only wanted there to have been.

Or liked that it existed, he corrected himself. Sternly. Because he didn't want things he wasn't going to let himself touch.

"I was about to ask you the same thing," he said mildly. "You should have come in last night. Griffin makes a mean chili. No need to lurk around at the windows, staring in like a lost puppy."

But if Kate was disconcerted that he knew she'd been following him around last night, she gave no sign. She charged up one step, then another. Then one more.

Until she was at his eye level.

And she made no move to switch off her headlamp, so he didn't do a thing about his, either.

"I'll ask again," she said, as if he were a naughty schoolboy. Something else he probably shouldn't have found hot. "Why did you choose to come out here this morning?"

"Two things," he drawled. He lifted one gloved finger. "First, everybody who runs around here runs these steps. This time of year it's safer than the trail, unless there's ice. But if there's ice, nothing's safe, so we all make choices. And second? If I was following you, Trooper Holiday, I'd be following you. And you wouldn't know it unless I wanted you to."

"That sounds like a threat."

"I don't make threats. I don't really have to, if I'm honest."

"And why is that? Is it because your organization is in itself threatening?"

"Kate," he said, and made a meal of that sharp, sweet syllable. "Can I call you Kate?"

"You may not."

"The thing is, *Kate*," he said lazily, because it wasn't a crime to call her by her first name, and he sure was finding those hints of temper in her addictive, "you're barking up the wrong tree here. I'm not a threat. Alaska Force is not a threat. There can actually be good in the world, even out here in the middle of nowhere, and even if it involves a collection of military veterans you're suspicious of, for some reason."

Her head tilted slightly to one side. "I can't think of anything more dangerous than a group of militaristic individuals, armed to the teeth, who are convinced not only of their own strength but of their own righteous goodness. Can you?"

Templeton shoved his headlamp back on his head and considered her, there before him on the step, dressed for a cold run and not in her uniform. He figured she'd take a dim view of it if he touched her the way he wanted to, so he kept his hands to himself.

And sighed. "I think you might want to ask yourself

why, when you look at a forest, you see a logging cult. When it's just trees."

"Thank you for that, Mr. Cross. You truly are a philosopher." Her smile was sharp. "Now, if you'll excuse me, I'm going to return to what I was doing. I have your cell phone number. I'll call you when and if I want to see you again."

And he should have let her go when she turned and started climbing the stairs again. He should have trotted back down to the village, but there was something about Kate Holiday that dug under his skin and hummed there. It wasn't that she'd followed him last night. He understood and respected the move. He'd clocked her when he'd stepped out of the Fairweather and had been impressed with her stealth as she'd tracked him through the fog to the little house that his Alaska Force brother Griffin had just moved into.

Are we going to do something about that? Griffin had asked, without looking toward the window.

Not a lot we can do, Templeton had replied. Lazily.

They'd both known when she'd melted away again. Later, he and Griffin had done a perimeter run of the village to make sure everything in Grizzly Harbor was as it should be, with no boats or storage sheds about to blow. And he'd spent longer than he planned to admit looking at the faint crack of light in the upstairs window at the Blue Bear Inn. Just making sure she made it through the fog, he'd told himself.

He'd come out this morning to run until he got his head on straight. To remind himself he'd given himself rules on purpose, and that he shouldn't have spent far too long last night coming up with reasons why she was an exception.

And then here she was. As if he'd conjured her.

Templeton wasn't one to look a holiday gift in the mouth, rules or no rules.

So for the hell of it, he followed her up the stairs

hacked into the side of the hill, matching his stride to hers, step for step.

And he could swear he saw the fury come off her in waves, bright and hot.

"I don't know what you think you're doing, Mr. Cross, but I would strongly advise you to stop. Now."

She was huffing a little bit as she threw that at him without stopping her jog, which he found a lot cuter than he should have.

"I take the safety of local law enforcement officials very seriously, Kate," he replied merrily, and kept going right alongside her. "I wouldn't want you to come to any harm here in Grizzly Harbor."

They still weren't at the top, but she stopped and whirled on him. And he was only one step below her just then, so that meant she was forced to look up at him. Which he liked. A lot.

"Again, that sounds a lot like a threat. What harm can I expect to come to, Mr. Cross? Do you think this is a game?"

"I think it's a run. A little morning workout to get the blood flowing. But we can make it a game if you want. I like games."

And he had spent his entire adult life strategizing. Calculating odds, assessing situations, reacting with pinpoint precision to the slightest alteration. He'd been taught to expect the unexpected. He reveled in conquering the unknown.

Yet he still had no freaking idea what it was about this cop that was making him act like he was still an eighteen-year-old kid, hopped up on hormones and a sense of his own immortality.

Isaac had told him to charm her, not flirt with her. Templeton couldn't seem to tell the difference.

"What do you think is happening here?" she asked him, but she'd lost that cop voice. She sounded . . . husky. Scratchy. Almost as rough as he did.

And Templeton knew they were standing on the side of a mountain, smack down in the middle of the great Alaskan wilderness, with only a few lights in the village down below to suggest that they were anywhere near civilization—but it didn't feel that way. The dark hemmed them in. The thickness of the air made it . . . intimate.

Or maybe that was his own blood, raising a ruckus in his veins and making him at least sixteen kinds of a fool.

"I know exactly what's happening, Kate," he said, his voice too deep and too low, no matter how much he wanted to tell himself that he was talking about Alaska Force and the people who were very clearly gunning for them. "I think the real question is, do you?"

And he didn't lift his hands and put them on her. He didn't smooth his hand down the length of her ponytail or adjust the bit of fleece she wore wrapped over her ears. He didn't put his hands on her shoulders or run them down the length of her arms. He didn't get a grip on her, letting his fingers test the lean muscle in her arms, and he certainly didn't pull her up on her toes so he could finally taste that mouth of hers that was driving him crazy.

He didn't do a single one of those things, because he'd put his personal set of rules into play for a reason. He had no intention of making the same mistake twice.

Templeton stood there like a saint, halo shining brighter than his headlamp, and reminded himself he was one of the most highly trained military operatives in the world.

He'd handled the collapse of governments, the brink of any number of disasters, and the so-called end of the world so many times he usually entertained himself and others by cracking jokes en route to the latest apocalypse. Just last week he'd been jumping out of a plane into a miserable jungle to relieve a nasty cartel of a few hostages and a caravan stuffed full of product, and he'd found the operation entertaining.

He could handle a girl. Even one with a badge and a dim view of his life's work.

Of course you can handle her, he growled at himself.

Her breathing changed as they gazed at each other in the light from the lamps they wore. And he knew that if he reached out and put his fingers in the crook of her neck, he'd feel her pulse. He knew that it would be clattering around, causing a commotion, just like his.

In addition to her cool-cop look, he'd seen flashes of amusement here and there, and maybe even temper. What he was not prepared for was the flash of something he would have sworn was vulnerability, making her eyes seem even darker out there in what was left of the night.

She didn't argue with him. She didn't try to brazen this moment out. Instead, she turned on her heel and raced toward the top of the stairs as if her life depended on it.

Every single cell in Templeton's body urged him to follow her. But he didn't. He waited.

He and Griffin had traded off watch patrols throughout the night, because who knew where or when the next strike would happen? When Griffin had relieved Templeton this morning, the temperature had been hovering around thirty-six, which made it perfect for working up a sweat and clearing his head. The last thing he'd expected was a little one-on-one time with his trooper.

But he couldn't deny that he liked it. He liked her.

Liking her wasn't the same thing as crossing the lines he'd drawn, he assured himself. Repeatedly.

And he didn't know what it said about him that the more she scowled at him, or tried to put him in his place, the more he liked it.

Nonetheless, standing still in the dark, frigid morning was as good as the cold shower he clearly needed. Better, maybe. He made himself breathe, long and deep. He didn't try to hide from the cold; he leaned into it, and hoped like hell that would make his body settle down, too.

And when he heard Kate's footsteps coming toward him again, he had himself under control. Or close enough.

She didn't stop when she got to him, so Templeton fell in behind her, which meant slowing himself down, given his size and stride—but not as much as he might have expected. Because, as he'd noticed yesterday, Trooper Holiday took her fitness seriously.

Almost as seriously as Templeton took the view of her from behind as she took the steps back down to town at a decent clip.

When they got to the main street, she started toward the inn, but wheeled around before she'd gone too far and glared at him. She reached up to pull the headlamp off her face now that there were all the Christmas lights twinkling on this and that building to illuminate them both.

"Was it my imagination, Mr. Cross, or were you fixated on my ass all the way down the stairs?"

"Is your ass a permitted topic of conversation? I can rustle up some commentary, if you like."

"I don't like." That flash of vulnerability he'd seen was gone now. She folded her arms over her chest, and the fact that she was wearing cold-weather running gear instead of her uniform did absolutely nothing to take away that cop vibe. "I'm less entertained than you might imagine by your antics."

"Impossible. I'm delightful. Everyone thinks so."

"I can only assume that I'm meant to flutter about, blushing and giggling every time you look at me, and forget the reason I came here in the first place."

"I've seen the blushing. When will the giggling start?"

"This isn't going to end well for you, Mr. Cross. You can call me Kate. You can make suggestive remarks. All it does is paint a picture of a man who thinks he can break the rules on a whim. A man who feels beholden to absolutely nothing save his libido and his pride. There's only one place that's going to go, and it's not the bedroom of your juvenile fantasies. It's a prison cell."

"It's okay if you think I'm hot," Templeton assured her in his mildest drawl. "You don't have to make it all about handcuffs and domination." He couldn't help his grin. "Unless that's what you're into."

"Hilarious. You're digging your own grave."

"It's okay, Kate. I think you're hot, too."

If a person could explode without actually moving, she managed to do it. He was sure he could see flames dancing around her head while all she did was take that death glare of hers to another level.

Predictably, he found that just as appealing.

"I can't express to you how little I care who or what you find hot," she said, so icily it was like a storm front moved in while she clipped out the words. "The weather reports suggest that wind conditions will shift and the fog will ease around eight. Enough to allow us to travel to Fool's Cove without risking our lives. I'll be ready to go at that time. I suggest that you make yourself ready, too, and if you have any sense of self-preservation whatsoever, I'd leave your inappropriate remarks at home."

And he watched as she turned—without any hint of temper or emotion even when he'd *seen* it all over her, because she really was good—and walked calmly up the street to the inn. Dismissing him as if he were neither the least bit interesting nor a threat to anyone, which should have offended him.

Maybe it would have if he'd believed her.

Templeton stood there awhile, letting himself get good and cold again because his body wasn't listening to a single thing he told it to do. Not where she was concerned. And given he was a highly tuned instrument that could be used as a weapon at a moment's notice, and often was, he found that . . . alarming.

He ran a loop of Grizzly Harbor, out along the hiking trail that led past the hot springs out to the point, then back. He lifted his hand in the direction of the place he knew Griffin was stationed, though of course he didn't see a single sign of him. Griffin was like smoke. Most targets never knew he was there at all. They just went down.

When he came back into town, Templeton let himself into the in-law addition off to the side of the house that Griffin used as an office. He had a shower and a couple of extra beds, where his Alaska Force brothers could crash when they found themselves staying in Grizzly Harbor overnight instead of making their way back across the water to Fool's Cove.

Templeton showered, then dressed again quickly. He realized as he did that he no longer stopped to wonder how, of all of them, someone he would have said was as closed off as Griffin had managed to find himself tucked up in all this domesticity. Griffin's Mariah had been a client on the run from her ex when she found Alaska Force, and had hidden out on the island for a while. And Griffin wasn't the only one who'd found someone, surprising everyone else in their tight little unit. Blue Hendricks, former Navy SEAL and all-around hard-ass, was actually engaged to a girl he'd grown up with, who'd tracked him down all the way out here when she found herself in some trouble back in Chicago.

Templeton would have bet real money that neither one of them would ever settle down. With anyone, ever. Or even pretend to. And Templeton wasn't used to being wrong.

He chose not to question why he was thinking about his friends' romantic relationships, because that was obviously heading nowhere good.

He called in, getting Isaac on the first ring.

"Incoming," Templeton said. "I'm meeting our trooper Holiday at eight, and we're headed straight for Fool's Cove."

"Affirmative." Templeton was sure he could hear Isaac roll his eyes. "What's your take on this?"

Templeton's take grew increasingly more X-rated the more he thought about his personal trooper, but he'd already handled himself in the shower. He certainly didn't need to share his upsetting lack of focus with Isaac, who, in his role as Templeton's best friend, would shamelessly exploit that weakness.

"Hard to say. I'm going to swing by Caradine's to see if I can get a sense of how her interview went yesterday after I left."

"I don't think you need to get a sit rep on Caradine." Isaac's voice changed, the way it always did when the topic of Caradine came up. Because the two of them had so much tension it could clear a room. And had. Templeton wished they would handle it already, but he only said things like that to Isaac when there were drinks around. And therefore less likelihood that his best friend might take his head off for mentioning that tension in the first place. "You can bet she was rude. The end."

"Still, I'd like to triangulate this a little bit, so we can see where the trooper's coming from."

"What I don't understand is how she failed to succumb to the patented Templeton Cross charm. Did the world end yesterday while I wasn't paying attention?"

That was even funnier when you knew, as Templeton did, how very close the world had come to ending in one way or another over the years but hadn't, thanks to Isaac Gentry's attention and interference. But that wasn't why Templeton laughed.

"Oh, she succumbed," he said. "What she didn't do was change her position on Alaska Force. Two different things, brother."

"Maybe try making them one thing, then," Isaac suggested. "Didn't you used to be better at this?"

"Now, Isaac," Templeton drawled. "You know there are rules."

"That's never been my takeaway from what happened."

"I called in a report, and you're trying to talk about ancient history." Templeton kept his voice light, though he wasn't amused. "Are you my commanding officer or my sorority sister?"

Isaac laughed. And Templeton knew that laugh. It meant there would be a reckoning—likely in the form of the physical challenges Isaac liked to set for their community workouts every morning, which Templeton would pretend to find exhilarating, just to irritate him.

"Go handle the trooper, please," Isaac said. "With or without pledging her to a sorority. Your choice."

Templeton would have loved nothing more. But instead of chasing down his trooper and continuing to polish his halo, he went over to the Water's Edge Café. And it was still dark this side of the tardy December sunrise, so the café part wasn't open. He went around the side and jogged up the outdoor stairs to the apartment that sat up over the restaurant.

His first knock went unanswered. His second did, too, but he got that prickly feeling he always did when someone was watching him. But Caradine herself didn't appear until his third knock, when she wrenched open the door and stood there in the crack with the chain still on, glaring at him.

"Is someone dead?" she demanded.

Her hair was standing up in places. She was wearing an oversized black sweatshirt that could have fit three of her, obnoxiously patterned flannel pajama bottoms, and what looked like knockoff Uggs. And still she was glaring at Templeton like *he* was the one looking like he'd just crawled out of a swamp.

"Would that make you happy?" Templeton asked. "Wait. Let me guess who you'd most like to be dead."

"If you guess yourself, congratulations." She rubbed a hand over her face. "I hate you, it's early, and yet you're here. Do something about that. Oh, wait. I will."

She went to close the door, but Templeton held it open with one hand. She stared at his hand. Then she lifted her gaze to his face.

"Keep your hand there and I'll start cutting fingers off."

Templeton believed her. He removed his hand. "I want to talk to you about your interview yesterday. I don't want to lose fingers."

"Are you afraid I told the mean trooper nasty things about your little club?" she asked in the usual tone she used when she discussed Alaska Force. The kind of disrespectful tone that a small man might take issue with.

But Templeton only grinned. "I'm not afraid of you, Caradine. I'm interested in what she asked you, that's all."

"She's very interested in my relationship with Alaska Force." Caradine sniffed. "And didn't seem particularly swayed when I told her that I've gone out of my way to avoid having relationships with anybody or anything, as is my right and privilege here in the Land of the Midnight Sun."

"Did you get a sense—"

"I don't work for you."

And the thing about Caradine was that she didn't raise her voice. She was reliably unfriendly, but she was not harsh. The look she leveled on him then was steady. Intense, maybe. But she wasn't kidding around.

"I don't care one way or the other if every single one of you ends up in a jail cell. What I do care about is the fact that letting you into my café has brought me to the attention of the Alaska State Troopers. That doesn't make me happy, Templeton. And when I'm not happy, I don't like cooking. So any way you do the math on that, it doesn't matter what she asked me or what I said or what the hell is going on. What matters is that you're all banned."

And this time when she slammed the door in his face, Templeton let her.

He headed back down toward the dock where he'd moored the skiff yesterday. He could tell his brothers right now that Caradine had banned them again—but where was the fun in that? It would be far more entertaining to have her share that information with each and every one of them herself. Right when they most needed coffee.

He entertained himself imagining those conversations all the way down to the docks through the weak new light of the lazy December sun, which cast the village in foggy blue before it cleared the mountains. He nodded at some of the fishermen he knew and the villagers waiting for the ferry to come in on its single stop per week this time of year. But his eyes instantly went to his trooper in her winter-ready gear, standing straight and tall next to the little building that functioned as a ferry terminal.

"All aboard, Trooper Holiday," he said merrily as he approached. "I hope you're ready for the bracing December seas."

"According to your file, you're from the South," she replied in a voice that was clearly supposed to tell him how unamusing she found him. Funny how he got the exact opposite from her.

"Guilty as charged, ma'am," he drawled, throwing some deep, slow, Mississippi vowels in there for good measure.

"Then let me assure you that I don't need preparation for Alaskan weather, Alaskan seas, or anything Alaskan at all. I was born right here."

It seemed to occur to her that she wasn't here to get in sparring matches with a man she suspected of criminal activity. He saw something flash over her face, then a little bit of heat in her cheeks that really could have been temper. Though he didn't think so. Whatever the cause, all she did was stand taller.

She nodded her head down the length of the dock

toward his skiff, and Templeton was fully aware she was issuing an order. "Are you ready?"

He took his time to pause and really grin at her like his life depended on it. "Kate. Don't you worry. Rangers are always ready."

And he didn't wait around to see her reaction, though he was pretty sure he could feel her roll her eyes at him. He sauntered down to the Alaska Force boat, then indicated that she should climb aboard before him.

"I'm going to need you to stay right there," she said cheerfully. "Both feet on the dock, and none of your body on this boat. Can you do that?"

"I can do it. Why would I want to?"

"I appreciate your assistance, Mr. Cross. I'm going to conduct a quick visual sweep of this boat. I'm sure you understand."

And the look she gave him was fully cop, no trace of Kate. Templeton waved a lazy hand, settled in to wait, and opted not to question himself as to what exactly the difference between *cop* and *Kate* was or when he'd decided he could tell the difference.

Because that led nowhere a wise man let himself go. Especially when the man in question had decided never again to mix business with pleasure.

It didn't take Kate long. She climbed on board, and he figured the point of her inspection was as much to make sure there was nothing on the boat that shouldn't be there—and no one hiding below deck in the tiny cabin—as it was for her to make it clear to him that she was in contact with her department. She got on her comm unit and broke down her inspection for dispatch, responding to several queries, and when she was finished; she kept her hand on her weapon as she beckoned for Templeton to join her on his own damn boat.

"Do I pass your test?" he asked her as he climbed aboard.

"Your boat passes muster," she said coolly. "I'm not prepared to make a judgment on whether or not you do."

But he was making a study of her expressions. And he was sure he could see the hint of the humor she didn't want him to know she had lurking there in her gaze, no matter what she said.

Templeton liked to think that he could pilot any vehicle on land or in the air, but what he really enjoyed were boats. Even at this time of year, when the sea was swollen and brooding in turn, he found it exhilarating. He liked the challenge of the swells. The dance between what he could see with his eyes and what his instruments told him as he piloted their way out of Grizzly Harbor, then around the rocky, steep, and inhospitable shore of the island toward the little cove he called home.

He expected Kate to fire more questions at him, taking advantage of the fact he had to concentrate on the water and the weather to interrogate him further. But instead, she was quiet. She stood next to him in the pilothouse, keeping her body at an angle and her hand resting casually enough on her hip, where she had her weapon strapped.

But she didn't say a word. Every time he snuck a glance her way, she had her gaze on the crashing Pacific all around them, as the uncertain daylight cast the world in gray and green.

And Templeton had lived in Alaska for years now. But she was right—deep down, he was still a Southerner, marked by the slow drawls and soft seasons of the land he'd come from, the damp heat of the summers, and the wide, brown Mississippi River that marked the eastern border of his part of Louisiana. He could tell that the woman beside him had been forged from this place instead. The resilient islands, the formidable mountains. Cool like the glaciers, and endlessly shifting like the sea.

Sweet Lord, he thought in amazement. He was coming over all poetic. Next thing he knew, he'd break into song and bring the rocky cliffs down around them with his tuneless voice. And then it wouldn't matter what rules he broke, because he'd be dead.

But the idea of him making like a troubadour had him laughing out loud, which had the added benefit of making the woman beside him jolt a little bit.

"Private joke," he told her, and grinned when she frowned at him.

He was still laughing to himself when he rounded the rocky outcropping and made his way into Fool's Cove.

He knew that the minute he powered around the bend there would be eyes all over his boat no matter the gloom of the morning. And he supposed that the Troopers weren't wrong to be worried about the kinds of things that could potentially be going on in a place like this. Fool's Cove was inaccessible to most of the world simply because of where it was. There was only one road in from Grizzly Harbor, though it was only passable every now and again over a tricky bastard of a mountain pass that the locals called Hard Ass Pass. Mostly, the road was washed out, and people who attempted to take it over the mountain didn't come back.

In fact, the only person in recent memory who'd survived it was Blue's fiancée, Everly. And the part of Templeton that leaned toward poetry liked the fact that the woman worthy of his brother Blue had proved herself in that way.

Something he said out loud only when he wanted to irritate the former SEAL.

The cove itself wasn't all that welcoming, should a person make it there. Isaac's ancestors had built themselves an out-of-the-way fishing lodge and hadn't done much to make anything about it appealing, because its draw was its location. Over time, they'd added cabins here and there. The lodge was a ramshackle, rambling set of connected buildings up above the high-tide mark over the water. It ran along the shore, with wooden walkways connecting the different buildings and cabins together. And there were separate cabins deeper in the trees, going up the side of the mountain, where the members of Alaska Force lived. Templeton's cabin wasn't hidden away in the woods like many of his brothers' were. He lived near the beach and what they called Isaac's box of pain, which is where they did their killer workouts every morning. He could see it as he got closer.

And it still felt like home, every time he laid eyes on it. Something Templeton didn't take for granted after his years being shuttled from one foster placement to another.

He navigated his way into the cove, headed for the docks below the lodge.

And as they got closer, they could see more of the lights on all over the cove, and the hum of the generators danced around with the sound of the waves.

"Home sweet home," Templeton said. And meant it, which never failed to surprise him. He'd been everywhere. But he liked it here, in all this gray and green, with the punishing winters and the months of darkness.

"Do you consider this your home?" Kate was asking. "Or is it more of a fiefdom?"

"The thing about your average medieval fiefdom is that it actually contained a lot of people's homes," Templeton said. "It's not an either-or scenario."

He was too aware of her gaze on the side of his face. "Interesting tack to take."

Templeton slid the boat into the slip at the dock and tied down the lines. He offered to help Kate off the boat once it was moored, received a trooper death glare in reply, and held his hands up in surrender as she climbed off onto the dock herself. Then he preceded her down the length of the dock to the land, wondering what she saw as she followed him. It was just another working day here at Alaska Force headquarters, no matter when whatever daylight they got this time of year decided to make itself known.

It was coming up on nine, and the sun was actually visible—but there were already clouds moving in. So it hardly mattered that it was slightly less dark, as far as Templeton was concerned.

And when they got to the end of the dock, where the beach ran off toward Templeton's cabin, Alaska Force's newest hire stood there waiting on the lowest step of the wooden staircase that rose up to the main part of the lodge.

Bethan Wilcox was one of the handful of women to ever make it through the army's elite Ranger School, which Templeton—as one of the very low percentage of men who had done the same—could only marvel at. The kind of dedication that it took to commit herself to an army that was still largely uncertain what to do with women in combat positions got nothing but respect from Templeton. Being a good soldier was tough enough without centuries of institutionalized sexism packed on top of it. Being an excellent one was even harder.

Also, she was a killer good shot, fast as hell, and held her own physically.

Templeton wasn't at all surprised that Isaac had brought her on board.

It was only Jonas, in fact, who seemed to have any reservations—but Templeton couldn't help thinking that was personal. Not that he'd dared to ask. Yet.

"Welcome to Fool's Cove, Trooper Holiday," Bethan said as Kate walked up behind Templeton to stand at the foot of the stairs.

Kate smiled, glacial and cool. "Are you here because you're a woman and that's supposed to put me at ease? Or because you're the newest member of this questionable little group and the least likely to implicate yourself?"

Bethan didn't blink. "I have to assume both, ma'am."

Kate actually smiled. Templeton absolutely did not stare at it, like a starving man, because that would be crazy.

He wasn't going to do this. He'd made a promise to himself a long time ago, and he intended to keep it, no matter how pretty his trooper's smile was.

Templeton ordered himself to get his head on straight. Then he and Bethan led an Alaska State Trooper who already believed they were suspicious criminals directly into the heart of Alaska Force.

Five

Once again, Kate's expectations were not met.

She climbed up the steep, well-made stairs to the lodge and found herself on one of a series of porches that ran alongside the connected or nearby cabins clinging to the side of the hill. She'd seen the surveillance photos and had looked at historical documents dating back to the arrival of the first Gentry into the area, and wasn't surprised that the place still looked like the rustic fishing lodge it had always been.

But she'd expected it to be *actually* rustic.

Instead, everything was weathered but clearly well maintained, if not new. She could fling herself facedown on the porch at her feet, rub her cheek against it, and very likely come up with no splinters.

She almost said that out loud, but . . . didn't. Because she made the mistake of looking at Templeton while she thought it, and everything seemed to tangle inside her. And she found herself wondering what sort of splinters she'd get if she leaned in close and rubbed her cheek—

Kate was so appalled at herself that she froze for a moment, there at the top of the steep stairs.

And Templeton's expression suggested he knew why.

The sun finally heaved itself a little bit higher, sending the pale winter light cascading over the trees but still leaving the cove in shadows. Kate felt shadowed herself, and compromised, and she hated it. So she called in her location, ostentatiously, holding Templeton's gaze while she did it.

"You do what you need to do to feel safe, Kate," Templeton drawled when she'd finished.

"I certainly appreciate your permission, Mr. Cross," she replied, sounding as cool as he had sounded lazy.

Then she nodded at Bethan Wilcox, who stood at attention on Templeton's other side, with her face perfectly blank, as if she, at least, hadn't fully shifted from the army into this ex-military life yet.

They led Kate into what must have once been the main lobby of the lodge when it was actually run as a fishing camp hotel. It was a wide space. There were chairs and sofas scattered here and there, and Kate had imagined that the place would be decorated much in the same style as her inn. One hundred percent, full-octane Alaska, complete with animal skins, hunting trophies, and taxidermy galore. Or more in the style of the compound of her youth, with an eye toward hunkering down and holding off armies rather than a living space that catered to humans.

Instead, the Alaska Force lodge felt both comfortable and professional, and she had to stop a moment to think about how they'd achieved that. It was cozy and inviting, yes, with all the ruddy-colored rugs tossed across the hardwood floors that were somehow as masculine as they were surprisingly sophisticated for this part of the world. There were sleek, modern updates that wouldn't look out of place in *Mountain Living* magazine, from the flat-screen TV on one wall and the big stone fireplace on another, down to the lack of clutter or anything extraneous.

"You look surprised," Templeton rumbled from beside her.

Too close beside her, because everything about him was inappropriate, and she understood that it was all deliberate. That was the game he was playing. She understood it, but for some reason, she seemed to be susceptible to him in ways that made absolutely no sense to her.

She ignored him—and her reaction—and walked farther into the great room, scanning it as she went.

"I wouldn't categorize my response as 'surprised,'" she said after a moment. "But I'll admit that this looks more corporate than cultish."

"Cultish?" Bethan laughed, though she had found another way to stand at attention just inside the door while Templeton prowled around like an oversized jungle cat. "I'm a soldier, ma'am. Not a cult member."

"Some would say boot camp is the same as brainwashing," Templeton pointed out. Conversationally.

"Not to my face, they wouldn't," Bethan retorted.

Kate smiled as she turned back to face them. "Did you practice that bit? Or am I supposed to believe it was spontaneous?"

"Again, ma'am," Bethan said, and Kate thought there was a little bite in that word. *Ma'am.* Especially since she and Bethan were much the same age. "I'm a soldier. Not in a cult. And not on a stage."

"Alaska Force is a business," came another voice, from the far side of the lodge's wide-open lobby, where doors clearly led to other rooms and the series of connected cabins Kate had seen from outside. "So whether or not you think we're evil probably depends on your feelings about businesses in general."

And there he was. The man she'd expected to see yesterday, who was at the heart of all of this.

Isaac Gentry stood there at the far end of the room, not at attention. In fact, he looked at his ease. Not in that pointedly lazy way Templeton always did, but like he was . . . just a guy. He wore a T-shirt with a drawing on the front of it, cargo pants low on his hips, and boots like everyone else's. Kate assumed that it was his goal to look unthreatening. Dismissible, even. His smile was genial. His eyes were bright. At a glance, he looked scruffy, bearded, and indistinguishable from any other male in his age demographic in Alaska.

Unless a person paid attention to how he was standing there, his weight equally distributed on the balls of his feet, spring-loaded and ready for action. Not to mention, he was in shockingly good physical condition. In perfect shape, even. And had the same kind of lean, dangerous muscles that Templeton had. The kind that were honed in battle, because the people sporting them didn't need a weapon. They were the weapons.

But what Isaac Gentry did not look like, to Kate's educated eye, was an unhinged survivalist cult leader.

Then again, things weren't always what they seemed.

"I'm not sure I know of anyone who has warm, fuzzy feelings about corporations," Kate pointed out. She kept walking until she had her back to a wall and could see all three Alaska Force members who stood in the room with her. It struck her how similar they all were, for all that they looked so different. Templeton was tall and wicked. Isaac looked so friendly. Bethan looked compact and tough. But all three of them had that same watchful stillness. The same hint of leashed power, just waiting to be set free.

Kate couldn't imagine how they ever convinced anyone that they were regular citizens.

"Corporations are made of people," Isaac replied. "If you hate them, you hate people. Do you?"

"It's a pleasure to meet you, Mr. Gentry," Kate said. "I have a lot of questions for you."

"Fire away," Isaac said cheerfully. He wandered in farther and tossed himself down on one of the couches, stretching out his legs in front of him and his arms to either side. Like a regular guy in his living room instead of a superhero—or supervillain—in his very own Batcave. "What do you want to know? I'm an open book."

"The first thing that comes to mind, off the top of my head, is why you find it necessary to stockpile an arsenal in a remote part of Alaska."

Isaac's laugh was as friendly and encouraging as the rest of him. It made Kate want to laugh along with him. She didn't.

"I'm fully licensed and entirely legal, Officer," Isaac assured her. "As is everyone who lives in Fool's Cove."

"If you weren't, I wouldn't be here alone, engaging in this friendly chat. I'd be here with a warrant and any number of fellow officers. But what I'd like to know is why you feel it's necessary."

"Alaska Force is a private security firm," Isaac said.

"You mean a military company."

"We're not big enough to feel *that* corporate, Trooper Holiday. Deliberately."

"Funny, I'm convinced there's a word to describe a ragged little band of private actors with militaristic leanings." Kate pretended to think. "Oh yes. Mercenaries."

"If we were nothing but mercenaries, I doubt local law enforcement would allow us to keep operating." Isaac grinned. "Would you?"

"I'll be honest with you, Mr. Gentry. I don't like private armies."

"Trooper Holiday is not a fan of armed men in remote, defensible positions," Templeton chimed in. "Makes her twitchy."

"It does make me twitchy," Kate agreed. "I'm sure I don't need to tell you that a lot of people think that they can come on up to Alaska, get far away from civilization, and make their own rules."

"A person might argue that's what Alaska's for," Templeton drawled.

But Isaac kept grinning at her. "Maybe they do, but

that's not me. I'm a local boy. Born and bred right here in Grizzly Harbor."

"And you trade on that," Kate said coolly. "But I'm not sure that aw-shucks routine can really stand in the face of repeated arson attempts."

"Why would I torch my own buildings?" There wasn't much *aw shucks* in Isaac's expression then. "That's not a rhetorical question. What benefit could I possibly get from it? I obviously don't want a lot of attention, or I wouldn't be here. I like the middle of nowhere. I don't like crowds. I don't like cities. I've seen a little too much to ever be comfortable with someone else's wall at my back. There's nothing in it for me to go around blowing things up."

"Unless this is all sleight of hand." Kate smiled. "If you're blowing up a boat here, what are you distracting us from over there?"

"I'm a marine," Isaac said, and she was sure there was an edge to his friendly grin. "Not a magician."

"There's no point to Alaska Force engaging in arson all over Southeast Alaska," Templeton said. And when Kate looked back over at him, she shivered into a different kind of awareness. It was something about the way his eyes glittered. She had the distinct, if ridiculous, notion that he didn't like her smiling at Isaac. But she shoved that thought away as soon as it formed. "The simplest explanation is that someone else is doing it."

"Claiming that some unknown entity is framing you is not the simplest explanation." Kate shook her head. "Why would anybody want to do that?"

"This might come as a shock to you, since you think we're an evil cult racing around doing harm," Templeton drawled. "But there are a whole lot of bad guys who would be thrilled if we weren't around to keep messing up their plans."

Kate sighed. "Do you think that you're in a comic book, Mr. Cross? Bad guys versus good guys? Wait, let me guess. You're actually made of steel, invulnerable except for that pesky kryptonite."

"Everyone has their kryptonite, ma'am," Bethan said then, with a laugh that made Kate too aware, suddenly, of how intensely she'd been staring at Templeton. "That's pretty much the first thing they look for in boot camp."

Kate ordered herself to take a breath. To center herself, remember why she was here, and stop . . . *reacting* to Templeton like this.

"What none of you seem to understand is that I can't effectively tell the difference between metaphoric, colorful language and a widespread, shared delusion," she said when she thought she had herself under control again, no matter the sensation shivering around inside her and making her so . . . jittery. "What I do know are the facts. A lot of arson, all of a sudden. And going back years, too many incidents involving questionable behavior and you. Is this a situation where all the smoke means fire? Or are you right that your hands are clean, if without official oversight? I have no way of telling. So far, everything has been very cloak-and-dagger or I've been treated to a number of performances, none of which I believe are genuine."

And she didn't look at Templeton when she said that. She didn't have to. She heard the bark of his laughter, and whether or not he was performing, she still felt it thud through her.

"I have nothing to hide." Isaac sounded as friendly and approachable as ever. "I'm private, not secretive. And you're here now." He opened his arms wider along the couch. "Knock yourself out. Investigate to your heart's content. Invite all your friends."

"Thank you, Mr. Gentry," Kate said, smiling wide herself, as if they were buddies. "I'll take you up on that offer."

Isaac rose to his feet then, with a powerful ease that showed who he really was behind all the grinning geniality. In case she was tempted to forget. "The only thing I'll ask is that you stay out of our active situation room, because we make a commitment to our clients to keep their personal information confidential. When I say *commitment*, I mean legal documents. You want to challenge that, be my guest. But it will take a judge's order."

"What I have to ask," Kate mused, "is why, if you planned to be so open and obliging all along, you avoided setting up this interview?"

"Because I'm not guilty of anything," Isaac said with a laugh. "How would you like it if the police wanted to comb through your life and business while hinting that you have terrorist leanings?"

"I'd assume they were doing their job."

"You're more trusting than I am," Isaac said, with that same friendly smile. And something in his gaze reminded her what kinds of things he must have done while in the service. What sorts of places he'd been. "But you're here now. Do your job at will."

"Thank you," Kate said, and smiled blandly. "I'm taking you at your word. I hope that's wise."

Templeton laughed again, and it didn't make Kate want to laugh along with him—it seemed to lodge itself inside her, daring her not to free-fall straight into it. Into him.

She scowled at him instead.

"We keep our promises and honor our word," Templeton told her. "That's the number one rule of Alaska Force. It's not a fight club. It's about honesty, or we can't do our jobs. We all take that seriously."

"I'm delighted to hear it." Kate whipped out her pad and clicked her pen. "Out of curiosity, how many times do you think someone has stood in front of me, monologuing about their commitment to honesty? And of the people who did, how many times do you think I've discovered that they were, in fact, lying to me?"

Templeton shook his head, and Kate told herself that

the gleam she saw in his dark eyes, golden and fierce, did nothing. It didn't make her feel warm. It didn't make a jangly sort of light dance around inside her.

It did absolutely nothing at all.

"You have a very dark take on humanity, Trooper," Templeton drawled. "Me? I'm an optimist. And this is the Christmas season. No better time to get your very merry on."

"I don't celebrate Christmas," Kate said crisply. "So I'm afraid I'm going to have to concentrate on evidence, not Christmas carols, to form my conclusions. If that's all the same to you."

Templeton didn't argue. What he did do was whistle every Christmas carol Kate had ever heard as he ushered her out of the lodge's main room and into the offices beyond, stopping only when they were in the presence of other people. In between renditions of "Let It Snow," "O Holy Night," and "Frosty the Snowman," Kate ran down a checklist of everybody she knew to be in Alaska Force, and met many of them on her tour of the Fool's Cove facilities.

She found Blue Hendricks and Jonas Crow hunched over schematics in one room, talking mission parameters. She met Alexander Oswald, otherwise known as Oz, who briefed her in a general way on current Alaska Force operations. Rory Lockwood still maintained he'd hurt himself last spring, and looked no worse for wear as he showed her one of their gun ranges and even offered her the opportunity to practice a few rounds herself. Kate declined.

While the fragile daylight held its own against the gathering clouds, Templeton led her down the beach to their workout facility, which was exactly what he'd said it was—an empty space with mats on the floor, a pull-up rig, free weights, and sandbags stacked against one wall. He pointed out various cabins up in the hills and told her their functions, whether they were private dwellings or part of the corporate footprint. If she wanted to look inside, he let her.

But anytime they weren't actually talking, he was caroling. At her.

When he cycled back around to "God Rest Ye Merry, Gentlemen" for the third time, they were marching along the cold beach, the breeze whipping in from the water and making Kate huddle deeper into her warm jacket. Templeton had been at pains to point out that the beach was part of a natural cove. It wasn't a fortress. Or if it was, they hadn't built it.

When she hadn't really responded to that, he'd started the freaking whistling again.

"I need you to stop," she told him.

Possibly she snapped it at him.

He looked innocent, which was a stretch. "I'm filled with holiday spirit. Given your name, I figured you would be, too."

Kate wasn't about to get into a discussion about her surname. Though what concerned her was that she felt the urge to do just that. What was the matter with her? Why did this man get to her when no one else had ever gotten *near* her?

"Is this how you run your non-mercenary missions?" she demanded. "You find your enemy, then pinpoint what irritates them to death?"

He considered. "Well, yes. More or less. Now that I think about it."

"I'm not sure what reaction you're going for here." She studied his face. The day was moodier by the second, and the sullen clouds were crowding out what little light there was. Kate could relate. "You keep treating this like a game. That makes me think that this *is* a game, which makes me wonder why you're all playing it. Once again I must caution you against taking my presence here lightly."

His smile faded, and what she was left with was that

face of his. The face she'd seen first, so powerful and intensely focused, his gaze intent. "I don't take you lightly at all, Kate."

And obviously, there was absolutely no reason that she should find it hard to breathe.

"Talk me through what you think is happening here," she managed to make herself say. "What exactly is your role? Somehow you don't strike me as someone whose primary purpose in life is wandering around, belting out Christmas carols."

"Pretty sure I was whistling. Not belting out anything."

"I understand that this is supposed to be a charm offensive. Why does Alaska Force think it needs to send you out to do your big laugh, *butter wouldn't melt unless you want it to* thing?"

He looked frozen for a split second, and that should have felt like a win. Kate didn't know why instead, she felt almost . . . apologetic.

A feeling she swallowed down. Hard.

"I'm here to be your point person, that's all," Templeton said. "The Christmas carols are just a bonus."

"I don't want Christmas carols." She was horrified to find that her voice was much too thick. Too . . . telling. "And I certainly don't want a man trailing me around and cozying up to me. I don't know what your agenda is. I find it off-putting and offensive."

"Okay."

". . . Okay?"

Templeton made a symphony out of a shrug, but his gaze wasn't lazy. Or mocking. It was much harder than that. "I am who I am, Trooper Holiday. I'm not going to close it up, lock it away, and pretend I'm someone else to make you feel better about your bogus investigation into my friends when you could be out there tracking the people who are actually responsible for these fires. Sorry if you find that offensive."

"I'm not asking you to stop being who you are," she managed to grit out, not entirely sure why her pulse was leaping around like he'd attacked her. "I'm asking you to stop with the overly familiar remarks. Or the use of my first name, when I expressly requested that you address me by my title."

"I'm a casual, friendly guy." And the drawl was so Deep South then, she was surprised she couldn't smell the grits. "You're the one who wanted honesty. Well, here I am. Honest and in your face."

"I suggest you change your unbridled so-called honesty to something more respectful," she managed to say, sounding almost like herself again. "And quickly."

"Here's the thing, Kate." And Templeton had the audacity to grin at her, and not the way he had before. Because this time he wasn't doing much to hide the glint of steel in his gaze. "I spent a long time figuring out who I was. I'm not about to change that on a dime because an uptight cop doesn't like me. You don't have to like me. In fact, I'd be a little insulted if you did, since I don't really speak cop and never have. But I'll remind you that calling you by your name—or by any name—isn't breaking a law."

There was no reason she should be gritting her teeth together. She made herself stop.

"That entire speech is problematic, Sergeant."

She expected one of his booming laughs, but instead he gave her more of that steel and intensity, and she found she was holding her breath.

"I was born problematic, Trooper. I don't know how to be anything else. And I didn't come looking for you. You came to us. To me. If you find all of this"—and he waved a hand in the general direction of his impossibly perfect torso, then out toward the rest of Fool's Cove and, presumably, all of Alaska Force—"a problem, go ahead and remove yourself from the problem anytime you like. But if you're going to stick around, maybe stop lecturing me. Maybe do your actual job and realize that we're not the threat. Just a thought."

And the worst part of that speech, she thought when he stepped around her and kept going, sauntering on down the beach as if it weren't cold and frigid and as if he could hang out outside all day long without noticing the temperature, or her, was that he was right. She'd gotten personal.

When had she allowed herself to get *personal*? Kate would have been the first to point out to anyone who asked that she didn't have that in her. She didn't get personal. She got to work.

She ordered herself to do that now, feeling a bit grim as she marched down the cold beach after him.

She'd come here expecting to find more evidence to indicate that Alaska Force was exactly what and who she'd assumed they were. Instead, she found them disconcertingly . . . sane. Her gut told her they were on the level.

It was her history that argued otherwise, and she didn't like that at all. She didn't understand it, either. The rugged Alaska wilderness did seem to lend itself to people who sometimes banded together with ill intent, and Kate had distinguished herself as the investigator best equipped to determine if the group in question was headed for the kind of danger zone that led people to throw around words like *cult*. She'd investigated a handful of other such groups already this fall. Two were family groups looking to live off the land, no matter how harsh. Another was religion-based, seeking to step away from the modern world. All were no danger to anyone except, arguably, themselves—if they weren't up to the rigors of the Alaskan winter.

But Kate hadn't *felt things* while she'd been investigating these groups, except a profound sense of gratitude that she was no longer an unwilling member of a group like theirs.

She had no idea why this was any different. She wanted to believe it was because Templeton and his friends were the questionable mercenaries she'd imagined they were, but she didn't think they were. She wanted to believe they were either sick or greedy, but that wasn't the impression she got anywhere in this pretty little cove.

The only problem she could find reliably was herself.

And she could blame it on Christmas all she wanted, but she thought that actually, the trouble was her. *In* her. And she didn't need to hang around these islands compounding her errors. She needed to get herself back to Juneau and her actual life and away from this man who for some reason made her feel like she was someone else entirely.

"I'd like you to take me back to Grizzly Harbor," she told Templeton when she caught up to him at the base of a different set of stairs leading up to the sprawling cabins farther up the steep hill. "I've seen all I need to here."

"Why am I guessing that's bad news?" he asked, but he didn't sound particularly worried.

"It's neither good news or bad—" she began, grabbing hold of her tattered professionalism as best she could, but his mobile went off.

And his entire demeanor changed. He went from lazy and easy to powerfully switched-on and completely focused the moment he picked up the call.

"Yeah, she's over here with us," he said, and his dark gaze locked to hers.

Kate stiffened. Templeton made a few noises, then hung up, never shifting his gaze.

"That was the harbormaster back at Grizzly Harbor," he said. "When was the last time you checked that seaplane of yours?"

"What do you mean?" But when he didn't elaborate, she blinked. "At approximately seven forty-five this morning, before meeting you on the docks. I stowed my overnight gear and called in."

"The ferry came in a little while ago," Templeton said. "And they thought maybe some fool got drunk and froze to death overnight, the way they do."

"Are you telling me there's a person in my plane?" Kate demanded. "Why wasn't I called directly?"

"They called the Troopers, Kate. But then they called here because people in town know you're already out here with us and a whole lot closer than the nearest Trooper station." Templeton studied her in a way she didn't like at all. It sent a dark, tumbling shiver of foreboding straight down her spine. "There isn't a person on your plane; there's a body. And he didn't freeze to death. He was stabbed."

Six

Suddenly, Kate felt as if she were starring in a movie about her own life, one she was both acting in and watching at the same time.

It was a movie about an Alaska State Trooper who had to make her way back by boat from a remote cove packed full of military operatives to a small fishing village where her seaplane was now a crime scene. And she had the distinct, dislocating sensation that she was watching this strange movie, shot through with dread and uncertainty, unspool right there before her.

Kate had felt like this before. She recognized it was what her court-appointed psychological counselor had called *disassociation*, back when she'd been a teenager. She'd just never imagined that she would ever have the occasion to feel this way again.

She could remember too well being fifteen and swept up into the criminal justice system when she'd finally made it out of the dark and cold and into that Trooper post in Nenana. It had taken years for her to stop feeling like she was playing a role instead of just . . . living.

She didn't really welcome the return of those feelings.

But this time, at least, she knew what needed to happen while she felt outside herself. This time she hadn't pulled off an impossible escape on a stolen snowmobile and then her own two feet; she was doing her job. She called in to report the potential crime. She relayed the information she had, then—once she'd arrived at Grizzly Harbor on a boat packed full of men she'd been ready to convict as criminals twenty-four hours before—she called in again once she'd done a preliminary sweep of the crime scene, to confirm that there was indeed a homicide in Grizzly Harbor.

Not only in Grizzly Harbor, but in Kate's plane.

Templeton hadn't been exaggerating. He'd been relaying facts. There was a man Kate had never seen before strapped into the cockpit of her little plane. With a hunting knife planted in the middle of his chest.

"Does anybody recognize this man?" Kate asked after she'd called in and then climbed back down to the dock, having made certain not to disturb anything.

The man Templeton had identified as the harbormaster shook his head. "He's not a local. And he's not dressed like a tourist."

Kate found herself looking to Templeton as if he were her partner, not an enemy. Something she was going to have to question herself about later, and sternly. Because her gut feeling wasn't evidence, no matter how often it was correct.

"Could he have come in on the ferry?"

"A question I intend to answer," Templeton replied, nodding at the harbormaster in a manner that had the other man bustling away as if he'd received a direct order.

And she should have asked what that unspoken order was, but it was already getting colder as the morning wore on. The clouds up above were dark and grim, and Kate couldn't tell if it was the weather that was making her feel so chilly or if it was the sheer creepiness of such a grisly discovery. Maybe both.

Kate was ordinarily more than prepared to handle any kind of crime scene on her own, but she couldn't think of a circumstance quite like this one. There was only a brief window of time in which this could have happened, and there had actually been some cloudy daylight then. And the reality of life in tiny villages was that it was very difficult to do much without someone noticing *something*.

Which meant, Kate thought, as she watched Alaska Force fan out into the village, that it was entirely possible it hadn't really looked like anything while it was happening. Certainly not like what it was.

But she didn't mention that, because it occurred to her that what she was actually watching as three of the men she'd met in Fool's Cove climbed the hill was Alaska Force interfering in an active murder investigation.

"You can't run around doing police work." She was standing between Templeton and Isaac on the dock, waiting for her colleagues to find their way here from Juneau and Sitka. "This is a murder investigation. You must know that you're civilians now, no matter how many tours of duty you did in the military."

"We're concerned citizens, that's all," Isaac said with a winning smile. "And this is our hometown. I'm not a big fan of burning boats, and I'm even less entertained by dead bodies."

"I'll have to ask you to wait for the troopers just like anyone else," Kate replied. Sternly. "Just like me."

"Let me go round up my men, then," Isaac said in such a friendly manner that it took her a minute to realize that all he did was walk away from her, toward the shore. What he did not do was rattle off orders into his comm unit, which presumably would have stopped his men in their tracks and had them return to the docks without . . . doing whatever they were doing.

And the craziest part was, she didn't even have it in her to argue with that the way she should have.

"I have to assume that the scene is staged," Kate found herself saying, because it was only Templeton there then, and he wasn't whistling any longer. His gaze was dark, his eyes gleaming with something it took her long moments to realize was fury.

On her behalf, she understood after a moment of shock.

She had never seen someone that angry *for her* before. Or angry for her at all. Ever. She had no doubt that if she gave the slightest signal, this man would do everything in his considerable power to assist her. Help her. Or whatever the hell else she asked him to do.

She didn't know where that thought came from. She tried to shove it away, but it was no good. Because Templeton was focused on her as if, were it in his power, he would start ripping apart the dock they stood on with his hands if that would get them answers.

Kate should have been horrified.

But that was definitely not the reaction her body had to all that focused, controlled fury.

"Agreed," Templeton was saying, because he couldn't know how he'd shook her. *He can never know*, she told herself resolutely. "The only question is whether this is a message to you? Or to us?"

"I don't normally receive messages in the form of homicides," Kate said, afraid she sounded less in control of herself than usual. "I'm not sure you can say the same."

"Why your plane, then?"

"My plane, yes. But not my plane while it sat here all night. My plane right after I left for Fool's Cove with you." She frowned. "Anyway, it doesn't matter. More troopers are coming, and we'll figure this out."

Templeton's gaze got harder. "We will."

Kate frowned again, looking up at him.

And when his mouth crooked up in one corner, it was like no smile she'd seen from him before. It made everything in her shimmer, then go still. Then seem to hum, as if she were spinning around and around to the music he made, though she knew he wasn't whistling any longer. Not out loud.

He reached over, and she was sure that he was going to do something inarguably inappropriate—

But all he did, very carefully, was flip the collar of her jacket into place. And she would have sworn he took particular care not to brush his fingers against the exposed skin of her cheek and neck while he did it.

Kate couldn't have said why that ache inside her seemed so large it nearly overtook her where she stood. Nearly took her right down to her knees.

Or why it took her another long moment or two to recognize that while she didn't approve of all this emotion, right out here in public, it was better than that dislocated feeling of watching herself on a screen.

And she didn't understand how he did that. How he put her back into her body.

"There's no *we*, Templeton," she managed to say, trying to keep her frown in place.

"Look at that," he said, his deep voice a rumble of satisfaction. It struck her as particularly male and too intensely hot for a cold December day as it wound around and around inside of her. "You do know how to say my name after all."

And then he left her there—out on the dock with the wind kicking at her but failing entirely to cool her down—as she took another call from her captain in Anchorage.

It wasn't until later, when her fellow troopers had handled the crime scene, and she'd flown back to Juneau and the temporary office where she'd been deployed to conduct her Alaska Force investigation, that Kate realized what a close escape she'd really had.

Not from whoever was running around blowing up buildings and stabbing people with hunting knives but from Templeton Cross.

Because back in Juneau, Kate couldn't access either

the strange feelings she'd had while she was out there or, even worse, the things Templeton himself had made her feel.

Deliberately and more than once.

She was happy, or maybe relieved, that she hadn't crossed any lines.

And then horrified, as she sat in her temporary office with her colleagues, talking through everything she'd done and seen since she'd headed out to Grizzly Harbor, that she'd even put herself in a position to consider the crossing of lines. Kate Holiday, who prided herself on following the law.

And sure, the troopers were given some fairly broad allowances, given where they lived and worked, but this was different.

Kate couldn't help feeling that if she hadn't left Grizzly Harbor when she had, she might have crossed not only the sorts of lines she maintained as a trooper but a good number of her own personal boundaries.

And she really couldn't think of anything that appalled her more.

That night, Kate let herself into the little apartment she'd rented. She'd chosen it for its efficiency and convenient location a few blocks away from her current office. She liked it. Or she had when she'd left it the other day.

Kate couldn't bring herself to live in the sort of stark, scary hovels like the ones where she'd been raised, so she always rented furnished places. But tonight she couldn't help but think that she was living in the odds and ends of other people's lives instead of making her own. Tonight it felt . . . makeshift and discordant.

Or she did.

"Get over yourself," she muttered, rubbing a hand against that weird hollow sensation in her chest.

She went to the bedroom, peeled off her uniform, and threw all her clothes into her hamper. She stood in the shower, let the hot water pour all over her, and told herself she was fine. Because she was always fine. Because nothing had changed, out there on those mysterious islands.

Because the one thing—the only thing—Kate had ever depended on was herself.

And Templeton Cross was a problem, that was for certain. But he wasn't *her* problem.

That was what she kept telling herself, all night long, hoping that somehow that would keep her from dreaming that same desperately erotic, wickedly dirty dream about him.

But it didn't.

That night or any of the nights that followed.

Ten days later, Kate pushed her way out of her office building into a blustery Juneau afternoon with no idea what to do with herself.

You haven't taken leave in years, her captain had told her over the phone from Anchorage, no doubt sitting there at the same desk where he'd promoted her time and time again.

I was under the impression that the fact I haven't taken leave is why I've been promoted as often as I have, she'd replied. Perhaps unwisely.

But it had been a long ten days. She wasn't entirely surprised when her boss sighed.

The thing is, Kate. This is a weird one. I don't want to suspend you.

You have no grounds to suspend me, she hadn't been able to keep herself from saying.

No one is accusing you of anything. But the fact of the matter is, somehow you're smack in the middle of this. Which means you can't be involved in the investigation. Which means I'm down the one person who could probably make sense of this whole mess. And look at that. It's the holidays. Perfect opportunity for you to take a holiday break, which gives us enough time to tie some bows around what we already know.

Kate had needed a moment to fight to keep her voice calm. *Which is that I had nothing to do with a body turning up in my plane.*

Of course you didn't, her boss had said. *This is procedure, nothing more.*

But she'd heard that note in his voice. That this was happening. That she had no control over it.

We'll reconvene in the New Year, he'd said. *Hopefully with some answers.*

"Merry freaking Christmas to me," Kate muttered to herself now, but the cold, damp wallop of the wind and the mountains took her breath away.

It had been snowy and in the twenties this morning. Now it was a relatively cozy thirty-seven degrees or so, though it was already tipping into twilight at two thirty in the afternoon. Kate could smell more snow in the air as she trudged out of the temporary office she was now no longer using, not far from the Capitol Building.

She went and got in her car. Then sat there, waiting for it to warm up.

Waiting to have some idea what she was supposed to do with time off she didn't want. During the one time of the year when she needed to be busy. When she depended on it.

Should she stay in Juneau? Or go back to Anchorage, where she could try to convince her captain to reinstate her when they were face-to-face? Though he hadn't sounded as if there was any wiggle room—

When the rap on her window came, she jumped.

She expected to see someone from work at her window, possibly out here to commiserate with her unwanted leave—not that Kate had made a huge number of friends in her couple of months here, chasing down Alaska Force leads. Not that she was much for making friends, full stop.

She fixed her work-appropriate smile on her face anyway—

But it was Templeton.

And for a long, hard kick of a heartbeat that made her a little too dizzy, she couldn't make sense of what she saw.

Templeton Cross. Standing in a parking lot in Juneau, when he was supposed to be roaming about the islands or off doing military maneuvers or running missions abroad.

And the thought that she was gaping at him like a starry-eyed schoolgirl made her jab her finger on the window's down button.

"What are you doing here?"

He smiled, infuriating man that he was. That big, careless grin. "Waiting for you, obviously."

"You can't lurk around outside—"

"I don't lurk, Kate. Men my size are too big to lurk."

"Does that mean that you had me under surveillance? Because that's not acceptable. And I should tell you that I take a very dim view—"

"Hey. Trooper. Breathe."

It was a distinct order, and Kate . . . obeyed him.

She actually obeyed him.

That gold, gleaming thing in his dark gaze brightened. Making her feel hot and itchy all at once, which she chose to interpret as a good opportunity to turn her car heater down.

"I know how to track people, if that's what you mean," he said. "I know where you live. But I would never turn up there, because that's exactly the kind of potential threat I think you really would take a dim, possibly armed, view of."

"You know where I live?"

"Juneau is not a big city. It's not hard to figure out where anyone lives."

"That's really not the point."

"Here I am at your current, if temporary, place of business, filled with various cops of all shapes and sizes," Templeton said. "As harmless as a lamb."

The idea of him as either harmless or any kind of lamb was so ridiculous that it didn't bear commenting on. Kate frowned at him instead.

"What could you possibly want? Let me rephrase. What could you possibly want that you couldn't achieve through a phone call? An e-mail? Or any of the time-honored forms of communication that do not necessitate a personal appearance at twilight?"

"Please. It's two thirty-four in the afternoon. Technical twilight is still the middle of the afternoon in Alaska."

"I don't need lessons on Alaska from an Outsider. I think we've already covered this."

"This is fun," Templeton said with that wicked drawl that licked all over her whether she wanted it to or not. "Matching wits with you always is. But I didn't come here for the entertainment. I have a proposition for you."

"I can't express to you how little interest I have in any propositions that come from—"

"Kate." He shook his head, just slightly. "We're past that."

She had no idea why she wanted to agree with him. But maybe it had nothing to do with him. Maybe it was that she felt so . . . unmoored. What was she supposed to do without work? Who was she supposed to *be*?

When he rounded the front of her vehicle, looking relaxed and at his ease and completely incongruous against the backdrop of downtown Juneau, she didn't know what came over her. But she unlocked her door and let him in.

And then Templeton Cross was sitting in her car.

Taking up entirely too much space. It was like a violation—except she couldn't pretend that it was anything so negative. It was just that she was so violently, painfully aware of him. All of him. He had to reach down to shove the passenger seat back as far as it would go, then tilt it back even farther in a bid to get his huge frame to fit.

And there was absolutely no reason that anything about the simple reality of a big man trying to fit into a relatively small SUV should have made her break out into a sweat.

"I feel like I'm in a mobster movie," she muttered.

"Am I the made guy in this scenario? I don't really think that works. I don't have the right accent, for one thing." Templeton nodded toward the office building. "Why don't you drive somewhere? Before you have to explain to all your cop buddies what you're doing playing mobsters with a person of interest in an ongoing and active investigation."

Now it was more like a cold sweat, and her stomach twisted. "I don't know why I let you in my car, but that moment of insanity has passed. You need to get out. You need to—"

"Kate. I have it on good authority that you're not on active duty yourself right now. Did they suspend you?"

"There are absolutely no grounds to suspend me," she snapped at him.

"Mandatory leave?"

"I'm enjoying the Christmas season," she gritted out, then turned to meet his gaze as blandly as she could. "Ho ho freaking ho."

"Drive," he told her, in that same commanding way, his eyes much too steady on hers. His voice too rich, too smooth, too . . . *much*.

But she went ahead and obeyed him all over again anyway.

Not, she was at pains to tell herself, because he'd ordered her to do something. She didn't take orders from him. But because he wasn't wrong about sitting there outside a building filled with law enforcement officials, practically begging them all to see what she was doing. And with whom.

She didn't take him back to her apartment. Instead, she drove up Starr Hill to one of her favorite spots in Juneau. It had a great view over the channel to Douglas Island when the sun was out. But the sun barely came up at all here at this time of year, and it disappeared quickly behind the mountains to the west when and if it did. By the time she got to her preferred place to park and sit awhile, the sky was dark and there was no view of any mountains or water. Just the lights from the houses tucked away up on the hill around them, and the city below.

And it occurred to her that either she was extraordinarily stupid to isolate herself with this man—again—or she actually did trust that Templeton was the man he said he was.

Or her gut trusted him, anyway, no matter how the rest of her tried to argue.

It irritated her, deeply, to admit that, even if her version of trust was fairly anemic. It had been beaten out of her early.

She turned to face him, scowling across the few inches between them in the dim interior of her car, with only the light from the dashboard to illuminate him. Like he was her own personal mountain.

"Well, you got your clandestine meeting. Here we are, like a couple of drug dealers."

"I don't think drug dealers hang out and talk," Templeton drawled. "I suspect that probably gets in the way of the whole *moving product and sampling their wares* thing."

"If you say so. I have no experience dealing drugs myself."

"Nice. Now I'm a drug-dealing mercenary. I keep on impressing you, don't I?"

She felt the hitch in her chest and told herself it was acid reflux. Stress. Something vaguely medical and having nothing to do with him. "Are you trying to impress me?"

Templeton turned and wrapped one big arm on the back of her seat as he moved, but she chose to interpret that as him making space for his big body, not . . . anything else. And the look on his face was an odd mix of sternness and what she was tempted to call surprise, mixed up with all that wicked sensuality that was just . . . him.

"You want to know if I'm trying to impress you?" he asked. "Are you sure we're not dating?"

The grin in the corner of his mouth and the way he said that made it clear that he was joking, but somehow, the air in the car between them was too stiff. Too tense. Too ripe with something Kate didn't want to understand.

But she'd dreamed about it.

Stop it. Now.

She pulled herself together. Or tried. "Why are you in Juneau? And why did you seek me out?"

"To ask you for a date, clearly."

"If you don't plan to answer my questions, fine. I'll turn this vehicle around, return you to my office, and you can explain to a roomful of Alaska State Troopers who want to date you as little as I do exactly what you're doing lurking around cars in parking lots at dusk."

"Sexy as that sounds," Templeton said, his grin deeper than before, "I'm here because of you. Because of who you are."

"You knew who I was in Grizzly Harbor. I've been an Alaska State Trooper for—"

"I don't mean your job. I mean you."

And she knew where he was going. Where people were always going when they were suddenly so interested in *who she was.*

This had happened so many times before that she'd taken to telling herself she was used to it. That it didn't matter. Ancient history that happened to also be a matter of public record was still history. She didn't have to talk about anything she didn't want to talk about, and she certainly didn't have to *feel* a damned thing.

But it felt different here. In the dark, again. With nothing in front of them but glaciers and frigid bays. Nothing around them but the looming mountains she couldn't see but knew were there.

And still there was nowhere to hide from her family.

Maybe, she thought darkly, this was how everyone felt during the holidays.

Templeton was studying her face. "Your father is Samuel Lee Holiday. *The* Samuel Lee Holiday."

"I know who my father is."

"The Samuel Lee Holiday who, with three of his brothers and two of his cousins, packed up all their wives and children and took them off into the interior of Alaska. Where they created a doozy of a little cult that was chiefly notable for sending explosive packages through the mail to a whole host of politicians some fifteen years ago. And might have kept on doing it if it weren't for his oldest daughter, who walked out of the Alaskan interior in subzero conditions, directly into an Alaska State Trooper office."

"The *walking out of the interior* part is always exaggerated. I stole a snowmobile and rode it until it ran out of gas. I walked for maybe ten minutes, and it wasn't that cold."

It had been negative twenty. She'd been dressed well for the elements. And lucky.

Templeton kept going. "When they went out to see what was happening in your father's compound, there was shooting. Two troopers died."

Kate had their names emblazoned on her memory, more potent and lasting than any tattoo. If she did any good in the world, if she made any kind of difference, it was to honor their sacrifice.

"Trooper Timothy David Gerard," she said quietly. "And Sergeant Jacob Anders Tolliver."

Templeton's gaze was too warm. Too bright. "You not only turned your father in, you endured each and every trial of your father, mother, uncles, and other relatives as the chief witness for the prosecution. While other kids were going to high school, Kate, you were going to court."

She stared back at him, somehow keeping her expression impassive. "Congratulations, Templeton. You have succeeded in telling me a great many things I already know."

"So here's what I have to ask myself," he said. "And what I need to ask you."

"If this is where you out yourself as some kind of ghoulish junkie of cult leaders, I warn you, I might shoot you."

"You can always try." His eyes gleamed, and she hated that she could feel it . . . everywhere. "But here's the thing. You've already distinguished yourself as somebody who took down groups like that when you were in your teens. I don't think it's a surprise to anyone that you followed the same path as an adult. From what I understand, when there are strange groups led by potentially dangerous men, you're the one they send. For going on five years now."

She wanted to argue that, but it was true. Or it had been true until today, when she'd been sent off on leave anyway.

"I have a lot of experience, that's all."

"I'm not asking you. I'm telling you."

Kate realized in that moment that she was seeing the business side of Templeton, right there in front of her. Not the public relations act. Not the flirt. But the man who had a thick file as full of medals and commendations as it was of redacted, classified material that all added up to a man who was remarkably good at what he did.

"If it's common knowledge that you're the one who's going to get sent out there when there's a questionable group that needs looking into, why are we assuming that the arson attempts, which are lame and annoying more than anything else, are aimed at Alaska Force?" he asked, his voice quiet but intense. Almost as intense as the way he focused all of his attention on her. And still not nearly as intense as the way her body reacted, with a shiver she had to fight to repress. "And why are we thinking that a body in your plane is somehow a message to us, or about us? Because the more I think about it, the more I think that this is all about you."

Seven

To say that Alaska Force didn't like it when people messed with Grizzly Harbor was an epic understatement.

Templeton hadn't liked it much when that lunatic preacher had come at them last spring. He really hadn't liked it when some hired muscle had neutralized Rory and helped himself to Mariah, their client. He took it pretty personally that someone was going around lighting their stuff on fire, and he hadn't much cared for it when that boat had gone up in flames at the beginning of the month.

But it was amazing to him how much less he liked it when it was all aimed straight at his trooper.

He studied her face in the dim shadows of the front seat of her car while Juneau did its early nighttime routine all around them. And the darkness might have felt endless at this time of year, but Templeton found he didn't mind much when Kate was there beside him, looking fierce and stubborn. Just the way he liked her.

"Of course this doesn't have to do with me," she said dismissively. As he'd expected she would. "And it certainly doesn't have to do with my father."

"What makes you so sure?"

It had taken them a few days to circle back around to Kate. They'd waited out the troopers and their initial investigation. They'd smiled politely and pretended to agree when told—repeatedly—to leave it alone.

Templeton was the one who'd done a deeper dive into Trooper Holiday's background. They'd already known she was the go-to for questionable groups. They knew all about her history with the Troopers, how she'd been rapidly promoted, and the cases she'd been involved with. That had seemed like sufficient information to have on hand for an initial interview.

But Templeton had wanted more. Not entirely because of the case, he could admit. But nonetheless, he'd dug in and found gold.

"The last time I spoke to any of my relatives was something like ten years ago," Kate said now. "I have nothing to do with them anymore. An arrangement everyone involved is perfectly happy with. Especially me."

"You think they're happy with you?" Templeton laughed, though he knew it wasn't his normal laugh. This one landed a lot more hollow. "I can tell you from experience, whenever prison is involved, there are bad feelings. That's just a fact."

Kate shrugged. "I'm sure they have bad feelings. I don't have any feelings. About them, about my childhood, anything. That's a closed chapter."

As usual, he had the urge to touch her.

And as usual, he didn't.

His halo was so bright by now he figured he could light up even the early Juneau night.

"Is that how it works?" he asked, his drawl a little too edgy. "You decide a chapter's closed and that's that? You must be the one person alive who gets to choose not to be affected by their childhood."

Her smile was thin, but he noticed it wasn't that same impenetrable cop smile he'd gotten used to back in Grizzly Harbor.

"Of course I'm affected by my childhood." Kate's expression became one of exaggerated patience. "It made me who I am today. But I don't flail around, constantly looking for reasons to be upset about things that happened more than half my life ago. I understand that's all the rage these days, but that's not me."

"Okay, fine. Great." His fingers curled around the headrest of her seat, taking what he could get. For God's sake. "But just because you're so psychologically sound, it doesn't mean they are."

She frowned and opened her mouth—no doubt to protest. Then she closed it again.

And Templeton waited as she thought her way through it. If he was surprised at how fascinating he found watching this woman *think*, well . . . He wasn't the sort of man who fought his instincts. He never had been. No matter what the rules were.

You have a crush on this trooper, Blue had said, laughing, in one of their morning briefings.

I don't have crushes, brother, Templeton had drawled. *I operate on intent.*

That had gotten him a lot of rolled eyes and muttered insults regarding his character, which he'd chosen, out of the goodness of his heart, to ignore.

I think that means that, yes, Templeton has a crush, Griffin had chimed in from across the room, where he liked to stand with his back to a wall, as if the enemy—any enemy—might crash through all their safeguards and be upon them at any moment.

Templeton has rules, Templeton had said, grinning broadly, as if he thought it was all a big joke. *Unlike some people in this room, I don't break those rules every time a pretty face shows up in Grizzly Harbor.*

Blue and Griffin had sized him up as he lounged there with his chair tipped back, like they were trying to figure out the best way to bum-rush him. He'd really, really hoped they would.

Isaac had called them all to order, but it wasn't the first time Templeton had enjoyed making the point that there was a difference between him and a number of his Alaska Force brothers. It wasn't that he hadn't seen the same dark stuff they had. And then some. He had, but he hadn't brought the dark out with him.

He figured it was because he'd gone in broken and the army had fixed him. He'd done what was necessary, and he didn't let the nightmares he had from time to time—because there were some things that a man couldn't forget if he tried—wreck his days. He didn't forget what he'd lived through, but it didn't own him.

And he didn't pretend he didn't want something when he did.

Wanting something was one thing. Taking it was another, especially when he knew better.

"Various family members made threats, particularly during the court cases," Kate said, snapping Templeton back to the cab of this SUV with the engine running to keep them warm. While the early night pressed in tight all around them.

Not the time, in other words, to be thinking this hard about all the ways he'd like to get his hands on this woman. And not only because it was against his rules. Or because he doubted she'd appreciate his thoughts in that direction. But, more practically, because he was entirely too large for any shenanigans in a closed car.

"Credible threats?"

She shot him a look. "I didn't think so. And even if I had, nothing came of them. It was years ago. Over a decade, in some cases."

"But not all of them are still in prison."

"I know who's behind bars and who isn't," Kate said in her steady, matter-of-fact cop way. "I said I hadn't talked to them myself, not that I didn't check in on what they were doing every now and again. As far as I can tell, they're all living exactly the squalid sort of lives they always wanted to live, only with less power over helpless family members, fewer death threats against national figures, and a whole lot more oversight from parole officers." She shook her head. "Mostly, they're just drunk and angry. But so are a lot of people."

"What we kept coming back to is the fact that they chose your seaplane as a stage for the body," Templeton said. "If this is about Alaska Force, how does that work? We literally had an Alaska State Trooper checking out our facilities when it happened, so we couldn't possibly have done it ourselves."

"Unless one of the unaccounted-for members of Alaska Force went ahead and staged the scene for the express purpose of shifting focus off of you."

"One, there are no unaccounted-for members of Alaska Force. You might not know where they were, but we do, and could prove it if necessary." Templeton shifted, because there was never enough room for his legs. "Second, walk me through how this works. If we're behind all this, we torch our own stuff and a random cabin, light a boat on fire in the place where we live, and then, after attracting all that attention, shove it away from us by staging a murder scene to implicate someone else. That seems pretty convoluted."

Kate's smile was icy. "The thing about criminals is no matter how smart they are about one thing or another, they almost always find a way to be dumb."

"Then lay out this case for me." Templeton nodded at the dashboard as if they were standing in an incident room. "Pretend I'm, God forbid, a lawyer, and you need to convince me to prosecute. What's the story?"

Kate rubbed at her forehead. "I'm not saying I have an airtight case. I'm saying that's the obvious first question when you tell me Alaska Force couldn't have done it because I was there. The fact is, I can't think of a particularly good reason why you and your friends would suddenly turn to abducting transients from ferries, murdering them, and leaving them around for people to find. Whatever else I might think of you, that certainly doesn't fit your MO."

"Damned with faint praise," Templeton murmured.

"I'll tell you what I told my captain." She tilted her chin up a little as she spoke, as if this was hard for her. "I think that it makes sense to give some serious side-eye to private military companies of any size, no matter their mission parameters or their glossy websites touting their commitment to their supposed values. Whatever those are. I have a deep and abiding distrust for secretive militias. But I've been studying you and your friends for the past six months, and I don't see it. I might not be an enthusiastic supporter of the work you do, but as much as it's possible to do that work aboveboard and right, I think you do it."

"Why, Trooper Holiday. You are fixing to make a grown man blush."

She frowned. "Once I accepted that I didn't think you were responsible for the uptick in arson—though I do think you require significantly more local oversight—I had to ask myself who was."

"Did you figure it out?"

"Yes, Templeton, I solve crime in my sleep. It's uncanny. I have a dream and just like that"—she snapped her fingers—"criminals are apprehended and justice is restored to the land."

"Your dreams are much more exciting than mine," he said.

And then watched, to his astonished delight, as his trooper . . . burst into flame.

He saw the bright red flush roll over her, making her eyes glitter even as the faintest beads of perspiration gathered at her temples. And along her upper lip. And he couldn't see the rest of her lean body, but he had absolutely no doubt she turned that same color everywhere.

Everywhere.

"Apparently much more exciting," he murmured.

She scowled at him and jabbed at her window, letting a burst of cold air into the car. "I always get overheated while sitting still in winter."

"Sure you do."

She jabbed at the window again, closing it. With prejudice. "I've investigated a lot of questionable groups. Any one of them could have regrouped in some form or another and focused their attention back on me. I have to admit it's not outside the realm of possibility."

"But you think your own family is outside the realm of possibility?" Templeton asked.

"What's your family like?" she retorted. "I notice you're sitting here in a car with me in Juneau a week before Christmas. Not planning to head back home to sing all those Christmas carols around the family tree."

"For all you know I could be flying out tomorrow."

"Are you?"

"There's nothing for me in the South," Templeton said, easily enough.

"Does that mean that you don't have any relatives? Or that you have a complicated relationship with them that you'd rather not go into detail about with a stranger?"

"You're the one who had all those background files. I think you know perfectly well that my father is doing a life sentence in Mississippi. And no, Trooper, I'm not planning to go take part in a Parchman family Christmas event. If I'm feeling sentimental I'll watch *Shawshank Redemption* a few more times, sing myself a Christmas carol, and call the whole thing merry enough."

And to his surprise, Kate laughed.

Had he heard her laugh before? Not in the course of asking more questions or proving how little affected she was by finding herself surrounded by people she considered desperate commandos, but a real laugh?

It hit him the same way that unexpected blush had. It seemed to arrow its way inside him, then headed straight for his sex—which was already a little too interested in how close they were sitting, here in this car with its fogged-up windows.

"I hope you don't spend a lot of time trying to convince people how fine you are while your father is sitting in a prison cell," she said when she finished laughing. "Here's what I know about having a father rotting away in jail. It sucks. It doesn't matter what I think about the man. It doesn't matter that I'm proud of the fact that I'm the one who put him there and consider that chapter of my life closed. Those are things I *think*. What I *feel* when I think about the fact that a good chunk of my relatives and both of my parents are either still in jail or ex-cons is shame."

Templeton felt his body shift, the way it did when he was ready for combat. He went still. Alert.

"You shouldn't feel any shame for what they did," he told her.

Her intent gaze slammed into his chest with the force of a bullet. "I appreciate that. But I think you know that I was talking about you."

"Here's the thing, Trooper. I'm shame-free. Shameless, in fact."

"Of course you are."

Templeton grinned widely and settled back against the seat. "You don't have to believe me. But that doesn't make it any less true."

"Let me see if I'm remembering your file correctly," she said, but she never shifted that steady gaze from his face. And once again, Templeton had the notion that there wasn't a whole lot Kate Holiday forgot. "Your father went to jail when you were very young. Your mother moved you out of state. And when she died, she had so successfully broken all ties with any remaining family members that you were put into foster care. But you have no feelings about that."

"You're not the only person who's come to terms with their childhood, Kate."

"You were eighteen the last time you were arrested, following your juvenile offenses that landed you in enough trouble that your only choice if you wanted to stay out of jail was to join the army."

"I considered becoming a priest. But there are some appetites a man doesn't want forgiven, if you know what I mean."

She rolled her eyes. And Templeton really couldn't have said why he found that more of a turn-on than any other woman's kiss.

"You have a chestful of medals, which they don't hand out for picnics in the park. We've already covered your childhood. But you're . . . fine."

"Is this a competition?" he asked mildly, but he was still too alert. Too ready for the next attack. Or any attack. For a full-on arsenal and an army to wield it. "Because you just finished telling me how fine you are."

"I said I don't look back. And I'm fine because I don't laze around, making sexually charged remarks, grinning and laughing like it's my job, and acting like life is a party."

"Maybe you should."

He could see the exact moment it occurred to his uptight little trooper that she'd veered far, far off course of anything that could possibly be called professional. Her eyes widened fractionally, and then there was nothing between them but the sound of the car's engine. The sound of her breath.

And the wild sensation it took him long moments to realize was his own pulse, racketing around like he wasn't a trained professional.

Like he didn't have rules.

But the rules were in place because once upon a time, he'd gotten involved on a job and it had ended badly.

Very badly. That hadn't kept him from having sex. It had made him very careful about having sex only with women he had no emotional or professional attachment to, so everyone stayed safe.

Now that he considered it, the emotional attachment had been the real problem. That had been what had messed everything up before, because he'd lost his focus. But Templeton was sure he didn't have that in him anymore. Sex didn't make him lose his focus these days. It made him better able to focus because he was relaxed.

This thing with Kate was fine, Templeton assured himself. Because tension like this would explode. That was what it did. And once it did, once he tasted her, this madness would subside and he could keep doing what he did best, which was solve unsolvable problems.

It was as good as done.

And he didn't want to talk about prison. Or any part of the past he'd merrily turned his back on years ago.

So maybe that was why he took his life in his hands—something he happened to be very, very good at—and moved his arm from around the back of her seat so he could slide his fingers lightly over those cheekbones that had been driving him nuts for more than ten days now.

She caught her breath. He thought maybe he caught his, too.

Everything between them tightened. The dark night outside pressed in harder, until there was nothing but her soft skin, her warm flesh. Her wide, pretty brown eyes. That mouth of hers that dropped ever so slightly open.

He traced the faintest pattern. Once, then again.

"Sergeant," she breathed. "If you do not remove your hand, I will take out my gun and shoot it off."

He believed her.

But he was also tied up in knots over this woman, which couldn't go on, and if that wasn't reason enough to risk a bullet, he didn't know what was. He risked his life all the time. What was once more, and for a far better reason?

To untie the knots. And fast-forward to the relaxing part.

Among other things.

"If you're going to shoot me anyway, might as well make it worth it," he drawled.

And then he bent his head toward her, holding her cheek right there where he wanted it, and got his mouth on his trooper at last.

Eight

This was impossible.

It was unacceptable.

It was—

Hot.

Templeton's mouth worked a dark and wicked magic, moving over hers with a lazy insistence that made Kate crumble.

Then melt. Everywhere.

Her head shorted out. That was the only explanation.

She was malfunctioning, clearly. That was why she was too hot all over again, flushed to the breaking point the way she'd been when he'd mentioned her dreams, except this—

This was so much worse.

Better, something gleeful and deeply feminine inside contradicted her.

He wasn't hesitant. He wasn't particularly careful. If he had a single inhibition, it wasn't apparent in the way he kissed.

Templeton Cross kissed her as if he already knew the fastest way to get her naked. He kissed her as if he planned to be inside her, and soon. He kissed her slowly, thoroughly, and with so much heat and fire that Kate didn't understand how they didn't both ignite where they sat.

He cupped her face in one big hand, holding her there with that same lazy ease, as if he was in no rush. As if he could sit there, tasting her like this, forever.

And Kate had been kissed before. The few times she'd attempted to have a relationship had involved all kinds of kissing, none of which she could remember now if her life depended on it. It all seemed so pale and fumbling in comparison. Tentative and forgettable.

But Templeton kissed the way he laughed. Big. Huge.

He took her over, crowding out everything else, until she thought that if she let go—surrendered—it might be possible to simply tip herself over into the kiss itself. And the more he kissed her, the more she found it hard to remember why that was probably a bad idea.

Meanwhile, sensations stormed through her, lighting up parts of her body she'd long since accepted didn't work. Not the way everyone else's did. As her last almost-boyfriend had been certain to tell her.

Templeton kissed her until she forgot her deficiencies. Until she forgot why it was so unwise to meet every slow, lazy thing he did with his mouth with her own.

Until she found herself pressing forward, demanding more, almost moaning with need—

But Kate didn't need anything. Or anyone.

That was the defining truth of her life, ever since she'd gotten away from her family.

The word *need* washed over her like an ice-cold shower, and she wrenched herself away from him, expecting there to be some resistance—

But there wasn't. Templeton let her go instantly, which made her flush all over again, because if he hadn't been holding her, and making that happen, that meant she'd been doing it herself.

"Have you lost your mind?" Kate demanded, her voice soft with rage. Horror. And all the rest of those jangly things that flashed around inside of her, so hard and bright she was half-afraid that her bones would break from the effort of keeping it all in.

"I don't think so," Templeton rumbled, all that laughter in his voice. "Though I expect I'd be the last to know if I had, right?"

"You put your mouth on an investigator—"

"I didn't simply put my mouth on you, Kate." And again, there was so much laughter in his voice and in his gaze that she almost felt as if she could hear it—or, more alarming by far, it was ricocheting around *inside* of her. "I got all up in there. Because I like kisses that matter. That require attention and commitment. Tongue, teeth, a moan or two. That's how I am."

Kate squeezed her eyes shut to block him out, but that made things worse. Because then she could do nothing but *feel* all that noise and nonsense inside her.

Her eyes snapped open again. She tried to focus and found herself frowning. "Stepping back from the appalling inappropriateness of this situation, you must realize that you've compromised this investigation."

"You're on leave," he reminded her, settling into that relaxed lounge that drove her mad, because he was too big. He should have looked awkward. Stuffed in like a sardine in a can. And he . . . didn't. "I didn't compromise any ongoing investigation, because you're not part of the investigation, and even if you were, you're not investigating me. And if it was that inappropriate, you probably shouldn't have kissed me back."

She wanted to put her hands to her mouth to see if she could press all that sensation away somehow. Or make her mouth feel like hers again. She wanted to do *something* about the taste of him, like some kind of terrible whiskey on her tongue, intoxicating and wild. But that would give it all away, and Kate had already given far too much away.

"We're done here," she told him frostily.

She wrenched herself back around to face her steering wheel and threw the car into reverse. But then froze when his big hand appeared in her vision and wrapped around the steering wheel, too.

"We got sidetracked," he rumbled from beside her. And around her. And in her, too, because he was that overwhelming. "But I didn't come all the way to Juneau to sit in a car and get a taste of you, fun as that is."

"Apparently you came all the way to Juneau to chat about family history, the judicial system, and the possibility that I might be the focus of one or another group of malcontents. Or in other news, it's just another Tuesday."

"Do you find dead bodies every Tuesday?"

She forced herself to stop gritting her teeth. "Obviously not. That's clearly an escalation, though I'm not convinced it's aimed at me. I live here, not out in the islands where most of these suspicious activities occurred."

"And now you're on leave. And as we've already established, not about to surround yourself with the big, happy, gun-toting family to help keep you safe over the holidays. What are your plans?"

"If you're inviting me over to watch *Shawshank Redemption* with you, Templeton, I'll have to take a hard pass on that," Kate managed to bite off, still glaring straight ahead at the city spread out along both sides of the channel far below them, sparkling in the dark. "I'm not sure I really understand the obsession men have with that particular movie, as I, personally, already know that prison is unpleasant and that I would not enjoy tunneling my way out through—"

"It's okay that you're dead inside," Templeton interrupted her. "My concern is with you turning up dead, not movie dates. Because if someone is escalating a campaign with you at the center of it, you sitting all alone for the rest of the holiday season is pretty much begging them to take that as an invitation."

Kate wanted to punch him for suggesting that she'd be sitting alone. Especially because it was true.

She focused on the other part instead of the urge toward violence—which, she had to admit deep down inside, no matter how she would prefer to pretend otherwise, could possibly be nothing more than an excuse to get her hands on him. "If someone does come for me, I'm more than capable of handling myself. Even if I hadn't spent my entire adulthood in law enforcement, I was also raised by paranoid survivalists. I knew more about weapons and self-defense by the time I was five than most people will ever learn in their entire lifetimes."

"Unless, of course, the people coming after you have the exact same history."

"Thank you, Mr. Cross," she said, biting off his surname like it was a weapon, because she wished it were. And that she could aim it at him because she wanted to take him out, and not because her body wanted things she had no intention of giving it. "I really do appreciate you coming so far on this, the first day of my unasked-for and unwanted leave. Not only to goad me into completely forgetting who I am and acting in a manner both deeply unprofessional and personally horrifying but also, clearly, to go out of your way to make me feel insecure in my own home. You're about as helpful as a December night in Juneau, aren't you?" She nodded toward the example right there before them, on the other side of her windshield. "Dark early, dark late, dark all the time."

"You can look at it that way if you like," Templeton drawled. "Or you could take your leave in Grizzly Harbor."

"What?" She blinked at him, because that didn't make any sense. Like everything else this afternoon. "Why would I want to spend more time in Grizzly Harbor?"

"Trooper. I know I spun your head around there, but you need to focus." And Templeton laughed when she glared daggers at him. "You and I both know that you're the best possible person to investigate the situation. And you can't do it if you stay here. Where you're also very likely at risk of actual, physical bodily harm. Whether you believe it or not. So come to Grizzly Harbor. Work with us."

"*Work* with you?" she repeated, as if he hadn't been speaking English.

"Unofficially, of course. We could use your help." Kate had always been under the impression that men, as a whole, were bad at admitting they needed help with anything. Ever. But Templeton looked relaxed and unbothered. "And it turns out I feel pretty personally invested in keeping you alive. Why not kill two birds with one stone?"

"I don't kill birds, with or without stones. And I don't work with questionable private military operators."

"Also," Templeton continued conversationally, as if she hadn't spoken, "I have every intention of kissing you again. A lot. Which is going to be hard to do if you're all the way over here in Juneau. Or dead."

Kate's head really was spinning, which was probably what he wanted.

But she didn't have time to do something about her spinning head. Or contemplate his astonishing offer. Because he was touching her again.

She told herself it was panic that seized her then, ripping through her like another brush fire and dousing all those flames she'd thought she'd put out—with kerosene. She pulled in a ragged breath, but then, belatedly, her brain asserted itself.

Yes, he was touching her. Templeton's big, callused hand was over hers on the gearshift between them. And he wasn't taking liberties. He was carefully easing the car out of reverse and back into park.

And later she would no doubt wish she hadn't given herself away so easily, but right now all she could do was whip her hand out from under his like he was a hot burner on a stove.

"Give me a list of pros and cons," Templeton said, still sitting there like he planned to lounge around in the front seat of her car forever.

So unhurried. So confident. So deeply sure that whatever it was he was doing, it was worth doing simply *because* he was doing it.

Why was she thinking about how he was *sitting*? Again?

"The pros and cons to what?" she clipped out at him. "If you mean your intention to kiss me a lot, there are no pros."

The look he gave her made that flush flare up all over again, and she had to force herself to unclench her hand when she realized how hard she was gripping the steering wheel.

"Now, Kate," he drawled. "Liars never prosper. Or so I heard one time while ambling past a church one Sunday afternoon on my way to engage in far more pleasurable activities."

She sighed. He grinned.

"But in this case, I wasn't asking you to tell us both lies about how much you liked kissing me. I already know. I was talking about you coming to work with Alaska Force for a little while. Which is less fun than kissing me, I'll admit."

"It's out of the question. Obviously."

"Why?"

She didn't understand why Templeton got to her like this, when no other man ever had. It had been bad enough out in Grizzly Harbor, when she couldn't help feeling that Templeton had gotten the best of every situation she'd found herself in with him. But at least then she'd had a better understanding of what she was supposed to be accomplishing.

Today she was off-balance. There was no other way to put it. The ground was shaky beneath her feet, and she was letting him take advantage of that. Or anyway, she wasn't doing a whole lot to stop him. Especially not when she'd leaned in and kissed him back.

Kate fought to repress her shudder. And told herself it was from revulsion.

But she knew better. Just like she knew—because she'd taught herself, step by precarious step when she'd still been a kid—that she was the only person who could get her balance back. That if she centered herself, nothing and no one could shake her.

She looked away from the temptation lounging there beside her. Out over her lit-up dashboard, down the hill, and across the lights of downtown Juneau, then off to the west, where the mountain blocked any view of the water and islands beyond.

Kate reminded herself how it was she'd come to be sitting in this vehicle in the first place, here in Juneau, an Alaska State Trooper and an investigator, whether she was on leave or not. Why it was she wasn't still marooned in that compound out in the snowy interior, knowing only the tiny little sliver of the frigid, isolated world that her father had wanted her to see. Or, more likely, long gone as another one of his victims. It was funny, because now and again she would meet tourists from the Lower 48, and they almost universally shuddered when they talked of Alaskan winters they'd never experienced and told her that they'd feel too trapped by the dark. Too claustrophobic. Or something along those lines.

But for Kate, endless dark or midnight sun, as long as she wasn't in that compound, she was free.

She was alive. She was away from her family. She was making her own life, her own choices, her own way. Sometimes that meant working through the holidays. Sometimes that meant accepting a leave she didn't want. Either way, she was living a life she couldn't have imagined when she was growing up. There had been very clearly defined roles for everyone her father controlled, and nothing in Kate's life now fit that bill.

That was the part she couldn't lose sight of, no matter what else happened.

This holiday leave might have been thrust upon her, but it was hardly the worst of the things Kate had survived in her time.

And the more she allowed herself to remember that, the more prepared she felt to try to look at Templeton's proposition—the one about working with him and his friends, that was—with a little more clarity.

"What exactly do you mean when you say *work with you*?" she asked.

"You've seen what we do. Or how and where we do it, anyway. Pretty certain you can figure it out from there, but if not, I could probably draw you a map."

How did he make that sound so . . . dirty? More worryingly, why did her own body react as if he were painting that map directly onto her bare skin?

"I'm not military. I don't . . ." Her throat was much too dry, and she blamed him for that, too. "Go out on missions or whatever it is you do."

"Kate. Please. You flew yourself to Grizzly Harbor to interview the members of a group you were sure had nefarious intentions and were moreover responsible for a series of explosions throughout Southeast Alaska. How is that not a mission?"

She drummed her fingers against the steering wheel, turning his offer over and over in her head. Because she should refuse, of course. She should already have refused. It was the responsible, reasonable thing to do.

"I'm not supposed to have anything to do with the investigation."

"And you won't." Templeton shrugged. "The official investigation. But as you already know, Alaska Force likes to do things our own way."

"I will not be a party to breaking the law." She turned toward him, making sure to look him straight in the eye. "That's a hard line I will not cross."

"No one's asking you to break the law."

"No breaking the law. No bending it. No gray areas."

"Life is gray areas, Kate. That's a fact. You like facts, don't you?"

"We already had this debate. I believe in choices."

"I realize this might come as a surprise to you," Templeton drawled, sounding deeply entertained. Though there was something about the gleam in his dark eyes that made her think he was possibly less entertained than he was acting. "But I don't actually run around encouraging people to break the law."

Kate frowned at him, still drumming the steering wheel with her fingers. She realized she was betraying her nerves, but she didn't make herself stop.

"I shouldn't be considering this. Not for a moment."

She didn't mean to say that out loud. And she didn't really understand why she hadn't dismissed the idea out of hand. The time of year was a factor, sure. Maybe she was afraid that if she didn't work, all those things she was usually so arrogantly sure she'd left in her past would bloom in her all over again. And not as a sharp little stab of shame, like when a new person pointed out her father's sins, but something bigger. More dangerous. Something that might lead her to end up like one of her cousins, living bitter and grim and, most of the time, blind drunk.

A fate worse than death, as far as Kate was concerned.

"The only reason I'm entertaining this notion is because if that body had been found in anyone else's seaplane, I'd be running the investigation. This sort of thing is what I do."

"I know."

"And I have to think taking my expertise off the field

entirely in a situation like this has the potential to make it worse."

"Yeah. Kind of like when you're one of the most highly trained and competent soldiers in the world, capable of doing things that make regular men think you're superhuman. And when you're done with the service you look around and think . . . maybe there are other ways I can use these skills for good."

"Are you comparing me to a band of—"

His dangerous mouth crooked. "Let's not call each other names, Trooper. It won't end well."

Kate looked at him. Just *looked* at him.

This impossible man, too big and too much in every conceivable way. And she understood that it was entirely possible that for the first time in her adult life, so far as she could recall, she wasn't actually doing something because it was right. That even though it was true that she had more expertise in this area than most of her colleagues, there was a Templeton factor as well. Her lips still tingled from his kiss. There were . . . *things* happening in her body because of him, when she'd been perfectly comfortable believing herself numb straight through.

There was no way to be sure that she wasn't acting on that same impulse that led to the kinds of stupidity she'd spent the early part of her career helping clean up, in one way or another. People did foolish things for sex. Kate had never been one of them, because she'd always had a clear head where such things were concerned.

Mostly because she'd had no idea it could feel like that. Until now.

Until him.

It's almost a 100 percent certainty that you're being an idiot, she informed herself.

But outside this overwarm, overly close car, it was as dark as if it were two in the morning, when it hadn't yet hit five p.m. Christmas was just over a week away and closing in fast.

And Kate felt, starkly, that she had to choose between the demon she knew too well—and the one she had only learned to fear today.

She knew how Christmas felt when she was working around the clock, focusing on the job to the exclusion of everything else. And she was so terrified of the prospect of not working that she'd not only allowed Templeton to climb into her vehicle, she'd made out with him like the kind of teenager she'd certainly never been.

She had to think that it was better to do what she could to handle the devil she knew before it took her down. And worry about this new demon if and when she had to, hoping all the while that what had happened here was an aberration brought on by her unexpected leave of absence from her job.

This was certainly not how Kate was used to doing things. But then again, nothing that had happened since she'd gone to Grizzly Harbor was how she was used to doing things. Maybe it was time to lean into it.

And maybe, if she went out there and worked with Alaska Force to figure out what on earth was really going on, she could settle all of this on her terms. Prove this had nothing to do with her past and make sure that she never had to take a break from the Troopers again, no matter what blew up in the middle of a dark December.

"You okay there?" Templeton asked, his voice a low rumble in the dark, and yes, she could feel every syllable inside her own body. Making her melt and shift a little in her seat.

But she could handle it.

Because if she had to handle something, she did. That was the story of her life.

She turned and looked Templeton full in the face, as

much to prove to herself that she could handle anything as to prove something to him. More, maybe.

"Okay," she said briskly. Before she could second-guess her decision. Or think better of it. "I'll do it. I'll work with you. Just as long as I'm on leave."

And she told herself she didn't feel a thing when Templeton unfurled that long, slow, dangerous smile that made her think she should have laid out a list of demands before she'd agreed.

Then made him sign it, no matter what that list might have told him about the things clamoring around inside of her.

As long as she kept them hidden, where he might guess at their existence but never know for sure, she'd be fine.

Perfectly fine, she told herself sternly.

And when all he did was nod in reply, slow and much too sexy, she pulled herself together and drove them both down the hill and back into what light there was in Juneau on this side of the December solstice.

Before she did something she couldn't blame on her least favorite time of year.

Nine

It didn't surprise Templeton that his trooper's response to what had happened between them in her cozy little SUV was to pretend it hadn't happened at all. He knew all about compartmentalization.

Once she decided to go back to Fool's Cove with him, she snapped back into her ultra cop mode. She drove down the hill and asked him only one thing as she navigated the streets through the evening snow: where she could drop him off.

Because she obviously didn't plan to spend one more moment of that evening with him than necessary.

"I was thinking dinner and a show," Templeton drawled. "Now that we're dating."

"Your options are to give me an address of a place I can drop you off or I'll leave you on the street right now," she replied, all clipped and cool and not there for his nonsense.

It was his own personal curse that he found her standoffishness refreshing. Especially when he still had the taste of her in his mouth.

Templeton laughed, then gave her the address of one of the places Alaska Force considered a safe house in

Juneau. Which was to say, a house belonging to one of their network of helpers and friends, who could be depended on to come up with an extra bed when needed.

And in the morning, Kate picked him up at the precise dot of 0900 and drove them both to the airport north of Juneau, where Templeton had a buddy waiting to fly them out to Fool's Cove.

It was another gloomy, gray day, but that didn't change the beauty of the landscape they flew through. All these years later and Templeton still couldn't seem to get enough of it. The clouds clinging to the mountainsides. The brooding sea.

And best of all, that stretch of cove that was the best and only home Templeton had ever had as an adult.

He waved off his buddy. Then he turned to Kate, who was standing on the end of the dock, looking up at the lodge and the assorted cabins with an expression he couldn't read on her face. It was windy today, making it feel much colder than it was, but Templeton enjoyed it. He liked the way the weather slapped him in the face, prickling him into life. He liked to be reminded that whatever else he was, whatever he might do in the course of his day, first and foremost he was alive.

He reached down and snagged her bag, hoisting it up and starting down the dock.

"I don't need you to carry my bag," she said in what sounded like a combination of surprise and outrage.

"Noted."

"I can carry it myself."

"Yes," he said patiently, without adjusting his stride. He could hear her feet hit the dock behind him. "I understand you're able-bodied. Good talk."

And he let her fume as he kept going, doing absolutely nothing to shorten his stride this time as he led her up the stairs and into the lodge itself.

The team was finishing up the morning briefing, which was an extralong one today, with the dead transient and arson to puzzle over on top of their other current missions. Templeton marched inside, tossing Kate's bag into an empty chair, then claiming one for himself. And he settled in to watch with maybe too much amusement as Kate looked around at the assembled collection of Alaska Force members, fixed that cool smile to her face, and stood where she could keep her back to the wall. At attention.

With them, but certainly not one of them.

Isaac was standing over by the flat-screen TV, where Oz normally put up various schematics and photographs. He smiled.

Because Isaac always smiled directly at any potential threats.

"Trooper Holiday," he said, with a genial sort of chuckle in his voice that made a wise man sit up a little straighter. "If you can't beat them, join them, right? It's a time-honored strategy for a reason."

But Kate did not disappoint.

"I may not think you're responsible for the string of crimes plaguing this division," she replied coolly. "But I'm certainly not joining your private army."

Blue let out a laugh from where he was sitting, his tablet in his hand. "You tell them," he said. "Never be a member of a club that would have you. Everybody knows that."

Templeton surveyed the room. He knew that Rory and Griffin were out doing some recon fieldwork around the sites of each fire. That was in addition to the teams farther afield, in play in more distant locations. But Jonas was here, sitting over by the big stone fireplace, while Bethan was about as far away as it was possible to sit from Jonas—diagonally across the great room—and still be in the same space.

Interesting things about Jonas and Bethan included Jonas's distinct, unusual objection to her hiring, when he typically offered either no opinion or quiet support to new members. Also the fact that the two of them never made eye contact. They never sat next to each other, close to each other, or anywhere that could even be loosely described as near each other. And when they were forced to speak to each other, or couldn't avoid partnering up for some reason during Isaac's horrendous workouts, they were so excruciatingly polite to each other that it could cause dental trauma to anyone in the vicinity.

Fascinating, Templeton thought, the way he always did, filing away the weirdness between the two of them.

"Now that you're here," Isaac said smoothly, still smiling, "we need to talk strategy." He raised his brows in Kate's direction. "Do you know the status of the Troopers' investigation?"

"I know that it's an active investigation," Kate replied in that calm way that was clearly meant to slap down anyone who came at her. And very likely did the trick, most times. "I'm not here to interfere with that, or them, in any way. I need that to be clear right now, or there's no point going forward."

Templeton found himself grinning.

"If you're not here to help figure out what's going on, then why are you here?" Jonas asked from across the room. He stood still. Too still, as always. He was a man who chose his words carefully, wasted few of them, and was perfectly happy to sit in silence otherwise. And the force of his attention was enough to make the unwary trip over their own two feet.

Templeton thought he saw Kate stiffen slightly, but she didn't back down. "I don't know what kind of bargain you all had to make to go from serving your country to serving your own interests," she said.

"That's not what we do," Isaac retorted, even as the tension level in the room ratcheted up.

Templeton, maybe because he was used to the kind of spice Kate liked to throw around, or maybe because he'd tasted her and knew exactly what it took to make his cool, prickly trooper melt, only laughed.

"Oh, do you work for free?" Kate asked sweetly.

"We're a business," Isaac said. And his smile was edgy, if you knew where to look. "Businesses rarely work pro bono."

"Call it whatever you like," Kate replied, and her chin tilted up a few notches. "I took a vow to serve, with honor, the people of the state of Alaska. I'm not going to do anything that compromises that vow."

Jonas seemed to turn to stone to match the fireplace behind him. Blue scowled. And even Bethan, who had so far maintained pretty much of a poker face in all scenarios, looked like she was thinking of breaking enough to frown herself.

"Settle down, Trooper," Templeton drawled. "Everyone in this room is committed and honorable. You're the only one making cracks about other people's promises."

And to his surprise, Kate inclined her head.

"You're right," she said in the same cool way. She folded her arms over her chest and then looked around to meet everyone's gaze for a moment. "I apologize."

Capable, kissable, and able to admit when she was wrong? Templeton thought he might have died and gone to the heaven he'd never believed in. Not for a man like him. Even when Isaac started talking, laying out possibilities, he couldn't seem to stop looking at Kate like she was his next meal. And dessert.

And a delicious hereafter.

This was nothing but a temporary holiday thing that would help him focus on the task at hand, he reminded himself. Or she would break his rules, and he couldn't have that.

"Oz went through your closed cases," Isaac was telling Kate. "He broke them down into three groups. Cases he thought were unlikely to produce this kind of reaction, cases he thought were either likely or at least possible, and then another set of cases that just got to him, one way or another."

"Got to him?" Kate asked crisply, as if she hadn't been chastised. As if she hadn't apologized.

Again, it made Templeton want to get his hands all over her. And while he was at it, taste her again. And this time, everywhere he wanted to taste her. Not only her wide, generous mouth.

Once he did, once he glutted himself on her, he'd be able to stop all of this obsessing. He was sure of it.

Isaac gave the impression of shrugging without actually doing it. "Things he thought were weird or that tweaked him a little. He would be able to tell you why."

"I understand. Gut feeling."

"Do you discount gut feelings, Officer?" Jonas asked, his gaze hooded.

Kate's smile was 100 percent police. "I wouldn't be much good at my job if I did."

Jonas nodded, as if that was settled. And maybe more than Kate's thoughts on gut feelings.

"We think it would be enormously helpful if you sat down with these lists and went through them to see what pops up for you," Isaac continued. "Then let's see what kind of overlap we have between Oz's lists and your lists."

"That sounds like a plan," Kate said.

"Templeton can show you where to set up." Isaac nodded at everyone else. "Let's get to it."

Templeton stayed where he was as the rest of the team went off to get to work. Only when everyone was gone did he get up, taking his sweet time and watching Kate's face while he did it.

"Are you pissed at me because I called you out?" he asked. Mildly.

"You weren't wrong, and I apologized," Kate replied in an infinitely serene way that Templeton didn't bother to pretend he couldn't feel all over him. He wanted more.

More of that mouth, because the last thing it was when it was under his was cool or calm or *serene*. "I'm not sure why we're revisiting the subject. Are you one of those people who can't take an apology?"

"There's not much I can't take, Trooper," Templeton rumbled at her. "As I'm happy to demonstrate at any point."

"I'm so glad that you reminded me about your penchant for off-color remarks," she said loftily, and he knew he wasn't mistaking the challenging gleam in her gaze. "We're working together now. So as inappropriate as it was for you to be doing this before, it's even more so now."

"We're not officially working together," Templeton replied easily enough. Because he'd thought about this way too much, clearly. "And even if we were, guess what? I'm a grown-ass man who makes his own decisions about his romantic life. My assumption was that you, too, were an adult and fully in charge of what you do and don't do. Or do you need to hide behind rulebooks so you don't have to feel anything?"

"I don't even know where to begin with that."

"Let me ask you a question," Templeton said, roaming toward her. He watched how her eyes widened, then heated. It was about the hottest thing he'd ever seen. And he didn't know how he kept himself from reaching over and getting his hands on her again. "What did you dream about?"

For a moment her face was blank. Then she flushed, bright and red enough to heat the whole of the lodge.

"Yeah," Templeton said with deep satisfaction. "That's what I thought."

He picked up her bag again, carrying it as he pushed out the lodge's front door. She came after him, and he could hear from the way her boots hit the deck that he'd pissed her off. A better man would probably not have found that as amusing as he did.

Oh well.

He led her along the intersecting wooden walkways until they reached the cabin that had been set up for her. He opened the front door, beckoning her in. And watched with sheer delight as the stiff way she preceded him told him all he needed to know about her mood.

It worked for him. Maybe he should have been concerned about how much it worked for him.

"I know this isn't much," he said as they looked around the cabin together. It was two rooms and a bathroom. The living room was furnished and winterized, and Oz had carefully laid out all the devices Kate would need to access the lists he'd made. There was a couch, a woodstove for heat, and a table in front of the window looking out over the misty cove. "But it's yours as long as you're here."

"No secret handshake?" she asked coolly. "No initiation rituals?"

Templeton let his gaze rest on hers too long. With too much heat. "I can haze you if you want, Kate. But you have to ask nicely."

Kate made a point of wrenching her bag out of his grasp. She marched into the other room, where Templeton knew there wasn't a whole lot. A bed, a dresser. Rustic walls with very little in the way of ornamentation. A thick rug to keep the cold out.

Every now and again a client came to Fool's Cove and stayed in one of these cabins. And then flipped out, because it was so stark and remote. And much too Alaskan.

But Kate wasn't a client. And better still, she was local born and bred.

He stayed where he was, propping up the wall next to the front door until she came back out again and stood in the doorway to the bedroom.

And Templeton was not a teenage boy. He needed reminding, because all he could think about was that bedroom. That bed. And how easy it would be to cross the cabin floor in a step. Pick her up and hold her against him, then bear her down sweet and certain onto that bed.

His mouth watered. His sex registered its enthusiasm.

But Templeton stayed where he was. Maybe to prove he could.

"No," Kate said.

Very distinctly.

"What do you mean, no?" Templeton protested with a laugh. "I didn't do anything. Or ask you anything."

"I can see your face. So I'll repeat myself. *No.*"

Now he was enjoying himself. More, that was. He lounged as he stood there, crossing his arms and propping one boot up on the other in front of him to look that much more languid.

He'd seen his trooper in various versions of her uniform. And in early morning, cold-weather running gear.

But this was the first time he'd seen her dressed as . . . Kate. Or what he assumed was just her, nothing else. She wore tough-looking technical pants that licked their way over her strong thighs and athletic calves to tuck into boots appropriate for anything Alaska could throw her way. On top she wore a jacket she'd unzipped when she'd entered the lodge, and a dark green sweater he'd guess was wool. Hardy and practical yet quietly elegant.

And it wasn't the kind of green that the locals wore, which could double as camouflage. It was more of a jewel tone, which suggested to Templeton that his trooper had more girl inside her than she liked to let on. Her hair was in a ponytail, sleek and neat, and she wore the kind of makeup that looked like no makeup at all. And he thought, *This is Kate on leave.* A woman who looked exactly like the cop she was, but with a few hints here and there that maybe there was more to her than her job.

More to her, full stop, that he had every intention of enjoying.

Temporarily.

"I don't need you to help me read through my old

cases," she said, her voice as even and faintly disinterested as her gaze was wary. And still too hot. "So if that's all . . . ?"

"Are you dismissing me?"

"It doesn't appear to be working."

"You're not here in an official capacity, Trooper," he reminded her. "Which means that unlike when you were, I don't have to jump to obey your commands, do I?"

"I don't recall you jumping. Certainly not at my command."

"You tossed me out of the Water's Edge Café. And my feelings are hurt that you can't remember that example of my perfect obedience."

"I don't think you know the meaning of the word *obedience*."

"That sounds a lot like an offer to teach me what I'm missing, Kate."

"It's really not."

Templeton didn't point out that for all her bluster, her eyes sparkled as they went back and forth. And he could see the smile she was trying to bite back. He didn't point out what he knew, which was that if he reached over there and got his hands on her, she would melt into a puddle.

And moan against him. And taste so sweet and hot he wasn't sure he'd recovered from it yet. Or would. Something he was pretty sure he knew how to remedy.

He didn't point any of that out; he just enjoyed it.

"Don't you have something to do?" she asked when all he did was gaze back at her. "Impressive physical feats? Various acts of controlled violence? Or maybe you need to go somewhere and . . . recharge all this."

She nodded at him when she said that last part.

"Recharge?"

"I don't know. I imagine you must need to take all that Templeton-ness and plug it in somewhere. So you can keep simmering away like this without interruption."

"That sounds a whole lot like a challenge to my masculinity."

She smiled. "If your masculinity is as fragile as a flower, sure."

"I'll say this as delicately as I can, Kate," Templeton said. With great deliberateness. "I don't need to recharge. I can go all night, tomorrow, and into next week if necessary. And nothing about it is fragile. Or delicate. Anytime you want me to provide you with a demonstration, just ask."

And, once again, he had the distinct pleasure of watching her turn several different shades of pink, edging over into red. There was nothing he didn't like about Kate in cop mode. But Kate flustered made his chest tighten in purely male anticipation.

"I'm going to have to take an extremely hard pass on that," she said after a moment, in a voice that was all woman. Rough and warm. No trace of trooper at all.

"As long as we agree it's hard," Templeton replied.

Because he couldn't seem to help himself.

And he left her then, before he couldn't, because her eyes were too bright and her cheeks were bright red. He shoved his way outside and found himself whistling all over again, though he knew, intellectually, that the day was gloomy and wet and cold.

But as far as he was concerned, it was the height of summer. The sky was blue, the sun was shining, and all the pretty birds were singing, because Kate was hot and bothered when she looked at him—and, best of all, part of the team in all the ways that mattered and yet not a coworker.

He was in no danger here. No danger at all.

As far as Templeton was concerned, Christmas had just come early.

What Kate wanted to do, though it was completely out of character, was dither around the cabin like a giddy teenage girl—the ones she'd watched on the television shows she'd studied when she'd first come out of her father's compound, to try to understand what she'd missed of the world—spinning around and around on another Templeton trip.

Luckily, she was actually the grown adult Templeton had reminded her she was earlier. And an officer of the law, thank you. Which meant that after only the tiniest little bit of dithering—which in her case looked nothing at all like the girls on television and happily involved nothing more undignified than staring at the door he'd closed behind him—she ordered herself to stop. Immediately.

She did not moon at doors after inappropriate men. It was time to stop overthinking all things Templeton Cross and get down to the reason she was here, neck-deep in the gray areas she abhorred with a band of commandos.

"Veterans," she corrected herself out loud, in almost as salty a tone as one of the Alaska Force members would have used. "Deeply committed veterans of our nation's elite special forces, that's all."

Kate found a mini refrigerator masquerading as an end table on the far side of the couch, stocked with a selection of cold drinks. Better still, there was a coffee-maker in the small not-quite-a-kitchen area, with a hot plate to one side and a bag of ground Black Cup Fisherman Blend coffee beans. That was really all she needed as she settled onto the couch and dived straight back into her past.

It took her the first little while to move past her uneasiness at how much information Alaska Force had compiled on her past cases. Meaning, they had everything but her personal notes, and they shouldn't have been able to access any of it, surely.

But once she let that go—because the point of Alaska Force, as far as she could tell, was their ability to do things they shouldn't, and if she wasn't prepared to handle that, she might as well go back to her impersonal apartment in Juneau while Christmas bore down on her like an angry grizzly—she sank into the task.

She started with the cases Oz had dismissed. As she went through them, she was pretty sure she'd figured out his methodology. The cases he thought were unlikely to relate to what had been going on here lately were the ones that mostly featured very small disorganized groups. A couple and their child, for example, off in a lean-to making noise one winter. Or lone-gunmen types, who tended more toward manifestos than military operations.

Kate read through the files, remembering the hours of investigative work she'd put into each case. The many witness statements, the careful compiling of evidence. She remembered long, cold stakeouts. The various interviews, ranging from tense to baffling to straight-up upsetting.

She wasn't a woman who wanted to look back. She worked so hard to avoid it, save for a few weeks in the darkest stretch of every December. But it didn't escape her notice that in looking through all these old cases, she might as well have hauled out the sort of happy, sparkly photo albums regular people kept on hand. These cases and the associated reports were the only memories that really mattered to Kate.

She read her own reports and remembered all the things she hadn't put in them. The ways she'd learned how to be a better cop. The times she'd disappointed herself and had failed to make the necessary connections in time, or at all. There were triumphs, too. The children she'd saved from unfortunate circumstances. Unhealthy families she'd helped dismantle, and broken families she'd helped put back together.

Some people collected pictures of themselves on sandy beaches or documented every time they went off on a run or to drink something, or so Kate's few forays onto social media had taught her. But Kate had always measured her life by what she did to make sure there were fewer bad people out there making other people's lives miserable.

Her old cases were like thick, complicated balls of gnarled yarn to her, but stitched together, they all made something greater than themselves. They made a career. And more than that, they made Kate's life more meaningful than the series of interchangeable furnished apartments she'd lived in or the relationships she'd never managed to hold on to or the thousands of ways she was never quite like all those regular people who'd grown up in normal families. No matter how hard she tried.

She'd made a serious dent in the list and was jotting down a few notes about her overall impressions next to Oz's when there was a knock on her cabin door.

"Come in," she called without thinking.

And immediately wished she hadn't, because she wasn't emotionally prepared for another round—

But it wasn't Templeton. The door swung open, and Bethan came in, bringing a swirl of the cold with her.

"I thought you might be getting a little bit of cabin fever," Bethan said when she'd closed the door behind her. "But you're still working."

Kate looked at her watch and saw that hours had passed. A lot of hours, in fact. It was edging toward seven o'clock at night. She stood and stretched, feeling the tension she'd been ignoring in her shoulders since the last time she'd gotten up and tended to her body's needs. Which could have been hours ago now. "I think I lost track of time."

Bethan looked open and friendly, which immediately put Kate on edge. Not only because she was always distrustful of friendly overtures, thank you, but because Bethan wasn't any old approachable neighbor in an apartment complex somewhere, randomly offering baked goods. She was one of the most accomplished women alive.

"I'm here to offer you some dinner options," Bethan said.

"There are options?" Kate blinked. "It just occurred to me that I'm on the part of this island that doesn't have any restaurants. Or bars."

"Correct." Bethan grinned, which might have been disarming if Kate hadn't been so aware of how the other woman was holding herself. Still and ready. "It's Jonas's night to cook in the lodge. We all take turns making dinner for whoever's on shift. I think you saw the mess hall on your tour when you were here before."

"It looked like more of a dining room than a mess hall."

"That's because you haven't eaten there yet with the men. Believe me, it's a mess hall. You're welcome to join in on the communal dinner and experience this yourself."

"I don't think I have enough information to make that determination," Kate said. She pressed her fingers into the place where her neck ached. "Is Jonas a good cook? What does he cook? If I don't like it, will I be forced to choke it down anyway?"

"He's actually a decent cook." Bethan sounded so resolutely even-keeled that Kate found herself frowning slightly, trying to figure out why a discussion of Jonas's cooking skills required diplomacy. "Tonight's offering is a stew. A beef stew, I believe."

"Okay. I like beef stew. But you said there were options?"

"Your other option is you come with me."

It was Kate's turn to smile. And hope she hit that open, friendly note that seemed to come so easily to others. "Again, I need more information."

"Blue is on shift tonight. His fiancée, Everly, invited me up to their place for dinner. You're welcome to join. I have no idea what she's going to make, but every time I've eaten with her in the past, it's been good."

Kate studied the woman before her. Her hair was pulled back into the typical soldier's bun at the nape of her neck. Her expression was neutral, her green eyes cool. She was dressed much the same way she had been the last time Kate had seen her. Sleek, competent, prepared for any variation in weather thanks to the layers of technical fabrics she wore. Every inch the elite soldier she was, in other words.

"I certainly don't want to crash into the middle of your . . . intimate friend time," Kate said after a moment.

And felt somewhat gratified when Bethan's expression changed to faint alarm.

"I don't know what 'intimate friend time' is." Bethan sounded horrified. "I'm going over to dinner because Everly is the only other female in Fool's Cove, until now, and sometimes I like to take a vacation from all the testosterone. And also eat. I like eating. With people. Who are sometimes friends, yes."

The awkwardness was like the dark outside. Total and complete and choking.

"I'd like to state for the record that I've never had intimate friend time," Kate blurted out, because the awkwardness was all her fault. "That's not a thing I do."

She realized she hadn't felt this way in a long time. Because she could navigate her colleagues well enough. Her work buddies. She could have a drink after her shift, tell stories, do the whole thing. She'd even, on occasion, let what happened in those congenial, after-work bars turn in to her attempts at relationships with men. Because she understood that, too. It was the same as the work-friend thing, but with sex. Transactional, really, because sex was just an interactive story people could tell each other. And whatever her faults, Kate could tell a story.

Where she fell down every time was intimacy. What the hell *was* that, anyway? Why would anyone want it? She thought maybe she was allergic to it.

But she was all too aware that sometimes there was a crucial moment in any level of friendship, especially with other women, when *something else* was clearly supposed to occur. If it was a man, Kate knew that sex usually bridged that gap, and she either did it or didn't and then dealt with the consequences. She knew how to navigate it, more or less. But with women, Kate was keenly aware that whatever was required in those moments of blossoming friendships, she failed to provide it. And once that happened—and it always happened—things got awkward, fast.

She'd apparently jumped more quickly than usual into that space today. She blamed it on the gray area she was currently occupying and Templeton and everything else that had happened this month that didn't make sense.

"If we could retire the phrase 'intimate friend time,' preferably forever, I would be good with that," Bethan said into the weirdness.

"Agreed," Kate replied quickly. Gratefully, really. "For God's sake."

Bethan let out a laugh, and Kate didn't know why she had the oddest sense that for once, she hadn't ruined the thing. That Bethan might find her weird and awkward and all the other things Kate always was without even trying when she was expected to suddenly be social. But none of those things appeared to be deal breakers tonight.

Almost like she was more one of these people than not. But that was impossible.

Kate nodded. "Right. So. Dinner with Everly?"

"Let's do it," Bethan said.

Kate stamped her feet back into her boots, tucking the cuffs of her technical pants in to keep her legs warm. She went into the other room to grab her hat, her headlamp—because she'd seen one around Bethan's neck—and the gloves she preferred. Then she shrugged on her coat and followed Bethan out into the night.

The lodge felt like some kind of mystical tree house, suspended there between the trees and the water with running lights to mark the pathways. But Bethan led her past the common room, then on past the last connected cabin. Then off the wooden walkways altogether, onto a trail. She stopped only briefly so they could both adjust their headlamps to see where they were going, and then she led Kate into the woods.

And Kate was already predisposed to like Bethan after that scene in her cabin, but she liked her even more as she followed her on this hike into the trees, and the other woman stayed quiet. So there was nothing but the murmur of the woods all around them. The darkness acted like an embrace, close and tight. The sounds of their feet crunching on the cold ground beneath them, over roots and stones and the frozen earth. The harsh sea in the distance, hurling itself at the rocky shore. And up above, the winter wind in the trees, the only kind of carols that Kate had ever known.

Kate felt something inside her grow still, then seem to open up wide. She could see Bethan's feet in front of her, right there at the edge of her light. Her headlamp cocooned her in its little ring of brightness. It felt like the intimacy she didn't know how to have with people.

And she was glad to move. To stretch her legs, feel her muscles kick in, and apologize to her body for keeping it curled up tight the way she had for so long today. She loved being outside, even though the temperature was dropping and the wind slapped at her face, leaving her cheeks feeling red and raw. It was invigorating, the way it always had been. She liked the crispness and the chill. The stillness inside and out.

It made that thing inside her open up wider, as if she hadn't realized that she'd been waiting all this time to take a real, deep breath.

She saw the cabin through the trees at first, giving off a bright light in the overwhelming darkness. As they came closer along the trail, she could hear the generators humming, and then they were in the clearing. The cabin was larger than the ones connected to the lodge, with a porch that she imagined looked back out over the water. She switched off her headlamp and pulled it down around her neck, following Bethan up onto the porch. Bethan knocked on the front door but pushed her way inside without waiting for an answer.

"I'm in a crucial pasta moment," sang out another woman's voice.

Kate shrugged out of her jacket, hanging it up in the entryway and stepping out of her boots. Then she padded in after Bethan, who had done the same, taking in the cabin the way she would assess any place she walked into. On the job or not.

It was a proper log cabin that felt cozy and expansive

all at once. The entryway led into a living area that had everything from a television to bookshelves packed tight with books and comics, to what looked like an artist's drafting table, to a set of neatly organized free weights. Yet somehow, it didn't feel cluttered. There were stairs to the second level on one side and on the other was a wide doorway that led into the kitchen, where Bethan had already gone and the woman Kate knew to be Everly Campbell was pouring out a huge double boiler of pasta water into her sink. Steam billowed up all around her, making the red curls she'd piled on top of her head seem to curl even further.

Everly set down the pot, wiped at her face, then turned around and smiled broadly at Kate.

"I'm Everly," she said. "But you're the Alaska State Trooper, so I'm guessing you already know that."

"Guilty as charged," Kate said. And reminded herself to smile. Friendly and open, which she was perfectly capable of doing when she was on the job.

And not to start carrying on about *intimate friend time* again.

"I should warn you right off the bat that cops make me a little anxious," Everly announced before Kate could do or say something embarrassing. She was wearing that faintly glazed look that always made Kate smile. She'd seen it so many times before. A little *too* alert. A little *too* worried. A little too ready to be arrested for no reason. "I can't help it. I had a whole thing with the Chicago PD. Although if I'm entirely honest, I've never been comfortable around the police, without ever having interacted with them much. Does that mean that deep inside, I'm a criminal waiting to get out?"

"You're talking a lot," Bethan observed.

"I am," Everly agreed. "I really am."

"Alternatively," Kate said calmly, "we could drink some of that wine over there. Like normal people do."

"Wine," Everly breathed, her eyes lighting up as if Kate had offered her the Holy Grail. "Of course, wine."

"You finish cooking," Bethan said. "We'll handle the wine."

Glasses were found and filled. Everly fussed around with the meal, putting a big bowl of pasta in the middle of the little table in the kitchen, and then, soon enough, they were all sitting down with wine in hand, freshly baked bread that smelled deliciously of butter and garlic, pasta with a red sauce, and a bowl heaped high with meatballs to add as desired.

And for a few moments, there was only quiet as they passed the bread around. Helped themselves to pasta, sauce, and meatballs. Then settled in to take the first few bites, with sips of wine in between.

The next time they all looked up and around at one another, Everly's shoulders had gone down from around her ears. Bethan was smiling. And even Kate felt nice and mellow all the way through.

"How do you like living in Alaska?" Kate asked them.

"This is my second winter here," Everly replied. "Blue keeps telling me not to get all full of myself that I made it through *one* winter. He says the second one is harder, because you can't pretend you don't know exactly how long the snow is going to last. And how dark it's going to be, and stay, until the spring ice breaks up."

"He's not wrong," Kate said with a laugh. "But that's a little dramatic. It's a hard winter, there's no getting around that. But the trick is finding out what you find beautiful about it. Even on the grayest, gloomiest, most bitter and uninspiring day, there's always something beautiful."

If she was sentimental about anything, it was Alaska.

"I'm personally excited," Bethan said. "I like a challenging environment."

Everly smiled. "Why does that not surprise me?"

"Not to ruin the challenge for you, but this is the coast, so you'll have a pretty mild winter," Kate told Bethan. "Relatively speaking."

"I'm from Chicago." Everly rolled the bowl of her wineglass between her palms. "I would not describe the winters there as mild. I can't decide which I found worse, if I'm honest. They're different."

"It always surprises me when people move to Alaska from places like Hawaii. Which they do a lot, for some reason." Kate shook her head. "It seems like such a bad idea. It's the absolute opposite."

"Opposites attract," Bethan said with a shrug. "I grew up in Santa Barbara. I used to think the weather was harsh if the thermometer dipped below seventy-two degrees."

"Alaska's a whole lot like California, really," Kate said, surprised to find herself grinning. And without having ordered herself to produce a grin for a specific purpose. "California has three seasons, as far as I can tell. Summer, Fire, and that one day of Rain. Up here in Alaska we also have three seasons. Ice, Mud, and Dust."

And it was much later when she waved Bethan off, back down on the wooden paths that connected all the cabins close to the waterline, that Kate realized she'd enjoyed herself. Really, truly enjoyed herself. That laughter and easy conversation that didn't center on work was what *enjoying herself* was. Most surprising of all, though she'd long since accepted the fact that she was neither charming nor entertaining unless she was playing a part in a work scenario, Everly and Bethan hadn't seemed to get that memo.

Maybe she would find that baffling, but not tonight, when she was nice and warm from wine and pasta.

Kate shoved her headlamp in her pocket as she made her way past the lodge and the still-lit cabins connected directly to it, where she knew Alaska Force members were taking their shifts and running missions all over the world. Somewhere inside, she knew she should look into that more deeply. Maybe nose around a bit, here in the darkness, with fewer eyes on her.

A week ago—even twenty-four hours ago—she wouldn't have hesitated.

But tonight she kept going, following the path away from the lodge and off to where her guest cabin sat back from the water, built into the hillside.

Because for once—just for once—she wanted to keep holding on tight to this odd, buoyant feeling. Maybe it was the wine. It probably was. But whatever the cause, Kate didn't have a lot of bright, happy sorts of nights tucked away in her memory. That wasn't what her life was like. She'd never sat around a table telling stories like that.

Her stories were usually depressing and told at the direction of attorneys. Or chock-full of grim gallows humor appropriate for conversations over hard alcohol with other cops.

She'd never found herself telling stories about her childhood that focused more on the gritty survival element—in a lighthearted sort of way, which she would have said was impossible. She'd never told anyone about what it was like to forage in the frozen tundra when she was a grumpy twelve-year-old who felt nothing but grotesquely misunderstood when her grudging contributions had been unappreciated, or what it was like to grow up so off the grid that her first experience with a television had terrified her into nightmares.

It had never occurred to her that she could tell those stories and make them funny.

And maybe that, too, was the wine. Maybe she would wake up in the morning with a headache and that same old sense that she was an alien in a world of normal, well-adjusted people. But she found that hard to believe when Everly had made them all laugh at her story of riding a pink bike around in circles until she made herself dizzy and scraped up her own knees, then lied about it to her parents.

I told them I had to dodge an out-of-control driver and they called the police, Everly had confessed. *Huh. Maybe that's why I have police anxiety.*

Then Bethan had told stories of trying to get one over on her very strict career-army father, who had reacted to the slightest infraction of his endless rules as if his family were a boot camp and he was its drill sergeant.

He made me drop and do fifty push-ups on the front lawn of my high school, Bethan had said in her dry way. *In retrospect, the fact I couldn't get a date to the prom isn't really all that mysterious.*

None of those stories was all that funny if Kate picked them apart. Just like her stories weren't all that funny in their particulars. But there was something about telling them to two other women who hadn't judged her or seemed to want anything from her, and then laughing about it all. Together. It felt like some kind of magic spell.

It felt retroactive, like the laughter had wound its way inside of her and changed her memories where she carried them. She wasn't likely to forget anything that had happened to her. But now when she thought of it, she suspected she might also think about sitting at the kitchen table in Everly's cabin, laughing until her cheeks hurt and her eyes felt damp.

If it was magic, she'd take it, she thought, as she walked the last little way toward her cabin. No matter how fanciful that might seem in the light of day.

Here, tonight, in the small hours of the endless Alaskan night, Kate didn't have to worry about daylight.

For once, she could let herself be as fanciful as she liked. She could indulge herself. She could let herself stay something perilously close to happy, with no one the wiser.

Tomorrow she could gather herself into familiar pieces again. Tomorrow she could remember who she really was, a bit too grim and always too serious, out of step with the world. Tomorrow was soon enough.

"Tomorrow," she muttered to herself.

Tonight she could let herself float a bit, whether it was magic or merlot. Tonight she could pretend she had it in her to be like other women for a change.

To be normal.

But when she got to her cabin and pushed her way inside into the warmth of it, she stopped dead.

Because Templeton was there, stretched out in the living room with a book like he belonged there, his big body dwarfing the six-foot couch. And his dark eyes glittering when he looked up at her, too wicked and too knowing all at once.

Kate felt more than warm then.

And the more layers she stripped off in the little entryway, the hotter and more flushed she became.

"Careful there, Trooper," Templeton drawled, looking lazy and unbothered and entirely too delicious to be real. "You're looking a little unsteady on your feet."

Kate should have been furious that he'd invaded her privacy. She should have been outraged that he thought he could make himself at home like this. She should have ordered him to leave, and she meant to. She was sure she meant to.

But instead of opening her mouth and telling him to go away, the way she knew she should, she thought . . . *magic*.

Because whatever else he was, the man was magic.

And she was going to have all kinds of things to regret tomorrow, from her comments in the lodge that had required she offer an apology to that *intimate friend time* horror to telling anyone anything about herself—much less two people she hardly knew and one she'd never met before. She knew that as surely as she knew that red wine gave her a headache, sooner or later, no matter how good it tasted going down.

But some things were worth the price, whatever it was and whatever it took from her. Kate had learned that a long time ago.

And there and then, flushed hot and red down to her toes, she decided that Templeton Cross was one of them.

Eleven

Templeton had run through this scenario in his head a thousand times already. It was one of his favorites.

Rules or no rules.

Kate, flushed and looking at him like she wanted to eat him alive, here and now. Kate, walking toward him with nothing but a bright gleam of need in her eyes and a sway in her hips.

But his imagination, always vivid, wasn't even close to the reality of his trooper stalking across the cabin floor to the sofa, where he sat like he didn't have a care in the world when really, he thought it was possible he might die of sheer longing. His imagination hadn't prepared him for the way she smiled at him, something he knew instantly he'd be replaying in his head forever.

And nothing could possibly have prepared him for Trooper Kate Holiday climbing on top of him and sliding her body. *All. Over. His.*

"Did I fall asleep?" Templeton asked, though his drawl sounded a whole lot less lazy than it usually did. And he was vaguely concerned that he was having a cardiac arrest. "Is this a dream?"

"Call it what you want," Kate replied. Gruffly.

Like she was finding the reality of her body on his body as hard to handle as he was.

And Templeton found that he didn't really have the words to call it anything at all, because she was settling against him. Stretching herself out along the length of him, making sure to rub a bit wherever she touched, and then propping herself up on her hands so she could look down at him.

Her skin was flushed, which he liked. There was a bright heat in her eyes that made every cell in his body go alert and awake. *Aware.*

And best of all, her mouth, generous, wide, and the faintest bit sulky tonight, was *right there.*

Templeton was so hard it hurt.

And that was before he processed the rest of it. Her torso flush against his, her strong thighs bracketing his hips and cradling him where he most wanted it.

It was *definitely* cardiac arrest, and he loved every second of it.

"Is this what a trooper looks like after a couple drinks?" Templeton asked. "Hallelujah."

Kate's eyes glittered, and not drunkenly. "Sure. Let's call it the wine."

She sounded almost angry, which didn't make a lot of sense. But Templeton couldn't say he cared that much. And his jubilant body cared even less than that. Especially when she bent her head, collapsed against him so he could feel the weight of her small breasts against his chest, and pressed her mouth to his.

She kissed him like she was desperate. Like this was all *desperation.*

Kate twined herself around him and moved her hips against his. And she kissed him, again and again, like her life depended on it.

Like they were both going to turn into stone any second and she needed to get as much of this in before it was all granite and regret.

Templeton wrapped his arms around her the way he had wanted to from the start. He reveled in the fierce way she angled her mouth against his, the sweet, hot glory of the way she rocked herself against him, and the feel of her—more solid than she looked—above him and astride him.

And Templeton had never considered himself a particularly good man. *Good* was the province of other men, whose hands were a lot cleaner than his had ever been.

He'd imagined this too many times. Too many and then more. And he liked the idea of his trooper desperate.

But *for* him. Not *at* him.

"Hey."

He held her away from him, lifting her up off his body as he jackknifed into a sitting position and then deposited her beside him on the couch. She caught herself and stayed on her knees.

And he thought his halo was so damned bright it was practically high noon on the equator somewhere up in this cabin.

"What's the problem?" Kate demanded.

"Is there a rush? A countdown of some kind? You seem to be in a hurry."

Kate glared at him. "I'll admit I didn't see this coming. All that talk, and that's all it was, wasn't it? *Talk.*"

"I beg your pardon. Are you calling me a tease?"

"If the shoe fits, Templeton."

He managed to keep from howling while his cardiac arrest kicked at him. He rubbed the hand he'd much rather put on her over his heart, like that might calm it down. And assured himself that was excitement, not emotion.

"Not at all. If you're ready to go, we can go. I only want a little bit of clarity as to why you're acting like we're in a death race to the finish."

Kate eyed him balefully from where she knelt beside him on the couch. "Are you critiquing my performance?"

Not for the first time tonight, Templeton found himself very nearly speechless. "It's not a critique. But why do we need to rush?"

"My bad," Kate said, but there was something dangerous in the way she tilted her head to one side. "That's how I like it. Fast. Hard. I thought you could keep up. But if not, no problem."

Templeton did not roar out his frustration, the way he wanted to do. Still, it was a close call. He laughed instead, loud and long, because it was almost the same thing.

"Now who's the tease?" he asked her.

Kate was still kneeling, her cheeks particularly red and deliciously rosy everywhere else. She was wearing the kind of long-sleeved shirt runners wore, tightly fitted to her high, compact breasts, her trim waist, and the slight swell of her belly. And she kept her eyes on him in a way that didn't require military training to know was dangerous.

Pure mayhem, in fact.

Kate didn't say a word. Instead, she reached down to grab the hem of her shirt and peeled it off her body. Templeton's mouth went dry. His head pounded, and there was that whole cardiac thing again. Definitely pure excitement. His tongue felt like someone else's, and he couldn't seem to use it the way he wanted.

And he was fairly certain Kate knew it, though she didn't smile. Not quite.

Her eyes gleamed brighter, and there was a certain satisfaction to the set of her lips, but she only reached up and tugged the elastic out of her hair. She ran her other hand through the dark strands, sending the mess of it tumbling down over her shoulders. Then, still staring him straight in the face, she reached down and unclasped the front of the bra she was wearing, which looked like a sports bra but held her like lingerie. She peeled it off and tossed it aside with her shirt.

And it was always possible that Templeton really was asleep and happily dreaming all this. Because he couldn't think of another reason Trooper Holiday would be kneeling before him in a log cabin in Fool's Cove stripped to the waist.

Offering herself to him as only she could. Daring him to touch her.

And *half-naked* clearly wasn't enough for her. Kate obviously had a much more significant level of torture in mind, because she flowed up to her feet and unzipped her pants.

Templeton, master of war zones, sat there frozen solid, staring at her while his heart performed mad gymnastics in his chest. And his blood pumped hot and wild.

And his sex did its level best to take matters into its own hands.

She stripped off her pants in a swift, easy movement, taking her socks with her.

Leaving her standing there before him wearing nothing but a bright pink pair of stretchy bikini panties, that satisfied curve to her mouth, and her dark hair flowing everywhere. Begging for him to get his hands in it. On her.

"What do you think?" Kate asked, her voice threaded through with amusement. Challenge. And more of that heat. "You still want to take it slow?"

And Templeton might have felt frozen solid for a moment there, but he wasn't dead. Not yet. He reached up and hooked an arm around her hips, hauling her to him. She came willingly, even eagerly, flowing into his lap and settling herself astride him there, too.

Templeton wasn't actually any kind of saint, so he indulged himself. He gripped her hair, holding her mouth right where he wanted it, and this time, he was the one who took charge.

Because it was about time.

He kissed her deep and long, dark and greedy. He

licked his way into her mouth, and then toyed with her until she was panting against his lips. He wasn't any kind of gentlemen, and he didn't kiss like one.

He kissed her dirty. Over and over again.

Templeton had been dreaming of the taste of her, and he drowned himself in it now, liking that she tasted a little bit extra tonight. Like wine. Like need.

Like his.

She rocked herself against him, getting the softest part of her flush against his sex, and then rubbing herself against him with abandon. Reminding him that she was tough and strong, sleek and fit and fast.

He thought he might die, then and there.

But he didn't.

Templeton pulled his mouth from hers, still gripping her thick, soft hair with one hard fist. He let the other hand roam, moving between them to test the weight of one perfect breast. And the proud nipple that stood between them, that he wanted very badly to pull into his mouth. But didn't, somehow. He moved around to her back, stroking his way down the line of her spine, then cupping that sweet, muscular ass.

He liked her sleekness. He loved her strength.

And he knew he wasn't likely to forget anytime soon the soft little noise of frustration she made as she writhed on him.

"Rush, rush, rush," Templeton rumbled. And he could hardly believe he was about to do this. But here he was, doing it. "Is this how it normally works for you, Trooper? Let me guess. A few shots in a bar, a rush toward oblivion, and that's it?"

"What do you mean, 'that's it'? What else is there?"

She sounded cranky and irritated, and Lord knew, he liked that, too.

"That's barely an appetizer," he told her. "And all this time you've been thinking it was a full meal? That explains a lot."

Kate stiffened, and her eyes changed to something far more dangerous, but Templeton wasn't afraid of her. Not when she was mostly naked, and he could feel how soft and hot she was against him with their bodies tight together, separated only by a few layers of their clothing.

"We can either do this or not," Kate snapped. "It's an offer that's unlikely to be repeated. So if you're not interested, terrific. You can go."

"It's not that I'm not interested." And Templeton wasn't a goddamned saint, so this was hard. Harder than she seemed to imagine while she sat on his lap and tempted him almost beyond endurance. "It's that I'm too interested. You want to bang me like I'm some guy you picked up in a bar? I'm going to have to pass on that."

"Oh my God," Kate breathed. "Let me guess. Deep inside, you're sweet and shy and *mushy*. You want *intimacy*. You want to *make sweet love*." She didn't actually gag at that, she only gave the impression of it, which wasn't much better. "Too bad, Templeton. Because all I want to do is—"

"You don't know what you want," he told her, cutting her off. "But don't worry, little trooper. I'm nothing if not a dedicated teacher."

She started to roll her eyes, but Templeton stood and took her with him. He was still fully clothed, something he reminded himself of as he moved, because it was like armor. Or something. It was going to save one of them, anyway, and he had the distinct impression that it might be him.

He carried her into the bedroom and tossed her into the center of the bed.

"Finally," Kate muttered. To the ceiling.

Because she was ungrateful. Ornery. Sullen. Surly—and that was when she wasn't acting the cool, controlled cop.

Templeton didn't think he'd ever wanted someone this

much in his life. Or ever would again. He needed to indulge that want, then move on before emotions got involved. He knew that.

But that wasn't the point of this. Not right now.

The bed was nice and high, perfect for his purposes. He reached down and took hold of her, dragging her toward the edge of the mattress. Then he peeled those ridiculously, delightfully girlie panties off her legs.

And he wanted to linger. He wanted to take his sweet time exploring every inch of her, getting to know the variances in the way she tasted. There behind her ear. In the hollow between her breasts. At her waist, her navel, and every sweet inch of her long, strong legs.

He wanted to make a meal of her. But he was going to have to settle for dessert.

And notify the Vatican on his way out, because he was clearly signing himself up for instant canonization.

He bent down, keeping her legs apart with the width of his shoulders. He scooped his hands beneath her butt to hold her in place, then lifted her up like she was on a platter.

Her breath went out of her with a gratifying stuttering sound that was sweet music as far as he was concerned. She lifted herself up on her elbows and scowled at him down the length of her own gorgeous body.

"Oh no," she said. Sounding even crankier than before. "I don't do that."

"Do what? You don't have to *do* anything but lie back and continue rolling your eyes at the ceiling."

"That sounds super fun, but I have a better idea. Why don't *you* lie back? I'll climb on top and make us both feel great."

"Sure thing," Templeton rumbled, and nipped gently at one of those strong thighs of hers. He felt her jolt beneath his hands. He discovered, to his delight, that when she flushed like that it covered the whole of her body.

Better still, goose bumps rose up everywhere. He could even smell her arousal, sweet and feminine. She shuddered. "But first, indulge me."

And then he leaned forward and got his mouth on her.

At last.

Tough, ornery Kate melted like candy. Soft and hot. He licked his way in, easing his way through her slickness, then finding the part of her that was the neediest. He teased her there. Using suction. His teeth.

Whatever worked.

First she went stiff. Then she went blazingly hot.

Then she started to lift her hips to meet each slide of his tongue, each scrape of his jaw.

Templeton was a man who indulged his appetites. And Kate was a feast.

He made her shiver, then he made her fall apart.

She shook and she shook, clamping her thighs around his head and making it that much better. That much hotter.

So he kept right on going.

And by the time he was finished with her, tasting her with his mouth and using his fingers to make it even more fun, she was limp. Shaking as if she'd never stop.

And best of all, making tiny, delectable little sounds in the back of her throat.

Templeton pulled back and stood, running a hand over his jaw as he stared down at the picture she made. Kate Holiday, his uptight trooper, splayed out on the bed before him. Every inch of her pink, rosy, and replete.

It wasn't that he was hard. He *ached*. He wanted her in ways he didn't have words to describe. He felt her everywhere, like some kind of vicious flu that could take him down to his knees if he let her.

He didn't.

Her eyelashes looked like soot against her cheeks, and her mouth was gently parted as she panted into the arm she'd thrown up over her head.

God, she was beautiful. That ache seemed to double, and Templeton would never know how he stayed where he was, standing there, not touching her. Not taking her.

"Go on," she ordered him as if she could read his mind, though her voice was wispy at best. "It's your turn."

"I don't believe in taking turns," Templeton told her, and he didn't sound like himself anymore. Too raspy. Too edgy with need and longing and that ache besides. "It's all fun for everyone or it's no fun at all."

"I don't know what that means."

He watched as she struggled to open her eyes, and when she did, she looked dazed.

And Templeton was glad for every last second of the intense training he'd undergone over the course of his life, because he was certain that was the only thing that kept him in check. When everything in him roared for more. To sink himself deep inside her, and never come up for air again.

But he'd practiced control. He knew how to exercise it.

And somehow, he did.

"If we were doing this my way," Templeton gritted out, "that would only be the beginning. A little warm-up before things got serious. I don't like to rush, Kate. I like to take my time. Every time."

"Is that supposed to be a threat?"

"I don't make threats."

Kate pushed herself up on one elbow, and everything about her was sultry, beautiful. He had no idea why he was standing at the side of the bed, fully clothed. What was he doing to himself? Why?

But then she smirked at him, and he remembered.

"I should have known," she said, looking far too sure of herself. "You like it when it's more of a game. You want me to play pretend. Beg. Act like I don't want it when I do, is that it?"

"Not at all," Templeton said quietly. "I want you to want *me*, Kate. Not *it*."

Her eyes opened wider as the smirk disappeared from her mouth, but he couldn't take that as a victory lap. Not when he was beginning to think that she was the cardiac event, and he was just going to have to get used to it.

"Let me guess how this usually goes for you," he said in the same quietly serious way, and she would never know what it cost him when he had the taste of her in his mouth. She was still naked before him, so beautiful he thought she might actually leave scars all over him. That she already had. "Everybody thinks you're uptight, untouchable. So you toss back a couple of drinks to prove them wrong. Someone makes a move and you think, why not? Because you know how to do this part. You know how to get naked, and fast. You know how to get exactly what you want, and how to avoid the things you don't want to deal with."

"Are you really going to pretend there's something wrong with that?" she demanded. "Since when is knowing my own mind a problem? I'm sorry if that intimidates you, Templeton."

He didn't rise to the bait. "You know exactly what to do with a man who wants it the way you do. Hard. Fast. You can do that, easy. But if I tried to hold your hand you'd try to shoot me. Wouldn't you?"

He watched her swallow, as hard as it was audible. "Don't psychoanalyze me. Especially after three glasses of wine."

"The wine is a great excuse, isn't it?" Templeton murmured, never shifting his gaze from hers. Pinning her there, naked and still flushed. "A lot like some night out in a bar for you. It's your excuse. Your alibi, if you need one. But I want you naked because I want you naked, Kate. I don't need an alibi. And I'm not going to blame anyone in the morning. Can you say the same?"

"I'm too busy blaming you for ruining tonight to worry about tomorrow morning. Thanks for that."

Templeton wanted to laugh, but he didn't. "Don't worry, we're going to revisit this topic. You can count on it."

"Like hell we are."

"I have the feeling it's all going to go down the way it did tonight. You're going to tell me how you don't do something, I'm going to show you that you do, and better still, that I don't care if you get mad at me about it."

"Will this all come with lectures? Because nothing's hotter than that. Every girl dreams of being naked before a pompous man who doesn't know when to shut his mouth. I know that keeps me up at night."

"It's going to keep me up, too, Kate," he told her, and this time, he didn't smile. Or laugh. Or try to make it better. "I can promise you that."

And he left her there, only cracking a smile when he heard her curse his name as he went. Then throw something hard at the door behind him. He suspected it was her boot.

That made him smile a lot wider.

It wasn't until he had taken the long, frigid-cold walk back to his cabin—where he doused himself in cold water, gritted his teeth, and reminded himself that he'd chosen his frustration—that it occurred to him he hadn't told her the reason he'd been waiting for her in the first place.

That someone had broken into Kate's apartment in Juneau earlier tonight.

That an individual dressed all in black had been lying in wait for her, which she would know as well as he did no one did when they planned to leap out for a hug and a cuddle.

Whoever it was had expected to find Kate there. Alone and off her guard. And when they'd been confronted by a neighbor instead, they'd taken off.

But they'd be back.

Templeton had absolutely no doubt.

Twelve

Kate didn't know where to begin processing everything that had happened that night. From her surprisingly carefree dinner with Bethan and Everly to . . . everything that had come afterward with Templeton. Which she would certainly not call *carefree.*

It was easier to focus on what had happened in Juneau instead.

One of her neighbors had walked by and seen Kate's door open, just a crack. Thinking that was unusual—because it was, of course, absolutely unheard of in all the months Kate had lived there—the woman had knocked and then walked in, calling out Kate's name.

Which was especially surprising, given Kate didn't know hers.

Her neighbor, who Kate now knew was named Alasie Benally, had startled whoever was inside. They'd rushed out, leaving Alasie shaken and knocked to the ground. Alasie was adamant that whoever the assailant was, she hadn't interrupted him in the middle of a robbery attempt—he'd been lurking there.

All the lights in the apartment had been off. He'd rushed Alasie when she'd moved far enough inside that, had she been who he wanted her to be, he could have gotten himself between his quarry and the door.

He'd growled something at Alasie when he'd seen her on the floor at his feet, then left.

This told Kate that whoever the assailant was, he was looking for Kate. He had broken into her apartment and he'd waited there, for her. Not whoever might happen to show up, but Kate herself. Kate specifically.

She couldn't pretend she liked how that felt.

The Juneau police had invited her to come back and do a walk-through to see if anything was missing, but Kate had declined. It hadn't looked like anything had been taken in the photos they'd sent her. And the good news was, it wouldn't have mattered if the man had stolen everything from that apartment. There was nothing in it Kate couldn't replace. Most of what was in it, in fact, wasn't hers to begin with.

Though she found that when she said things like that to the police or her colleagues, there were those uncomfortable silences that reminded her—powerfully—that she really wasn't like other people. And there was nothing that screamed *Christmastime* with more forced, uncomfortable cheer than being made to feel, yet again, like an alien.

I'm glad you took your leave seriously and got out of there for a while, her captain had told her gruffly when they'd spoken on the phone. *You deserve a vacation, Kate.*

And the truth was, Kate didn't really like how *that* felt, either. As much because she wasn't actually on vacation as because, when her captain had asked where she was, she'd said she was holed up on an island in the Inside Passage to ring in the New Year.

That wasn't a lie. Kate couldn't tell lies directly to anyone. She refused. But it wasn't exactly the truth, either.

It felt a lot like one of those gray areas she'd avoided

her whole life. She hated it. She hated that it made her wonder if she was on a slippery slope that led directly to megalomaniacal homesteading in the Alaskan interior like her father, ranting at captive family members about *purity*. Something that also did not feel great.

Kate was full up on *feelings*.

And that was before she got to thinking about what else had happened that night in Fool's Cove.

She'd woken that morning with the expected drumbeat in her temples, though it wasn't bad enough to allow her to feel truly sick, which would have been a terrific way to not face up to the previous night's behavior. Sadly, the couple of ibuprofen she'd swallowed had dealt with the headache but done absolutely nothing to wipe away the details of what had transpired between her and Templeton. On that couch, and then—worse by far—on her bed.

She'd chugged a huge glass of water. Then another. She'd made herself a strong pot of coffee as she checked her phone and learned what had transpired in Juneau while she'd been eating pasta and then rolling around naked with a completely inappropriate man, letting him do things that she would have sworn up and down she wouldn't like at all. Except she had.

Her unmanageable feelings churned around inside of her, no matter how hard she tried to shove them back down, into place.

Especially since it was a text from Templeton—sent late the previous night, after he'd left her—that had very tersely outlined what had happened in Juneau.

By the time Kate had finished her rounds of endless phone calls, she was edgy. So she'd dealt with all of it—her issues and her hangover and those unwieldy, unwelcome *feelings*—the way she'd always dealt with such things and always would.

Kate had gotten back to work.

And by the time Templeton ambled back around to

find her, it was already dark again on Friday afternoon. Only a rainy, insubstantial little spit of daylight earlier had indicated that Kate had worked almost all the way through the night, nibbling on a power bar when she thought of it. She'd passed out on the couch for a few hours around four in the morning, then jumped right back in when she'd woken a few hours later.

Kate had finished going through Oz's lists and all her old cases. Which was a good thing, because she could see that questioning sort of expression on Templeton's face and wanted nothing to do with it.

"Whatever you're about to say," she said briskly—professionally—when she opened the door to his knock and that knowing gleam in his dark eyes, "it's going to have to wait. I'm ready to talk about these lists."

She expected him to argue. Because didn't he always argue?

But instead, Templeton grinned big and wide, as if he'd expected her to do exactly this, which was deeply irritating. He didn't say a word. He didn't tease her or make suggestive remarks. He didn't glance in the direction of the couch, or her bedroom, or even her body.

He made her want to scream.

Kate did not scream. Because she'd decided that all she could really do was exude professionalism from every pore and treat Templeton the way she'd treated any of the other cops she'd gotten involved with in one way or another over the years. With distance and disinterest until they got the message and went away.

And the fact that Templeton had made her feel things she'd always thought were the sort of overheated, overwrought, deeply unrealistic fantasies best suited for romantic movies was something Kate planned to keep to herself.

Templeton waited—still grinning, damn him—while Kate pulled on her jacket and boots, then he led her back to the main part of the lodge. He brought her through that main lobby area and into the back rooms that she'd seen briefly when she'd toured this place that very first visit. And it was in one of those back rooms that she sat with Oz himself, who looked like no computer geek or man behind a curtain that Kate had ever known, with clever eyes and the build of a world-class athlete.

Together, she and Oz had gone through the lists again until they'd hammered out one they both agreed on. Out of all the cases that Kate had worked on in her career, they narrowed it down to three potentials.

One was a family of human traffickers who'd operated a "pleasure cruise" out of Ketchikan, up through the Inside Passage. Another was a group of religious separatists whose base on a communal farm outside of Anchorage had been the center of a number of abuses and alleged exploitation of minors and laborers. Kate had been instrumental in dismantling both and putting the leaders in jail.

The third was her own family. Samuel Lee Holiday, his three brothers and two cousins, and their foiled plot to alter the political landscape with homemade pipe bombs. Her uncles and second cousins were in jail, along with her father, and Kate had been more than "instrumental" in making that happen. She'd cracked the case wide open when she'd walked into that Trooper station and told them who she was and why she'd stolen that snowmobile to get away from her father's compound.

Not that Kate wanted to believe her personal history was relevant to explosions fifteen years later and an intruder in her Juneau apartment. But she couldn't say with certainty that it *wasn't.*

She and Oz had dug into all three of those cases—and more important, the current whereabouts, if known, of every person connected to those cases—ever since. They'd pulled another near-all-nighter, with Kate crashing out for a couple of hours on one of the couches in the lobby, lulled to sleep by the crackling fire. Then she'd been back at it, breaking only to experience the mess hall conditions Bethan had been talking about.

And the best part of throwing herself into all this research was that it left her absolutely no time to consider the ramifications of getting naked in front of, and all over, Templeton Cross.

But she'd be lying to herself—and not in a gray area, slippery-slide sort of way, but an all-out, full-scale lie—if she pretended she ever really got anything that had happened that night out of her head.

Whatever she was doing, whatever lead she was trying to follow, she would always find herself lapsing back into the memory of Templeton's mouth between her legs, those huge shoulders of his holding her legs apart, and his hands—

It was not helpful. The memory might kill her. Kate was a little surprised it hadn't already.

But it was also drawing closer to Christmas.

Blue and Everly had left for Chicago Friday morning. Griffin and Mariah had headed off to tour their respective hometowns together on Saturday. Because they all might be elite special operatives, but some of them had families. And normal families did normal things come Christmastime, which usually meant congregating in groups. Together. This Kate already knew from a thousand movies and all the online reports of happy, glowing scenes involving iced sugar cookies, twinkling lights strewn over evergreens, and hapless reindeer statuary.

"I didn't expect Alaska Force to be the sort of place that closes down for the holidays," Kate said, possibly more grumpily than was necessary, at the briefing on Sunday morning. Saturday had been the winter solstice and the longest night of the year, which meant that today was the first day in the long climb out of the dark.

But it was nine in the morning and cloudy, so Kate was going to have to take that on faith.

Her trust was anemic. Her faith was nonexistent.

"We don't shut down," Isaac told her. "Ever."

"You said you were going to Anchorage," Kate pointed out.

Or threw in his face, to be more precise.

And no one actually gasped out loud at her temerity in talking back to their commanding officer. But they didn't have to. Kate knew better.

Isaac smiled. And the room around her changed almost imperceptibly. Kate reminded herself that Isaac Gentry was a wolf in sheep's clothing at the best of times. Above and beyond that, he was also not her friend. She hadn't served with him. She'd come here in the first place to find a way to arrest him, not befriend him.

All those thoughts chased through her head as he smiled at her, and she wished that she'd slept a bit more and fought off her Templeton memories less. Also that she'd kept her mouth shut.

"Yes," he said, with that endless amiability that she now knew enough to find alarming. "I have family to visit. But the good news is, I can take point on what's left of the separatists and their farm commune, since I'll be up there anyway. You're welcome."

She did not point out that she hadn't thanked him, though it was on the tip of her tongue to do so. Because apparently, Kate on a forced vacation liked to live dangerously.

And it wasn't until they'd left the lodge together, as ordered, that Templeton shook his head at her as if she'd had a narrow escape. As if she didn't know she'd had a narrow escape, to be more precise.

"I wouldn't lose focus and mess with Isaac," Templeton said out on the deck outside the lobby. Below, the waves were making a ruckus on the shore, and Kate wasn't sure she liked the fact that she was starting to find that soothing when she'd always preferred to admire the ocean and its raw power from a safe distance.

It felt like another metaphor she'd rather not poke at.

"I wasn't messing with him," she said, fighting to keep her voice even. "It was a valid concern. Bear in mind that I'm here, ready and willing to work. Perfectly focused on the task at hand. I thought we all were."

Templeton studied her a moment, and there was no smile on his face. No gleam in his dark eyes. Kate knew that once again, she was seeing his real face. And maybe it should have scared her that he didn't do anything to conceal that fact.

Maybe what Kate really didn't want to admit was that it did scare her.

"I would follow that man anywhere." Templeton's voice was as serious as his expression. "But I don't ever forget who he is. Or what he's capable of. Neither should you."

Kate accepted that she'd been duly chastised and decided the best course of action was not to dwell on it. She nodded once, jerkily. She said nothing. She turned and went off to her cabin, packed her go bag, and met Templeton back down on the docks.

It had started to rain, but that hardly mattered. Because they were headed north, where rain would be the least of their problems. Everyone in Alaska Force had agreed that anyone could handle traffickers or religious separatists, but whether she liked it or not, Kate was best suited to deal with her own family.

And when she set aside her own revulsion and considered it the way she would if she were advising someone else on how to handle the situation, Kate knew they were right.

Which meant Kate and Templeton were headed to Fairbanks. To see a cousin she hadn't seen since they'd both been teenagers. Kate had been testifying against their parents in court. William had been two years younger than Kate and not exactly supportive of her position. Or her willingness to discuss, in open court, the things they'd been repeatedly told were private and for family only.

Kate and Templeton flew to Juneau first, then caught a ride on a private plane to Fairbanks. The sun was already setting as they flew in a little before three o'clock that afternoon. She'd put in a year or two as a brand-new trooper here, but it was the winters of her childhood that she remembered the most vividly, with sun dogs in the morning and afternoon, when ice crystals in the atmosphere made the sun into art against the ever-present snow.

It was already snowing when they landed, and the snow kept coming as they climbed into the waiting car, then headed toward one of the less desirable neighborhoods within the city limits, which contained Kate's cousin's last known address. He'd gone from the compound outside Nenana to Anchorage, where he'd spent the remainder of his adolescence, then moved farther and farther north every time he'd changed addresses until he'd ended up in Fairbanks a couple of years back. And as far as Kate could tell, he'd been here ever since.

"You seem tense," Templeton said cheerfully as he navigated along the road, leaving the relative traffic of the Fairbanks airport behind and driving along streets that Kate recognized from the years she'd been stationed here. "Want to talk about sex?"

Kate laughed despite herself. "Why would I want to talk about sex?"

"Why wouldn't you want to talk about sex? I always want to talk about sex."

And for some reason, his outrageousness struck her as so ridiculous that she forgot to be angry. She shifted in the passenger seat, shaking her head at him as he drove the way he did absolutely everything else. Lounging there, one hand draped lazily over the steering wheel, looking like he might drift off to sleep at any moment when what he was actually doing was navigating a fairly treacherous road through inclement weather.

"So while sitting there, right this minute, you thought to yourself, *I know. While on the way to meet up with a family member who might actually express his disinterest in seeing her, violently, what Kate really wants to do is discuss sexual escapades that didn't even really happen.*"

"Oh, let's not play that game. It happened."

Kate rolled her eyes. "I told you that you had an opportunity. You wasted that opportunity. That's it. It's gone, never to return."

He threw her a dark look that brimmed with his particular brand of amusement, which made her want to smile back. Obviously, she frowned instead. But that look danced around inside her, making her feel all the things she'd been telling herself she didn't feel since she'd woken up that morning-after with a hefty dose of buyer's remorse.

"Tell yourself whatever you have to, Trooper," Templeton drawled. "We're just getting started."

"And again, that's a giant pass from me." Kate smiled at him, cool and faintly malicious, which she found settled her nerves considerably. "*You* can start whatever you want. You have two hands. Go wild. But I very rarely repeat myself. And I never repeat mistakes."

His laugh filled the SUV. It filled her, too, and she told herself she hated that feeling. But that was a lie. A definite, no-wiggle-room, full-on lie. She was melting inside and between her legs, she suspected he knew it, and now she was *lying* to herself.

Talk about slippery slopes.

"Keep telling yourself that," Templeton murmured with that total confidence of his that should have made her want to heave. But that wasn't the reaction she had at all.

And when they pulled up to a squat little house, with

a variety of questionable outbuildings and surrounded by run-down looking cars, Kate realized that she'd forgotten to get as anxious as she might have otherwise.

Kate told herself Templeton couldn't possibly have done that deliberately, that there was no method to his madness, but she couldn't quite make herself believe it.

She shook that off as best she could and tried to concentrate on the task at hand.

Her cousin lived in the sort of community that troopers always found challenging. It was impossible to have any element of surprise, pulling up in recognizable state vehicles, particularly when the people who lived in places like this were typically well acquainted with all the local law enforcement officers.

But this wasn't Kate's division. And Templeton's SUV didn't look like it was Trooper issue. It was too glossy. Too impressive.

"They're going to think you're a drug dealer," Kate pointed out.

"Whatever gets them to open the door," Templeton replied as they both pulled on their gear and adjusted their weapons.

Kate had studied her cousin's file. She knew that he was on his third wife. That he had all kinds of kids. But he didn't live with them off in the bush somewhere, under harsh conditions and even harsher rules that he made to exalt himself. And he didn't direct them all to break laws and try to literally blow up the government, so she was inclined to think of his life as an upgrade.

It didn't feel much like an upgrade when she climbed out of the car, pulled her hood tighter around her face to block out the snow, and trudged toward the uninspiring front door of the prefab house painted a sullen, peeling blue, with its huge icicles hanging down, proclaiming its lack of insulation. She ignored the anxious churning in her belly, made sure to stand close enough to the door to avoid the icicles if they fell, and knocked. Hard.

"We're being watched," Templeton said quietly. That didn't surprise Kate at all. She'd seen the lights in the other frosted-over windows in this sad little neighborhood, and particularly in the house in the next clearing. She knew that the neighbors were watching. It was par for the course.

She knocked again.

"William?" she called loudly. "It's your cousin Kate. I just want to talk to you."

She heard the usual sounds of shuffling and banging around inside. A loud television suddenly muted. She waited, angling her body, as the dead bolt was thrown.

The door swung open, and the light spilled from inside into the drawn-out twilight with the snow coming down. And then Kate was face-to-face with a family member for the first time in years.

William wasn't the kid she remembered. He'd grown up. He looked like an odd mix of Kate's father and his own, and he sported a dark mustache, a scraggly beard, and a visible neck tattoo that crawled up toward one ear.

And he looked about as thrilled at this reunion as Kate was.

"What the hell, Katie," he said after a long pause, his dark eyes glittering in a way that reminded her, against her will, of her father's long monologues and the cold, stark rooms they'd all huddled in for warmth on days a lot like this one. "If I wanted the family over for Christmas or whatever this is, it wouldn't be you."

Thirteen

Templeton watched Kate's reaction while he kept one eye on the cousin who stood in the doorway looking anything but welcoming, but she didn't crack. She gave no indication that the guy staring down at them from the step above her was anything to her besides another person of interest in an old investigation.

What he couldn't tell was whether Kate was simply showing her professionalism or if it was true.

And this was definitely not the optimal time for Templeton to consider all the things he didn't know about Kate Holiday. As opposed to obsessing over the things about her he did know. Like her sweet taste. Like those sounds she made, there in the back of her throat.

Once again, dumbass, he growled at himself. *Try to focus. This is not the time.*

He was still pissed at himself for losing his focus entirely when he'd gone to Kate's cabin to tell her about the break-in at her apartment and had lost himself in her tipsy come-on instead. God, had he lost himself. But he'd vowed he wouldn't let even Kate's naked body distract him from work again, and he'd given himself one last chance.

He had no intention of blowing it now.

Templeton focused on the cousin. William Holiday did not strike him as any kind of significant threat. The overly large neck tattoo looked to Templeton like a small man's attempt to look bigger than he was. And the guy's general demeanor struck Templeton as sad-sack territory. He would be very surprised if this guy was running around blowing things up or potentially killing transients to leave them lying around like bait.

People were always surprising, it was true. But Templeton rarely read them wrong to that degree.

"It's great to see you, too, Will," Kate was saying, in exactly the same tone her cousin had used when he'd called her *Katie*. And Templeton didn't have to delve too much deeper into the mysteries of Trooper Kate Holiday to know that she really, really did not enjoy being called by a nickname. "I figure the last time has to be, what? Eleven years ago, at least."

"You know how long ago it was." Templeton wasn't fond of the way the cousin glared at Kate like she was personally responsible for his bad decisions, including that neck tattoo. More interesting, he didn't look at Templeton at all. The kind of man who was deep into firebombing and murder would likely pay some attention to a huge, clearly tactically proficient individual who was taller than eye level even though he was standing two steps down. "It was ten years ago at Mom's appeal."

"How is your mom?" Kate asked. She made a little show of including Templeton in the conversation with the way she inclined her head, but she didn't actually shift her gaze from William. "I haven't thought about Aunt Darlene in ages."

"You know how my mother is." William made a derisive sort of noise, like he was sucking on his teeth. "She's an ex-con. The minute she could leave the state, she did, and she's never been back. She's never even met her grandchildren. Merry Christmas, Katie."

William went as if to close the door, but Katie stopped him. She didn't throw her hand out or use her body weight. She only smiled and shifted her body enough that it made her seem broader somehow. And William stopped what he was doing.

"I'm afraid this isn't a social call, Will," Kate said quietly. "As much fun as it is to catch up out here on your doorstep, I'm going to have to ask you to invite us inside."

William snorted. "What a surprise. Another Holiday throwing weight around. I'm shocked."

He sounded bitter. But in keeping with Templeton's judgment of his character, he did nothing but step back and wave his hand in ironic invitation, beckoning the two of them inside.

Kate marched in with great confidence, but Templeton figured that was for show. She knew he was behind her, proceeding more slowly. Checking out the scene as he went, looking for booby traps and other potential problems that could blow up in their face. Maybe literally, if William Holiday was more fire-happy than Templeton's gut thought he was.

But it was like any crappy house Templeton had ever walked into. The only booby traps here were the residents. The front door opened up into a shabby living room, piled high with the detritus of unfolded laundry, unwashed dishes, piles of dirty snow boots, and cereal boxes upended on the floor, their contents strewn across the dingy rug. Someone had stapled plastic over the windows to try to create some insulation. It was charming, in other words. Templeton felt like he was back in one of the foster homes he'd been desperate to escape when he was still a kid.

One more reason to dislike Cousin William.

Templeton closed the front door behind him, then stood with his back to it, his gaze moving around what he could see of the rest of the house. A kitchen straight ahead, open to the living room. A small hallway, with a couple of doors leading off it. A back door at the far end of the hall that would provide easier access to the plugged-in vehicles out back.

"Who else is here?" Kate asked. "I wouldn't want to miss a chance to say hello to your family."

"I'll go introduce myself," Templeton said.

"If this is official business," William said, still glaring at Kate, "why aren't you wearing a uniform?"

Templeton left his post by the front door. He scanned the rest of the house in minutes. There was a dull-eyed, lank-haired woman in the bigger of the two bedrooms, who did nothing but glower at Templeton when he poked his head in. Then blew smoke rings as much toward the ceiling as at him. He saw no sign of the kids that had been mentioned in the files. And he had no way of telling whether that was a good or bad thing.

He walked back out to the living area, where Kate was standing in the center of the room, her hands on her hips and that cop smile on her face. He lifted one finger and saw her barely perceptible nod in reply.

"You keep glaring at me like I did something to you, Will," she said, sounding friendly and encouraging, if still cool. "You're going to have to explain that to me."

"Really? It needs an explanation? Or did you somehow forget that you ripped our family apart?"

Templeton eyed Cousin Will, who was a little more yoked than he liked the average person of interest to be, but nothing he couldn't handle. And nothing Kate couldn't handle, for that matter. But he still didn't get that kind of vibe.

If there weren't blown-up buildings and boats, and that pesky dead guy, Templeton would have accepted the fact that he was witnessing a messed-up family reunion, thought no more of it, and waited in the car.

Kate, meanwhile, looked about as unbothered as it

was possible to be. "'Ripped our family apart,'" she repeated. "That's an interesting way to put it. How can you rip something apart that was already sick and broken to begin with?"

"I already know your opinion, Katie," her cousin growled. "I don't think there's a courtroom you didn't share your thoughts in when you had the chance. I don't need to hear it again here." He stretched his arms out along the back of the couch where he was sitting, in a manner Templeton could only describe as aggressive. Which made him marginally more interesting. But not interesting enough that Templeton felt he needed to move to a more strategic position. "I don't care."

"I really want to believe you," Kate said. "But is it true that you don't care? Or are you pretending that you don't care, when actually all you really want is to finish what our parents started?"

Will made a derisive noise. "Finish what they started? Like what? Does it look to you that I'm living off my wits in the bush?"

"I don't know what you're doing," Kate said calmly. "To me it looks a whole lot like wasting your potential."

"You try getting a decent job when your name is William Holiday."

"My examination of your file suggests that it's holding down the jobs that's a challenge, not getting them."

"It's not exactly a walk in the park to convince people to give me a chance. They always believe the name, not me."

Kate, also named Holiday and gainfully employed for years now, gazed back at her cousin. "The name hasn't gotten in my way. Not that I'm aware of."

Her cousin sneered. "Yeah, well, we don't all get to ride that whistle-blower glory, do we?"

"It seems to me that you've walked away from relationships, kids, spouses, jobs, *and* cities when things got tough. But that's your business, Will. You can conduct your personal life any way you want. What worries me is the stuff that makes you a danger to others."

"A danger to others?" William scoffed. "What is this? You're not satisfied with putting an entire generation of our family behind bars—now you want to start in on the next?"

"That all depends," Kate replied. "Is the next generation law-abiding? Or is it chock-full of criminals like our parents?"

"That probably depends on what you mean by *law-abiding*."

"No one cares if you smoke weed, buddy," Templeton drawled from where he stood.

"Oh, I get this now," William said. He flicked his gaze to Templeton, then dismissed him, turning that glare back on Kate. "You don't actually have anything on me. You're just afraid."

"Do I look afraid?" Kate asked. She sounded genuinely curious. "Because I haven't been afraid in a long time. Not since I left the compound and discovered that there really was a whole different world out here."

William only rolled his eyes. "I'm not your guy. I'm not interested in you or anyone else I used to be related to. You can all go to hell together, as far as I'm concerned. In fact, I'll light the match."

"There's that wholesome, tender Christmas spirit," Kate murmured. "It never disappoints."

"You got to go off and make yourself over into some kind of hero, didn't you?" William asked. "That's real nice for you. But I didn't get that option. I bet no one asks you if you're any relation to *that* Holiday. And why would they? You don't look like them. I might as well be freaking Samuel Lee Holiday himself. I'm his spitting image."

"I don't remember Daddy having a tattoo like that one all over your neck. What is that, anyway? A rat?"

"It's a wolverine." Will bared his teeth. "You always were the funny one, weren't you?"

The way he said that made Templeton suspect that there had been consequences for being the "funny one." Possibly consequences simply for distinguishing herself from the rest, if he knew his messed-up, dysfunctional families.

And the prospect of a young Kate suffering said consequences made Templeton feel a good deal more grim about the whole situation.

Come on now, an inner voice chided him. *No one gets as tough or as good as she is without a little suffering. You should know.*

"Of course they ask me if I'm related to him," Kate replied, her voice as deliberate as if she were talking to a possibly inebriated perpetrator. The fact that this was her family member appeared to have no effect on her at all. "I have the same name you do. And it might surprise you to learn that, given my profession, people are far more interested in my links to known criminals than they might be otherwise. They tend to bring it up. A lot."

Templeton had brought it up himself not long ago. Though he didn't jump in to share that information with whiny cousin Will.

"Let me dig out my violin," William threw at her. "The difference is, you did this. You made it all happen. I don't remember asking you to make me a pariah."

"I'm glad you brought up memory," Kate said, as if she were musing over the whole thing. As if this were one of those cheerful family moments Templeton had never seen outside of the *Family Circus* cartoons in the paper, that he sometimes read in sheer disbelief. "Because I don't remember doing anything to you, Will. I thought we were friends as well as cousins. I asked you to go with me that day. You refused. How is that on me?"

William shook his head. He rubbed one hand over his face. Then he stood, and Templeton moved with him to keep him in his sights. And, more important, to make sure the guy knew that Templeton was ready to take him down if he breathed funny.

But William's attention was on Kate. He let out a hollow kind of laugh. "No," he said in a low voice. "I didn't go with you. But I wanted to."

"You should have."

Templeton cut his gaze to Kate, who sounded less like a cop then. The least like a cop in all the time he'd known her, in fact.

"I've had to live with that," William threw back at her. "And don't tell me I should have testified."

"Why didn't you?"

Her cousin shook his head as if this all caused him pain. Or distaste. Or maybe both.

"I thought I could hold on to the family. I wanted to hold on to something. You don't know what it was like when they came. That raid. The way they stormed in and took us all away . . ." He shook his head again, but this time like he was trying to shake the memory out. "But there was nothing to hold on to. They all thought I was a traitor, just like you. We had *ideas*. They would have made us answer for that sooner or later."

"Sooner, not later," Kate said softly. "Why do you think I left?"

Her cousin blinked. "They weren't going to put you through the ritual. I would have heard."

"It was coming. They'd discussed it. My father was pretending to be the holdout vote."

William swayed a little on his feet.

"I'm missing the subtext here," Templeton belted out into the sudden tension in the room, and was gratified when both Kate and William shifted their positions, like he'd succeeded in breaking that chain with the past. "What ritual are you talking about?"

"The ritual was a favorite practice, doled out to traitors." Kate smiled at Templeton. It went nowhere near her eyes. "In case you're wondering why my father was transferred back here from his stint in federal prison for the mail fraud and the tax evasion to do his life sentences for murder, it wasn't only for the troopers he shot during the raid. It was the ritual. It was his way of rooting out a traitor, because a traitor was an offense to the bountiful land that gave us all we should need."

"Any man, woman, or child who could withstand nature's fury could prove beyond any reasonable doubt that they weren't actually a traitor," William intoned.

Kate was still smiling at Templeton. "You know how cold it gets up here in winter. Guess how many traitors lived through the night when they were forced to stay outside? Naked?"

Templeton thought of fifteen-year-old Kate and muttered a curse.

"Exactly," William said sourly. "That many."

"And it was all, always, my father's idea. But he was really, really good at getting other people to convince him to do what he wanted to do in the first place." Kate shifted her gaze back to William. "A master manipulator to the end."

"There is no end," William said, his voice rough. He swallowed hard enough to make his Adam's apple bob. "They all still love him the way they always did. They're never going to see the light. And that means I get it from both sides. No one who knows who my family is wants anything to do with me. And no one in the family wants anything to do with me, either."

If anything, Kate's smile got wider. "Let me guess. That's all my fault, too."

"I know it's not your fault, Katie. Believe me, I know. But I blame you anyway."

And the look on William's face then tore at Templeton. Because he was terribly afraid that he knew what that felt like. A terrible yearning mixed with sorrow, bound up in anger that had nowhere to go.

He'd had similar feelings about his own father his whole life.

Templeton didn't like recognizing it on another man's face. He didn't like admitting he knew what it was. And he couldn't decide if he felt empathetic or if what he really wanted to do was punch William—hard—until that awful look went away.

And what did that make him?

"Someone left a dead body in my seaplane," Kate said quietly. And her voice was different—harder, maybe—but Templeton was too busy looking into a mirror he wanted to deny existed to glance over at her. "And then someone broke into my apartment in Juneau. Maybe the same someone. Only that time, it looks like they were waiting for me to come home, presumably so we could throw a little Christmas party. Or who knows, perform the ritual after all. And yes, it seems pretty clear that they were waiting for me specifically, because I wasn't the woman who walked in on them. Do you know anything about any of that?"

"You think I have access to dead bodies?" William blinked. Then a mottled sort of color washed over his face, making his neck tattoo stand out even more. "Oh, wait, you think I'd *murder* someone? Then come at you in your own apartment? All these years later, that's what you think of me?"

"You're either like them or you're not, William," Kate said, and she sounded tough again. Giving no quarter, no matter that this had to be eating away at her. If Templeton was seeing his own ghosts in this room, what was she seeing? "I have no idea what the years have done to you inside. Only you do. But you either know information that could help me or you don't, and that's why I'm here."

William's fists curled at his sides, but even as Templeton clocked it and shifted to a higher gear, he could tell that the other man was fighting himself. He wasn't about to swing at his cousin. Which meant Templeton didn't get the opportunity to show him why that would be a terrible idea. William swallowed hard. Again. Like it hurt him.

"I told you. They don't want any part of me."

"That doesn't mean you don't hear things."

"I hear things," William admitted. Grudgingly. "And last I heard, Liberty and Russ went back. To Nenana."

Kate was too still. It was the first time since they'd gotten here that Templeton thought her cousin had really made it under her skin. "Not the compound."

"No. Not that far out."

"I thought they were in Palmer."

"Now they're farming. Kind of. Living off the land, but within driving distance of supplies."

"Will."

But that was all Kate said. Just her cousin's name.

"I don't know," he said, begrudgingly. "I haven't gone looking, and I'm not sure you should, either, without an invitation."

"Is it starting again?" Kate asked softly. "Has it already started?"

"You know everything I know."

She made an impatient noise. "Are you really telling me that it could be happening again, right now, and you're sitting up here an hour away doing absolutely nothing to stop it? Again?"

It was that *again* that was the hit. It made her cousin flinch.

And Templeton watched as that same expression moved over the other man's face once again. Loss. Pain. Maybe it was grief, simple as that.

Though nothing about it looked simple to Templeton.

"You look like you're doing well, Katie," her cousin said, his voice rough. "It's nice that one of us is. I'm sure that once I think about it, once you're gone again, I'll be real glad about that. But tonight I want you to go back where you came from. And stay there."

Fourteen

Templeton was quiet as they trudged back out to the SUV. He spoke only when he called in to update Jonas, who was running point on the two or three Alaska Force cases that were still active at this time of year.

Dirtbags don't take a vacation, Templeton had told her when Kate had asked him directly why they didn't go dark over the holidays the way it seemed the rest of the world did. *Neither do we.*

A sentiment she'd appreciated, since the Troopers certainly didn't take time off during the drunkest, darkest part of the year. Even if Kate had been personally ordered to take a step back at present.

But she appreciated it even more that he didn't say anything to Kate directly as he drove back down the short, snow-packed drive toward the road, leaving Will and all Kate's bad memories behind them.

She tried pretending she was grateful. That she was *pleased* he was giving her the space to sort it all out in her own head.

But when he pulled out of her cousin's drive and paused there to look both ways through the falling snow at the edge of the tree line, *grateful* was not the word that came to mind. If she didn't know better—if it wasn't ridiculous—Kate would have said that she was actually in something of a fury.

Kate had no right. She knew that. Templeton wasn't her friend. He wasn't even really a colleague. They had common interests, that was all, and he didn't have to pretend that they had any sort of closeness—she refused to use the word *intimacy*—just because there had been some nudity. All hers.

And she hated the fact that it mattered to her. That he was treating her differently, suddenly, and it bothered her. That anything he did bothered her.

She wrestled with herself for another long moment or two because the kind of disconnection that she could feel between them now was what she had always wanted from her working relationships. No banter, no invites to family cookouts in the summer, no disrobing in log cabins.

Why should she feel hollow that she'd finally gotten what she wanted?

"If you're waiting for me to offer some commentary about your family," Templeton said as he drove along the road, leaving Will firmly behind them, "or judge you in some way because of what you got away from, you're going to be waiting a long time."

And Kate didn't understand how that hollow sensation could turn so quickly into a sort of aching heat instead.

"Will was the cousin I was closest to, growing up," Kate heard herself say, which was astonishing because she was sure she'd intended to say something very dry about strategy. Or their next move. Something very deliberately impersonal. "Looking back, I guess I could have tried to stay in touch with him. Or the others. We were all kids, after all. But when no one reached out to me after the trials, I thought that was what they wanted."

She didn't know where that came from, either. She'd

kept tabs on every last member of her family. Distantly. She'd always assumed that if they'd really wanted, they could have kept track of what she was doing, too. And it wasn't a secret that she'd become a trooper. The newspapers had run big stories when she'd graduated from the academy, dredging up all the Holiday family history.

Then again, perhaps Kate was being unkind. According to every movie she'd ever seen that addressed the topic, family wasn't meant to judge such things. Family was meant to be accepting, no matter what. No matter the different life choices relatives made, everyone was supposed to gather together for cheery meals and act like they loved one another. Particularly at Christmas.

That hadn't exactly been one of her father's preferred manifestos.

"Your cousin is a grown man, Kate," Templeton said. And when did she start thinking of his low, deep voice as comforting? *When have you thought of* anything *as comforting?* she asked herself. "Perfectly capable of reaching out if that's what he wanted."

"That goes both ways."

"Sure. You and I can sit here and come up with a thousand scenarios about how he should have done this and you should have done that. And maybe that's all true. But it also means that if he's not to blame, neither are you."

Kate stared out into the darkness, Templeton's headlights picking up the snow coming down and the trees rising high on each side of the road, while her heart kicked at her as if she were running for her life. "I didn't ask you to forgive me."

"And here I am, doing it anyway."

Kate opened her mouth to say something rash, along the lines of *That's what you do, isn't it? You ignore what I say and do what you want anyway.*

But she didn't. Sanity reasserted itself, or more likely, she accepted that the real, honest truth was that she liked that about him. She liked that he seemed to know exactly how wicked she wanted him, no matter what she might say to the contrary.

That kind of contradiction felt a whole lot like a deep, smoky gray sort of area, and Kate had no idea what to do with it. She wasn't supposed to feel things like that. She was black and white, right or wrong, all the way through.

Though she didn't feel like that at all when Templeton was around.

"It's dark," Kate said instead. "But it's not that late. We could be down in Nenana by dinnertime."

"You think that's the right move?"

"You don't?"

Behind the wheel, Templeton slid a look her way. "That wasn't a loaded question. I'm not afraid of a little brainstorming. You know the people in question better than I do."

Kate thought about her cousins. Liberty had been the next oldest girl, eighteen months younger than Will, her brother. Kate's memories of her were patchy, threaded through with her feelings about her father and her own growing realization that the Holiday family wasn't the force of good her father claimed it was. She remembered being jealous of Will and Liberty's father, Uncle Joseph, who had always seemed so much kinder and more approachable than her own father. But she'd also always thought that Liberty too closely resembled her mother, the pinch-faced Aunt Darlene.

Their cousin Russ was a wild card. Six years younger than Kate and the son of yet another Holiday brother, he'd been her responsibility in her role as oldest girl and therefore caretaker of the younger kids. It was hard to imagine chubby little Russ as a grown man, filled with opinions and capable of barricading himself in another place like the compound. By choice.

She said as much to Templeton, and for a long moment there was nothing but the sound of their tires against the snowy road and the *thwack* of the wipers against the windshield.

"It's hard to ignore that they went back to the scene of the crime," Templeton said.

Kate would have said that she liked teamwork, in a general sense. She considered herself a part of the Trooper family. She'd enjoyed working with the partners she'd been paired with at different points in her career. Templeton was another assigned partner, nothing more, and the kind of brainstorming that he and his Alaska Force buddies liked to do in the lodge every morning was a perfectly valid way of working through problems with a case.

But it felt a lot like more of that uncomfortable intimacy when she turned a little in her seat, in the cab of yet another SUV hemmed in on all sides by the Alaskan night, and agreed with him.

"Something about it doesn't sit right. And that's before I even get eyes on the situation. My father's compound wasn't the sort of place to inspire nostalgia."

Templeton nodded. "The other thing that jumps out at me is that cousins don't normally set up house together."

"Insert Appalachian joke here," Kate said dryly.

Templeton's laugh filled the vehicle. And Kate would have to be truly dead inside not to feel a little warmer because of it. But she tried to deny that, too.

"My inclination is to wait until tomorrow," Templeton said after a moment, traces of that laughter like an undercurrent in his voice. "My thinking is that it takes longer to get anywhere in the snow, so that puts us in later tonight. And that's if we don't get worse weather on the way or spin out on the ice somewhere. Then we have to do a little basic recon, because I'm not walking into a potential Samuel Lee Holiday situation in the dark. I think it would be a lot easier to do it in whatever kind of weak-ass daylight we get tomorrow." He made a low noise, as if he was mulling it over. "Then again, could be your cousin Will is on the phone right now trying to ingratiate himself by telling them we're coming. Maybe it would make more sense not to give them extra time to prepare for our arrival."

Kate frowned out the window, not quite seeing the streets of Fairbanks before her. "I honestly don't know which way he'll go. But Will could have called the minute we left. We have to assume they've already been alerted."

"If your gut feeling says that we need to go tonight, let's go tonight."

Kate waited, but that was it. That was all he said. And there was nothing the least bit passive-aggressive or challenging in his tone. Of all the things she was worried about when it came to Templeton—or anyone in Alaska Force, for that matter—it wasn't that garden variety *I know more than you because I'm a man* nonsense that she'd been drenched in as a child and had learned how to handle when she'd started in law enforcement.

"You're not really a big mansplainer, are you?" she asked.

Templeton threw another look at her, something glinting in his dark gaze. "Was that a compliment? I don't know if my heart can take it. You might need to call the paramedics."

"I'm not sure it's a compliment to have someone tell you that you've achieved the bare minimum of common decency. But sure, take it as one if you want."

"I'm impatient with people who should know their stuff but don't." Templeton's voice was even. His gaze was on the road. "That doesn't apply to you."

"That sounds like straight-up flattery." But she couldn't deny that it warmed that same once-hollow place inside her, even so.

"No, ma'am. If I was talking about sex, sure. I might

pretty it up. But when it comes to the job? The only thing I'm interested in is competency. Believe that, if nothing else."

And the crazy part was, she did believe him. *Or maybe,* a more caustic voice inside her butted in, *it's more accurate to say that you* want *to believe him. Because you want this man to think of you as competent. If not as highly skilled as he is—because who could be?—then at least pretty damn good at your own job.*

"I don't know if what I have is a gut feeling," Kate said after a moment, because his flattery deserved an honest response. Or as honest as she was capable of being, anyway. "Or if I just want to get this part over with."

"Which part? The investigation?"

"The part that involves anyone I'm related to. I didn't think I was signing on for this twisted little inversion of a family Christmas, but I'd like it to end. As soon as possible."

"Roger that." Templeton nodded toward the back of the SUV. "Aside from what I have in my go bag and what I assume you have in yours, we also have what amounts to a minor arsenal in the back. It's not a full SWAT team situation, but we could have ourselves a little party."

Kate smiled. "I do like a party."

But it was already after five p.m. The temperature was plummeting, the snow was falling, and Kate had no idea what they would be walking into in Nenana. Her cousins might very well be nostalgic for the compound, as impossible as that seemed to her. Human beings were complicated, as she knew all too well. They spent significant parts of their lives yearning for things that they not only couldn't have but that were actively bad for them.

Kate had always claimed that she didn't understand that sort of self-destructive urge. But that was before she'd met Templeton.

She rubbed a hand over her face.

"I hate waiting. But I think it might be the better

move." She cleared her throat. "I'm happy to put us up in hotel rooms and then try again tomorrow."

There was a silence that was certainly not *electric* in any way. Kate told herself she was overtired from her research all-nighters and clearly imagining things.

"First of all," Templeton said, his voice as dark as the night, "you don't need to foot the bill."

"This is my family we're talking about."

"Trooper. Get your head back in the game. Your family might or might not be the jackholes responsible for blown-up boats and dead men. But either way, this blackmail attempt is aimed straight at Alaska Force. And we take defending ourselves pretty seriously."

"I would feel better if I was contributing."

"Second," Templeton continued, as if she hadn't said that last part, "we have a place in Fairbanks. No hotels required."

Kate wanted to argue. But she was afraid that launching into an impassioned argument about why she needed the relative protection of a hotel room, rather than the perceived intimacy of some house, would do nothing but show Templeton exactly how much she was freaking out at the prospect of being alone with him again in a place where there were beds. And every instinct and gut feeling she had, all of which were silent on the issue of her cousins, bleated out exactly how bad an idea it would be to let him know such a thing.

Besides, she was pretty sure he already knew.

So she stayed silent, as if she didn't care where they stayed. She said nothing as he drove them across the city, then turned down a heavily snow-packed lane that wound through the trees and stopped in front of a dark little house, locked up tight.

"It's going to be cold at first," Templeton said as he bumped them over the snow that covered the clearing. "But it'll warm up quick."

Kate bit her tongue rather than throw something back

at him, reminding him that she knew all about cold houses and woodstoves here in Alaska. More than he would know, anyway, with his history in the deep, warm South, even if he seemed to know his way around the block heater and timer that he connected to the SUV.

Keep it professional, she told herself.

Because clearly that was going to be the only thing that saved her. If anything could save her, that was. And assuming that particular genie wasn't already out of its bottle, as she was so desperately trying to convince herself.

Templeton opened the front door of the cabin by keying a code into a heavy-duty padlock. He led Kate inside, flipping on the lights as he went. She could see a living room, a small study, and a kitchen at the back to make up the main floor. And to her surprise, it was a cheerful, modest sort of house that looked as if a family might walk in any second. Not a black ops team.

After kicking off her boots and hanging up her jacket, Kate drifted over toward the pictures all along the mantel, which looked as if it should sit over a fireplace but framed a TV instead.

And was shocked when she saw a smiling, much younger version of a man who could only be Isaac Gentry.

"This is Isaac's sister's house," Templeton told her, once the woodstove was lit and roaring away. He rubbed his hands together as he came to stand beside Kate. He squinted at the picture of Isaac and the woman who was presumably his sister, grinning at the camera with packs on their backs and, behind them, one of Alaska's blue glaciers. Kate could almost hear the ice crackling.

"Isaac has a sister?"

Templeton laughed. "Doesn't seem possible, right? But yes. He's not only mortal, he has a family and everything."

"Is she Wonder Woman? To continue the family theme."

Templeton laughed again, sounding even more delighted than before, which Kate assured herself didn't affect her in the least.

"That depends on your definition. Amy raised three decent kids, which isn't easy. Now she and her husband are exploring the country in their fifth wheel. But Isaac maintains the house."

"How many houses does Isaac have?"

"As many as he needs." Templeton grinned. "He likes to make sure there's always a safe place to stay."

Kate turned from the mantel. She squared her shoulders as she looked at Templeton, almost unconsciously. Almost.

"Why don't you like hotels?"

"I like hotels fine. But I can't always control the access points. And, funny thing about me, I like to know who's coming and going. Wherever I am."

Kate didn't know how he made that sound dirty. The way he made everything sound dirty. She only nodded and pretended not to hear it. His gaze got that golden gleam that made her feel alarmingly melty inside, but all he did was lead her upstairs and show her which room was hers for the night. They both stood in the narrow hall looking at the full bed beneath the slanted ceiling. Kate felt much too warm. But Templeton didn't make any suggestive comments.

Once again forcing Kate to question why she felt more disappointed than she did relieved.

She tossed her bag on the end of the bed, sat down next to it, and made a few phone calls to her contacts down in Anchorage, to see if they could help her figure out where exactly in Nenana Liberty and Russ were living. To start a little basic recon before they drove down there tomorrow morning.

When she went back downstairs, Templeton was heating up canned soup on the stove. Kate accepted the bowl he offered her and absolutely did not think about the domesticity of it all. Or how much it reminded her of that cozy scene at Griffin and Mariah's house she'd spied through a window in Grizzly Harbor.

It was amazing how far away that seemed to her now.

Kate put her spoon down and cleared her throat. "A friend of mine contacted the Trooper station in Nenana and asked after my cousins. In a roundabout way. And the word is they're living about ten minutes out in what the trooper on duty called 'a group situation,' whatever that means."

She rolled her eyes, because she knew what she thought that meant. It screamed *cult* to her. Manifestos, a marked interest in taking down the current government, and her father's fingerprints all over everything. But maybe that was her baggage. A girl only had to grow up in one cult and she saw them everywhere.

"The house isn't entirely off the grid, they said. But you know that could go either way."

Wholly off the grid could mean trigger-happy and a difficult time raising any backup should that become necessary, like the raid on her father's compound. But *on the grid* could mean access to more sophisticated expressions of trigger-happiness, rendering any backup moot. There was no way of knowing what they would be walking into.

"Do you have a specific location?" Templeton asked.

Kate took out her phone and pulled up a map. That inspired Templeton to go and get his tablet, and they spent a largely congenial hour or two, talking through scenarios and generally marinating in that professionalism that Kate was so sure she craved.

And when there was a lull in the conversation, and it seemed to her that they'd covered all possible bases, she shot to her feet and made a show of checking her watch.

She assiduously avoided reacting to that knowing look in Templeton's dark gaze as he sat there across the table in the cheerful little kitchen, with his long legs thrust out before him and his hands piled on the back of his head. Like he was on a beach somewhere, taking in the sun.

"I'm glad we decided to do this tomorrow," she said, oozing professionalism from every pore. "It will give me a chance to catch up on some sleep."

"Good idea, Trooper," he rumbled at her. "Better make sure you're good and rested."

Unsurprisingly, she didn't think about her family members or the life cycle of a cult when he said things like that. She thought about being spread out on a bed before him. Any bed. The one upstairs, for example. She thought about lifting her hips for closer contact to that wicked mouth of his. She thought about that wild, marvelous shattering and all the dark intent on his beautiful face when she'd finally managed to open her eyes again.

And her thoughts must have been written all over her face, because the corner of his dangerous mouth crooked up in what she was terribly afraid was invitation.

Kate smiled coolly. "I'll see you in the morning."

With regal dismissiveness, if she did say so herself.

She made herself walk sedately from the room. She climbed the stairs at the same unhurried pace, as if her heart weren't lodged somewhere in her throat and her palms weren't damp with the desire to touch him again.

Everywhere, this time.

Then she locked herself up tight in her bedroom, because she was Trooper Kate Holiday, and she didn't do desire. She never had. And this was no time to start.

Fifteen

When Kate came downstairs the next morning, Templeton was already awake and dressed in running clothes, and she had to lecture herself, sternly, that Templeton was just a man. He didn't know he'd starred in every one of her very dirty dreams last night. He didn't know anything that went on inside her unless she told him.

He nodded toward the coffee machine, and she felt nearly giddy with relief as she poured herself a mug, blew on it, then took a big gulp. It was very strong, full of flavor, and she thought that another woman—one with significantly less of a sense of self-preservation—might fall in love with the man for that coffee alone. Then and there.

Kate was obviously not that foolish.

Though her second swig of the coffee he'd made certainly tempted her to change her mind.

"It's hours to daylight yet," Templeton said, his gaze out the back window, where a security light showed the pristine snow piled high in what Kate assumed was a yard. So high it met the pine branches that were weighed down with even more snow. "Are you up for another run?"

He didn't smirk, and his gaze wasn't any more knowing than usual, so it seemed like a straightforward question. But it felt anything but straightforward to Kate.

She wasn't one for group activities. She never had been. Kate had run with other people during her training, of course. There'd been a lot of that when she was a recruit at the academy in Sitka. But the primary reason she liked to run was because it was something she could do alone. And because now and again, it made her feel connected to the world.

She could remember all too well running the stairs with Templeton that morning in Grizzly Harbor. He'd appeared out of nowhere. He'd challenged her. Then chased her.

That was how she chose to remember it, anyway.

Her body seemed to have a whole different set of memories, and she scowled down at her coffee mug.

"It's a yes-or-no question, Trooper," Templeton said, and she heard his laughter then. Humming through her whether she wanted to admit it or not.

"Of course," she said, because there was no rational reason not to go running with the man. It would be great to get a run in and work off some of her nervous energy before she returned to Nenana. And it would be silly to run separately if they were both heading out at the same time.

Because heaven forbid Kate ever allow herself to be anything less than rational.

"Of course?" he asked, and she thought that he was actually . . . teasing her. Pushing, at the very least. "Why not say, *Templeton, I would love to go running with you*? Or would the world screech to a halt if you showed the slightest bit of enthusiasm for something?"

"I would love to go running with you." She glared at him. "Templeton."

He grinned. "Excellent."

When Kate was done with her coffee, she jogged back

upstairs. She checked the weather on her phone and pulled together her running clothes. It was ten degrees below zero out there, which meant an extra pair of compression socks, her studded running shoes, and a pair of mittens to pull on over her regular gloves so she'd be able to keep her fingers together and generate more heat. A Buff around her neck she could pull up over her face, and several layers to encourage heat and keep out the wet. Nothing too thick, because Kate knew from experience that if she felt warm when she started running, she would overheat and get wildly uncomfortable shortly thereafter. No matter the temperature.

When she met Templeton by the front door, he was dressed almost identically.

"How fast do you normally run?" she asked him.

He didn't look at her as he jerked his hat into place. "Whatever pace you want to go is fine with me."

"I'm quite fast, actually."

That made him give her his full attention, which instantly made Kate question whether or not that had been her motive all along.

"I'm sure you are," he said in a low rumble that affected her the way his mouth had against hers. And lower. "But you don't have my legs or my training. You set the pace. And don't try to show off at these temperatures. I wouldn't want to have to carry you back."

"That will never happen."

"Because you're not at all competitive and would never try to show off, especially after some guy said he was faster than you?"

"You will never have to carry me anywhere," Kate clarified. Icily.

And shoved her hat down hard over her ears as they headed outside, though that did nothing at all to block the sound of his laughter.

It was definitely a Fairbanks winter morning. The cold sucker punched Kate instantly, then seemed to settle hard in her bones. Breathing in was sharp, like a machete. It felt like clarity.

The snowfall had stopped for the moment, and the lights from the front of the house showed Kate that Templeton had been out already this morning, shoveling grooves into the few feet of snow that had fallen in the night, which would make it easier for them to drive out later. And made it easier now for Kate to set off toward the main road.

Running in fresh snow was fun. Kate had always enjoyed it, in her years in cold and snowy places like right here in Fairbanks. It was the potential ice packed beneath the snow from warmer temperatures that was the problem, so quickly could it take a runner down. And then the real trouble happened, out in the dark with a broken ankle or worse, risking hypothermia with potentially no cell phone service.

But Kate wasn't worried about that today. On the main road, the snowplows had already been out this morning. Kate could run in the street, parallel to the snow berm the plow had pushed to the side. It was as much a test of agility as it was of regular endurance, with her headlamp casting a little circle of light before her and the strange, somehow comforting and yet unsettling awareness of the big man keeping pace with her at her back.

She didn't know what she expected Templeton to do. Make noise, make his presence known the way he always did. *Something.*

But all he did was run. The only sound was her breath and his and their feet crunching against the snowpack. It was like they were the only people alive and awake in all of Alaska, when Kate knew better.

Once again, Kate felt the embrace of it. That damnable intimacy, wrapping around her like the sort of hug she would decline if it was offered to her.

It made her mad. It made her run faster, as if she

could outrun it—and not because she was trying to show off to an ex–Delta Force Army Ranger whose very physicality was a testament to his commitment to keeping himself battle ready. Kate had spent almost fifteen years building up her walls, creating and bolstering her boundaries, and policing the vast gulf of distance—physical and emotional—she kept between herself and other people. She'd weathered the uncomfortable silences, the "lost" invitations to group activities she didn't want to attend anyway, the whispers behind her back when her "attitude" inevitably caused offense. She was happy with where she'd ended up in her career, able to do her own thing without worrying about office politics.

Kate was well known as an ice queen, and she liked it that way.

And all it took was one visit to Templeton and his friends and it all started crumbling.

Like it had been dominoes all along, instead of stone walls and sheets of arctic ice.

She wasn't a good judge of the male half of the species, but everything she'd witnessed as a child suggested that Templeton was nothing like the men in her family and was much more like the troopers who had listened to her, understood what was happening, and made sure she never had to go back out into the bush to the compound she'd escaped. Then died because they'd protected her. And the more adult truth she had no desire to acknowledge was that she already had more of a relationship with Templeton than she'd had with any of the other men who'd walk-on roles in her life.

Kate wanted absolutely no part of this, whatever it was.

Seeing her cousin yesterday had crystallized that for her. Will was family. He was the least offensive member of her family, as a matter of fact, and she had no desire to do anything about the state of her broken relationship with him. If it hadn't been for her Alaska Force investigation and that body in her seaplane, she never would have looked him up. She would have let that bridge burn down into dust, and if she'd thought about it at all, she would have roasted marshmallows in the flames.

Kate didn't want intimacy. She didn't want cozy chats over red wine in cheerful log cabins with women she barely knew. And she had never been all that interested in oral sex, with all that forced vulnerability. She still didn't want any of it, she snapped at herself.

She pumped her arms, moving faster over the frigid ground, because her body was warm and limber now despite the cold—and she didn't like the fact that Templeton seemed to have his own private access to her body and its reactions no matter what she thought about it. She didn't like that at all.

Kate liked sugar, too. A lot. Yet she knew that it was far better to moderate its use than to indulge herself, because no matter how good it tasted, it was never worth how she felt afterward. Templeton was no different. He was just . . . sugar in male form. Tempting, impossible to consume without that little bit of a head rush, but no good for her.

She was solitary like a rock and alone like an island, like the old song had always told her.

"Are you running toward something?" came Templeton's amused voice from behind her. That was when she realized she was practically sprinting at breakneck pace down a snowy, treacherous road with only the faintest stirrings of approaching daylight lightening up the dark sky. "Or is something chasing us?"

"I was thinking about sugar," she said, having to yell a bit to make sure her words made it through the covering she had over the lower part of her face.

"Sugar makes me cranky," Templeton observed. Kate noticed that he wasn't out of breath. At all. That was so annoying that she ran even faster. "It doesn't make me feel like I need to try to break the land speed record."

She made it to the turn of the road that led farther into

town. That put them at about two miles from Isaac's sister's house—which Kate would count as four, because she always counted miles as doubles in weather like this. It was that much harder to move. She stopped running, and hated the fact that she was panting a bit. She could see his breath in the air, too, but he looked as if he could run at twice the pace she'd set, straight up the side of Denali and on into forever.

And sure, that was the entire point of his existence. That was who he was.

But it still irritated her.

"And I'm thinking about communities," she told him. The sky really was getting brighter, so she pulled her headlamp down around her neck and scowled at him, not caring that her eyelashes were frozen. His were, too. It only made his eyes that much more formidable. "Some people are put on this earth to bond. To make connections. To form big and little groups, or whatever you want to call it."

"I call it being a person, actually."

"But as I've already proved more than once, my purpose on this earth is to seek out unhealthy communities and either set them on the path to a healthier future or take them apart. That's good work. It's my work. There aren't a lot of people who can do it."

"Is this your résumé?" She didn't hear that signature laugh of his, but it still seemed to fill the air between them, like the puff of his breath against the frigid air. "I already know what you do, Kate. It's why we're up here in subzero weather, preparing to take on the second coming of Samuel Lee Holiday's freaky family compound."

Kate hopped from foot to foot to keep her body temperature from dropping. "All I'm saying is that some people, because of who they are and what they do, need to maintain certain distances. Surgeons are cold and off-putting. People make jokes about their bedside manner. It's a big cliché, but the reality is, they have to be more scientific than social. Or how could they do what they need to do?"

"You're going to have to leave me a trail of breadcrumbs here," Templeton said, though he didn't sound confused. He sounded entertained. And maybe a little chilly. "Because you lost me long before you got to bedside manners."

"Not everybody can sail through life with a big belly laugh and a few off-color remarks, Templeton."

That landed awkwardly. And distinctly, in that space between them.

"You know what the song says," Templeton drawled. "We couldn't all be cowboys, no matter how much we might want to be. Some of us, it turns out, were always going to end up clowns."

"That sounds like a stupid song."

"Only because you've obviously never heard it."

Kate turned then and ran even faster back toward the house. And she couldn't have said what she was running away from at that point. That tone in his voice. The look she was sure she'd seen on his face. Much too kind. Far too understanding.

Or worse still, the sure knowledge that once again he had her acting irrationally.

And making all the things she didn't like about this situation *even worse* despite her efforts to stop what felt like a terrible avalanche into emotion and sensation, connection and intimacy, and all the other things she wanted no part of. Ever.

But once they were back at the house, it was almost like those strange, embarrassing moments in the dark hadn't happened at all. They both took showers, then packed up and met downstairs again. Kate rustled up a relatively decent breakfast from the kitchen cabinets while Templeton made more coffee, and she could almost pretend that she didn't keep revealing herself to this man.

Over and over and over again.

"Are you ready to do this?" Templeton asked.

Like they had a little holiday shopping planned on the twenty-third of December. A merry run to the stores for unnecessary items to wrap in shiny paper and foist upon others, or mysterious things people seemed to want only at this time of year, like mulled wine or fruitcake. Instead of a strategic approach to a potentially dicey, cultish operation that would be all the more fraught because said cultish operators were related to Kate.

Kate had the deeply uncharacteristic and irrational urge to jump all over that question. She wanted to parse it to death and ask him why exactly he was implying that she might not be ready.

But she bit her tongue. Literally bit it.

Because it occurred to her that it was possible she was the teensiest bit anxious.

"Let's go," was all she said.

Templeton called in as he drove, updating Isaac and then Jonas. And Kate knew she should feel pleased that he kept them on speaker, so she could take part in the conversation. Or pleased that she didn't have to ask him to include her. Because this was a job, after all. Just a job, nothing more.

No matter all those edgy and awkward and distressingly *melty* things that felt like a whole lot more than a job kicking around within her.

"Are you thinking it's going to be a full-fledged party down there?" Isaac asked, something on his end making noise, which was unusual. Kate remembered then that even Isaac did a family thing over the holidays.

She should have been more excited to finally be doing something regular people did, even if she was doing it with that typical Holiday family spin.

"I think it's going to be an interview," Kate replied.

"Perhaps slightly more awkward than most, given the family connection."

"But we're going in with party favors," Templeton assured his leader. "Just in case."

The drive from Fairbanks to Nenana was slow but unremarkable, except for the inevitable idiot driving way too fast for the wintry road conditions. The sun came up as the Parks Highway split from the railroad that headed left toward the railroad bridge and followed the road over the separate bridge for passenger vehicles. And when they drove into the village of Nenana, over the frozen Tanana river, with its glimpse over the hardy river town on the southern bank, Kate couldn't help but remember what it had been like to come into this same town that Christmas Day long ago. She'd spent hours on that snowmobile, following this same river in from the east. She'd ditched the snowmobile on Front Street when it ran out of gas, then walked—stumbled—south to find the Troopers.

It had been fifteen years since that walk in weather as unpleasant as today's. In the dark, after her terrifying ride away from the compound. And yet Kate felt it lodged there beneath her ribs this morning like a deep bruise. As if coming back here, for this reason and at this time of year, had dislodged something inside her. Something hard and heavy that left marks.

But she didn't say a word.

They drove past the village, then turned at the mile marker Kate's contacts had indicated would lead them to the new Holiday compound. The road was more of a suggestion than anything else, and the rest of the directions were very Alaskan. *Drive out past the power lines, then go about five miles until the burned-out cabin. Take a left and go another few miles—when you see all the spruce trees, you're close.*

"My plan is to drive right up to the front door and see what happens," Templeton said as they left the power lines behind. "Any objections?"

"None whatsoever."

Though Kate could think of approximately nine hundred objections, none of them rational. All of them emotional.

She checked her weapon, found it as satisfactory as the last three times she'd checked it, and secured it again.

The day was good and broken by the time they found the spruce trees and saw the curl of smoke that indicated a nearby cabin. The winter light was pale and pretty, lighting up the snow-covered hills and making the confluence of frozen rivers gleam in the distance.

And Kate didn't have any particular memories about this stretch of the land around Nenana. The family compound hadn't been in this direction. Still, as they bumped along toward the house, there was something about knowing that she was going to see her family members. It made a clearing she knew she'd never been in before in her life seem familiar. Maybe it was the house itself when they reached it, built in ramshackle Alaskan style, with outbuildings and additions slapped on here and there.

But no people.

Templeton pulled up in front of the house and cut the engine.

"This doesn't feel right," Kate said.

The back of her neck tingled. She couldn't put her finger on why.

"No lights on," Templeton said in his low voice. "It's December. The sun just came up. Where are the lights? And why don't we hear a generator?"

But Kate didn't have time to think that one through.

Or even answer him.

Because that was when the shooting started.

Sixteen

A split second after the first bullet slammed into the ground in front of the SUV, Templeton and Kate were moving.

Like one.

Kate threw herself down, reaching for her weapon as she scanned the scene outside. Templeton tossed the car into reverse, wheeling them back so the SUV was at an angle to the house and could offer some protection.

"One shooter," Kate reported. "He's on the roof."

"I see him."

Templeton slammed the SUV into park, tossed his door open, and then rolled out of the vehicle. He opened his mouth to order Kate to follow him, but she was already right there, moving smoothly to duck down next to him, with the SUV between them and the house. He was glad they'd both suited up for exposure to the outdoors shortly after they'd turned off the highway—because you never knew—or they would be in a lot more trouble than they already were.

And then, without discussing it, Kate kept eyes on the

idiot playing sniper from the roof while Templeton checked the surrounding area for any other trigger-happy maniacs.

"All clear," he told Kate in a low voice after a few tense moments and another shot that, like the first few, slammed into the frozen ground in the space between them and the house. "I think that joker is the only active threat."

"That's one way to put it," Kate said grimly. "I'm seventy-five percent certain that's my cousin Russ up there."

"Only seventy-five percent?"

"The last time I saw him he was a chubby kid. The man on the roof is bearded and could be anywhere between twenty and forty years old." Kate blew out a breath. Then another. "Cover me."

He had an inkling of what she was about to do when she holstered her weapon. And had to check himself, because if any other member of Alaska Force had made the same move, Templeton wouldn't have blinked. Yet here he was thinking about how much he wanted to keep her in one piece.

But a man could think like a Neanderthal without acting like one. Or giving in to the things that churned around in him that couldn't possibly be emotions.

So he propped himself up against the SUV, ostentatiously pointing his own weapon right at no-longer-chubby Cousin Russ. If that was who it was. All Templeton saw was one more backwoods fool with a beard longer than his common sense.

"If I start shooting, friend," Templeton called, letting his voice ring out into the quiet of the frigid morning, "I'm not going to hit three feet in front of you."

"I missed you on purpose," came the reply from the roof. "I won't miss again."

"Then it looks like we have a stalemate," Templeton drawled, loud enough to reach to the windows all over the front part of the house, where he could see the suggestion of shadows and knew that whoever else lived here was watching.

"Russ?" Kate called, sounding remarkably friendly as she stepped out from behind the car, her hands up in the air. "Is that you?"

The Neanderthal in Templeton distinctly disliked the way she stepped out even farther, marching a few paces closer to the house. It left her completely exposed, and he hated it.

The strategist in him, on the other hand, admired both the move itself and how coolly she executed it.

"It's me, Russ," she called again, like she was someone's elderly neighbor on a television show. "Your cousin Kate."

The man on the roof spat. In disgust, presumably.

And for a long, tense moment, nothing else happened.

"What do you want?" the man demanded right when Templeton was beginning to feel itchy, like maybe he should shoot something to keep the ball rolling.

He could tell that Kate figured that question was a tacit agreement that the guy was, in fact, her cousin. Or he assumed that was what her serene trooper smile was all about.

"It's the holiday season," she said, loud enough to bounce back from the house. "People are ripe for reconciliation and reunion this time of year, don't you think?"

"What I think is that you're trespassing," Russ called down into the clearing. He let out a disgruntled sort of noise. "Cousin."

"It's good to see you, too," Kate called back. Like she meant it.

It was impossible not to admire his trooper. Templeton didn't try.

There was the sound of locks being thrown, and then the front door of the cabin opened. Templeton moved his gaze from the idiot on the roof for no more than a split second, but it was enough to get a picture. A woman stood there, a regular shotgun in her arms and a scowl on her face. She looked nothing like Kate. She was rounder and softer, though her face looked more like a long-haul road in winter, cracked and hard and salted besides.

But he recognized that scowl. This was clearly Kate's cousin Liberty.

"Are you hunting us down," Liberty asked, her voice hard. "Again?"

"If I was hunting you down, I would be here with a SWAT team," Kate replied, still sounding cheerful. As if they were exchanging Christmas cookie recipes, not gunfire.

Liberty motioned to Templeton with the muzzle of the shotgun, another thing Templeton did not care for. At all. "What do you call him?"

"My insurance policy." Kate's smile widened. "Seeing as Cousin Russ is lying on the roof with a shotgun, I suspect you know a thing or two about insurance policies."

"We haven't broken any laws," Liberty said, though she lowered the shotgun. Fractionally. "Since I know that's what concerns you, Miss Law and Order."

"Trooper Law and Order, thank you," Kate said, still smiling. "I saw Will last night."

"My brother isn't welcome around here." Liberty's voice was hard. "And neither are you."

"All I want to do is talk." Kate looked from Liberty to Russ then back. "We can do that, can't we? Just talk?"

"Not until your goon puts down that gun," came Russ's voice.

Templeton let out one of his better laughs, long and loud. "You first, buddy."

"How about everybody puts down their guns?" Kate asked, a little more edge in her voice. "Like whoever is lurking there behind you, Liberty."

Templeton had already clocked the man lurking in the shadows and suspected there was at least one more adult in that house. But he didn't see any more obvious weapons.

"We don't like strangers," Liberty snapped. "And that's all you are to us, Kate. A stranger. Worse than that, a stranger who used to be family before you sold us all out."

"If I'd sold you out, I would have gained something from the experience," Kate said, as if this were a pleasant conversation, not an armed confrontation in the bitter cold. "I can't say I did."

"You got the attention you always wanted," Liberty retorted. "You had no trouble stepping right into that spotlight, did you?"

"I was a fifteen-year-old girl. Terrified for my life." Kate shook her head, and Templeton thought her smile was a little edgier than before. "We don't have to do this, do we? I know why you hate me. I don't think we need to do a point-by-point analysis of all the reasons why I think you shouldn't. We're unlikely to reach an agreement. Still, I'd like to talk to you. Maybe somewhere where we're not all risking frostbite or worse."

There was another long, tense silence. Templeton kept his eyes on the roof. Because as much as he wanted to keep watch over Kate—maybe he wanted that too much, a detail he was going to have to examine when he wasn't some idiot's idea of winter target practice—he knew that this was like any day on the job for her. And that she knew what she was doing. She'd lowered her hands to her sides, and he'd bet everything he had that his trooper was quicker on the draw than her cousin. Than either one of her cousins.

"Fine," Liberty said.

She let out a piercing whistle. Templeton watched Russ scowl but lower his weapon. Templeton took his sweet time doing the same.

Liberty watched him closely, like she was expecting a trick. "You can leave your insurance policy outside."

Kate smiled. "That's not going to happen."

Templeton was surprised that there was no argument. Liberty glared at him, but then jerked her chin in what he chose to take as an invitation, though the way she stepped deeper into the house could have been read as ominous.

He ambled inside behind Kate, and it wasn't lost on him that once again, they fell into the kind of patterns that usually took a hell of a lot more time to develop. She marched in with all the confidence in the world, putting on a show. He followed, looking and acting lazy and aimless, and took in all the details.

"I see you share the same decorating taste as our parents," Kate was saying. Templeton glanced around the stark room with no furniture, which that would have been a living room in any other house. It was empty, the way it looked at first glance, save for the huge yellow flag covering most of one wall with a snake coiled in the middle of it and the words DON'T TREAD ON ME emblazoned across the bottom. There were mats along the walls, but no television or comfortable sofa. And the wall across from the flag appeared to double as an armory.

"Do you all sit around and meditate together?" Templeton asked. "This looks like a great yoga room."

All he got in return were a few stray growls. And that gleam in Kate's gaze when she glanced over at him.

But all that muttering kept the attention on his outrageousness. He was more interested in the individual who stood behind Liberty, whom he could now see fully. The man was all dark brows and another epic beard to match. And up at the top of the narrow staircase that led to the open loft area above, there was a woman even rounder and softer than Liberty. She looked like a fertility statue as she corralled two surprisingly quiet kids under ten or so, a tearstained toddler, and the baby she wore in a sling.

At least the presence of potential spouses meant things

here were a lot less Appalachian than they'd seemed on paper, he thought. Because Templeton had made a whole career out of finding the silver lining anywhere he looked.

"Kate was terrified by our childhood," Liberty was saying. It took Templeton a moment to realize she was responding to his ridiculous yoga remark. "We weren't."

"So you and Russ figured you'd move back to the old stomping grounds?" Kate asked, and once again, she was in total trooper mode.

As if this weren't her family. As if she were answering a call, didn't know these people, and hadn't grown up in a room a lot like this one.

An image Templeton really didn't like at all.

Because he wouldn't like anyone growing up here, he assured himself. Sternly. Including the kids who lived here now. It had nothing to do with any inappropriate emotional connection to—

Shut up, dumbass.

Templeton concentrated on the information he was receiving from the house around them. He could hear Cousin Russ's thumping progress down off the roof, then in through a back door. He could hear it every time someone shifted position. It took maybe two full heartbeats for him to pinpoint where every person in the house was standing and to determine that there very likely weren't any surprise visitors hiding in the rooms he couldn't see. Still, *very likely* wasn't an *all clear*. He kept his back to the wall so that, if he was wrong, he could disarm Liberty and the man he assumed was her husband with maybe three moves. Then help himself to one of the weapons displayed on the wall behind them, if necessary.

"It's beautiful here," Liberty was saying, a harder note in her voice that made it seem highly unlikely she was an avid hiker, outdoor sports enthusiast, or, say, an arctic photographer. "We were homesick."

"You either have a heart for this land or you don't," Russ said, stamping in from the back of the house, looking red from the cold and bitter straight through.

"I was unaware that hearts were involved in anything that happened out here," Kate replied lightly. "I thought it was mostly manual labor, hunger, and my father's endless, unhinged lectures."

"Your father is a great man," Russ said darkly. "A *great* man. You watch your mouth when you talk about him."

"Or what?" Kate asked. But she managed to make it sound like it wasn't a direct challenge, more that she was musing on the topic. "The thing is, Russ, you might think he's a great man, and you're welcome to your opinion, of course. But the state of Alaska and the federal government disagree."

"This isn't the right place to rehash all your lies," Liberty said, and she did not sound light or musing. "Is that why you came here? You think you can poison us the way you did my brother?"

"Will didn't seem particularly poisoned to me," Kate observed.

"You're both traitors," Russ growled. "End of story."

"Once again," Kate said quietly, "the state of Alaska disagrees. They don't like it when people kill their law enforcement officers. And they took a dim view of the ritual that claimed the lives of two people that all the adults in this family allowed to happen. I'm not sure truly great men come with a body count."

"Lies," Russ shouted. "We all know how you twisted it. But no one in this family is responsible for two grown adults who chose to walk out into a winter storm."

"Naked," Kate reminded him. "And so far out in the bush that even if they changed their minds, it wouldn't have mattered."

"You can't blame our family for other people's

choices," Liberty chimed in, the same impassioned—or unhinged—note in her voice.

"I understand that's what you believe," Kate said after a moment, and maybe Templeton was the only person in the room who could hear the fury she was obviously trying to conceal. She took a breath, then smiled. "There's no need to litigate it here."

Because, Templeton knew, she had been cross-examined on this subject repeatedly. Her parents, her aunts and uncles, her father's cousins—Kate had been a star witness for the prosecution in each one of their trials. She'd been called to the stand at their appeals.

And none of that changed the fact that of the small handful of nonfamily members who had been a part of this group all those years ago, two had ended up dead. Both after participating in what the Holiday family called *the ritual*. The one Cousin William had referred to yesterday, which involved a so-called test of worth against an Alaskan winter. The remains of Christine Cotter had washed downstream two summers before Kate walked into the Nenana Trooper station. The remains of her husband, Gerald Cotter, had never been found.

"Let's say that the ritual was benign in every way," Kate said now. "That doesn't change the fact that the family was also sending out explosives through the mail. And it certainly doesn't change the fact that when the troopers came out to the compound, our parents refused to surrender."

"Why are you here?" Liberty asked again, impatiently. "We're not the audience for your lies. We know what actually happened."

"You invaded private property with weapons; you shouldn't be surprised if what you get is an armed response," the man behind Liberty chimed in. "We're within our rights to defend our land."

"I take it this is your husband, Liberty," Kate said. She smiled sunnily at the man. "I'm Liberty's cousin Kate. I'm guessing you've heard of me."

"This is Scott." Liberty exchanged glances with him. "Life went on without you, Kate. Like you never existed. And let me tell you this right now. You might have ruined our childhood, but you're not going to ruin the rest of our lives."

"I'm not here to ruin anything."

"We're not breaking any laws," Russ said.

"I think you'll find that shooting at an Alaska State Trooper is generally frowned upon, no matter the circumstances." Kate was still smiling. "But because we're family and it's almost Christmas, I'm prepared to overlook that."

"We don't need any favors from you," Scott growled.

"The other option is that I call for backup and have the Troopers swarming all over this place within the hour, which I'm guessing you won't like," Kate said dryly. "So really, it's up to you."

"If you want something, say what it is," Liberty threw at her, her pitch rising. "If you just came here to stir things up because you need more attention, you need to go."

"Do you have your own plane?" Kate asked calmly.

"What do you care?" Russ demanded. Next to him, Scott muttered something he was very lucky Templeton couldn't quite hear.

"It's a yes-or-no question," Kate said, and continued to gaze expectantly at her cousins.

Templeton swept the room, looking from the cluster of children at the top of the stairs—and the blank-faced woman who watched the proceedings down below as if none of it affected her—to the trio of adults standing together on the other side of this weird room, as if they were guarding something. Some kind of temple or treasure.

He put his money on drugs of one sort or another. Or illegal weapons.

But what he bet they didn't have was a plane.

"And no," Russ said, as if he was offended by the question in the first place. "We don't have a plane. We don't have the same uppity needs that you do."

"What uppity needs do you mean?" Kate asked him, sounding slightly less calm. "The ability to do my job?"

"I'm more interested in how you know what kind of needs your cousin has, uppity or otherwise," Templeton said then. "Living all the way out here the way you do and not having spoken in years."

Liberty rolled her eyes. "I don't think there's a single member of this family that doesn't think it's in their best interests to keep up with what Trooper Holiday is doing. Seeing as how she went and built a whole career out of betraying her nearest and dearest. Who's to say she won't do it again?"

"What do you think would have happened if I hadn't left that night?" Kate asked her softly. But this time that softness was temper, not entreaty.

"You think we don't ask ourselves that same question every damned day?" Russ demanded.

Liberty nodded her agreement, her eyes narrowed. "For one thing, the family wouldn't be in pieces."

"It's always a pleasure to learn how little my life matters when stacked up next to the rest of the family," Kate said dryly. "All of our relatives are still alive, Russ. If I hadn't left that night, I'm not sure I'd be able to say the same."

"Boo freaking hoo," Russ growled. "You look fine to me."

"I want to hear more about the tabs you keep on Kate," Templeton said then. He didn't move from where he stood. But he did widen his stance, and found it entertaining when the two other men in the room stood taller, puffing out their chests like he couldn't take them both with his hands tied behind his back. "Because that sounds a lot like a kind of threat."

"It's not a threat to type a name into a search engine," Liberty snapped. "Seems like we can't go more than six months without another glowing write-up on the life and times of everybody's favorite Alaska State Trooper."

Kate smiled again. "I appreciate your support."

"All we want is to be left alone," Liberty hurled at her. "You and Will don't seem to get that there are consequences to actions, like Father Samuel always said. I would have thought that you, of all people, would know that."

"What kind of consequences are we talking about here?" Kate asked her. "Because everybody in the family seems to be unduly fire-happy. You blow anything up lately?"

"You reap what you sow," Liberty intoned, a lot like she was throwing down her version of a prayer. "You can count on that."

"Again," Templeton drawled. "That's hitting me like a threat."

"Oh, that's what this is," Russ said then. He let out a little laugh. Like a huff of satisfaction. "Someone threatened you, you got your panties in a twist, and your first thought was us. What that says to me is that you know what you did, no matter what lies you tell in court. You know that the first place to look is at the people you wronged."

"The first place we're looking is at the lowlifes and lunatics," Templeton said conversationally. "So."

"I don't think I wronged any of you, Russ," Kate said, and her voice was crisp now—possibly in an effort to keep Russ from doing something truly stupid like launching himself at Templeton. A quick and fun way to knock himself out, to Templeton's way of thinking. "I'm interested, in a distant sort of way, in the psychology it takes to consider yourselves victims while supporting the people who are responsible for the deaths of two individuals they called friends. Not to mention the outright murder of two men who were only doing their jobs. That takes some willful suspension of disbelief." She made a show of looking around the room, from the ugly flag to the shrine to the Second Amendment. Then back at her cousins. "However, it's clear to me that's what the two of you are good at. I can't imagine what you think you're going to get out of re-creating the horror of that compound. I feel sorry for your children. But you're right, you're not breaking any laws. Not yet."

"Let's circle back to reaping and sowing," Templeton suggested.

"That's the beauty of this," Liberty said then, her gaze like stone and her mouth twisted. "I don't have to do anything to you, Kate. We're just out here, living our lives the way we want. Lives you tried to take from us years ago."

"It's funny, though, that only one side took lives, and it isn't me."

"You're filled with guilt and shame, and you should be," Liberty continued, and her voice changed. It got . . . calm. In a creepy way that made Templeton's neck itch. "You need to make us the enemy. When I think you know better, Katie. The only real enemy is you."

"A merry Christmas to you, too, cousin," Kate murmured, something like grief in her gaze, though she was still smiling.

Russ snorted. "Why am I not surprised that the family traitor is a capitalist?"

Kate shook her head. "You sound just like him."

"I take that as a compliment," Russ snarled. "Father Samuel is a great man. A true martyr for the cause. I'm honored to follow his example."

Templeton restrained himself from pointing out that martyrs usually died.

"Does that mean you want to spend the rest of your life

in prison, too?" Kate was asking her cousin. "Because that can be arranged, Russ. Just give me an excuse."

"It doesn't matter where Father Samuel is," Liberty said. "His messages are in here."

And she tapped on her chest. Hard.

"When I check his visitor logs down there in Spring Creek, am I going to see your name?" Kate asked. She tilted her head slightly. "Or does he communicate directly into your heart?"

Her cousins looked at each other, then back at her. And when Liberty smiled again, it was . . . unsettling.

"*We* don't turn our back on our family," Liberty said. "It's a privilege to be able to visit Father Samuel when we can. Will's afraid to go. Just like he's afraid to come here. I bet he didn't mention that when he sent you here."

"Never could choose a side," Russ said derisively.

"I never thought we'd lay eyes on you again." And Liberty's voice was almost a singsong. Templeton's neck itched again. More than before. "But Father Samuel knew different. He always promised that you'd return to face judgment."

"I won't be back again," Kate assured her. "And if I am, Liberty, make no mistake. It will be to escort you to your own jail cell. If that's not the judgment you're looking for, my advice to you is to follow less in the footsteps of a crazy person."

Liberty laughed. "He was right about you. Back then, and now. He was right about Will. He's right about *everything*. Don't you get tired of pretending otherwise?"

"He's a creep," Kate said softly. "An unhinged narcissist who preys on weak-minded people, Liberty. Like the children he groomed to be his willing accomplices. Like you."

And that was how Templeton knew that all of this was getting to Kate, no matter how calm and collected she pretended to be.

Her words were like a lit match tossed down into a

puddle of gasoline, and he had to think she knew they would be.

Liberty snarled in outrage. There was a shocked sound from the landing up above, but Templeton kept his gaze on the two men. It took approximately one second for Kate's words to sink in, and then Russ moved.

He launched himself toward Kate like he planned to beat his feelings directly into her face.

Kate sidestepped him, smooth and easy.

Which meant the only face Russ had in front of him was Templeton's.

Templeton put him down. Harder than necessary. Then held him there, with a foot at his neck. Happily filtering out the screaming from the loft above and the blue streak Liberty's husband was swearing up and down.

Liberty herself moved toward Kate as if she intended to finish her brother's job, but it was Kate who stopped her dead.

"One more step," she told her in a voice that was entirely steel-edged trooper, "and you too will be facedown on the floor with a foot on your neck. My foot. Do you understand me?"

Templeton hadn't gotten around to asking Kate if she had any martial arts training or self-defense experience. Probably because he was far more interested in all that sleek fitness of hers on a very personal level. But he could see from the way she stood, on the balls of her feet and perfectly ready for whatever might come, that she did.

Of course she did. She knew whose daughter she was. He imagined that on some level, Kate had been preparing for a day like this since that night she'd lit out of that original compound on a snowmobile in the winter dark.

Something he couldn't really let himself think about too hard, especially not when he had her cousin at his mercy.

"If I wanted to," Kate said into the tense silence, "I could bring all of you in. There are always consequences for behavior, on that we agree, but I won't strip you both down and throw you outside to see if you can magically survive the elements. I'm not a monster. You can't say the same about yourselves. Or the man you think is so great that he planned to sacrifice his own child because I dared to have thoughts of my own. I hope you remember that when your own kids start acting up, the way kids do."

"I hope I never see you again," Liberty gritted out. "Unless it's reading your obituary."

"Keep making threats," Kate suggested. "It's not going to end well for you."

But she didn't ask any more questions. She stepped away from Liberty and headed toward the door. She slid a look Templeton's way as she went, and he understood it at once.

He let Russ up, grinning when the other man scrambled to his feet, red-faced and puffing with fury. He looked as if he was about to take another swing. Templeton wished he would.

"I'd think twice if I were you, friend," he drawled, because he really was a saint. "I have six inches on you, not to mention enough training to knock you out before you hit the ground. Twice. Choose wisely."

"You better pray to God I don't shoot you in the back on your way out of here," Russ all but shouted at him.

"I hope you do," Templeton replied lazily. "I'll die a happy man, knowing you'll join the rest of your creepy family behind bars. Which is where all of you belong, as far as I'm concerned."

And then, because it was insulting, Templeton turned his back on the room and took his time sauntering outside, following Kate to the SUV.

Her cousins followed them out, standing in their

clearing with different degrees of rage and hatred all over their faces.

And later, Templeton would look back and pick this as the moment that his heart sustained a fatal blow.

Because beside him, his prickly, tough, ridiculously beautiful trooper smiled big and bright, then gave her family a cheerful wave as they drove away.

Seventeen

"It makes me sick to say this out loud," Kate said about halfway through their drive back to Fairbanks, while the low sun hit them too bright to last and the temperature sank like a stone, "but I think I have to visit my father."

She'd been fighting it since they'd left Russ and Liberty's nauseating new version of the same old compound. She hadn't wanted to think it, much less say it out loud.

And she was holding her breath, she realized, as she waited for Templeton's answer.

"I'd like to visit your father," Templeton said shortly. "But not in a prison where we'll be monitored."

That was gratifying. She was surprised at how it worked its way through her like separate strands of warmth, braiding together and wrapping all around her. And she hadn't understood how cold she felt until he heated her up a little.

"But yeah," Templeton said after a moment. "That seems like a reasonable next move."

"Russ and Liberty seem as deluded as I remember the entire family being, back in the day," Kate said, staring out the windshield in front of her at the wintry, snowy highway, because that still felt safer than looking directly at Templeton Cross. "But they said they don't have a plane. That fits with what the troopers told me about them. They don't have the capability to fly themselves in and out of the Panhandle to make mischief for Alaska Force or break into my apartment. They would have to fly commercial, which I doubt they can afford. Or involve a third party. And none of that gels in my head with freaky little wannabe cult members, hunkered down for the winter out there. But not too far out there, so they can drive into Nenana for supplies."

"Agreed." Templeton shifted his big body in his seat. "Oz is already doing deeper background checks. If any of them flew commercial in the past six months, we'll know soon. And knowing Oz, he's going to dig into all the private planes that left the airport in Nenana over the last month. I'll nudge him on that, too."

The winter road was loud, no matter how quiet it was inside the car.

"I think Liberty wanted me to feel threatened, but I don't think she was being specific so much as mean," Kate said after another little while passed. "On the other hand, I'm not sure I see my father masterminding any of this from behind bars. For one thing, how would he even know what Alaska Force was, much less where you keep old storage facilities?"

Templeton grunted. "Excellent point."

He made another call into Alaska Force HQ while Kate stared out at the road. The temperature kept dropping, mirroring how cold she felt, but she ordered herself to remain calm.

Will last night. Liberty and Russ today. And now, potentially, her father tomorrow?

It was more family than she'd been forced to contend with in years. It was too much family, by any tally. And the real trouble was, being around them was even worse than thinking about them. They made her feel dirty. Tainted.

As if proximity to her cousins had exposed her. The messy, unhinged, potential-cult-member truth of her that she'd spent her whole life trying to hide.

What she didn't understand was why she wasn't doing everything in her power to put distance between herself and Templeton, if not physically, then verbally. Because he'd seen. Because he knew. Because there was no pretending now.

She wasn't going to fling herself out of a moving vehicle on the Parks Highway in the middle of winter while a cold front moved in. Kate had always hated theatrics. But she couldn't help noticing that she hadn't shut down. She was talking to him, when he wasn't on the phone with the rest of Alaska Force. She *wanted* to talk to him. Her brain wasn't madly spinning, trying to come up with escape plans.

When her pulse kicked up, drumming panic throughout her body, she had the sneaking suspicion that it wasn't Templeton or what he'd seen that was making it happen. It was the fact that she didn't mind that he'd seen the truth about who she was as much as she should have.

She was still stuck on that anomaly when they made it back to the little house they'd left this morning, what seemed like whole lifetimes ago. Kate remembered their run, in the razor-blade cold, but it almost felt as if that had been someone else.

She felt cracked wide open like an egg.

And the last thing in the world Kate wanted to do was muck around in all that yolk.

Okay, she told herself testily after Templeton plugged in the car so it would start again in these temperatures when they needed it, then jabbed in the numbers to open the padlock on the front door. *Enough with the egg.*

"Isaac is setting up a flight right now," Templeton told her. "Can you be ready to go in fifteen?"

"I'm ready to go now," Kate replied. And was somewhat astonished that she sounded like her regular old self. As if nothing much had happened today. As if there were no yolk risk. "I'll grab my bag."

Templeton's phone buzzed as they got inside, out of the cold. She ran up the stairs while he answered it, picking up the bag in question and starting back down.

"Why do you have that look on your face?" she asked him, coming to a stop halfway down the steps.

"Ice fog," he said succinctly. "We're not going anywhere."

Kate blinked. The sun had already been down as they'd driven up to the house. The dark was coming in, swift and dangerous, with the temperature already at negative forty and dropping, and she didn't need Templeton to explain to her why ice fog blanketing Fairbanks would keep them grounded. The ice particles in the air made it far too dangerous to fly. It had trapped Kate before, and would again.

She made a show of shrugging and pretended she couldn't feel the way her own heart started to beat too hard, too loud, and too slow beneath her ribs. "That's Alaska," she said, trying to sound as unbothered as she should have felt. "I guess if I was ever really in any kind of hurry, I'd have to think about living somewhere else."

"You've never thought about living anywhere else?" Templeton asked, his voice curiously . . . blank, almost. Maybe it was that he was being careful with her, and she wanted to let that ruffle her feathers. But she couldn't quite get there. "I can see you not wanting to stay in the state where most of your family lives."

"I thought about leaving," Kate admitted. "A lot, when I was younger. Trouble was, I couldn't think of any place I wanted to go badly enough. There are nice places out there, don't get me wrong. But none of them are Alaska."

Something shuddered deep inside of her when Templeton failed to smile. He didn't flash that grin. He didn't let out one of his huge laughs. He stood there at the bottom of the stairs, an almost stern expression on his face.

And there was no pretending he wasn't an attractive man. A beautiful man. When he was smiling, laughing, throwing that booming voice of his around, he was like a thunderstorm in the summertime, washing everything clean all around him whether it wanted it or not.

But when he was still, he reminded her of all the reasons she loved it here in her home state. He was that astonishing. Rugged and infinitely dangerous. And he made something deep in her belly tremble every time he looked at her.

"I'll get the stove going," he said quietly. Hushed, even, as if he felt it, too. This heavy tension between them that coiled inside of Kate until she was afraid it might pop at any moment.

He moved off toward the kitchen and Kate pulled in a breath, only aware then that she'd been holding it. She felt a loose kind of relief, but she didn't sit there and dig around in the feeling to see what it was made of. Maybe she didn't dare. She turned around, carried her bag back upstairs, and marched herself into the bathroom to splash a little water on her face.

And get herself back under control.

The rest of the evening slid easily enough into another night that Kate might have called pleasant if she weren't so on guard. Against herself.

And against how easy it was to spend time with Templeton.

They spent a long time going through all the files Oz had compiled on Samuel Lee Holiday and his prison records—which Kate knew she should have objected to Alaska Force having in the first place. But she was far more interested in preparing herself for the confrontation with her father.

"Maybe I'm kidding myself," she said much later, after they'd both read more or less everything there was to read about the man who'd given her life and had tried to take it away, too, fifteen years and two days ago. "Maybe this has always been inevitable."

"You don't have to do it."

Templeton sounded so matter-of-fact it made Kate blink. She studied him, lounging the way he always did, as if a mere armchair could not contain him. As if he were called upon to demonstrate his bonelessness at every turn. His legs were thrust out before him. He'd kicked off his boots and, like her, had nothing on his feet but wool socks to cut the chill. Though she doubted he felt that much chill, since all he was wearing was a T-shirt.

And she didn't want to admit how much energy she was expending *not* ogling the corded muscles that made up his arms, or the way his biceps stretched against his sleeves.

"You don't have to do it," Templeton said again. "You're not in this alone, Kate. I get this is your family and it feels personal, but it's only as personal as we let it be. Alaska Force is behind you. I'm here. And I'm perfectly prepared to have a friendly chat with your father." His mouth kicked over into one of those dangerous curves. "Perfectly prepared and raring for the chance to go at him, if I'm honest."

Her heart flipped over. Because Kate couldn't think of another time in her adult life that someone had told her that she wasn't alone. That she was part of a team, and it wasn't contingent on her doing a job or impressing everyone with her commitment.

No one had ever made sure she knew that they were willing to jump in if she couldn't do something, for whatever reason. And not only jump in. She'd had partners before. She'd relied on them, to one extent or another, as appropriate.

But she'd never trusted that if she truly needed help, they wouldn't use that against her down the line.

Something twisted, deep in her gut, at the notion that

she trusted Templeton in a whole different way. Not only to have her back, or to step in here if needed. Kate knew—she just *knew*—that he would never hold something like that against her. Never.

She felt a little bit light-headed.

"We have to decide what the best strategy is here," she made herself say.

"I love me some strategy," Templeton drawled. "But what's important is the fact that there's an emotional component to this. It's not some random drug bust. You're putting on a good show, but I can tell that your cousins got to you."

She made herself smile. "I'm choosing to view them as a warm-up. The way to dip my toe in before jumping into the ocean for a little polar bear dip, like we do up here in the frozen north."

Not that she, personally, had ever flung herself into frigid water for no apparent reason.

"Kate. It would be weird if it wasn't emotional."

"I'm not denying that there's an emotional component," she said briskly. Knowing full well that she would absolutely have denied it if she thought she could do so convincingly. "I'm wondering if it makes more sense to use that emotion or not. Do we let my father think he's winning whatever game he imagines he's playing? Or do we sidestep all that and let you go in instead?"

"Why, Trooper. Be still my heart. Are you voluntarily brainstorming with me?"

She tried to frown sternly at him, but the way her mouth twitched probably ruined the effect. "I don't mind letting my father think he's rattled me if that gets us what we want."

"I do."

And there it was again, that intense connection between them, so strong she could almost see it shimmering there above the coffee table.

"You were the one who suggested we look into my

family," she said. "I could have told you that turning over these rocks would lead us straight to the worms." She pulled in a deep breath. "I don't know, maybe it's healthy. Otherwise it all festers there, doesn't it?"

"The past is just the past." Templeton's gaze was intent on hers then. "It's not healthy or unhealthy. It happened. It's over."

"We're all steeped in our past all the time, Templeton. The past makes us who we are. I have to think it's better to poke at it every now and again, to make sure it's a scar and not an open wound."

"If things hadn't started blowing up in Southeast Alaska, you wouldn't have touched your family with a ten-foot pole."

"Maybe not in person." Kate felt her gaze narrow as she looked at him. "But this conversation is starting to feel less about what I did, or might do, and a little more about you."

He shrugged. "I don't look back, Trooper. Ever."

"Right. You're a shark. If you stop swimming forward, you die."

"Do whatever you want." And Kate was fascinated that he grinned then. Bright, easy. And, without a doubt, completely fake. "All I'm saying is that one of us is a prickly, uptight, lonely trooper who's gotten so used to being all alone in this world that she thinks it's a virtue. And the other one is me. Which one of us do you think is healthier?"

He didn't wait for an answer. He got to his feet in one of his typically, absurdly powerful displays of offhanded might and ease, ran a hand over his head, and let out a booming laugh.

"Right," Kate said, doing a fair approximation of his drawl. Because it was obnoxious. "Mr. Don't Look Back, the Past Has Fangs That I Must Outrun at All Costs, is the epitome of healthy and well-adjusted. But nice try."

Templeton let his gaze move over her, as if he was trying to decide what to do with her. Or what to say, and she braced herself because she knew that whatever he did, it would be a weapon—

But he only shook his head. "I'm going to go see if I can rustle up something a little more filling than a can of soup for dinner. Why don't you stay out here and think about whether you're talking to your father because it's the right move—or because you don't know how to play well with others."

"Super well-adjusted," Kate murmured. "Not taking your ball and going home, or anything like that."

"Keep it up, Trooper," he advised her, and she was sure there was something dangerous in his gaze before he turned and headed for the kitchen. "And I won't feed you."

But he did, of course.

Kate expected him to be surly about it, but that wasn't Templeton's style. He produced a hearty dinner of lamb chops and spinach he liberated from the freezer, mashed potatoes from a box, and even a bottle of wine.

And instead of sitting there, sullen and broody with his nose out of joint, he regaled her with stories of Alaska Force adventures. He was charming. Funny. He certainly knew how to tell a story. But when all the food was gone and they were sitting in the cozy little kitchen that felt like a home, even if it wasn't theirs, all the laughter subsided and Kate gazed at him across the one glass of wine that she'd taken care to nurse, not drink. Because she certainly didn't need a repeat of the last time she had a few glasses of wine around him.

"That's a strange look," Templeton said.

"I'm wondering why you felt you needed to put on a performance tonight."

She expected him to argue. To huff and puff and tell her she'd been imagining things. But instead, that mouth of his crooked up in one corner and made her short of breath.

"Everybody likes a little dinner theater," he drawled. "I figured we could take a break from discussing the Holiday family. You're welcome."

Kate was keenly aware that these kinds of conversations with Templeton were dangerous. *He* was dangerous. All of this was woven through with that highly charged thing that hummed between them and felt a lot like *inevitability*, and it would take very little to blow it all up.

Very, very little.

She did the dishes instead. She washed and Templeton dried, another thing they seemed to fall into as if they'd choreographed it, but without saying a word.

Kate blamed the house. The fact that it felt so cozy, so lived in. A real home, unlike any of the places she'd lived in over the years. And there was something about being here with Templeton that tugged at her. The fire was so warm, the light was so bright, when there was all that darkness and ice fog outside.

The man had made her dinner. Twice. And had made her laugh, because he could and because there had already been a little too much nastiness.

Kate wished he would grab her. Make a pass. She knew what to do with that kind of overtness. It was kindness that she didn't know how to digest. It was the fact that he was good to her for no discernible reason except that, beneath all that danger and skill he wore so casually, he was actually the good man she'd been sure he couldn't be back when she'd met him in Grizzly Harbor for the first time.

And even thinking that *did things* to her.

They'd eaten late, which meant it was the easiest thing in the world to excuse herself when the dishes were done and hustle straight up the stairs before she was tempted to sink into all that heat he generated. Before she gave in to all those strange sensations that swirled around and around inside of her and made her imagine that heat like his could swallow her whole yet not burn.

She was sure she would drop off to sleep in an instant after such a strange and emotional couple of days. But instead, she read on her phone until late. She heard Templeton come upstairs, then the door across the hall from hers open and shut.

Kate slept fitfully when she finally closed her eyes, falling in and out of anxious dreams that she knew were about her family, though none of them appeared as themselves. It was all faceless monsters and frightening beasts. And when she woke in the morning, she was annoyed that she hadn't had one of those deliciously wicked dreams about the man across the hall instead.

She went downstairs, not surprised to find that the lights were on and a fresh pot of coffee sat there, already brewed. She wondered if Templeton slept at all or if he simply *waited*, like that Chuck Norris joke. She suspected the latter.

She poured herself a cup of coffee and was getting around to asking herself if she should be alarmed that there was no sign of him when the front door opened and he shouldered his way in, bringing a blast of frigid air with him.

"Still the ice fog," he told her.

She made a noise in commiseration, because the weather meant there would be no run today unless they went out and found a gym with those boring treadmills. It also meant they would be stuck here until it got warmer.

And with no way to work off all your excess nervous energy, a voice inside her said. *Unless . . .*

But she couldn't go there. Particularly not this early in the morning.

"All flights are still grounded," Templeton said, which

she'd expected. "It doesn't look like you and I are getting out of here anytime soon."

"Stranded in the interior. My favorite."

Templeton shrugged out of his cold-weather gear. Then he started toward her. And her heart did that thing again. That low, hard kick filled with a slow, drugging heat, in time with the way he moved.

"This gives us extra time to determine the best strategy to take." She was pleased with how professional she sounded. How pulled together, when she was still on her first cup of coffee. "The reality is that my father was in a prison cell and therefore couldn't possibly have personally blown anything up or killed that poor man. Much less attempted to assault or abduct me. We'll have to wait for Oz's confirmation, but I think we'll find that none of my cousins were in the area, either. I would be very surprised if Liberty and Russ took any excursions. And I'd be shocked if Will did much of anything."

"Fair enough."

"That means someone else is out there, either doing my father's bidding or, like Russ and Liberty, interpreting my father's old wishes to suit themselves."

"Did you stay up all night thinking about this case?" Templeton asked.

And she'd been so busy congratulating herself on her professionalism that she'd somehow failed to notice how close he'd gotten. He was standing next to her at the counter. Right next to her. She kept expecting him to reach past her and help himself to the coffee he'd made, but he didn't. He only looked down at her.

All too-dark eyes, those wicked brows, and cheekbones for days.

"Yes," she lied, and met his gaze as blandly as she could. "I allowed myself some time to process the family emotions it all stirred up and then tried to look at it more analytically. Didn't you?"

"No, ma'am," Templeton said, in that drawl that she

could feel all the way down into her toes, so much so that she had to curl them to keep from shuddering. "I was much more focused on picturing you naked. Again."

"Wh . . . what?"

She heard herself stutter and would have slapped herself, but she was still holding her coffee mug. Something she remembered only when it nearly slipped out of her suddenly nerveless fingers.

Templeton reached over and gently eased the mug from her grip, then set it down on the counter.

"I think you heard me."

"What I heard was so inappropriate that I'm sure I must be mistaken."

"Threaten to shoot me again," he suggested, grinning slightly. "It's hot."

And then he bent his head, snaking one arm around her to haul her toward him, and crushed his mouth to hers.

This time, there was even less build than before.

It was instant immolation.

The shock exploded into need, longing, and the kind of full-body *yes* that had Kate shooting up on her toes, wrapping her arms around his strong neck, and kissing him like her life depended on it.

He picked her up, high against his body, so it was the easiest thing in the world—and somehow natural—to wrap her legs around his waist. And she understood the benefits of a man like him, built huge and powerful, because he held her as if she weighed nothing at all. He broke the kiss to tilt his head back as he carried her out of the kitchen.

"I figured I'd carry you at some point or another," he told her, his dark eyes gleaming. "And I do like to be right."

"Shut up, Templeton."

He laid her down on the soft rug in the center of the living room. And better still, came right down with her.

And then everything was heat and wonder. Her hands all over him, and his hands on her. Testing, tasting.

She stripped off his T-shirt, humming a little in joy and anticipation at the ridged muscles she exposed. Then she bent to the task of tasting each and every one of them. She thought she could have done that forever, but he lifted her after a while and pulled her shirt up and over her head, tossing it aside. Then sent her bra along with it.

And this time, Templeton held her above him. Then tipped her torso toward his mouth so he could get first one nipple against his tongue, then the other.

Sensation streaked through her, like a crackling live wire. She felt his mouth against her breast, and she felt the surge of heat lower still. Between her legs, where she melted and clenched and nearly threw herself over that edge then and there.

They both fumbled with each other's pants until Templeton laughed, pulled her hands from his waistband, and put them on her own.

"Race me," he said.

Kate won. But then they both won, because they were naked together.

Finally.

And for a long, beautifully aching stretch of forever, they just . . . reveled in that. Skin against skin. All the glorious differences in their bodies. The hard wall of his chest against the softness of hers, with the nipples he tasted like bright points of sensation between them. He moved his heavy, muscled thigh between her legs, and both of them groaned when his corded strength met the place where she was softest. Hottest.

And in some distant part of her head, she thought maybe she ought to feel self-conscious about the way she rode his thigh, but she didn't. She couldn't.

Because he kissed her again, and his hands were so big as he cupped her face that it was the easiest thing in the world to rock herself against him, then fling herself over that cliff.

When she shuddered back into awareness, Templeton was fishing a packet out of the pants he'd tossed aside earlier. Then he rolled protection down the steel length of him.

"You're greedy, aren't you?" he asked her as he crawled back to her side. "I like it."

And that was a good thing, because she intended to go right on being greedy. She was still panting, but she pushed herself up and threw herself at him. She pushed at his shoulders, laughing when he toppled over, because she knew full well that if he hadn't wanted to fall backward, she could have pushed against him all day to no avail.

"Lie back," she told him. "Think of baseball or something."

His voice was rough, deep, as she crawled on top of him. "I'd rather think about you."

Kate's hands were shaking. Or maybe she was shaking, inside and out. It was hard to tell.

She didn't know if it was greed or something bigger, wilder. Her heart was still pounding, and she could feel her blood racing through her veins. And she didn't think she would last the hour if she didn't do this. If she didn't make this mad, insane thing in her go away.

And there was only one way to do that.

She settled there astride him, then braced herself against his powerful chest with one hand. With the other, she reached down between them and wrapped her fingers as far around him as they could go.

"Look at me," he commanded her.

And she couldn't help but obey him. Her gaze snapped to his, even as she worked him inside of her. She saw the muscles in his neck go tight. She saw a wild glitter in his gaze, triumph and victory at once.

He had one hand on her hip and the other fisted in her hair.

And Kate knew with every cell and atom in her body

that it was taking every inch of the formidable control this man had to let her do what she was doing. To let her take her time, settling her body against his as she worked that length of him inside her, bit by bit.

And when they were finally flush, she was red everywhere, shaking, and even sweating.

And Templeton smiled.

"Good job, Trooper," he said. "You want to go fast, don't you?"

She wanted to answer him in kind, but she couldn't seem to find the words. Her breath was a tangle, and she couldn't seem to stop shaking.

"Take it slow," Templeton said. "I dare you."

She accepted the challenge.

He held her, but loosely. So she lifted herself, then settled back down on him.

And it was almost too much to bear.

Pleasure speared through her, an intense wallop that might have knocked her sideways if he weren't holding on to her.

She found that the more she moved, the better it felt. Until she could roll her hips, slide herself against him, and it was like magic.

And all the while, Templeton talked.

As if he'd been inside her head for all those dreams and knew things she didn't know about herself. For example, that she'd always wanted a man with a dirty mouth and a whole lot of wicked commands.

Each and every one of which she followed, because they felt good.

Because he felt good.

"Go on," he told her when her breath was ragged and she was shivering against him. "Go over."

That time, when she came apart at the seams, she shouted out his name. Or sobbed it, maybe.

And when she could think again, barely, Templeton was turning them over, coming up over her and taking both her hands in one of his. He stretched her arms up over her head, then grinned down at her, but it was a hard sort of grin, his face carved into a kind of heady sensuality that made Kate shudder all over again.

"My turn," he growled at her.

And then he surged into her.

Once, then again, with a tightly reined ferocity that stormed through Kate. She arched up against him, her hips rising of their own accord to meet his.

And the rhythm he set was blistering. Beautiful.

She thought she was done, but he taught her otherwise. He taught her exactly how much she'd been holding back. And Kate felt moisture form in the corners of her eyes, because she'd never imagined anything could feel like this. So deep. So full. So perfect.

He dropped his head to the crook of her neck, and still he pounded into her. And she held on tight, meeting every thrust.

Connected. The word glimmered in her head, not quite making sense and yet making too much sense at the same time.

All her life she'd wanted this. This close. This intertwined. This incapable of telling one body from another.

She already knew that she never wanted this to end.

And she shattered so hard this time, so intensely, she wasn't entirely sure she would survive it.

But she didn't care, because he was right there with her.

It could have been days, then. Years.

Slowly, dizzily, Kate opened her eyes. Templeton was beside her, sprawled out and breathing hard at last.

He jackknifed up, going all the way to his feet. And she had the distinct pleasure of watching him walk away, gloriously naked. He went into the bathroom, and she heard the water running. She knew she should move. Get up, do something. But she didn't. And when he came back into the room, he stood there for a moment, gazing down at her as if she were a gift.

"I'm gearing up to say something depressingly practical," she told him, but her arms were still thrown up over her head, and the way his smile deepened, she could only imagine what she looked like. Thoroughly debauched, she was sure. "Appropriateness. Working relationship. Blah blah blah."

"Gear up all you want, my little trooper," Templeton said, his voice the deepest and darkest she'd ever heard it. And something almost fierce on his face, as if this wasn't as easy for him as it seemed. "The weather outside is legitimately frightful. And I have plans for you. A lot of plans."

Kate meant to object to that. She really did.

Templeton dropped down to the floor, then prowled toward her on his hands and knees, and she definitely wanted no part of his plans.

She needed to tell him that. She meant to.

But instead, when he wrapped her up in his arms and lifted her up against his shockingly beautiful body again, all Kate could seem to do was melt against him.

Eighteen

"Merry Christmas to you, too, jackhole," Isaac growled into the phone at four thirty in the morning. "Who died?"

The obvious half-asleep crankiness in his best friend's voice made Templeton that much happier that he'd decided to give the boss a call at his typical wake-up time.

"Are you sleeping in?" he asked, laughing. "I'm sorry, who is this? Isaac Gentry? Or some soft-bellied civilian?"

Isaac made a disgruntled sound. "Whether I sleep in or don't is my business and definitely not something I plan to discuss on the phone. At this hour. While crashing on the pullout couch in my grandmother's house."

Isaac sounded . . . almost like a normal human, really. A regular guy—and not because he was putting on a show, for a change.

It was like Santa really had come.

"We spent an extra day in Fairbanks," Templeton said. "Ice fog."

Isaac grunted, because who hadn't found themselves stuck in Fairbanks's inversion layer at some point or another. Templeton opted not to give his friend a play-by-play outline of how he'd spent that extra day.

Trooper Holiday had taken the back of his head off. Repeatedly. Templeton was amazed that he'd managed to wake up at his usual time, shifting from a sound sleep to total alertness instantly, as was his way. And he'd known exactly who was curled up against his chest, nestled into him as if they'd always slept together like this, jigsaw puzzle pieces snapped together.

He'd never been the kind of man who reacted like a scalded cat at the very hint of affection or suggestion of intimacy. He'd never snuck off in the middle of the night, the better to avoid a conversation when the light came in. He left with a smile in the full force of daylight.

But the way he and Kate fit together made every single alarm go off inside him, loud and long. The way they had yesterday—but he hadn't cared then. He'd gone outside to run a perimeter check and get a sense of the predawn weather, and he hadn't been prepared for her when he'd come back inside. She'd been standing there in the kitchen, her brown eyes sleepy and her mouth soft, and Templeton had lost his fight there and then.

He very distinctly remembered thinking, *Rules? What rules?*

Waking up this morning, all he could think about were those rules. And how he'd broken every last one of them.

Over and over again.

He wanted to linger longer there, in the heat of the bed with her soft weight all over him, her hair drifting across his chest.

His heart had kicked at him—hard—like it knew things he didn't about the mess he'd made. That was what had gotten him up and moving.

Because Templeton didn't deviate from his routine. Deviation led to disaster.

And discipline was a practice, not a punishment, as he reminded himself when he went downstairs. Though maybe he was in the mood to punish himself, too, as he banged out his morning set of push-ups, crunches, and burpees, then two extra sets besides to get the blood flowing. He checked the weather, ran the frigid perimeter to make sure there were no uninvited guests of the human variety, then checked to see the status of potential flights.

He'd actually forgotten it was Christmas today. And that Christmas made disgruntled pilgrims out of every man with a family that still held on to expectations of a gathering. Blue was back in the suburb of Chicago he'd once vowed he'd rather bomb than visit, thanks to Everly. Griffin, the coldest and most remote individual Templeton had ever known—until the recent, gradual thawing that Mariah had brought about in him—was subjecting himself to his annual trip home to pretend to his family that he was normal, like them. That had always baffled and entertained Templeton, who had nowhere to go and no one to perform for.

But it was always the thought of Isaac, one of the most dangerous men alive, on a pullout sofa surrounded by his grandmother's relentless Christmas cheer, that made his heart sing.

"Are the planes still grounded?" Isaac asked.

"Negative. They're starting to let flights out at nine."

"Are you headed back to Fool's Cove?"

Templeton stood in the kitchen while the coffeemaker churned and sputtered, scowling out at the dark. "We're heading down to Seward for a touching reunion with Samuel Lee Holiday."

"There's no love here in Anchorage," Isaac said, sounding less grumpy. "Any religious separatist aspirations have taken a back seat to medical bills. Cancer, a couple car accidents. I'm hearing it's the same story in Ketchikan. These malcontents look good on paper, but dig down into it another layer, and there's nothing there."

"We're not finding a different story here," Templeton told him. "The cousins were trigger-happy douchebags yesterday, but I don't see them putting together anything sophisticated enough to sneak beneath our perimeter. We're missing something. Still."

"You figure Samuel Lee Holiday is pulling the strings?"

Templeton considered it. "I think Kate's cousins wish that he was. But everything in Nenana felt more like a vigil than any seething hotbed of vigilante justice for past wrongs. And again, there's only so much one old man can do from a cell."

"What does your trooper think?"

Templeton ran his free hand over his head and hated that lurching sensation in his chest, which felt a whole lot like his heart carrying on in all the ways he'd been sure it never would. Ever again. Because everyone he'd ever loved, or felt something about, ended up dead.

But that wasn't what Isaac had asked him.

"I think she's torn," he said. "Part of her wants it to be him, because she's familiar with that. She took him down once, so she probably thinks she'd do it again. On the other hand, it's obviously better for everyone concerned if he's as impotent as he ought to be."

It was only after he'd answered that Templeton reflected on the fact that Isaac had called Kate *his* trooper.

Crap.

"What's your read?" Isaac asked. He no longer sounded even remotely sleepy. Or, more precisely, he no longer sounded irritated that Templeton had supposedly woken him. Templeton wasn't sure he'd ever heard Isaac sound *truly* sleepy. There was some debate as to whether or not the man actually slept. "Whether it is or isn't her father, do you think she can handle the face-to-face?"

"She can pretend to handle anything. What price she'll have to pay for that later, I don't know."

Isaac was quiet, which gave Templeton an opportunity to play that back to himself. What he should have said was that Kate was a well-trained Alaska State Trooper who could and would conduct herself in a professional manner no matter the circumstances. That's exactly what he would have said if he'd been talking about any other law enforcement officer he might have been partnered with—right after he scoffed at the question even being asked.

He might as well have taken out a billboard to announce his relationship with Kate. He basically had.

"This is none of my business," Isaac began.

"Like that's ever stopped you before."

"Here's what we know about your trooper. She had one of the worst childhoods imaginable, and it's not like you had a great one yourself. She emancipated herself at fifteen, literally. Put every adult in her life in jail. Unlike every other member of her family, she didn't go crazy, didn't spiral into darkness or a repeat of what she left. She became a trooper instead. Climbed the ranks, dedicated her life to taking down groups like her family. Thought that we're one of those groups, so came on out to Grizzly Harbor and subjected herself to the Templeton Cross charm offensive."

"I read her file, Isaac. And was there. I didn't forget any of this."

"Are you telling me that of all the women in the world—a revolting percentage of whom seem to find you attractive, for reasons unclear to me—"

"Bite me."

"—*this* is the woman that you've decided to get close to? After all the carrying-on about your precious rules for all these years?"

"I didn't tell you that. Deliberately."

"Yeah, too bad I know you." Templeton could *see* Isaac shaking his head over three hundred miles away in Anchorage. As if he were standing next to him in this cozy kitchen in Fairbanks. "Big laugh, big show, but if you didn't care about her, you wouldn't be psychoanalyzing what she's *pretending* to feel. You wouldn't have called me at four thirty to update me on your mission parameters when a text would do."

"I was filled with the Christmas spirit," Templeton lied. "I wanted to make sure Santa and his handy elves brought you the coal you deserve."

"It doesn't take a genius to figure out that this woman has some trust issues, genius. What's going to happen if she decides she can trust you?"

Templeton thought of their easy, unspoken choreography. At the scenes they'd visited and, better still, right here in this house. He found himself rubbing at his chest and slammed his hand down on the counter.

"Of course she can trust me."

"To have her back in a firefight, sure. To work on a case together, great. But unless something has changed since—"

"I really don't need you to remind me."

Isaac was quiet for a moment. "You know my position on this. It wasn't your fault. Sometimes missions go bad. That's just the deal. I've been telling you this for years."

"This situation has nothing to do with that." But his voice betrayed him. It was too rough, too dark. It gave him away completely.

"It shouldn't," Isaac agreed. "But here's what I know about you, Templeton. You've been beating yourself up since the day that car blew up. You've been squirrelly about working with local law enforcement ever since. Has something changed?"

"Please. I'm entirely too large to ever be called *squirrelly*."

"Because I don't think anything has changed," Isaac said, answering his own question. "You like this woman. Great. But sooner or later your guilt is going to kick in, because it always does. And when that happens, you're going to do what you always do. You're going to flip that switch. No more happy-go-lucky Templeton. No more easygoing, big smile, too-lazy-to-breathe guy without a care in the world. It's going to feel like a bait and switch to her because, guess what? It will be. She won't like it, and you'll leave anyway. Meanwhile, all of this could be avoided."

Templeton rubbed a hand over his face and told himself that the churning in his gut was outrage, not the sneaking suspicion that all of this was an uncomfortable truth he didn't particularly want to hear. "This is great stuff, Isaac. Really. And all the more poignant coming from a man whose only true long-term relationship is with his mobile phone. Oh, right. And with a woman who can't stand the sight of him."

It was a low blow, throwing Isaac's messy situation with Caradine into the mix, but Templeton felt like low blows were going around. And right now, he felt a lot like kneecapping his best friend.

"Are you going to tell me those things aren't going to happen?" Isaac asked, and Templeton was glad that there were so many miles between him and the leader of Alaska Force. Because he had the feeling that if there weren't, that note of dark disapproval in Isaac's voice would have been the least of his problems. "Kate is smart. She's good at her job. And if this entire thing hinges around her and her family the way we think it does, she's already on course for a crappy New Year. The last thing she needs is your Dr. Jekyll and Mr. Hyde act."

"I never know which one of those is which," Templeton replied, more growl than anything else. "But this conversation is over. I'll update you after we talk to the father."

"Or you could not be a dumbass. Try that one on."

Templeton hung up before he said something he'd regret. Something else he'd regret.

And he wished, maybe for the first time since they'd started Alaska Force, that Isaac wasn't one of his oldest friends. Because if he had the same relationship with Isaac almost everyone else did, Isaac could remain the wise, distant leader. Diplomatic, but never involved. Instead of the friend who felt it necessary to tell Templeton things he really didn't want to hear.

He moved from the kitchen into the living room of Isaac's sister's house, no light anywhere except for the flames in the woodstove. He stared in the general direction of the fire, but he didn't see anything. He was far away, back in the past, neck-deep in yet another mission he couldn't discuss in a place he couldn't name. His contact had been a high-ranked aide to one of the local president's cabinet ministers. She'd served as part of the man's security team, and she'd been good at her job. Better still, she and Templeton had made an excellent team. In and out of bed.

And no one, not Isaac or the United States military, could convince him that it wasn't that teamwork that had gotten her killed.

A last-minute call had kept Templeton out of the convoy he'd supposed to be in. He remembered the sound of the explosion and his split-second realization of what it meant. Then he'd been running to the wreckage, hoping for survivors, and denying the evidence he could see with his own two eyes.

And later, after the shock had worn off and Templeton's team was back on American soil, he'd understood the real truth. It was him. It was his fault. He was some kind of walking Bermuda Triangle—let a woman care about him and she was doomed. His mother had been the first, the aide was the second.

Yeah, he had some past trauma around working with anyone not trained the same way he was. About letting a woman care about him when he knew what would happen next. He'd made a lot of rules around that, for everyone's safety.

Which meant he knew exactly what he had to do here.

Now. Before what was going on with Kate got any more intense.

"Why are you standing in the dark?" she asked from behind him.

And he nearly jumped out of his skin, which was embarrassing. He should have heard it the moment she sat up in bed upstairs. He certainly should have heard her come down those stairs. He couldn't actually recall the last time anyone had managed to sneak up on him.

There was only one thing to do about this. He needed to pull the trigger. Now.

Templeton turned around, and Kate was standing there before him. Not a ghost. Not shades of his own past, his own guilt.

Just . . . Kate.

Beautiful Kate, who tasted sweet everywhere. She had her hair up in a lopsided knot on her head, her shoulders were high enough to suggest she was trying to ward him off, and she was scowling like she was having similar internal debates with herself. Right now.

Templeton should have sung a few hallelujahs. Instead, he . . . didn't like that idea at all.

Kate rubbed at her face. "You're staring at me. It's weird." She said that matter-of-factly and didn't sound as if she was looking for a response. Good thing, because he didn't have one. "It's much warmer this morning. I want to go for a run. A hard one, if you're up for it."

And he could have psychoanalyzed her. He could have pointed out that it made sense to go test herself on a snowy road in "much warmer" ten-degree weather, because a much bigger test was coming her way later today. Or that working up a sweat was a terrific way to clear her head and pretend last night hadn't been one big, epic jumble of crossed lines.

But he didn't say any of that. Because he didn't want to look too closely at himself.

"Bring it on," he told her instead.

And they ran.

They ran together until Templeton's muscles actually protested and Kate looked about frozen through. When they got back to the house, she went upstairs to shower, and Templeton thought he'd prove to himself how in control he was of everything by leaving her to it.

But the idea of Kate up there, naked and warm, was too much for him to bear.

He was halfway up the stairs before he meant to move. He found her with the hot water beating down on her, turning her skin that rosy pink that he'd acquainted himself with so thoroughly all day yesterday.

He pulled her into his arms, gazing down at her as she melted against him. She tipped her chin up to look at him as the spray from the showerhead kicked up steam all around them. And she didn't smile. She looked almost solemn, and it made his ribs hurt.

He didn't grin down at her. No big laugh, lazy performance, or whatever the hell else Isaac had said.

And it was the easiest thing in the world to pick her up, tilt her back against the tiles, and find his way between her legs. She was already slick and ready for him. And he felt himself shudder, deep. He told himself it was simple need. And that was all it was.

"I don't have a condom," he managed to grit out, vaguely surprised he could speak when his chest ached like this and she was slick and naked. "Here in the shower with me, to clarify."

And for the first time in his entire life, Templeton wasn't sure if he had the strength to pull himself away to go do what needed to be done. But he started to.

Instead, Kate rocked her hips up to him and didn't let go from where she hung around his neck.

"I'm on the pill," she told him. "I get tested regularly. I believe in preparation, Templeton."

And he knew that was a bright red flag. A screeching, deafening alarm. He didn't have to ask whether or not his practical, rule-following trooper had ever let another man touch her without a condom. It had certainly never occurred to him to have sex with anyone without being properly protected before, for both their sakes.

She trusts you, a voice in him pronounced, like a death knell.

Just like Isaac had said.

He needed to step away. He could carry her out of the shower and toss her down on the bed. They could roll around out there, condoms in reach and both of them wet and slippery. It would be fun. He could see it.

But here in the shower he was hard where she was soft. She wiggled against him, lifting and then lowering herself. And rubbing her heat up and down the length of him.

Everything was jumbled up inside of him. Sex and trust. Guilt and need.

And in the middle of everything there was just Kate.

He shifted his hips that little bit, then thrust himself home.

And it was the cold light of day now, or the Fairbanks version, which meant a hint of dawn outside. Either way, he'd had her what felt like a thousand times yesterday. The itch was scratched, surely.

He should have been done with this.

But deep inside her, with nothing between them and her strong, supple body wrapped around his, Templeton felt as if this were the first time all over again.

"Merry Christmas, Trooper," he said softly against her mouth. "You are definitely on the naughty list."

And by the time he was finished, naughty and nice were tangled around each other, Kate was sobbing out his name like the prettiest carol he'd ever heard, and he wasn't sure he had it in him to survive the Trooper Holiday effect.

He had the sneaking suspicion he'd already sustained a mortal blow.

Luckily, Templeton had a long flight to get himself back under control. Or under control in the first place, if he was being brutally honest with himself. He was a highly trained military operative, for God's sake. He had handled himself and kept his cool in situations that would turn most people, most normal people, to shrapnel. And he was still standing.

His past was not his future. Kate was a colleague with benefits, that was all. Isaac should spend more time sorting out his own complicated romantic life and less time making dire predictions about other people's business, especially when Templeton was *fine*.

By the time they got to Spring Creek Correctional Center, a maximum-security prison smack down in one of the prettiest places in the world, Templeton thought he'd handled it. Any stray emotions had been packed away. And Oz had called in with confirmation of the things they'd already assumed to be true the night before.

"Liberty Holiday is married to one Charles Scott McGarity," Oz told them on speaker as Templeton drove from the airport in Seward across the water to the prison. "Native of Wyoming. Some political activism before he was kicked out of the University of Montana. Radical libertarian, but not one to really put his money where his mouth is. About what you'd expect."

"I didn't really see Liberty with a mild-mannered, average accountant," Kate said in that quietly sharp way.

"I can't guarantee that they didn't find a way to get under our radar and slide over to Grizzly Harbor and back. Or whatever else they would have had to do to be the people responsible for everything that's been happening over the past few months." Oz blew out a breath. "But I really don't think it's likely. I don't think they do much besides a supply run into town every few weeks. I could be wrong. I've been wrong before."

"When he says that, he means maybe once," Templeton told Kate.

"I don't like them for it, either," Kate said, crossing her arms as she sat in the passenger seat. "It would be convenient if it was them, certainly, but as far as I can tell, they're just out there living my father's dream to the best of their abilities. Which I can tell you from experience is a whole lot of unpleasant daily labor that leaves precious little time for pleasure flights all over the state."

They sat in silence when the call with Oz was done, and Templeton cursed himself when he reached over and rested his hand on her thigh. Especially when she gazed down as if she hardly knew what to make of it. As if no one had ever touched her without wanting sex.

Because that was another thing he knew without having to ask her. He'd already discovered his trooper knew her self-defense. He could tell that she'd trained, which meant she'd endured physical contact. He bet she knew how to tolerate it on the mat and in a training exercise. And she certainly knew what to do when she was naked.

But Kate—the emancipated fifteen-year-old who'd made her own way in this life, entirely on the force of her own will, who had grown into a very good cop—wasn't much for physical affection. Thinking about why made him want to break things. Even while Isaac's voice was ping-ponging around in his head, throwing out accusations Templeton wanted to refute but couldn't.

Still, he left his hand where it was.

"You okay?" he asked her, gruffly.

He felt her shift slightly beneath his palm. But she didn't push him away.

"I'm fine," she said after a moment, and it wasn't a throwaway, automatic response. He could hear all the feeling in it. All the things he should have cut off already. "Really."

"I wish it was your cousins, too."

"Even if it was, all roads would lead here eventually." Kate sounded almost rueful. Maybe wary. "One way or another."

He drove on, letting the complicated quiet rest between them.

And Templeton didn't take his hand off her leg until they made it to the prison.

Where everything got bureaucratic and institutional in a hurry.

"Nothing says Christmas like jail," Kate said when they'd made it through the series of doors and gates and locks and guards, her voice dry.

Dry and almost amused.

But Templeton didn't buy it the way he might have only a few days before. Because he knew things about Kate now.

And in any case, he was having a little trouble getting his own game face on. Because even visiting a prison, in Templeton's experience, made a man feel like less of a human. He couldn't imagine having to come here and *stay* here.

Sometimes he thought his father had given him a gift by insisting that he never, ever visit.

"I'm not sure it being Christmas makes being in prison any worse." Templeton kept his voice low as they followed the guard who led them down a corridor that smelled of industrial-strength cleaners and human misery. "I think prison is the problem no matter what day it is."

"My mistake. Here I was under the impression that Christmas was the season of miracle and wonder. For everyone. Isn't there a song about that? Resting merry gentlemen or whatever?"

"Hey."

She turned to look at him, and her brown eyes looked troubled no matter how she tried to keep her expression blank.

"You don't actually have to do this," he told her.

She looked as though she was about to fire off a reply, but she blinked. Then swallowed, as if she were trying to settle herself down. "I think I have to do it."

"Because your cousins got in your head?"

"Because I don't know if they're in my head or not. Whether he is or not. And I think it's time to find out."

Templeton couldn't argue with that. Far be it from him to keep a person from confronting their demons head-on. He knew his demons. He knew each of them by name, he knew where they lived, and the fact that he didn't want to go and get all up in their faces didn't mean he didn't handle his stuff. It was the fact that he didn't have issues with his stuff that meant it was handled.

Stop having arguments with yourself, dumbass, he growled at himself. *Especially when you're losing.*

Then the guard led them into the private visitor space that some combination of Kate's connections and Alaska Force's persuasion had gotten them. A table with two chairs on one side and one chair on the other. Windows for the guards to keep watch through and a panic button. Standard.

"Ready?" Templeton asked.

"Oh, sure," Kate drawled, just like him. "You know me."

"I do," he said. More seriously than he should have. "But remember, he doesn't."

Kate smiled at him. And any hint of trouble he'd seen on her face, in her eyes, was gone now. She was fully a cop. The cop he'd first met, in fact, back at the Water's Edge Café.

And it was that cop—Trooper Kate Holiday, investigator for the Alaska Bureau of Investigation and all around badass—who smiled at the man who shuffled in the door a moment later, flanked by two guards. They settled him in his seat, nodded to Kate and Templeton, and then left them to it.

Kate didn't say a word. She kept on smiling, flinty and fearless, and Templeton wanted to eat her up like dessert.

Instead, he took the opportunity to get an eyeful of one of Alaska's most notorious criminals.

Like most men, he looked diminished in jail. But in

Samuel Lee Holiday's case, it was because he'd gone gray over the past fifteen years. He didn't sit like a man who'd been beaten down. And Templeton could see the family resemblance that Will had been talking about, no matter how much he wanted to dismiss everything Kate's cousin had said as so much whining. Where Will had looked wild, his uncle's hair and beard were trimmed. And the old man sat ramrod straight, as if he felt he needed to announce his meticulousness. As if it gave him power, despite the fact he was in chains.

Samuel Lee Holiday did not smile at his only child.

"Hello, Katie," he said, his gaze alight with malice and his voice a rich sort of rasp. "I knew you'd come crawling back to me. Sooner or later, I knew you'd come."

Nineteen

The last time Kate had seen her father, he'd hissed the word *traitor* across the courtroom as they'd led him away, his face twisted and mottled with hatred. Today, by contrast, he looked very nearly sedate. She would have thought he really was sedated if she didn't know his thoughts on the dangers of numbing his own genius.

And if she overlooked that familiar, burning hatred in his gaze when he looked at her.

"Cat got your tongue?" her father asked in that same voice she remembered. Dark and deceptively flat when she'd learned young that he was always *this close* to raising it. "You had no trouble shooting your mouth off in court, as I recollect."

Kate eyed him for a moment, then let out a light laugh that made his eyes narrow.

"This is so funny," she said, shaking her head and even smiling like she expected him to join in. "It's so hard to remember why you were intimidating. I mean, look at you. Gray, old, locked away. And pretty much forgotten entirely out in the real world, unless someone's writing a book report on easily caught local criminals."

His furious gaze got more intense. And Kate couldn't

pretend it didn't get to her. It did. She remembered what had always come next. How he liked to administer his form of judgment and retribution. But the difference was, now she knew how to hide her reactions. And, better still, she wasn't a dependent child that he could hurt on a whim.

She was a grown woman. One he didn't know at all.

That thought made her smile a little wider.

"Forgotten by everyone except you," he said after a moment.

Kate nodded at Templeton. "I wouldn't have thought of you at all, if I'm honest. It was this guy."

And it wasn't as if they'd planned out what they would say. But Templeton grinned wide, the way he always did.

"Funny thing," he said. "But in the state of Alaska, if you start talking about whackadoo groups who tried to get all culty, your name comes up every time."

Samuel Lee—because Kate really didn't think of him as her father—glowered.

Kate made herself take a breath. She remembered that bitterly cold snowmobile ride in the dark, fifteen years ago this very day. How scared she'd been. That she would die out there. That she wouldn't. That she would make it all the way to the police only for them to take her back. That what her father had told her more than once, sometimes with his hand around her throat, was true—she would never escape him. Her life was his, to elevate or extinguish as he pleased.

The fifteen-year-old she'd been had held on tight to the feeling—little more than a fantasy—that whatever was out there in the big, wide world, it had to be better than the life she knew. *It just had to be.*

That terrified, determined, defiantly hopeful teenager would never have believed that this was the way it would all end up. Samuel Lee locked away forever. And Kate left to live her life exactly as she pleased.

Is that how you live your life? something inside her

asked. *Or have you been reeling around in fear since that night—locking yourself away as surely as if you were the one who ended up behind bars?*

But this wasn't the time for a chat with her inner turmoil. Not after the day she'd spent with Templeton, which had lit her up in so many different ways she was more or less scorched straight through. And certainly not when the boogeyman she'd feared all her life was sitting right there in front of her at last.

"I shouldn't have to tell you this, Dad," Kate said then, with an emphasis on the word because she knew he hated the familiarity and preferred to be called Father Samuel, even by her. *I am everyone's father, Katie*, he'd told her during a spanking she'd earned because she'd cried when told she couldn't call him Daddy. *Only a selfish, wicked girl would want to claim me as her own.* She'd been six. "But if you're found to be up to your old tricks in any way, it's going to make your time here a lot harder."

Her father didn't respond the way she thought he would. He stared at her for another long while. His eyes burned with a malice that seemed to hook into her and pull at her flesh.

And she'd forgotten this part. When she thought about her father, it was always the lectures. The rants and the punishments. His thunderous volume and all the words he used. Or the cruelty of his hard hands.

She'd forgotten about his silences. How he could sit and stare until you would do anything at all, anything he asked and all the things he didn't ask, to get him to snap out of his furious silence. To shift that gaze somewhere else.

Kate stared back at him, ready to sit across from him and hold his gaze forever, if only to prove she could.

But she realized she wasn't prepared. She'd forgotten his deliberate, deadly silences, but she could handle that.

Because while he'd been sitting in jail, she'd been trained in all manner of interrogation techniques.

That wasn't what got to her. It was the family resemblance.

She'd forgotten that they had the same nose, though hers was daintier. She'd forgotten the similarity in the shape of their hands. And, more disorienting, the similar gestures she hadn't realized she'd picked up from him. Her father sat with his hands folded in front of him and his back straight, and it was like looking in a mirror. She could see all the times she'd sat exactly like that, staring down one of the subjects of her investigations.

She had gotten so used to thinking of him as a monster and nothing else, nothing more. She'd forgotten all the ways that he was human. And she'd completely blocked out the fact that he'd contributed half of her DNA.

Maybe she'd never really thought about that, back when she was a kid. She certainly didn't enjoy thinking about it now.

"I know why you're here," her father said, and Kate allowed herself the faintest smile, because she'd won. He'd been forced to break the silence. And the faint red flush on his face told her he knew he'd lost. "Deep down, Katie, you must know that you're well overdue a reckoning for the things you've done."

She heard Templeton shift behind her, but he didn't say anything. He didn't jump in. And even though he'd been oddly quiet and contemplative this morning, she knew that he was fully prepared to let her take this wherever she needed to go.

"I've already had a public reckoning in court," she said, mildly enough. "They called me a hero. They still do. That's not a word they use for you, Dad."

"You can pretend to be of the world all you like, Katie. Inside, in your bones, you know the truth."

"That you're mentally ill?" She let her faint smile

widen. "A malignant narcissist with hefty doses of psychopathic impulses and sociopathic tendencies? I knew that a long time ago." She decided that rather than fight the link between them, she should lean into it. She settled her hands on the table, lacing them together in that way that mirrored his. And when that flush of temper got a shade or two darker, she knew he'd seen what she had. And liked it about as much as she did. "I visited Liberty and Russ yesterday."

Was that a flash of irritation on her father's face? Or was it something else?

"Your cousins were always obedient. They honored their parents and the family above all things, as good children should. It would never have occurred to either of them to betray the family's trust. Not like you."

"You say that, but you never threatened them with the ritual, did you?"

"The ritual is a gift," her father intoned, as if he were trying to stir them up the way he'd liked to do back in the compound. "That you don't see it that way only proves your unworthiness."

"If that were true, there'd be no need to keep threatening me with death by exposure. Would there?"

"Deep down," he said. "Deep down, you know where you're going. You know what waits for you. You know."

That was creepy enough that Kate had to remind herself that they were sitting in a maximum-security prison. One her father would never leave unless he was transferred to another facility. Because he might have a long memory for all the slights he felt had been visited upon him, but he had nothing on the police.

They never, ever forgot their own.

"I wasn't visiting Russ and Liberty to catch up on old times," Kate told him. "I'm in the middle of an investigation. And this time, the target appears to be me. Guess who tops the list when I start thinking about who might have a psychotic little grudge?"

"Are you scared?" her father asked, that sick gleam in his eyes. "Did you beg?"

"All of the attempts on me have failed, of course," Kate said, dry and unbothered. Because he didn't get to see her stomach clench. He didn't get to know that her palms were slightly damp. "This should come as no surprise to you. You're an old man rotting away in a jail cell, becoming more irrelevant by the day. I'm a highly regarded law enforcement officer who lives in the real world, not the one you made up for us all those years ago. Whatever scraggly little plot this is, if you're involved, it only makes you look that much more sad."

"And yet you're here," her father said. "Why would you bother to come see a sad old man you're not afraid of?"

That was an excellent question.

Kate discovered that she didn't have an answer.

She stood, holding her father's gaze while she rose.

"I forgot," she told him quietly. "All these years, I built you up in my head. I forgot what it was like in all those courtrooms. You were so small and angry, and for once, it didn't matter. No one listened to you or waited, breathlessly, for you to speak. You were only ever powerful when I was small and stranded." She didn't look away from him. She didn't cower or avert her eyes. She didn't shrink in any way. "I'm not small any longer. And I'm definitely not stranded."

She turned and nodded to Templeton. His intense gaze touched her face as if he were checking for marks, but once again, he moved as if they'd done this a thousand times. He went over and knocked on the door for the guard.

"You can tell yourself any stories you like," Samuel Lee said bitterly. "But believe me, Katie, you might run from the consequences for your actions, but they'll catch up to you. They always do."

Kate turned when she reached the door, looking back over her shoulder at this man who had loomed so large all her life. But it was high time she stepped out of his shadow, even inside her own head.

"I'll be sure to check back in with you more often," she said, smirking a little at him. "So I can get a close, personal look at all those consequences. Because they look good on you, Dad. They really do."

Testifying against him in court had been satisfying. But she'd been so much younger then, so unable to imagine that there really could be an existence without him choking the life out of her. Kate was older now. This was better.

She should have visited him a long time ago. Because if she felt alien, cut off from the world, it wasn't because she was off and wrong, as she'd always assumed. It was because that was what he'd taught her.

And she didn't have to allow a single thing this man had taught her to take hold. Her childhood was nothing but weeds, choking out the real plants. And she was ready to do a little blooming.

Templeton nodded for her to lead the way out the door. Neither one of them looked back, as if the man they walked away from was nothing. Because that was exactly what he was.

And she heard the satisfying sound of her father's hands—too much like her hands—slamming down hard on the tabletop.

The man who claimed that he was ruled by reason and righteousness was locked in a cage and forced to express himself like any common criminal. Impotently.

Kate wasn't sure she'd ever understood the magic of Christmas until this very moment.

Once they were back outside and tucked up in the front of yet another SUV that had been waiting for them when their plane had landed, she let out a long, cleansing sort of breath.

"That was fun," she said. "But that's all it was. He

might wish that he could get to me. Create some kind of reckoning, or whatever he wants to call it. But he can't."

The Templeton she thought she knew would have laughed. Made a joke to lighten things, maybe put his hands on her. But today's new, brooding Templeton only looked straight ahead as he started the engine, no trace of a smile on his face.

Not that it made him look anything but delicious.

"I couldn't tell if he knows that someone's coming after you or if he wanted to pretend he did."

Kate shrugged. "Either way, the only thing he could contribute to the situation is potentially ordering it. It's not like he's out stabbing people."

Templeton fished out his phone, frowning down at it. "Oz is taking a closer look at his visitor log. Our initial examination didn't turn up anything interesting, so he's going deeper, but he thinks it's unlikely to turn up any bombshells. Your father is pretty closely monitored."

Kate settled back against her seat and let out another breath. She was letting go of her childhood today. Just opening up hands she hadn't known were balled into fists and releasing everything in them, straight up into the air.

She was sure that she was going to need to spend some time curled up in the fetal position somewhere with everything that had happened recently, but she couldn't seem to access the storm now. It was too much, maybe. It had blanked her out. She'd lit up and burned straight through. All the adrenaline and anxiety had melted away into something blessedly numb.

Or not numb, exactly. That wasn't right.

She was aware of everything. All the words her father had used, which she'd be sure to parse and worry over in the days to come. The shift in Templeton's behavior that made her stomach drop, suggesting as it did that once again she'd missed whatever clues she should have seen. That she'd dropped the ball the way she always did, only this time she hadn't even realized it. He'd been different from the first moment she'd set eyes on him this morning. Before she'd even been fully awake.

Even now, as he drove them away from the prison, a wool hat tugged down on his head, he looked . . . grim. No big, inviting smile. No infectious laugh. And she could tell that he was highly unlikely to turn around and tease her with something outrageous to lighten the mood today. That Templeton was gone.

You did it again, she chided herself.

But even as the thought formed, she rejected it. That was a Samuel Lee Holiday line of thinking. That was weeds and mess, having everything to do with a man behind bars and nothing to do with her.

Her normal go-to when things shifted beneath her feet like this was to sink herself into work and pretend she was an Alaska State Trooper robot. She was good at it.

But today, she didn't have it in her.

"Let's drive," she said, staring out the window across Resurrection Bay at the actual town of Seward. The Kenai Mountains loomed this way and that, wearing their snowy winter best against the sudden sunshine.

Templeton shot her a look. "Drive where?"

"You seem to be able to magically produce a plane wherever we go. What about Anchorage?"

He hesitated slightly. So slightly she almost thought she'd imagined it. "There are always planes in Anchorage."

"Let's drive there. It's only a couple of hours, and the road is usually clear."

She thought he would argue. He gave her an intense, long look, but he didn't say a word. He just drove. He headed north on Seward Highway instead of back south toward the airport. Straight toward the mountains that would lead them over the spine of the Kenai Peninsula and then into Anchorage, some 130 miles to the north.

At first she thought she would jump in and start interrogating him. Demand that he tell her what had changed between yesterday and now. Ask him if she had done something.

But she didn't.

She dug out her phone instead, connected it to the SUV, and played some music.

And she could feel all the things she needed to think about. All the things she needed to feel. They were right there, looming. Waiting.

But here, now, on one of the prettiest roads in Alaska, she played music. She stared out the window at the scenery that made her heart leap. From Moose Creek to Turnagain Arm. And with every mile, the silence they sat in seemed less punitive and more . . . perfect.

Because nothing could happen here, on this road that wound over mountains and past alpine lakes. No one could shoot at them as they drove up from one side of this beautiful peninsula and down to another, with views of the Gulf of Alaska and its offshoot inlets. Her family was only here with her if she let them take over her head, so she didn't. That left her with the man who had somehow wedged his way beneath her skin, this beautiful state she loved so much on a pretty winter's day, and nothing to do but bask in both.

It almost made her believe in Christmas.

Because for a little while, Kate could suspend herself in the sweetness of it. The winter day unfolding around them, moody in the distance but bright where they were.

For a little while, she pretended that she had always been like this and always would be. Whole. Happy. Fully human, like everyone else.

Kate knew it couldn't last. Real life might not be the hole her father had wanted to bury them all in, but that didn't mean that it was this, either. Still, she tipped her head back and let herself fall head over heels into all the happiness anyway.

Because she doubted that she would ever feel like this again. The only other time she'd come close was in

Templeton's arms. And she wasn't sure, given the way he'd closed down today, that she'd get to experience that again, either.

She couldn't bear that thought. Kate reached across the center of the vehicle and put her hand on Templeton's leg. The way he'd done before they'd hit the prison. And when—after a long, frozen moment—he covered it with his, she smiled. And for a couple of hours on the strangest Christmas of her life, Kate didn't worry about what came next. She basked in the now.

And she knew she'd made the right decision when they made it back to the island that night. Because instead of landing in Fool's Cove, the plane diverted to Grizzly Harbor instead.

"I hope we're going to the Fairweather," Kate said when they landed. "I could really use a drink."

Templeton was staring at his phone, the way he'd been doing since he'd leaned forward and told the pilot to head to town instead of the cove. It seemed to take him an ice age or two to lift his gaze to hers. And what she saw there made her chest feel funny.

"You have a visitor," he told her. Tersely, no hint of a grin. "Waiting for you at the inn."

"Most of my colleagues know that I'm on leave," Kate said. She tossed her bag over her shoulder as she crawled off the plane, then waited for Templeton to jump down to the dock beside her. "But I wouldn't think—"

"It's not one of your colleagues." Templeton's gaze had grown even darker. More intense. And Kate was terribly afraid that what she saw on his face was a sort of kindness that edged too close to pity for her tastes. "Kate. I wish . . ."

Her chest felt more than funny. And now she really did feel numb.

But he shook his head, tossing off whatever he'd been about to say. "It's your mother."

Twenty

Templeton watched her change in an instant. From the almost dreamy Kate he'd spent the afternoon with straight back into full-on trooper, like she had flipped a switch.

"My mother," Kate said, as if she had to say it out loud to believe it. Her voice was flat and laced with steel, but she didn't sound like she'd been gut-punched. "Tracy Warren Holiday."

"That's the one."

"She's supposed to be in Anchorage. Enjoying her life as an ex-con while still being married to one of Alaska's most notorious criminals."

"She came in on a seaplane about an hour ago, walked into the Fairweather, and asked for you."

Kate looked as if she were sorting out math problems in her head, and Templeton didn't know what to do with the mess inside of him. Everything Isaac had said kicked at him, mostly because he wanted to deny it. And couldn't.

He was right on schedule to do exactly what Isaac had predicted he would. An argument could be made that he'd already done it, given how distant he'd been acting all day. But none of his rules seemed to matter when his trooper looked so deflated. Even if it was only for a moment.

But this was Kate, so when the moment was up, her chin lifted. Something flashed over her face, and she didn't waste another second. She charged off the dock, then started up the hill into town, clearly prepared to storm the Blue Bear Inn right this minute.

"You're just going to go in there?" Templeton asked, keeping pace with her as she sprinted along the road, such as it was. "Guns blazing?"

"Metaphorically." She stormed past the Fairweather. "Unless she gets mouthy."

"You already had a face-to-face with one of your parents today. You don't need to deal with both of them."

"It appears that I do. Because it never rains, it pours. And in my family, at the first hint of moisture you can expect a flash flood."

If anything, she picked up her pace.

"Kate." But she didn't slow down. She didn't stop. "Baby, come on."

She stopped so fast then that Templeton almost tripped over his own feet as he tried to stop along with her. Almost. The Christmas lights were sparkling, making the wooden boardwalk beneath their feet seem to gleam, and the way Kate looked at him made his heart stutter in his chest.

"*Baby*?" she repeated in what sounded like disbelief. And maybe something angrier. "Now I'm *baby*? You could barely look at me all day."

He wished she'd hauled off and punched him. He would have handled it better. "I looked at you."

The look she gave him then was withering.

"Here's a word of advice, Templeton. You've already witnessed one half of the greatest gaslighting duo in the history of the world today. You're about to witness the other. My suggestion is that you not try to step into any perceived void here. I was raised by two people who spent their lives trying to convince me and everyone else around them not that we were all insane but that *the entire world was insane*, except for them." She shook her head, that mirthless smile almost too much for him to take, especially with twinkling lights all around. "Don't jump on board this train."

"I have rules," he told her. And then couldn't believe that sentence had come out of his mouth. Here, now. She glared at him, waiting. "I don't get involved with women I work with."

Kate scowled. "Weirdly, I remember saying something similar and getting a lecture about being grown up enough to make my own decisions."

"I decided it would be fine as long as I didn't get emotionally involved."

He expected her to look as if he'd kicked her. To swing at him, maybe.

What he could not have predicted was her laughter.

It wasn't a bark of hollow laughter, tossed out into a night that, at about thirty-five degrees, felt warm and cozy after a visit to Fairbanks. She really laughed. So hard that she stepped back, covered her face with one hand, and eventually had to wipe at her eyes.

Templeton was pretty clear that this did not bode well for him. But all he could do was watch.

"I'll give it to you," she said when she could finally speak. "I did not see that coming."

Templeton gritted his teeth. "There was an op a long time ago. I can't tell you where. I got . . . involved."

"And the hilarity continues." She shook her head at him. "I'm not awesome at relationships, or whatever this is, but even I know that you don't start talking spontaneously about your past flings with the current one."

"She died." He belted that out. Because apparently he could control himself in every single scenario on this earth unless it had to do with Kate Holiday. Something he was going to have to find a way to come to terms with. Apparently. "I dropped the ball, she paid the price. I decided one way to make sure that never happened again was to put down a few ground rules."

"That's great for you." Kate stepped closer, and the hand that held the strap of her bag over her shoulder balled into a fist. "I'm delighted that you're having some kind of emotional moment here, Templeton, instead of laughing maniacally and pretending you don't care about anything. I'm sure it's really meaningful for you."

"I'm trying to tell you what's going on," he said stiffly.

"That's really good of you," she said in that sharp way of hers that was as hard as a blow. And did more damage. "I'm sure you even think that's true."

"I know I'm going to regret this," he growled, his eyes narrowing as he stared down at her. "But what the hell do you mean by that?"

"I understood how you operated the first time I met you," Kate told him, and there was no trace of laughter on her face then. "You put on a big light show, Templeton. But it's precisely calculated to make sure you only ever give anything away, if you ever give anything away, on your terms."

He kept being amazed by all the ways she could land a punch without swinging. And he shouldn't have been. "Great. A character assassination."

"I don't have time to assassinate your character, actually. I'm in the middle of a joyful family reunion. Maybe you missed that part." Her head tilted slightly to one side, and her expression was as scathing as her voice. "It's been one for the books. Who doesn't want to get shot at in a creepy compound, follow it up with a little prison time, and then come back to what's supposed to be a safe space only to discover that your favorite gorgon is waiting for you?"

"You skipped right over Christmas Eve. I found that part pretty memorable."

"Yes, Templeton, we had sex," Kate said, and he told himself that she was trying to sound that patronizing. She was doing it deliberately, trying to poke at him, get under his skin, play her little cop game. "And yes, it was good." She jutted out her chin at him. "Too bad it clearly scared you half to death."

"Army Rangers aren't scared of anything, Trooper. Especially not sex."

Something moved over her, intense enough to make it look as if she was reeling for a moment. And Templeton had to fight himself to keep his hands where they belonged. Meaning, not on her.

"I learned something important today," Kate gritted out at him, and it took him a moment to realize why he was reacting to her voice the way he did. As if he were under attack. It was because she didn't sound like a cop. She sounded like a pissed-off, emotional woman, and Templeton couldn't decide if he wanted to get the hell away from that or celebrate it. "I've spent my whole life feeling like an alien walking among humans, trying to figure out their ways. At a certain point I gave up. Sometimes it's easier to let people call you all the usual names instead. *Ice queen. Aloof. Intimidating. Unfriendly.* Or worse."

"You're not any of those things."

She shifted closer to him and jabbed a finger toward him, as if she was thinking about thumping him on the chest. He wished she would. He had always excelled at the physical. It was the emotional where he clearly didn't know what he was doing.

"That's the point I'm trying to make. I'm not any of those things. Maybe I became those things, in reaction. I don't know. But I was raised by sick, twisted people. That doesn't make me one of them."

"Kate. You're not. You're nothing like your father."

She wrinkled her nose. "And yet I can look back at every relationship I've ever tried to have with another person and see the moment where it all turns. Because it always turns."

Templeton understood where this was going now. He stopped battling himself and his urges and reached over to wrap his hand around her shoulder, holding on to her through her coat. Just because he needed to touch her.

"This isn't a turn. You came out of nowhere and broke all my rules. I'm recalibrating, that's all."

"Congratulations. Your recalibration efforts read a whole lot like a man who got what he wanted, then got really grumpy about having to continue to spend time with the woman he'd gotten it from."

"You can't think that's who I am. I know you don't."

"Who you pretend to be?" she asked with that unerring accuracy that he appreciated a lot more when it was aimed at someone else. "Or who you really are?"

Templeton stared back at her, aware of too many things at once. The pounding of his heart. The way his pulse racketed around, like the enemy was upon him and it was time to bring out the big guns. All things he was great at.

He could have single-handedly sorted out all kinds of war games. But staring down at this woman, he couldn't find the right words. Not one.

Kate's mouth twisted. "That's what I thought. Maybe it's time the great, eternally happy-go-lucky Templeton Cross dealt with stuff for a change."

She shrugged his hand off her shoulder, then turned to continue up the street toward the inn.

"Today sucks," Templeton growled after her. She stopped, but she didn't turn around. "I get that. But I was right there with you, Kate. You didn't have to do it by yourself."

"Merry freaking Christmas to me," she replied, her voice perfectly audible and razor sharp on the cold breeze. "You're basically Santa Claus in this self-congratulatory scenario, aren't you?"

And he got that she had stuff of her own. They had been tracking that stuff all over Alaska. But there was something about the way she said that—unnecessarily snide, he thought, with a bright surge of temper—that hit him the wrong way.

"I would kill someone for the chance to see my mother again," he told her harshly, because she wasn't the only one who could hit below the belt. "But I can't. And there's no shame in taking the opportunity to see if a broken thing can be fixed, Kate. Maybe not with Samuel Lee Holiday. But with your mom, who knows?"

Kate turned slowly. Very slowly. That prickle on the back of his neck warned Templeton, the way it always did, that there was incoming gunfire. Shooting straight out of those brown eyes, if he had his guess.

"Is that why you've never visited your living, breathing father?" she asked. "With or without the shame you claimed you don't feel because you're so dedicated to living in the now?"

Templeton would have preferred her cousin's automatic rifle in his face again.

"That's different."

"Sure it is. It's completely different. We have nothing in common at all. Certainly not a father in prison. Serving a life sentence. With very little contact. How could I possibly begin to imagine what you might think or feel about anything?"

"You have no idea what you're talking about."

"Because you and your friends are the only people who can do background research, is that it?" Kate shook her head. "You actually have an advantage over me. You have no idea if you have a good father or not, you only know that you have an incarcerated one. But at least you can be fairly certain he doesn't want to kill you."

"I have no idea what he wants or doesn't want."

"I don't have that comfort. Because even if my father isn't responsible for all the nonsense that's been going on around here lately, he's always wanted to kill me. And would have if I hadn't escaped. So you tell me, Templeton. Should I really go try to repair my relationship with the woman who chose him over me, her only child, again and again and again?"

"Go right ahead and be pissed at me because I didn't talk to you enough today, or whatever you're mad about."

Kate laughed. And this time, clearly not because she thought anything was funny. If she'd been someone else, he might have thought that glassiness in her eyes meant—

But not Kate. Not his trooper. He'd only ever seen her cry because she was laughing.

At him.

"I bet that works for you usually." She laughed again. "I bet all of this works for you. And I'll admit, it's quite a package. But the problem is, I've actually seen more than one of the faces you wear. I know that the Templeton Show is a way to avoid the kind of intimacy you pretend you want. You're not fooling me."

"I'm not trying to fool you, Kate. I was trying to explain."

"I don't need your explanations." She lifted her chin again. "You don't have to follow me up to the inn. I can handle this by myself. I'm used to handling things by myself."

That was clearly supposed to land like a punch, and it did. Templeton stalked toward her, aware that for the first time in living memory—or at least, since he'd been hotheaded and a teenager—his temper was getting the better of him.

"You think because we're fighting I'm going to throw you to the wolves?" He shook his head. "You don't know me as well as you think you do. That's not how I roll."

"Then let me request that you roll with a little less male posturing," Kate threw back at him. "Let me handle the endless family situation I seem to be in the middle of, and I'll be sure to schedule some time for your ego and unexpected emotions when it's done. If that's all right with you."

Suddenly he didn't care if his Alaska Force brothers were arrayed around the town, watching all this unfold while they watched the perimeter. He'd handle their inevitable responses later. And he'd take his ribbing like a man.

But right now, his attention was on her.

This woman with the cool gaze and that hard-edged trooper's smile, who had turned his world completely inside out.

"I never planned on wanting anyone this much, Kate," he told her. "I didn't think I was capable of it. And, believe me, I have no problem whatsoever standing right here in the middle of the street and telling you, the entire Alaska Force team that's probably listening in and watching us right now, and every citizen of Grizzly Harbor every last thing that I'm feeling on this topic. But I'm pretty sure you don't want that."

She scowled at him, but that glitter in her gaze was different. "As I said. I can pencil you in for sometime next year. Lucky you, that's in a week." Her hand tightened around the strap of her bag. "Now, if you don't mind, I'm going to go talk to the second-to-last person I ever wanted to see again. Much less in one day."

Templeton didn't intend to hold her here. But he reached out anyway, curling his hand over the nape of her neck beneath the hat she wore against the weather, and pulled her even closer.

"Templeton," she began, sounding impatient.

But he didn't care if she was impatient. He didn't care if she wanted to yell at him some more, or always. That was what he'd been wrestling with all day. Everything inside of him made no sense. It was too big, too out of control, temper and emotion muddled together with things he really didn't want to think about at all, like his father.

And wrapped up in all of it, the bright bit of color stitching it all together, was her. Kate. His very own trooper.

He'd known she was trouble the minute he'd walked into that café.

And that was why he bent down and pressed his mouth to hers. It was the memory of that first meeting. It was an acknowledgment of Christmas Eve.

It was him and it was her.

He had the sinking feeling he knew exactly what that ache in his chest was. He'd been fighting it off since he'd woken up this morning, and it had only gotten worse. Until it felt less like an affliction and more like an acknowledgment.

"Don't pencil me in. Use a pen," he told her, against her lips that softened only for him. "And you're going to need to block out some time, Kate. When this is over. You and me."

He expected her to argue with that. He expected her to argue, period.

But instead, her gaze searched his for another moment, in the darkness, with Christmas lights sparkling all around her like a halo.

She didn't say a word, and still he felt as if she'd said a thousand things. Somehow, he heard them all.

When she turned around this time, he followed her. Up the rest of the hill to the inn, where the lights inside made it look cozy. Inviting.

Kate didn't pause on the threshold. She pushed her way inside, nodding coolly at Madeleine Yazzie, who stood behind the desk in the lobby, looking neither cozy nor inviting. Templeton nodded Madeleine's way, able to tell by the way her red beehive trembled that she was outraged that she'd been dragged out of her house—all of three minutes' walk away—to work on Christmas.

But he couldn't do more than smile at her.

"There you are," came a woman's voice from the lobby. "My sweet Katie."

Kate stood in her trooper stance in the doorway to the common area, one hand hovering near her weapon and the other ready to go for her comm unit. And Templeton took his place at her back, getting a glimpse of the woman who had married Samuel Lee Holiday, given him a baby, and followed him out to that compound.

Tracy Holiday looked rough. Templeton would have known at a glance that she'd spent time in prison even if he hadn't pored over her record. Even so, he could see where Kate had come from. The same brown eyes. The same forehead. But where Kate was sleek and strong, her mother was unhealthily skinny. Wiry in a way that spoke to Templeton about bad choices, tough living, and too many cigarettes.

"My sweet, sweet little girl," Tracy cried in her smoker's rasp with apparent delight. Though she stayed where she was, sitting on the couch in the Blue Bear Inn's living room. As if to make sure she didn't turn her back on the stuffed grizzly by the fireplace. "Look at you, all grown up."

And this was the trouble with emotional involvements. Templeton couldn't tell if this woman was setting off his alarms because she was up to no good here or because her presence clearly bothered Kate.

"Okay, Mom," Kate said after a moment. All police, no give. Her mother could have been a drunk driver by the side of the road for all the emotion she let into her voice. "You're laying it on pretty thick, don't you think? What do you want?"

Twenty-one

Kate's mother stared back at her for a moment, her face still set into what looked like concern. Or some other emotion. Something in the neighborhood of tender and affectionate, maybe.

Kate assumed she'd seen it on TV.

The next moment, it cracked. Tracy stopped wrinkling up her forehead. She stopped her attempt at an encouraging, tremulous smile. She coughed, and that took Kate back. It was her smoker's cough, the music of her mother, and Kate filled up fast with the swamp of emotions she associated with all things Tracy. Revulsion, hurt, and the leftover ruins of long-lost hope.

"As self-righteous as ever, I see," Tracy said. Her canny eyes flicked from Kate to a point behind and above her, where Kate knew Templeton stood. And Kate would have ripped out her tongue before she admitted how comforting she found it to have a man the size of a mountain at her back. No matter how irritated she was with him. "Can't a mother have a change of heart? A desire to see her only child?"

"I'm sure mothers can and do," Kate replied. "But we're talking about you."

There was a flicker of something in Tracy's eyes, but she only shrugged. "It's been a long time. People change."

"I've changed," Kate agreed. "But none of you seem to be any different from how I left you. Will is a mess. Liberty and Russ are overzealous. And Dad is exactly the same as he was back then. The only thing that's changed is his audience."

"I did my time," Tracy said stoutly. "My debt is paid. It's not unusual to want to rebuild a life after prison, is it?"

"You've been out of prison for three years."

"I had to get on my feet."

Kate shook her head. "I don't buy whatever this is. Even if you were rebuilding your life, you wouldn't be doing it here." She narrowed her eyes at the woman in front of her. "Do you have a bomb strapped to your chest?"

Tracy sighed. "I guess I deserve that."

She stood up, and Kate felt those same swampy things spiral inside her. She could see too much of herself in this woman. In the shape of her. The way she jutted out one hip when she stood. The way her shoulders sloped. She'd despaired of these things years ago. Today it made her feel hollow.

But somehow not as dislocated as she might have expected she would.

Tracy smirked. Then she lifted the hem of the shirt she wore, exposing her abdomen. Then higher to show her bra. There was nothing visible there except her rail-thin body, with her ribs poking through. Kate could almost feel the impression of those bones against her face, the way she had as a child on the few occasions she could remember being sick enough, feverish enough, that her mother had actually held her.

"I hope you enjoyed the show," Tracy said, and Kate couldn't tell if that was directed at her or Templeton. "One thing prison does real well is make a person less self-conscious."

"You have five minutes," Kate told her. "If you have something to say, say it."

"This is awkward for me, too, Katie." Tracy shook her head, looked at Templeton as if he were on her side in this. "I'm sorry that you feel you can't talk to me alone."

"You didn't ask to speak with me alone." Kate had to work very hard not to bite her mother's head off. "I don't feel one way or the other about it."

"Caradine's is open today," Templeton said.

Kate didn't want to look at him. She wasn't ready to think about all the revelations they'd tossed at each other on their walk up from the docks. Certainly not when her mother was around, like a hovering toxic event. But because her mother was there, and watching, she aimed a cool smile his way.

"On Christmas? That's surprising."

Templeton's gaze was too dark, but it was that golden gleam that caught at her. "Not when she can charge double."

What he didn't say was that it was likely wise to have this conversation with Tracy in a public place, which could be monitored by Alaska Force and other witnesses. Instead of going off for a cozy chat somewhere private, where who knew what might happen? He didn't say any of that, but since Kate felt exactly the same way, she nodded.

"Perfect." She looked back at her mother. "Look at that, Mom. We get to celebrate our first real Christmas together. Can't you feel the joy?"

The Tracy she'd known back in the day would have slapped her. Or worse. But this version of her mother was less readable. More contained, maybe. As if she'd learned to temper herself along with casual disrobing during her incarceration.

"I've prayed for you every day we've been apart," Tracy said, with a certain edge to all her piety that made Kate grit her teeth. "I've prayed to change your heart."

"I've prayed for different parents," Kate shot back. "I guess none of our prayers have been answered."

Tracy took her time putting on her coat and then walked jerkily out of the inn, back out to the cold street. Kate followed behind her, keenly aware of Templeton moving along with them, soundless and intense.

"I'll see you and your friends later," Kate said to him in an undertone as he closed the door of the inn behind them. She thought it was highly unlikely that her mother's appearance was a coincidence, which meant Tracy probably knew exactly who and what Alaska Force was. Samuel Lee had been the showboat out there in the bush, but it was always Tracy who'd set the stage. Kate wouldn't put it past her mother to have spent the past three years plotting revenge. But on the off chance she hadn't—and was somehow uninvolved in what was happening—Kate saw no reason to advertise who and what Alaska Force was.

Templeton's dark gaze touched hers. "Count on it."

And Kate hadn't been being melodramatic when she'd told him she was used to working alone. Or not too melodramatic, anyway. She was. That was part and parcel of the job.

Except she couldn't deny that she liked knowing she was in Alaska Force territory now. That when Templeton nodded to her mother, then melted off into the dark, he wasn't abandoning her. He was calling in reinforcements.

"How did you know where to find me?" Kate asked briskly as she led her mother down the cold street toward the Water's Edge Café. Which was lit up and open for business, just as Templeton had said. She had clearly been too annoyed at him to see it on the way up.

"If it was a secret that there was a body in your plane, they probably should have kept it out of the papers," Tracy replied.

"Since when do you read the papers?" Kate walked next to her mother, but not too close. She didn't think

Tracy would take a swing at her, but you never could tell. "I would have thought you'd object to them on philosophical grounds. Heaven forbid you get current cultural ideas implanted into your brain."

Tracy sniffed. "I keep telling you. Things change."

When they arrived at the café, they weren't the only ones there. Caradine—dressed in head-to-toe black, complete with thick black eye makeup, in case anyone was tempted to mistake her for an elf—scowled at them when they walked inside.

"Christmas prices," she said without preamble. "No bargaining or bartering."

"Is that double the usual?" Kate asked.

Caradine smirked as she swiped at her forehead briskly enough to make her dark ponytail bounce. "It's whatever I say it is. Based entirely on how annoying you are."

"Then I'll be certain to be as annoying as possible," Kate told her, because she was apparently irreverent now. "As a Christmas present."

Caradine didn't actually sneer, though Kate had never met another person who could give the impression of sneering without actually doing it. She stomped away, and Kate waved a hand toward the nearest empty table. Tracy took a seat.

Kate looked around the café. In one corner there were what looked like two couples, each with small babies—though the longer Kate looked, the less she could tell which configuration of couples was together, and whose baby was whose. There was a weathered old man sitting alone, but he was engaged in conversation with the rowdy table to his left. Kate recognized the harbormaster at another table. And a couple of other faces at yet another table that struck her as familiar, but they were hardy-looking men in outdoor gear, so she assumed they were local fishermen she might have seen in passing on the docks.

That made her mother and her the only tourists. The

only outsiders, and given that Kate had been an outsider her whole life, no matter where she went, she couldn't think of a single good reason for that to sit on her the way it did tonight. This wasn't her home, no matter how comfortable she felt here.

"Don't bother ordering anything," she told her mother. "You'll get what she gives you."

Tracy sniffed again, but she didn't argue. And Kate settled across from her, shrugging out of her coat to hang it on the back of her chair.

And she wasn't surprised that her mother did nothing but stare back at her, silently. Because, really, what was there to say?

"How is your father?" Tracy asked. Also not surprising as an opening gambit. "You said you saw him."

"He's older." Kate studied her mother's face, looking for cracks. Clues. "Did he send you here?"

"I haven't seen your father for years."

"Yet, last I checked, you were still married to him."

Tracy moved a bony shoulder. "Too much paperwork."

Kate wanted to pepper her mother with questions, but that urge came from the daughter in her. Not the trained cop. So instead, she waited. Caradine stormed over and slammed down water glasses between them. Then a basket of bread.

Tracy made a production out of taking a thick slice, then buttering it as if she'd never seen either dairy or bread before.

The door to the café opened, and Bethan walked in. She looked dressed for a winter hike, not a battle, with her hair down. As if she were a regular person.

When she looked past Kate like they'd never met, Kate understood she was the reinforcements. Kate watched as Bethan and Caradine exchanged a total of three syllables, then Bethan took a table for herself.

And the fact that she was here made Kate feel a little lighter.

Almost as if wine and pasta in a cabin mattered after all.

"I told you five minutes, but now you have a whole dinner," Kate said when Caradine came out with big plates for them, heaped high with prime rib, roasted potatoes, and roasted brussels sprouts. "Use it wisely. Why are you here?"

Tracy picked up her fork and pushed a roasted potato around on her plate. "I know you won't believe this, but I wanted to see how you were doing."

"You're right. I don't believe it. And if I was inclined to think you had that kind of sentimentality in you, the fact that it's bubbling up now? On the fifteenth anniversary of the night I escaped you?" She shook her head. "I think we both know that's not who you are."

Tracy stopped pretending to eat and stared at Kate instead. Kate cut herself a big bite and was aware that it was far and away the best prime rib she'd ever had in her life. But she couldn't quite enjoy it. Not under the circumstances.

If anything was going to make her cry today, during this seemingly endless marathon of ghosts from Christmas past, it was that.

"I know it's been fifteen years," Tracy said with an edge in her voice again. "To the day. Of course I know that. I just wanted to see my daughter."

"Now you have."

Tracy's lips moved, but it wasn't a smile. Not really. "You've always seen me as your enemy. You still do."

"I don't see you at all, Mom," Kate said softly. "By choice."

Tracy sniffed. "The judge was pretty clear that it was your father making all the decisions. Telling us all what to do. But you blame it all on me, not him."

Kate opened her mouth to refute that, but stopped herself. Because Tracy wasn't wrong. And she had to sit with that a moment.

"You knew what he was," she said, when she could put words to it. "And you liked it so much that you married him. Had a baby with him. Moved out into the middle of nowhere with him, where he could do whatever he wanted, unchecked. He is who he is, and believe me, I don't have anything nice to say about him or to him. But you." She shook her head. "Sorry, Mom, but sometimes I can't help thinking you're worse."

Tracy looked down at her plate. "I'm the only reason you're alive." Her voice was quiet, and the cop in Kate wished she could see her expression. The daughter in her was glad she couldn't. "Your father wanted to put you out when you weren't much more than seven."

"It's exactly that kind of tender memory that makes me wonder about you." Kate put her fork down, her appetite gone entirely. "What kind of mother stays with a man who even discusses putting a child out into an Alaskan winter? Or at all?"

"I don't expect you to understand the choices I made."

"Good. Because I don't. And neither did the judge, which is why you spent twelve years in prison."

"Sometimes I miss prison." Tracy's faint rasp barely rose above the sound of the other diners all around them. "The same way I miss the compound. All that clarity."

Kate made a noise that wasn't quite a laugh. "Oddly enough, I prefer freedom."

But her mother didn't reply. And Kate stared down at her food, wishing that when she took a bite she could taste it again, but she seemed to have lost her taste for anything.

"You have to pay for that anyway," Caradine said, when she came by to refill water glasses. "Triple if you don't eat it."

Kate sighed when she was gone. She shrugged her coat back on.

"Are we going somewhere?" Tracy asked.

"I don't know what you're doing," Kate said, and hated that it was hard to sound calm. "But I don't see any practical reason to extend this interaction. We have nothing to say to each other. I don't want to talk about the past. It doesn't sound like you have any new perspectives to share. As a law enforcement officer, I find it concerning that you could spend twelve years in prison and have nothing to say for it. But your rehabilitation is not my problem."

She stood, tossing some money on the table that she hoped would cover the bill in triplicate. She didn't wait for her mother. She didn't catch Bethan's eye. She just headed outside.

And for a moment, she faced the embrace of the December cold, squeezed her eyes shut tight, took a breath, and wished . . . for all those things she'd never been able to name. And the thing she could name but didn't bother to ask for anymore.

One breath, in deep, then she let it go.

When she opened her eyes, her mother was pushing out of the café door behind her.

And for what felt like forever, they stood there, facing each other across the gulf of their history, the night, and the few feet between them.

"I only wanted to see your face," Tracy said. "Is that wrong?"

And if she'd said it the way she'd said everything else tonight, with that aggressive undercurrent, Kate would have gone full trooper on her. But it was so plaintive. Almost lost.

Kate had to remind herself that her own feelings aside, Tracy Warren had been as much a victim of Samuel Lee Holiday as anyone else. Kate had spent so much time focusing on the ways she was complicit that it rarely occurred to her to remember that her mother had met her father when she was all of nineteen years old. She'd been pregnant at twenty-one. What did she know of the world that wasn't shaped by him? Could she have been an entirely different woman if he hadn't gotten his hooks into her so early?

Kate would never know. But maybe it wouldn't kill her to find a little compassion somewhere inside herself for this woman. She could do that, surely. It didn't mean she wanted a relationship with Tracy, or really anything to do with her, but she could certainly try a little empathy.

Something she knew wouldn't have occurred to her if it hadn't been for Templeton. Who might not be as *perfectly fine* as he claimed he was, but that didn't mean he wasn't a little more evolved than she was when it came to these interpersonal matters.

Like everybody else, as far as she knew, except the woman standing across from her.

"Mom," Kate said softly, without the usual irony she usually threw into that word. "I appreciate you coming all this way. I do. Thank you for looking me up after all this time."

Because she could, too, be the bigger person, she assured herself.

For a moment, Tracy didn't do anything but continue to stare at the ground, her phone in one hand. Kate wondered if she might actually see her mother get emotional about something that wasn't Samuel Lee—

But Tracy didn't look the slightest bit lost when her gaze lifted to meet Kate's. Or when she smiled. She didn't look sad or soft. She looked . . . smug.

Every instinct Kate had screamed at her that something was wrong. Very wrong.

Tracy hit something on her phone, and her smile got smugger.

And that was when the night split in half and the harbor caught fire.

Twenty-two

The explosion went off, the blast loud enough to rock the windows of all the houses along the street but not enough to shatter them.

Templeton registered that, but he was already moving from his position on the stairs that sat up high and looked out over the harbor. Running like he was daring the ice to try him.

People were pouring out into the street, staring at the bright column of fire down on the beach. Or running toward it, like Templeton. Like Jonas, who appeared out of nowhere from wherever he'd been keeping watch, barreling down the hillside.

A seaplane was on fire. Fumes and flames burned, and there was confusion already, the way there always was, as the volunteer firefighters—some official, some not—appeared and did their thing.

"Bethan." Templeton gritted out her name into the comm unit as he ran back up the hill toward the café. "Report."

Because everyone in town was coming outside, clustering together on the hill or lending a hand to the effort to put out the fire below. But Templeton didn't see his trooper.

And he didn't need that extra kick in his gut to make it clear to him that there was no way Kate would fail to react to something like this. No way in hell.

His worst fears were confirmed when Bethan met him outside the Fairweather, a wary look on her face.

"Kate stepped outside with her mother," she said. "I haven't seen her since the explosion."

And somehow, he'd expected that.

Something in Templeton had known this would happen the minute he'd gotten the call that Tracy Holiday had appeared.

"Does anyone have eyes on Kate?" he clipped out into his comm unit, already moving. Fading back from the crowd, his eyes scanning the darkness. "The explosion is a decoy."

He repeated that, in case he wasn't clear the first time.

Templeton didn't go back up into town, because Bethan and Jonas had that covered. He headed down to the beach instead, past the docks and out toward the rocky point that marked the end of Grizzly Harbor. The farther away he got from the fire, the more his heart kicked at him.

It was like clockwork. All he had to do was feel something, and sure enough—

Lock it up, dumbass, he growled at himself. *You can wallow after you find her.*

"I have it," came Jonas's voice over the comm. "Chris Tanaka and his bottle of whiskey saw a dinghy headed out right around the time of the blast."

"A dinghy." Templeton managed to get the words out past the cold, gnawing fury that had him in its grip. Somehow. "In the dark at this time of year."

"It looked to be headed out to sea," Jonas confirmed, with zero inflection. "No running lights."

And Templeton was breathless.

There was silence on the comm because everyone knew what that meant. In even the most experienced hands, a little boat was hard to handle out where the harbor gave way to the swells of the open water of the cold Pacific.

In anything but the most experienced hands, it was a death sentence.

Templeton stared out at the water, scanning the darkness. But he saw nothing.

It was happening again. *It was happening again.*

But this time, Templeton had every intention of dying himself if that was what it took to make sure Kate was okay. If he had to swim out there and find that boat himself. Whatever it took, this was not ending the same way it had last time.

He was an Army Ranger, and he would not allow this to end badly. He would not lose her. The truth he beat himself up with from time to time was that he barely remembered the woman he'd lost. He had known her so briefly, lost her so quickly.

But Templeton knew that Kate was burned on his bones. There was no forgetting his trooper.

Not tonight, Templeton vowed, still scanning the dark water for signs of her. *Not ever.*

"Rory," he growled into his comm unit, to the Green Beret who was running point back in Fool's Cove. "Bring me the helicopter."

The explosion rocked her, then confused her.

Kate had forgotten that creepy smile of Tracy's as she'd tossed herself at her mother and brought them both to the ground. She'd rolled up to her feet again and had automatically started cataloging the scene as an odd silence hung over the town. One beat. Another.

Then people started to come out of their houses. Some were already running, with fire extinguishers in hand. Others looked more wary.

Tracy grabbed at Kate's arm. "This way!"

Kate was scanning the buildings they passed, looking for structural damage. She let her mother lead her away from the café and down the hill. But when Tracy started to tug Kate away from the fire, away from the beach at the other end of town where everyone else was heading, she resisted.

"We have to help," she said.

Tracy didn't let go of her arm. "Don't you hear the children crying?"

Kate heard the waves against the beach. The shouts from those fighting the fire and higher up on the hill. But she couldn't hear any children.

And by the time they made it to the far side of the harbor, where the waves were even louder and a little boat was waiting, it was too late.

There were no children. There never had been. Shc was an idiot.

The two men she'd seen in the café and thought were familiar-looking were standing there by the boat. Another man stood between them, though he was holding his body at an awkward angle.

But as the flames down the beach climbed higher against the night sky, Kate could see that the awkward-looking man was tied up. With duct tape.

More important, he was her cousin Will.

Everything slid into place, with a little click that sounded like a gun.

A real gun, Kate amended, when she felt the muzzle of a handgun in her back.

"I wanted to see your face again," Tracy said from behind her, "because I wanted to see if you still needed cleansing. If you were still wrong all the way through. And you are worse, Katie. Filthy and twisted and *unworthy.*"

Unworthy.

There had only ever been one way to handle *unworthiness* in the Holiday family.

Kate stared at Will. At his expression, sad and something like resigned. As if he'd always expected to end up here, on a dark beach, on the longest Christmas in recorded history, caught up in this crap all over again.

"Are you sure, Mom?" Kate asked. Conversationally. "You make it sound like you came all this way to see if you needed to perform the ritual. When I think you and I both know this is nothing more than revenge."

The other men laughed. And Kate belatedly realized that they might have insinuated themselves as fishermen here in Grizzly Harbor with the rest of the men who came in for the seasonal jobs and sometimes stayed, but they were in fact her second cousins. The little ones she barely remembered, all grown up now and no longer drinking themselves into a stupor in Anchorage, apparently. And she'd bet they knew their way around some C-4. If she recalled anything about them correctly, it was that the two of them had always loved playing with fire.

Her mind raced. It would take so little. Just hunker down, spend time in the Fairweather, and they'd hear enough about Alaska Force to track them. Mess with them the way someone had been this last year, but making sure that mess triggered a review by the Alaska State Troopers. Because the officer who was usually dispatched to look into groups out in the Alaskan wilderness making trouble was Kate.

They'd done all of this to get her and Will here, where they could perform that damned ritual and make the pair of them pay the way they would have years ago if Kate hadn't escaped.

And Kate should have remembered that Tracy might have been Samuel Lee's victim at first—but these days she was a willing one. And this kind of thing had her fingerprints all over it. Kate had no doubt she'd left prison, found these two and dried them out, then started plotting.

Kate couldn't believe she'd walked right into it.

"Whatever works," Tracy said, with her smoker's cough as punctuation.

One of her long-lost cousins duct-taped Kate's hands in front of her, and then Tracy encouraged her to climb into the boat. By jabbing that gun hard into her lower back.

The boat was smaller than the Alaska Force skiff that Templeton had used to take her to Fool's Cove. Much smaller. Worse, it was completely open to the elements. And a temperature that seemed warm and practically springlike on the ground, after a tour of the interior the past few days, was going to be significantly less pleasant out on the water.

Something Kate got to experience in full, because she and Will were placed side by side on the bench in the bow of the boat. Tracy sat behind them with her gun. Kate's cousins pushed the boat out and then jumped into the stern to pilot it with an outboard motor.

When the first slap of water splashed over her, Kate steeled herself and tried not to hide behind Will like a princess. The second time, she understood exactly what her mother was planning.

The only question left was whether Kate and Will would succumb to hypothermia before Tracy got around to making them strip and jump overboard to drown. Jumping into the ocean at this time of year was as close to the original ritual—strip, then get dropped out in the frigid bush to freeze—as it was possible to get. The water was usually around thirty-six degrees in December. The air tonight was about the same, if not colder. It was a half hour to exhaustion and potential death if submerged—and that was a best-case scenario.

"I can't believe you're going to make us walk the plank," Kate said, because she needed to extend this. To stay on the boat as long as possible. "That suggests a level of whimsy I didn't think you had in you, Mom."

She had to shout to make sure her mother heard her.

And all she got for her efforts was that gun in her back again, a hard jab that she suspected would leave a bruise.

"Enjoy that mouth," Tracy told her, raising her voice so the wind didn't steal it. "You won't be using it much longer."

Next to her, Will kept fidgeting. Kate assumed he was cold. And getting colder, as the December air and the ocean spray got beneath the layers she wore. Which spelled certain doom. Exposure to water plus a winter night in Alaska led nowhere good.

Kate supposed she really ought to feel a lurching sense of betrayal. But instead, all she felt was pissed. At herself.

She should have known. She should have gone with her initial instincts instead of suffering through prime rib and her mother's terrible performance of fake emotion. Tracy had kept a low profile since she'd come out of prison three years ago, and that was a warning sign right there. Because Tracy had always lived in Samuel Lee's shadow, sure. But she hadn't exactly withered away there.

Kate hadn't expected her to get in touch when she got out, but now, with the benefit of hindsight, Kate could see that the fact Tracy had seemed to take so meekly to postprison life was a big clue. One she should have picked up on.

Tracy hadn't changed. Maybe she couldn't change.

But Kate still should have seen this coming.

Beside her, Will kept moving his legs restlessly. Kate didn't want to get close to him, or anyone else in this suicidally small boat that seemed tinier the bigger the swells got, but she found herself huddling against him anyway. Because it was warmer. Marginally.

She reviewed their situation. Cold. Wet. The boat was heading away from Grizzly Harbor, and not to navigate its way around the side of the island toward Fool's Cove. If Kate, personally, was a homicidal maniac bent on enacting a twisted revenge on her own child, she wouldn't choose one of the islands in the archipelago. She would go right for the ocean. And she would motor out as far as possible, to make sure that there was no coming back.

She had to assume that was what her mother had planned. And if all else failed, Tracy could shoot them both, drop their bodies overboard, and be done with it.

The boat kept chugging toward open water. Kate stared down at her hands and the duct tape wrapped around her wrists. Given a little time and some effort, she thought she could work her way out of it. But even if she couldn't, they'd thoughtfully left her hands in front of her body. That gave her more options.

And the ace in her pocket, of course, was Alaska Force. Templeton.

Something yawned open inside her, dark like despair, but she slapped a lid on it. And shoved it away.

Because the minute she thought she wasn't going to see him again—the minute she believed she wasn't going to get out of this—that was the moment she lost.

Fifteen years ago, some seven hundred miles north of here, she'd told herself something similar, and she'd made it.

Kate couldn't say she particularly liked the poetic symmetry. But she intended to keep it symmetrical. She *would* escape this.

And while she figured out how to handle what was happening on this boat, Alaska Force was doing its part. She knew it. Templeton would notice she wasn't there. Bethan had been in the café and would know she'd disappeared with her mother. Kate couldn't imagine it would take them long to figure out what had happened.

All she had to do was keep herself out of the ocean.

The sound of the motor changed, going down to a low sputter. That was not a good sign.

Next to her, Will and his restless legs got a little more frantic. The first time he kicked her, she ignored it, because they were all doing the best they could out here. The second time, she glared at him.

"That actually hurts," she said.

And got that gun jammed in her back again, in the very same spot. Which Kate fervently hoped she lived long enough to complain about. She would welcome the opportunity to attend to the ugly bruise that she could already feel spreading across her lower back.

"Sorry," she threw back over her shoulder to her mother. "I can see how us talking will really put a crimp in your execution schedule."

Once again, Tracy came in close. Gun in the back, mouth at her ear.

"This isn't an execution, Katie. This is a simple ritual. I don't understand why you've never been able to grasp this."

"I don't know. Possibly because it's crazy?"

Another jab. Harder.

"All your father and I ever wanted was a simple life. You took that from us."

"You want to take my *actual* life, Mom," Kate said. She braced herself for that jab, but even when it came she couldn't seem to stop. "I think even you would have to agree that's worse, right?"

"Your life was ours," Tracy said, and she didn't sound angry. She didn't sound particularly unhinged, or as if—given a black-and-white movie and a railroad track—she might start twirling a mustache. She sounded absolutely matter-of-fact. Completely devoid of the knowledge that what she was saying was, at the very least, a little outside the mainstream. "Ours to make, and ours to take."

It was amazing how clear everything became at gunpoint.

Because while it was true that both of her parents were manipulative and deeply unwell, obviously, they weren't actually trying to make the people around them feel crazy. They didn't think that they themselves were crazy. Her parents had always believed that Kate was theirs to do with as they wished. It wasn't an act. It wasn't put on. They had moved all the way out into the literal middle of nowhere so they could do what they pleased. With themselves, with their child, with their own lives.

Kate had always assumed that because she had fiercely believed that there had to be something other than the world they showed her, they must have known better themselves. But maybe they didn't.

It was odd, the things a person could find comforting when she was about to be executed.

Her mother was a true believer. It was possible everyone else in the family was. Maybe that was why Will had always struggled so hard. And maybe the thing that was wrong with Kate was that she couldn't bring herself to believe in anything simply because she was told to believe in it.

Kate had never trusted the things she couldn't see. She wasn't wired that way.

In her whole life, there was one person who had promised that she could trust him and then proved it.

She was trusting him now, in fact. But Kate knew the danger of free-falling into blind trust. She knew where it led.

She was looking at it.

"You are my only child," her mother was saying, in the kind of tone Kate assumed regular mothers used while chatting to their happy, run-of-the-mill daughters about delightfully bland normal things, like a grocery list. Or what to wear to church. Or something else Kate couldn't even imagine, because what the hell did she know about normal?

"What I hope for you, more than I could possibly tell you, is that you walk through this ritual and find yourself cleansed," Tracy said. "That's all I've ever wanted for you, Kate."

"Does it work if you swim through the ritual? Or do you need to stagger around in the snow? I wouldn't want to face my unworthiness the wrong way."

Another jab. And that one felt like the muzzle of the gun hit bone. *Ouch.*

Tracy hissed in her ear. "Nothing would make your father more proud than if you proved yourself to be one of us after all."

And this time, Kate said nothing as her mother sat back, presumably to ready the final details for this exercise.

Kate scanned the water around them. Dark, forbidding. Swells too high and relentless, and only the light every now and again of the far-off land that was Grizzly Harbor.

Up above, the night was cloudy, and off in the distance, she couldn't really see much of anything. Because there was nothing but the sea.

If she and Will went over the side of this boat, there was zero chance that they could be swept to safety. Or swim to it.

Which clearly meant that they couldn't go over.

This time when Will kicked her, it was so hard that she had to screw her eyes shut to keep from shouting. She glared at him as best she could out of the corner of her eye, not wanting to turn her head and get that gun slammed into her back yet again.

Will caught her gaze, out of the corner of his. And almost without moving at all, his hands taped behind his back, he indicated the floor at his feet. Kate looked down.

To see the flare gun he was half covering with his trussed-up feet.

A flare gun in a watertight bag with what looked like at least three cartridges.

Kate's heart began to beat in that hard, low way that meant adrenaline was moving through her. She knew

Alaska Force would be looking for them. For her. What she didn't know was whether they'd be checking the water.

But they would certainly see it if she set off a flare gun.

She could hear her mother and cousins talking in the back. She could feel Will tense beside her. Far off in the distance, she swore she could hear the faint whirring of helicopter blades, but she couldn't tell if that was wishful thinking.

So she kept her eyes on the flare gun, not the sky, because the sky couldn't save her. But the flare gun might.

There was movement from the back, and the boat rocked.

Will threw a glance at her, and she nodded.

And she guessed he'd finally chosen his side, because he surged up to his feet, making the boat rock alarmingly.

"I'm ready!" he bellowed toward the back, turning around so Kate could see that he'd worked his hands out of his duct tape but was holding them there anyway. "I've been ready for years. You were in prison, Aunt Tracy, but I spent all this time waiting. Wondering."

"You're a traitor," one of the second cousins spat at him.

"That's for the elements to decide," Will threw right back. "Not you."

Convincingly, Kate thought.

But she wasn't about to waste her opportunity. The next time the boat rocked, she rocked with it, falling down to the bottom of the boat, slimy and smelling of low tide and rust. She fumbled with the slippery plastic, yanking the closure wide. She pulled out the gun, then a cartridge, cursing the one second—then another second—it took her to fiddle her hands around into the right space. And then to get the job done.

"This land makes its own choices!" Will was shouting, sounding so much like his own father and hers that if she let herself, Kate could have tumbled back in time to yet more terrible memories she didn't want to revisit.

Not while she was in the middle of reliving one.

She blocked him out. She listened. And this time, she didn't think it was wishful thinking—she was sure she could hear helicopter blades in the distance. And when she looked, she could see a searchlight dancing along near the shore, as if they were scouring the waves.

Her mother hadn't seen it yet. But she would.

It was now or never.

Kate surged to her feet. She kept Will between her and her mother, and she shot the flare gun into the sky.

She didn't wait or watch. She loaded another cartridge, almost dropping it as she tried to work with her tied-together wrists, and shot off another. Then loaded the third, final cartridge.

It took seconds.

The flares lit up the sky above them, broadcasting their position in no uncertain terms. Someone screamed—probably her mother. Kate didn't look to see if the helicopter's spotlight was headed this way.

She had to believe it was.

She had to believe in something, and it was this.

Will shouted out some kind of noise and threw himself down the length of the boat, body checking the cousins like he was bowling with his whole torso. One cousin fell overboard. The other fell down hard but came up swinging.

Will freed his hands and fought back.

Somehow, the boat didn't capsize, though it lurched from side to side in the waves.

And that left Kate and her mother face-to-face.

"The ritual is too good for you!" Tracy howled at her, struggling to her feet as the boat rocked this way, then that. "I should have put you down like a dog years ago!"

Kate snuck a look, because belief only went so far. The helicopter was coming.

"I can remedy that right now," Tracy said, and lifted her gun.

Kate aimed the flare gun directly at her mother's face.

"Go ahead, Mom," she said. "See if you can shoot me before I light you up like a Christmas tree."

Tracy scoffed. "Have you forgotten I'm the one who taught you how to shoot?"

There was no shame, no guilt, no second thoughts. Kate had spent too much time this month indulging her inner child, that poor kid. But here, now, she was the policewoman she'd made herself out of that kid. She had already risen like a phoenix once. She would damn well do it again, if necessary.

She couldn't say she particularly wanted to kill her mother. Of course she didn't.

But she would.

"You taught me a lot of things," Kate replied, keeping herself balanced and her hands steady. "But I got over that a long time ago."

Tracy screamed like a banshee. Bloody murder, rage, and all that crazy besides. She lunged forward and brandished her weapon at Kate as if she wanted to pistol-whip her, then maybe get around to shooting her a few times.

But Kate saw her opening. Tracy overbalanced and nearly toppled into the water. Kate shifted to the side, then reached across the bench seat where she and Will had huddled, and smacked the handgun out of her mother's hand.

The gun clattered across the boat's floor. It skated around, then hit Will in the side. And Kate had to hope that Will was the one who picked it up, not their grunting, bellowing second cousin. But she couldn't concentrate on their fight. Not when Tracy was screaming even louder now, grabbing her hand as if Kate had cut it off.

"Give it up," Kate advised her. "You can't win this."

The spotlight picked them up as the helicopter flew closer, lower. The boat rocked wildly. Tracy jerked her head up, as if she couldn't believe her own eyes. Kate wanted to look up herself, but she could tell where the helicopter was by the look on her mother's face and the way she swayed.

"You're going back to prison," Kate told her. "For good this time. You might as well accept that here and now."

Out of the corner of her eye, she saw ropes dropping down from above, with men on the ends of them. A figure jumped into the water to go after the cousin who'd fallen overboard. But the man on the other rope moved closer.

It was dark, she was looking only with her peripheral vision, and she still knew it was Templeton.

She felt him, like a natural disaster, deep in the core of her. Like that ritual that really, she'd survived twice.

And once again, he'd proved that she could trust him absolutely.

Something in her stuttered at that. But she shoved it away, slammed the lid on it, and compartmentalized it with the strength of years' practice.

In the back of the boat, Will was holding the gun on their remaining second cousin. His face was beat up and he had a bloody nose, but the look he threw Kate was proud.

Because this time, he knew who he was. Not a traitor. Just done with this Holiday family crap once and for all.

Kate knew the feeling.

Templeton came closer, hanging at the end of the rope over the brooding, dangerous December sea the way other men might take a casual walk on a flat road.

But that was Templeton.

Always a freaking light show.

"You're not worthy," Tracy shouted at Kate. "You never were. But I know I am."

Kate snapped her attention back to her mother. And when Tracy moved, Kate couldn't make sense of what she was doing. She leaned down and screamed again as she sort of squatted.

"What are you doing?" Kate demanded. And then she saw what she was doing. "Put down that anchor!"

She braced herself, waiting for her mother to swing the anchor at her—calculating how much it would hurt and whether it would knock her overboard or not—

"I know my worth!" her mother screamed at her.

Then, holding the anchor tight to her chest, Tracy threw herself overboard.

And sank like a stone.

Twenty-three

They tried, but they couldn't recover Tracy Holiday's body.

Templeton was inclined to think that was a good thing. Because when a person chose their grave, they should be left to it.

But he had no idea how Kate felt about it.

"Are you okay?" he'd asked when he'd finally gotten to her. When he'd finally put his hands on her in that small, swamped boat. Where she was already too damp and risking exposure by the second.

But she was Kate. So she'd scowled at him while he pulled the emergency blanket around her shoulders, as if he were the one who'd assaulted her.

"I'm fine."

"Kate, you watched your mother—"

"I said I was fine," she'd snapped at him. "That wasn't *your* mother. That was the lunatic who raised me, who never should have had a child in the first place. I'm not crying. I'm not going to cry."

"Kate—"

"Did you come here to save me?" she'd thrown at him

while the wind from the water and the helicopter rotors churned all around them. "Guess what, Templeton? I saved myself. Again."

And Templeton's personal tragedy, aside from the burn of her words, was that he'd had his comm unit on when she'd said that. Loud and clear, so that all his Alaska Force brothers could hear it, internalize it, and use it to mock him forever.

That was exactly what they did. Starting right then, with a low, dark, delighted laugh that Templeton didn't recognize at first as it lit up the comm channel. And then realized that the reason he didn't recognize it was because it was Jonas doing the laughing. And Jonas never laughed.

Terrific.

But then the practicalities took over. There were dirtbags to handle and the authorities to call to the scene. Troopers and paramedics and anyone else who wanted to come to the party. Isaac was already on his way, having mobilized out of Anchorage within minutes of that first explosion.

They brought everyone to the Blue Bear Inn, bad Holiday cousins and good Holiday cousins alike. Kate disappeared briefly to change her clothes, then came back downstairs with that same blank expression that Templeton remembered from the first afternoon they'd met.

All Alaska State Trooper. No Kate.

And he was so happy she was alive, it didn't matter which one she was.

But he was revising that opinion even before the Troopers arrived. There were statements to give, the usual bureaucratic nonsense to wade through. Medical checks to undergo.

All of which intensified when Isaac showed up, because it looked like he was ready, finally, to stop pretending to the Alaskan authorities that he was nothing more than a local boy with a gun collection and some similarly enthusiastic friends.

Christmas night wore on.

Caradine, the grouchiest Good Samaritan Templeton had ever encountered, kept appearing at intervals. She dispensed coffee and her trademark glares and usually left behind a plate of this or that to keep everybody's strength up as they sorted through what had happened tonight. And in the months leading up to it.

Tracy had blown up her own plane. Kate had seen her do it with her mobile phone. The blast had been bright but largely self-contained, which cut down on the property damage.

Everyone's best hypothesis was that she'd wrapped the anchor chain around herself as she sank, so that even when she let go when her air ran out, she couldn't come back up to the surface.

"*If* she let go," Kate said when the theory was advanced to her. "Which I doubt."

Templeton kept waiting to get another moment with her. For her to seek him out and maybe smile at him the way she had when it was just the two of them, driving on those mountain roads on the Seward Highway. He kept waiting, but she didn't come to him.

And even when her eyes met his, it was like the Kate he knew wasn't there.

It wasn't until the troopers began to pack their things up, many hours later, that it occurred to him that Kate was going to . . . just leave. Without a word.

And he couldn't accept that. He couldn't *believe* it.

He caught up to her in the upstairs hall of the inn. This was Grizzly Harbor's most eventful Christmas since the year a moose got into the general store, and folks were still milling around near the smoldering remains of Tracy's plane. The Fairweather was doing a brisk business, well into the night, as locals gathered to tell ever more fictionalized tales of their bravery tonight.

If Templeton squinted, he might mistake the crime scene for one of the typical Alaskan festivals that the locals loved so much they threw them all the time. Bundle up well enough, after all, and even a cold December night could feel downright jovial.

But his attention was on the woman who came out of the guest room at the top of the stairs, her bag on her shoulder and not one thing he recognized in her cool brown gaze.

"Did you want something?" she asked him.

"That's how you want to play this? Like you don't know me?"

"Maybe you should call me baby," she suggested. "That worked so well the last time."

"Kate," he began.

But she shook her head. "I'm not doing this."

"Having a conversation?"

"A conversation. The rest of it. Whatever it is, I don't want it."

He started to argue, but she shook her head. And her thousand-yard stare was what cut at him the most.

"Tonight was actually validating," she said, sounding as if she were already gone. "All this time, I've been beating myself up for not getting the things that everybody else seems to. For not understanding the world. But it turns out, I understand it fine. I know who people are. And I know what they do."

He couldn't understand why that sounded like good-bye.

"The fact that you can trust me should be a good thing, shouldn't it?"

"I trust you to do what you do, in your corner," she said, which wasn't the same thing. "If tonight proved anything to me, it's that I do best in my own corner, doing my own thing. That's what I'm good at. That's what I know."

"That's an interesting takeaway." He wanted to reach

out and touch her, but he didn't. Somehow, he kept his hands to himself. "Meanwhile, what I learned tonight is that I'm falling in love with you."

She smiled at that, and it broke his heart.

"No, you're not," she said, with a quiet certainty that broke the pieces of his heart all over again. "You like a damsel in distress. It's in your blood. It's who you are. But that's not me."

"Kate."

He could hear how torn he sounded. How destroyed. He knew she could, too. He didn't care if his comm unit was on and the whole world heard him.

And still, when she walked away from him, she didn't look back.

It took four days for Templeton to come to a decision.

One day to get pissed. Another to drink. A third day to analyze the situation the way he would a tricky op.

On the fourth day, he and Isaac were lying on the floor of the so-called box of pain, down by the water's edge. The brutal morning workout had left everyone gasping. They'd all staggered off when it was done, cursing Isaac's name in that way that brought him his greatest and deepest joy. That was why Templeton refused to do it himself.

Instead of heading back to his cabin to sit in silence and further contemplate his life choices, Templeton had decided to do a little cash-out instead. He pushed his body until his muscles couldn't take it anymore, and he nearly crushed his own foot with his kettlebell. Only then did he drop down to the floor himself. And then lie there, waiting for his heart rate to get back under control and his breathing to even out.

And to see if the clarity he'd gotten would fade.

But it didn't.

He lifted his head and looked around, but it was still

only Isaac sprawled on the floor a small distance away from him. And Horatio, Isaac's entirely too smart border collie, who was never too far away from his master.

"I'm going to need some time," Templeton said.

Isaac lifted his head. "To recover from your workout? I know you're only an army man, but I expected better, Templeton."

Templeton grinned. And then gave his best friend and superior officer a one-fingered salute.

"I need some vacation."

Isaac laughed and rolled up to his feet. "Didn't she blow you off?"

Templeton took his time rising. He stretched. Then he went and rubbed Horatio's ears, because he knew exactly how to do it to make the canny dog roll and kick like a silly little puppy. It was their little secret.

"I didn't ask you for your commentary on my romantic life," he told Isaac. Genially enough. "I'm informing you that I'm going to take some of the time I have coming. I know you want to assign me to that extraction thing, but I'm going to have to pass."

"That's a lot of pushback," Isaac pointed out. "Especially when I'm the one person—the only person—around here who hasn't been all over you about that I-saved-myself thing."

"We both know that's not out of the goodness of your heart. It's because you don't want to hear what I have to say in reply."

The name *Caradine* hung there in the air, the way it often did. Templeton thought it was further evidence of his sainthood that he didn't say it out loud. And a few choice other things while he was at it.

"It doesn't matter why," Isaac said loftily. Also not saying her name. "I'm pointing out what an excellent friend I am. And how maybe I don't deserve you talking to me like I'm a redheaded stepchild."

"I don't know how long I'll be," Templeton said, grinning. He did not apologize for his tone. "As long as it takes, I guess."

He gave Isaac a real salute then and headed for the door of the gym.

"She seemed pretty definitive," Isaac said from behind him. "That's all I'm saying."

Templeton looked over his shoulder and grinned even wider.

"Isaac. Buddy. I know you're only a marine, so this probably won't make any sense to you. But I'm an Army Ranger. We get what we want, or it can't get got."

He headed to Juneau first.

But when he got to Kate's building, he found her apartment open, empty, and undergoing an intense cleaning.

"The last tenant moved out," the woman cleaning the place told him. "The day after Christmas."

She didn't know where to. Or care.

It took Templeton one call to figure out that Kate was probably headed back to Anchorage, her usual base of operations. And a second call to get himself on the next plane. But once he landed in Anchorage, it took a little doing to figure out her whereabouts.

Because his trooper liked to live in throwaway furnished apartments that she could trade in at a moment's notice. Which meant he had to wait until she showed up at her office, then trail her home. It was old-school but effective.

When he finally made it to her door, it was New Year's Eve.

She swung open the door before he knocked on it and stood there, her arms crossed over her chest. Those pissed-off, go-to-hell eyes on his like a pair of daggers. And a welcoming scowl on her face.

Oh yeah, Templeton thought. He was head over freaking heels for this one.

"I knew that was you." Her voice was just the way he liked it. Calm, unimpressed, and 100 percent his favorite

Alaska State Trooper. "You might want to reconsider a career as a covert operative when you insist on renting the flashiest, highest-tech SUV you can find everywhere you go."

"Baby," he drawled. "I got to be me."

"Go be you in Grizzly Harbor," she replied.

But she didn't slam the door shut. And Templeton smiled.

"Here are the facts, Trooper," he said, leaning against the doorjamb. "I'm in love with you. And you didn't slam the door in my face, which, as far as I can tell, is your version of a sweet nothing. So I'm feeling pretty good about the whole love thing."

He expected her to snap at him. Maybe punch him, which should be fun.

But instead, all she did was shake her head. And he watched as those cool brown eyes filled up with what looked like sadness.

And how he managed to keep from hauling her into his arms and making sure she was all in one piece, he would never know.

"Don't you understand yet?" she asked softly. Almost defeated. And yet very, very certain, because that was Kate. "I can't."

Twenty-four

Templeton was the most beautiful thing Kate had ever seen, but then, he always was.

She'd been angry in Grizzly Harbor. That anger had carried her all the way to Juneau. She'd packed up her pitiful selection of possessions, informed her landlord that she was moving on, and been on her way back to Anchorage the next morning. In her plane, released at last from police custody.

Kate had taken a couple of days to fly herself back to Anchorage, keeping that anger kicking all the way.

Her mother had been declared missing while they waited to see if a body turned up, though no one was optimistic. And Kate tried her best to mourn, she really did.

But she'd grieved her mother a long time ago.

Her two second cousins were arrested and booked. Kate's captain called her in, behaving as if her leave had never happened because he needed her advice as her relatives confessed to all the arson, the murder, and the break-in at Kate's apartment. And it was as Kate had thought. Tracy had spearheaded the whole thing. She wanted Kate and Will to pay—but especially Kate. And they'd settled on Grizzly Harbor—and Alaska Force—as the perfect trap after a dishonorably discharged friend of theirs had come back from the navy with a story about the secretive ex–special forces group that was still running missions out of the Panhandle.

Kate's captain was inclined to make Kate's cousins pay. And to make Alaska Force a whole lot less secretive, too.

She was happy to share her thoughts. She was happy to work.

And it was easy to keep her anger going strong while all of that went on. Even when Will and she attempted to stop treating each other like part of the problem, for a change.

Because they'd survived.

And really, they were the only ones who'd survived. Because others might have lived through the Holiday family, but she and Will had escaped them.

"I guess that means we're stuck with each other," Will said, scowling into his beer in one of Kate's favorite bars in Anchorage. They'd beaten him up, but the bruises would fade. Kate thought he looked like a different man. Because he, too, had fought the family ghosts out there on the water. And, like her, he'd won.

They'd both changed, maybe.

"We can be stuck with each other," she said, fiddling with her drink. "But there will be no rituals of any kind. Ever."

"God, no."

"I don't need to visit Nenana again." She even smiled at him then, and it wasn't a fake one. "And I'm not getting a wolverine tattooed on my body."

Will smiled back. "I think I can live with that."

After that, the anger shifted into something heavier. Harder. Kate was working again, but she couldn't seem to lose herself in it the way she wanted to. At night she would go home and sit on more furniture she hadn't chosen herself, surrounded by things that weren't hers and meant nothing to her, and think of nothing but a man as big as a mountain.

And all the ways he made her feel, which rivaled all the mountain ranges in Alaska. Put together.

That was the problem.

"What do you mean you can't?" Templeton asked now. And he didn't wait for her to invite him in. He brushed past her, looking around at the apartment and rolling his eyes. "If this is going to work, we're going to have to upgrade from this sad, lonely, furnished-apartment crap. It makes my head hurt."

"It's not going to work."

"Well, not with that attitude."

"Templeton."

If he heard the warning in her voice, he gave no sign. He was too busy stripping off his coat, kicking off his boots, and then sauntering over to her sofa and flinging himself down.

"I'm not built for this," she told him, and frowned. "And I don't need an argument."

"There's no point arguing with sheer insanity," he replied. "You are, literally, perfectly built. For this. For me."

There was a smile on his mouth, but it was the intensity of his gaze that made her shudder.

"I've had time to think about this," she said.

"You mean you've had time to come up with excuses."

"That's your department, if I recall correctly," she shot back at him before she could think better of it. And knew she'd lost ground when his eyes began to gleam, gold and dangerous.

"You can come at me all you want, Trooper," he drawled. "I like it. I like you. I like the whole Trooper Holiday package. I don't think you're an alien. I don't think there's a single thing wrong with you, except maybe that you're standing across the room from me."

"I'm broken," she announced matter-of-factly. "If I

had any doubt about that, I toured every aspect of my family and childhood in the past month, and it was made perfectly clear to me. That's where I come from. That genetic swamp."

"What it should have proved to you is that you're absolutely nothing like any of them."

She shook her head again, because she could feel the emotion sloshing around inside of her. And she knew how terrifying it was. She knew where that led.

"But don't you understand? I'm exactly like them." When he looked like he would argue the point, she shook her head again, insistently. "I never understood it while I lived there, and I didn't understand it after I escaped. Because all I could see was the crazy. I'd never felt it myself."

"Because you're not crazy."

"You make me feel completely out of my mind," she threw at him, and the proof was there in how she sounded. Too loud. Too uncontrolled. "I was standing on a boat in the open sea in December. Moments from my own death. Do you know what I kept thinking about?"

"If it's not me, Kate, I'm going to be gravely disappointed."

"Of course it was you." She threw up her hands. "Who does that? I'm a trained law enforcement officer. I should have been thinking strategy, tactical options, how to save my own cousin. I probably should have saved my mother."

"You saved yourself," Templeton reminded her. "And not for the first time."

"When you came down on that rope, I wanted to jump on you and let you carry me away forever." When he only looked at her as if he thought that was a fine idea, she made a sound of frustration. "I might as well be my mother. She would have followed that man anywhere. She did. And look what happened."

He shifted as if he was going to say something, so she kept going.

"That's how people love in my family. Into prison, out of prison, through murders and assaults and criminal conspiracies. Until they weigh themselves down with an anchor and drown. That's what's in here." She put one hand over her heart, aware it was beating too fast. And aware that her breathing sounded a little too much like sobbing. "That's what I have to offer."

But Templeton didn't react the way he should have. He shrugged. "I accept."

He said that lazily. Easily. She might have thought that he wasn't taking this seriously if she hadn't been able to see the fierce expression in his gaze.

"You can't . . . *accept*," she sputtered. "This is an escape hatch, Templeton. You need to take it."

"I think you just told me you're in love with me," he said, in that dark, low voice that shivered around inside her and made her feel like a different woman. One who was really free, not simply . . . no longer trapped. One who was his. "Buried in all that, somewhere. I don't need an escape hatch."

"The only way that I managed to not end up like all the rest of them is by keeping to myself," she told him, and she was aware that her voice was cracking. That her hands were in fists at her side. "I work. That's it. That's the only thing that lets me stay *me*."

Templeton sat up. He leaned forward so he could rest his elbows on his knees and dangle his hands between his legs.

"Do you trust me?" he asked her, without a trace of a smile on that beautiful, wicked face of his.

"I don't really see how that's relevant."

"I think we both know that means that you do, but I want to hear you say it."

"I trust you to show up when you say you will," she said grudgingly. "You keep your promises, I'll give you that."

He dropped his head a little and laughed, but it wasn't his usual foundation-rocking laughter.

Then he came to his feet in that way that never ceased to make her catch her breath. And the only reason she didn't cut and run when he started toward her was because she knew that he would catch her.

Or she told herself that was the reason, anyway.

When he got to her, he took his time reaching down and taking her hands in his.

And that was unfair.

Because his hands were so big, and hard, and hot around hers. She could feel his heat, and that electric thing that had buzzed between them from the start.

And this time, she knew exactly where it went. She knew exactly what he could do.

She had to remind herself that was the problem.

"It seems to me that the real problem here is Samuel Lee Holiday himself," he said after a moment.

"He usually is," Kate said. Maybe a little dourly.

"What worries you is that you might be like your mother."

Kate shuddered. "Yes."

It was one of the hardest things she'd ever said.

But Templeton didn't condemn her. He didn't seem to notice.

"The real issue is that when your mother fell in love, it was with a psycho. So here's what I promise you." His hands tightened around hers. And she was suddenly sure that he could see all the way inside her. Every secret. Every fear. Every scrap of hope she'd ever gathered inside herself and hidden away. "You can love me as much as you want. As big and as wide and as crazy as you like. I can take it."

Kate couldn't breathe. Still, his name was on her lips.

But he wasn't finished. "And in return, there will be no whackadoo ritual to prove your worth. I already know that you're worthy. You're more than worthy." He pulled her closer, and she went. Easily. "You're beautiful. Tough. You make me laugh, and you're not afraid of me. I have the feeling that if I let you, you'll make me into a better man. I don't need you to prove a single thing to me, Kate."

"Templeton . . ."

"Maybe I can't save you. But I promise you, I will always keep your heart safe. You will never end up on a compound, and I will never end up in prison. Loving me is not going to lead to you with an anchor in the middle of a winter sea."

Kate never cried, but she could feel the tears on her cheeks then. One more thing she would have sworn she'd never do, and then did.

Because of him.

"I want to believe you," she whispered. "But I never have believed in anything I can't see."

"Then stick around," Templeton urged her, his voice low. And, she realized, certain. As if he already knew exactly how this was going to work out, and she would love it. And him. Forever. "All you have to do is stay, baby. I promise."

He moved his hands until he could lace his fingers through hers. And she was the one who raised up their linked hands, so she could move closer to the great wall of his chest. Because when she tilted her head up, his mouth was there.

Right there.

Templeton looked at her as if he were some kind of sun. Bright enough to make even the darkest December in Alaska feel like summer.

"And what about you?" she asked, even though she was afraid she didn't want to know. "What do you get out of this?"

Templeton's grin was big and wide.

"You, Trooper. I get you." When she scowled at him, she got his real laugh. And it was beautiful, just like him. "You might not need saving, baby, but I do. Pretty much all the time. You think you can handle that?"

And Kate had never been one for faith. But the difference here was that it wasn't blind. And better still, she was choosing it.

She had seen so many of his different facets already. She wasn't afraid of what others she might discover. He was the most dangerous man she'd ever known, but unlike the other men in her experience, he had only ever used his power to protect her.

He hadn't punished her for her own.

If anything, he seemed to like it.

He loved it. And her. And he made her feel . . . giddy.

Which, in turn, made her understand that however much her mind couldn't grasp the things that Templeton had told her, her heart believed him completely.

Her heart had loved him from the start.

"You don't have to think that hard," Templeton said. He wrapped his arms around her, and they still fit the way she'd convinced herself she'd only imagined they did. Like they'd been made for this. For each other. "All you need to do—"

"Is love you," she finished for him. "I have that part covered." She gave into the giddiness, throwing herself straight off that cliff. Straight into his arms. Then she smiled up at him and felt a lot like sunshine herself. "Did anyone ever tell you that you talk too much?"

His laugh boomed between them, and it felt better than faith. It felt like a promise.

And when he kissed her, he tasted like forever.

So Kate held on tight, kissed him back, and set about loving the only man she'd ever known who made her feel safe.

And better yet, always would.

He'd promised.

And Templeton Cross kept his promises.

Twenty-five

Six months later, Templeton unfolded himself from yet another SUV he'd had waiting at the airport, stretched, and breathed in the wallop of the Mississippi heat.

"Are you nervous?" Kate asked, coming around from the passenger side to stand beside him.

"That's not the word I'd use," Templeton said. "It's a little more layered than that."

And she understood him, so all she did was slip her hand into his.

He'd had half a year with her, and it already felt like a lifetime. Two lifetimes. And not nearly enough.

They'd both agreed to start things slow. If that was what it could be called when they were both so thirsty for each other.

"You live almost a thousand miles away," Kate said one afternoon while they were shopping for furniture. For the unfurnished apartment she'd reluctantly rented, because Templeton had convinced her it was time. "You'll sit on whatever sofa I buy . . . maybe twice."

"Trooper," he replied, grinning. "Challenge accepted."

And they figured it out. Mission by mission and case

by case. Kate flew to Fool's Cove when she could. Templeton went to Anchorage.

"I don't know how you do long distance," Blue said one morning while they were suffering together through a heavy sandbag carry.

"Because it doesn't feel like long distance," Templeton replied without thinking.

But even when he thought about it, it felt true.

One night, about three months in, they were in Templeton's cabin in Fool's Cove. It was technically spring, but there was no evidence of that outside. Alaska liked to hold on to her winters. They'd been talking through the raid the Troopers had undertaken on Russ and Liberty's property the month before and the cache of illegal arms recovered. The children removed from their parents' custody.

"I understand why you want things this way," Kate said abruptly. Templeton eyed her from across his kitchen, seeing his woman, not his trooper. "The fact is, the gift of the Holiday family keeps on giving, and it likely always will."

"Baby." Templeton shook his head. "Your family is noise. You're the gift."

"Things are better separate," she insisted, scowling at him. "You maintain plausible deniability, and I—"

"Hey."

He went to her then, pulling her into his arms and trapping her there, so she had no choice but to look at him. But it was Kate, so she glared.

"We can be realists about this, can't we?" she asked.

"I told you a long time ago that I'm an optimist," Templeton reminded her. "What do you think is happening here?"

"I . . ." And he loved that the only time his strong, smart, capable woman ever got flustered was when her heart was involved. He loved her. Though he had to pick and choose when to tell her that, because the words made her flushed and red and soft, and he preferred to keep that to himself. And act on it. "I'm trying to . . ."

"You have a job that means everything to you," Templeton said. "So do I. We won't have them forever. What's a little travel?"

"It's not that easy."

"It's as easy as we decide it is," he told her.

And then he showed her just how good he could make easy feel.

A few weeks after that, her captain made Kate the Troopers' special attachment to Alaska Force. That gave her even more reason to go to Fool's Cove and stay there while Alaska Force handled various missions of interest to local law enforcement.

"Something strange came up," Kate told him one night in their Anchorage apartment. Not that she called it theirs, but Templeton had his stamp all over it. A lot like the stamp he had on her. "I need your thoughts."

And she looked like Kate, but she had her cop face on, so Templeton decided not to see if he could get his hands on her. That moment.

"Hit me," he said.

"After my interview with Caradine in December, I asked for her records," Kate said. And rolled her eyes at Templeton's expression. "Like you don't have Oz run background checks on everybody you see on the street."

"That's different."

"You know it's not." She wrinkled up her nose. "The thing is . . . Caradine Scott doesn't exist. She appeared out of nowhere some years back."

But when Templeton turned that over in his head, all he thought about was Isaac.

"Has she broken a law?" he asked.

"Not that I know of."

Templeton shrugged. "People come to Alaska to be someone else, far away from anyone who knows better. You know that."

"I do. And I like her. I really like her cooking. I just . . ."

He grinned at her, because she was so cute and she looked so lost. "Welcome to the gray areas of life, Trooper. Complicated, isn't it?"

She answered him with a challenge no man could resist, and Templeton made sure that in the end, they were both winners.

As far as he was concerned, things were moving along just fine.

Especially on the nights in Fool's Cove when Kate came back from dinners with Bethan and Everly a little tipsy, shooting her mouth off about red wine and *intimate friend time.*

He always took that as an opportunity to experiment with intimacy. On an epic level.

And it was entirely because of Kate that he found himself in Mississippi. Heading into Parchman to visit a man he'd been pretending was dead his whole life.

Because he'd watched Kate deal with all of her ghosts. He'd watched her walk away from old demons, and he'd watched her forge a new bond with Will, who was doing his best not to live up to the family traditions.

How could he do any less?

And when Kate and he were shown into a private visiting room, Templeton wondered how the hell she'd seemed so calm back in Alaska when she'd done this. Because he was about to come out of his skin.

She sat next to him, looking cool and calm. She put her hand on his leg beneath the table, and Templeton instantly figured out how to take himself down a few notches. How to breathe.

The doors opened, and a man came in. Templeton stood.

Johnny Cross looked . . . like him. Tall. Big.

With the same damned face.

It hit him like a gut punch.

Johnny looked at Templeton a good long while, like he was searching for breath himself. Then he slid his gaze to Kate, who smiled that cop smile right back at him.

"Your wife?" Johnny asked, his voice deep like Templeton's.

"Not yet," Templeton said, aware that they even sounded alike. "She's not ready. But she will be."

Kate glared at him. But she didn't argue.

And Johnny Cross laughed. Loud and long and deep.

Until Templeton joined in.

"My God," Kate said crankily, though her brown eyes were suspiciously bright. "There are two of you."

Templeton thrust out his hand, and his father took it.

And he couldn't say that he suddenly remembered those early years of his childhood. He wasn't suddenly drenched in images of the two of them together.

But it felt like a homecoming.

"It's nice to see you, Dad," Templeton said. He looked his father in the eye. "I promise you, I'm going to get you out of here."

And Templeton was a man of his word. He kept his promises.

He got Johnny out three years and two months later.

And he married Kate a few months after that, on Christmas Day, right there in Grizzly Harbor where they'd met.

"I love you," she told him, smiling ear to ear.

He kissed her the way he always would, deep and real. Forever.

"Get ready," he told her. "Because, next up? We're making a family of our own."

She scowled at him, there in her white dress and snow boots with her hair down, the Christmas lights making her shine.

"Absolutely not," she told him, all trooper. And pissed-off woman. "Carry on the Holiday nonsense? Never."

Templeton smiled.

And that time, it took him nine sweet months.

Acknowledgments

Thanks as always to the marvelous Kerry Donovan for being so much fun to work with, and everyone else at Berkley for supporting this series! I love writing it. And more thanks—all the thanks, always—to Holly Root for supporting me in all things.

As always, I owe a deep debt of gratitude to Lisa Hendrix for reading my manuscripts and finding the gaps between my research and actual life in Alaska. I'm also thankful to Nicole Helm and Maisey Yates, who read as I go and are usually responsible for me finishing.

Most of all, I'm thankful to you for reading these books and loving Alaska Force as much as I do!

Continue reading for a preview
of the newest Alaska Force book,
coming in Summer 2020!

BOSTON
TEN YEARS EARLIER

Julia had already ignored her father's summons as many times as she could. It was time to go back home or face the consequences.

Or, knowing her father, both.

Twenty-two-year-olds about to graduate from college *should* assert their independence. That was the excuse she planned to use when he lit into her about it, assuming he was in a mood to listen to excuses, anyway. Because he was going to be furious; there was no getting around that.

No one was suicidal enough to ignore Mickey Sheeran for too long.

Julia was one of the few people who dared pretend otherwise, and, filled with bravado while safely on campus and protected by university security, she'd decided to prove it.

She was already feeling sick with regret about that as she turned onto her parents' street in the unpretentious neighborhood outside of Boston proper that was filled with the "regular Joes" her dad claimed he admired as "true American heroes." Julia knew that what he really meant by that was that all their neighbors were as in awe of him as they were afraid of him. Just the way he liked it.

Most people were just plain-old afraid of him, Julia included.

Moreso the closer she got to the house she'd grown up in and hadn't been able to leave fast enough. And never seemed to be able to put behind her, whether she lived there or not.

There wasn't a single part of her that wanted to go back. Ever. And particularly not when she'd deliberately provoked him.

Sure, all she'd actually done was ignore a couple of phone messages ordering her to leave her dormitory and come home. But she knew her father would view the delay between the messages he'd left and her appearance as nothing short of traitorous. She was expected to leap to obey him almost before he issued a command, as she well knew. He didn't care that she had exams. He probably didn't *know* she had exams.

But Julia knew it was foolish to imagine her father was dumb. He wasn't. It was far more likely that he knew full well it was her exam period and had waited until this, her final semester of college, to force her to take incompletes and fail to graduate. He was nothing if not a master at revenge-served-cold.

Mickey hadn't been on board with the college thing, something he made perfectly clear every time he sneered about Julia's "ambitions." He'd also refused to pay for it, and had gone ballistic when Julia had found her own loans and a job in a restaurant to help with costs.

She still thought it was worth the bruises.

Her sister Lindsey was fifteen months younger and had never made it out from under their father's thumb. She still lived at home, grimly obeying his every command in the respectful silence he demanded, because females were to be seen, never heard.

She'd even started dating one of Mickey's younger associates.

You know where that's going to lead, Julia had muttered, under her breath, when she'd been forced to put in an appearance on Easter Sunday. *Straight to an entire life exactly like Mom's. Is that really what you want?*

You're the only one who thinks there's another choice, Lindsey had snapped right back, her gaze dark and her mouth set in a mulish line. *There's not.*

Julia had looked across the crowded church, filled with the people who came to Mass one other time each year, and stared at the back of Lindsey's boyfriend's head. She wished her gaze could punch holes in him.

I don't accept that, she'd said quietly. *I refuse to accept that.*

Next to her, her sister had sighed, something weary and practical on her face. Julia had recognized the look. Their mother wore it often. Soon it would start to fade and crack around the edges, until it turned into beaten-down resignation.

He's not a nice guy, but at least it gets me out of the house and away from Dad every now and again, she'd said. *That's not nothing.*

Their brother Jimmy, the meanest of their three older brothers, had turned around from the pew in front of them. He looked more and more like Dad by the day, and the nasty look he'd thrown the two of them had shut them both up. Instantly.

Sometimes Julia lied in her narrow cot in the dorm, squeezed her eyes shut so tight she expected all her blood vessels to pop, and *wished*. For something to save her. For some way out. For the limitless, oversized life her college friends had waiting for them, with no boundaries in sight. No rules. Nothing but their imagination to lead them wherever they wanted to go.

Maybe she'd always known that she wasn't going to get any of that.

And maybe her father had been right to oppose her going off to college, because all it was going to do was break her heart. Worse than if she'd been a good girl like Lindsey and had done what was expected of her.

Hopelessness only hurt if you were dumb enough to hope for something different.

Julia couldn't remember, now, when she'd first realized that her father was . . . unusual. That he was the reason the other children kept their distance from the Sheeran family. But she could remember, distinctly, the first time she'd googled her father's name and found a wealth of information about him. Just right there, online. For anyone to see.

She'd always known her father was a bad man.

Still, it was something else to find all those articles detailing the criminal acts he'd been accused of over the course of his long career. She thought sometimes that a good daughter would have been appalled, disbelieving.

But she'd looked at her father's mug shot in an article from the front page of *The Boston Globe*, and she'd believed. She'd known. He was exactly as bad as they claimed he was, probably worse, and that likely meant she was bad, too. Deep in her blood and bones, no matter what she did.

Every year they failed to catch him in the act, the bolder and more vicious he became.

And the more she accepted that his DNA lived in her, too.

Because if Julia was as brave as she pretended she was when she was across town on a pretty campus where she could squint her eyes and imagine she was someone else's daughter, she would have called the FBI herself.

But she wasn't brave. She didn't point the car in some other direction, drive for days, and disappear. Instead, she was obediently driving home to face her father's rage. And the back of his hand. And whatever other treats he had in store for her.

Her throat might be dry with fear and her heart might be pounding, but she was still doing what he wanted. In the end, she always did.

All things considered, maybe Lindsey's grim acceptance was the better path. Julia liked to put on a good show, but they were both going to end up in the same place.

Her stomach was killing her. Knots upon knots.

She eased her car to the curb, cut the headlights, and forced herself to get out into the warm spring night. It was a force of habit to park a ways down the block. There were always flat-eyed men coming and going from the house, and it would go badly for her if she inconvenienced any of them. And Mickey was never satisfied with small displays of strength when bigger ones could cow more people and show off his cruelty to greater effect.

In his circles, the crueler he was—especially to his own family—the more people feared him. And fear was what made Mickey come alive.

She leaned against the closed car door and pulled her phone out of her pocket. It was cold enough that she wished she'd worn more than T-shirt, but there was a part of her that liked the chill that ran along her arms. It would keep her awake. Aware.

You couldn't really dodge one of Mickey's blows, but there were ways of taking it, and falling—that lessened the damage.

She'd learned that lesson early.

She pulled up Lindsey's number and texted her, announcing that she'd parked and was about to walk in to face the music.

Don't come in, her sister texted back almost instantly. It's weird in here.

A different sort of prickle worked its way down the

back of Julia's neck and started winding down her spine. Her hair felt as if it was standing on end in the breeze, except there wasn't a breeze.

I'm coming out, Lindsay texted.

Julia found herself holding her breath, though she couldn't have said why. The night felt thick and dark suddenly, though she could see the streetlights with her own eyes. Something about that caught at her, and she moved away from the nearest pool of light to the shadow of a big tree. She stood there, keeping still. She put her back to the trunk, hoping that if anyone was looking they wouldn't see her.

And she tried really hard to convince herself that she was just being paranoid.

But when her sister appeared out of nowhere and grabbed her arm, she bit her own tongue so hard to keep from screaming that she tasted copper.

"What are you doing?" she whispered fiercely at Lindsey. "You scared the—"

"You should go back to your dorm," Lindsey said, and this time, there was something stark in her gaze. Too much knowledge maybe. Something unflinching that made the knots inside Julia's belly sharpen into spikes. "And stay there."

And all the things they never talked about directly seemed to swell in the cool spring night. The truths that no one spoke, for fear of what it might unleash. Not just because they were afraid of Mickey and his friends who he often called his brothers but treated with far more respect, but because acknowledging a thing made it real.

It had never occurred to Julia before this very moment how deeply and desperately she'd clung to the tattered shreds of her denial.

She and her sister stared at each other in the inky black shadows of the ominous night, and she couldn't tell anymore if it was the dark that threatened her or if it was the truth.

Whatever was coming, there was no escaping it. Had she always known that? Whether it was this night or another night or twenty years down a road that ended up with her seeing her mother's tired, fearful face in the mirror, this life she'd been so determined to imagine as a path she could choose had only ever been a downward spiral. To one single destination.

Sooner or later, they were all going to hell. Or hell was coming for them. It didn't matter which. She was going to burn either way.

Julia wanted to throw up.

But at the same time, a heady sort of giddiness swept over her, and it took her a second to realize what it was. Freedom, of a sort. Or relief, which amounted to the same thing.

She reached out and laced her fingers through her sister's, the way she used to do when they were little. Back when it was easier to pretend.

"Come with me," she said fiercely.

And Lindsey looked as if she wanted to cry.

"It's too late," she replied. Her voice was soft. Painful. "He asked me to marry him."

"You don't have to say yes."

"I love that you think it matters what I say."

"All the more reason to come with me," Julia said stoutly. "We can figure it out. We can . . . do something."

Lindsey's smile pained Julia, like someone had prized her ribs apart.

"Julia," she began.

But when hell came, it came out of nowhere.

A bright, hot, terrible flash of horror.

They were both on the ground, dazed and stunned, and Julia lifted a hand to her temples where she felt something sticky. But she couldn't find her way to caring about it much. Something was wrong with her ears, her head. Something was *wrong*.

Car alarms were going off up and down the street,

there was a siren in the distance, and she couldn't remember how she'd gotten to the ground. She pulled herself to her hands and knees, grabbing for Lindsey as she went.

And they knelt there, hugging each other even though it hurt, and stared at the roaring fire where their childhood home had been.

Their mother. Their brothers. Even their father—

Julia couldn't take it in.

Lindsay made a shocked, low sort of sound, like a sob.

And somehow, that crystallized things. With a wrenching, vicious jolt inside of Julia. Half panic, half resolve.

She turned to her sister, and took her shoulders in her hands, ignoring the stinging in her palms.

"This is the other choice, Lindsey," Julia said, her voice harsh and thick and not her own at all. But she would get used to it. She would grow into it. If she survived. And she had every intention of surviving. "But we have to choose it. Now."